MW00975898

The
Living
Stone

The Chronicles of Eres Book 1

by M.B. Mooney

© 2013 MB Mooney
All rights reserved.

www.mbmooney.com

ISBN: 978-1492245681

This book is dedicated to Micah, Elisha, and Hosanna. May you never lose your creative spark and always endeavor to share it with the world. You have already made me wealthy beyond comparison with your joy and imagination, but it is too much for me alone.

And to all that dream of a Kingdom where everything is good and right and just – keep striving and hoping for that which is beyond our comprehension but the deepest cry of our hearts.

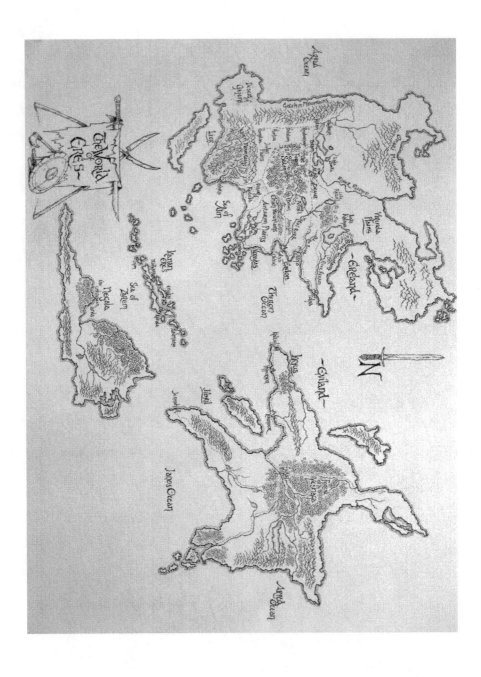

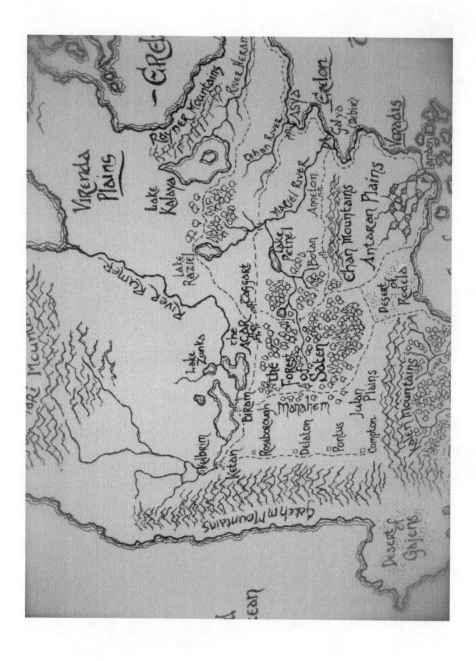

"I have come so you may live," Yosu told them. "Your heart beats, your lungs take in breath, and you have your own thoughts. You think you are alive, but you are dead. You must trade your death for my life. You cannot hold both. Few will understand and fewer will choose. But if you choose my way, it is a life no one can take from you. Then you will be truly free."

Mochus drew closer to the Master. "So is this the end of death foretold by the ancients? The end of all things?" Mochus asked.

Great sorrow overcame Yosu, and he said to Mochus, "No, my friend. This is only the beginning."

- From the Ydu, 5th Scroll, translated into common tongue by the Prophet

Chapter 1

Home Again

Caleb De'Ador's steel gray eyes squinted against the late afternoon sun as the boat beneath him docked in the harbor of Asya, the largest city on the continent of men. Kryus, a kingdom of elves, now ruled the land. It was the land where he had been born, and where he would also meet his end.

The *Far Lover*, a sleek vessel built by the elves with black Liorian wood, came to rest at the end of a busy pier, and Caleb stood at the bow. He turned his bearded face from the wind to watch the human crew secure the craft to her moorings, his shoulder length brown hair falling across his eyes for a moment. The shirtless and barefoot crew each bore small eagle tattoos on their left wrist that marked them as corporate slaves.

Caleb paid for his passage but slept in the hold with the slaves, making a few friends among the crew on the long voyage across the ocean from Kryus. He wanted to say his farewells to the slave crew as he left the boat, but he decided to satisfy himself with one of the men nearby, a man by the name of Dun.

He had spent the most time with Dun along the journey. A gregarious man, Dun was hardened but quick with a joke; his favorite punch line was, "Whether a shog or a crit, you're the one that chooses it!" His hearty laugh was good company, especially over a good game of Tablets. When Caleb shared ancient stories of heroic men and women, Dun listened but dismissed the tales as wave whispers. He did ask to hear more, however, almost every night. Caleb did his best to remember the stories of the ancient scriptures, tales told by his father and his Uncle Reyan.

Caleb approached Dun, and the man now lowered his eyes and hunched his shoulders up on deck in sight of the elven Captain driving the men to their work. Caleb stretched out his hand. Dun took it in friendship.

"Remember to keep your ear to the wind, my friend," Caleb said. "And do not be surprised if you hear that things are beginning to change one day."

"I will," Dun said. "Well met."

"Well met," Caleb said.

The momentary pause in the labor caught the Captain's attention, and he hurried in their direction. Caleb adjusted the backpack on his shoulder and left Dun to his work.

The Captain was average height for an elf – a head shorter than the average man – with cropped blond hair and pointed ears that both leaned to the right. He wore a plain, long white robe and leather sandals, and he walked with a slight limp, which he proudly claimed to have acquired in the War of Accession. Caleb was skeptical, however. Elves possessed long lives and aggrandized memories.

As they passed each other, the Captain turned and shot Caleb a glare. After centuries of Kryan control, men learned to bow to the elves. However, Caleb didn't avert his stare but stood straight, reaching over with his left hand to hold leather bracer that covered his right forearm. The elf frowned as Caleb held the gaze.

The Captain broke away first and spun, cursing and yelling at the men moving quickly about the ship, a nine-thronged whip held in his right hand. Caleb began to move to the plank that led off the boat. Out of the corner of his eye, he saw the elven Captain rush Dun.

"Come on, you piece of crit! We haven't got all breakin' day!"

Dun simply nodded, bowing to the Captain and looking at the deck, pulling a line with all his might to furl a large white sail.

The Captain took another two steps and raised the whip in his hand, bringing it down upon Dun's bare back. The man tied off the line and knelt in a huddle, his arms crossing to protect his head. The Captain continued to whip him.

Caleb froze two paces away from the walkway off the ship. He rolled his shoulders as the scars on his own back from an elven whip began to itch beneath his white shirt, the cloak, and the burden of the canvas pack. His fists clenched at his side. He spun around to face the Captain and Dun.

The Captain continued to beat the man. Caleb could see blood dripping from several rips on the man's flesh and onto the deck. The rest of the human crew slowed in their work, their faces blank. Dun yelled in pain through gritted teeth. The Captain began to grin.

Caleb sprinted, his feet barely making a sound across the deck, and he stopped in a crouch between Dun and the Captain. The Captain brought down the whip in his hand, and the leather thongs were caught by Caleb's covered right forearm. The whip wound around his wrist with a snapping sound; he reached out and grabbed the lash with his right hand. The Captain stood rigid. Dun groaned and caught his breath, collapsing to the deck.

Sneering at the elf, Caleb pulled on the whip. The Captain held fast to the handle and was drawn into a left-handed strike between the eyes, his head snapping back. Gasping as he faltered, the Captain stumbled, and Caleb yanked the whip away, standing from the crouched position and rotating into a flying right kick across the side of the Captain's head. The Captain legs buckled, and he dropped to the deck in an unconscious heap.

It all happened so fast. The human crew was motionless, watching him with fear in their eyes. Caleb unwound the whip from his forearm and threw it overboard. He heard yelling from down below in the hold, the First Mate preparing the cargo to be unloaded. "What's going on up there?"

Time to go, Caleb thought.

"Break me," he said. He adjusted his pack, nodded to Dun and the rest of the crew, and walked toward the plank leading to the quay.

Caleb heard the voice of the elven First Mate from the deck as he stepped on the pier and strode away from the ship. "Hey – what the shog?" Caleb reached back and pulled the hood of his cloak over his head, moving as quickly as he could - without looking desperate - down the pier towards the bustling docks north of the white city walls.

The cacophony of sounds in the harbor surrounded him: loud voices, profanity, wooden crates shifting, horses and mules and wagons traveling back and forth to ships and the city. He could smell dung and sweat. Most of the humans also wore the eagle tattoo on their left wrist.

At the end of the pier, Caleb turned right and inclined his head enough to see the First Mate of the Far Lover pushing through the crowd and following him, calling angrily with a short sword in his hand. Caleb cursed and maneuvered the throng of people and cargo toward the wide gate into the city. Two elven Cityguard stood at the gate, clothed in their gray tunics, light steel armor and helmets, the elven gladi – short swords – at their side. The guard, engrossed in their conversation, didn't even look at him as he passed through the gate.

Caleb knew the First Mate followed him, however, so he pressed into the northern quarter of Asya. Old, dilapidated warehouses rose on either side of him, human workers busy while elven supervisors stood over them. He stole a glance behind him after two blocks, and two steel Cityguard helmets bobbed through the crowd in his direction. He took a deep breath and ran.

Leaving the warehouses behind, he found himself among tenements, gray rectangular buildings that had once been painted bright colors. Kryus had burned Asya down while conquering the ancient city, and they rebuilt it to show their compassion. But that was centuries before; the paint and color faded to nothing long ago. The smell of human waste and decay overpowered Caleb, nauseated him. The few humans in the streets were in rags, hollow-eyed and bone thin.

Turning left down a side alley between two tenements, he looked back. The two Cityguard gained on him, only five mitres away. He no longer saw the First Mate, though.

The alley narrowed along the length of the tenements, littered with debris, and beyond the shadows, Caleb peered ahead. It was a dead end. He slowed to a stop, sighing, and he whirled to see the Cityguard jogging towards him. The two guard completely blocked the way in the narrow alley, their gladi in their hands.

Caleb let his pack drop to the floor of the alley, and he kicked it to the side. He removed his cloak, his eyes never leaving the Cityguard in their approach, and he draped the mantle over his pack. He stepped forward and stood with his hands relaxed at his side.

The two elves halted two mitres away. They caught their breath, both scowling. "You need to come with us," the first Cityguard said.

The Cityguard triggered a distinct childhood memory: holding his weeping baby sister in his arms in a dark cave, hearing the distant screams of his mother as the Cityguard did things to her that he could only imagine, an imagination that had only become more detailed as he grew into manhood.

He thought about the letter in his pack, and the gold, but it was fleeting. With his mother's screams in his head, he kept silent and sneered back at them. He angled his body with his left foot slightly forward, his knees bent, his feet shoulder width apart.

The two elves hesitated, blinking and sharing a glance in surprise when they saw his eyes. But their frowns deepened at his gall. Trained to work as a team, the two guard tread forward with their gladi before them. Their faces were both intent on their prey, sobered in the duty before them.

But Caleb had been trained, as well, and by better masters. The Cityguard on his right stabbed forward, and Caleb easily leapt backward out of range of the gladus. The elf on the left immediately struck out with his sword behind his partner's move, and this time Caleb slid to his left, stretched out with his right hand and grabbed the sword arm of the elf. He lashed out with his left hand and crushed the Cityguard's windpipe. The Cityguard gurgled, trying to gasp, and Caleb spun the elf towards his partner, using the wounded elf as a shield and pushing both guard back against the wall of the alley.

The second Cityguard's gladus was caught between himself and his partner, and he struggled to free it as Caleb twisted the wounded elf's right wrist. He heard a snapping sound as the sword fell to the dirt of the alley. Caleb let the suffocating elf fall while he jumped straight up and brought his elbow down into the face of the second Cityguard. The elf sputtered as blood spouted from his nose, but Caleb wasted no time in crossing his arms and grabbing the elf by the neck. The elf blindly swung his gladus and slashed across Caleb's left forearm. In one fluid and violent motion, Caleb turned and threw the elf over his shoulder against the opposite wall of the alley and heard the spine break, the elf dead before he hit the dirt.

Caleb almost tripped over the other elf at his feet, still clutching desperately at his neck. He walked over to his pack, opening it and picking out a new shirt. He tore the one he wore off his body, ripped it into a few strips and dressed the gash on his left forearm. It wasn't deep but bled heavily. He tugged the new shirt on, placed the cloak into the pack, and he slung the backpack over his shoulders.

Both elves were dead by the time he exited the shadows of the alley and turned left onto the main street, looking both ways and seeing it free of any other threat. But the First Mate might have gone for help, and when the Captain returned to consciousness, the elves of the city would be looking for him.

He would need somewhere to hide tonight, but it had been more than seventeen years since he was last in this city with his uncle. He could only think of one place. He hoped he could find it.

—

Crossing the city, he used as many side streets as he could. The sun fell behind the city wall as he traveled, the western horizon changing to shades of orange and red. Caleb paused in front of an apartment building closer to the Merchant District on the southern edge of Asya. He stopped a young man on the street, a thin youth with bushy dark hair, pallid skin, and dilated pupils. Caleb could smell the sickly sweet scent of Sorcos on the young man. He was deep in the thrall of the drug.

"Excuse me," Caleb said. "Do the Re'Wyl's live in this building?"

"Whu?" the youth said, his body swaying as his head turned to look at Caleb. The Kryan Empire generously provided Sorcos as a drug they claimed entertained the mind and healed the body. What medicinal effects it had, Caleb had never seen, but it was highly addictive and produced a tranquil and somnolent population.

Caleb spoke louder now that he had the boy's attention. "Jyson and Rose Re'Wyl. Do they still live here?" He pointed to the apartment building.

"Oh, yeah," the youth said. "Up on third be the rooms o' Jyson; rooms three-four." He pursed his lips in satisfaction.

"Thank you," Caleb said, walking into the building. After he climbed the narrow stairwell up to the third floor, the hallway was dim and he had trouble making out the numbers due to the lack of light. But he walked to the fourth door, on the corner of the building, and he knocked.

He remembered Rose as a handsome woman, and that hadn't changed. She wore a baggy red tunic over a brown pleated skirt.

Running a hand through her graying blond hair, she smiled at a man she thought a stranger. "May I help you?" she asked.

"Rose," he said. "It's me. Caleb De'Ador."

It took her a moment to register the name, but once she did, her eyes widened. She froze and her face tightened. "Caleb?" she said. "What – what are you doing here?"

Caleb heard a man's voice from within the apartment. "Who is it?" the man asked.

Caught between her husband and the man at her door, Rose hesitated, but after a moment searching his eyes, she grabbed Caleb's left arm, the one with the fresh wound. He winced as she pulled him into the room. "Come in, quickly." She closed the door behind him.

The main room was small and sparse but functional: a small table with four chairs stood in the corner next to a wood stove and there were cabinets on the wall. A short couch and two ragged but inviting cushioned reading chairs sat on the opposite side of the room; books and parchments were piled on the floor.

A man with wavy white hair and a full white beard regarded Caleb from one of the chairs. He stood. Jyson was still fit for his age, and he wore a simple crimson tunic over brown pants.

Rose hovered next to Caleb and faced her husband. "Jy, he says he's Caleb De'Ador."

Jyson frowned at him. "Hard to believe. That boy disappeared more than fifteen years ago."

"Yes, I know. But I'm back now," Caleb said.

"He has the same eyes," Rose said, her voice low.

Jyson scoffed. "We'll need more than a likeness of the eyes to believe a man is someone we thought long dead." Jyson's glare challenged him.

They want proof? Caleb thought. Very well.

"My name is Caleb De'Ador. My uncle is Reyan Be'Luthel, also known by many in Erelon as the Prophet. He is an enemy of Kryus for traveling to nations, cities, and towns and preaching the truth of El, the Creator, truth that the Empire has tried for centuries to suppress or eradicate. He teaches men that they were created to be free. After the Kryan Empire burned my parents at the stake, my little sister and I lived and traveled with the Prophet and his family. I was last here seventeen years ago. I was thirteen years old, and my sister and I slept on that floor with your two kids."

"Only a handful of people know that, Jy," Rose said. "Only a handful in the world."

Jyson's jaw clenched. "What happened to you?"

Caleb took a deep breath. "I was kidnapped by the Kryan Empire while we were in the city of Landen sixteen years ago. I am back."

"You escaped?" Jyson asked.

"Not exactly. I was being trained by the elves, and my Master sent me away once my training was finished."

"You work for the elves?"

"No. I am free and here on my own." Caleb held up his left arm, rolled back the sleeve of the shirt and showed them the bloody cloth around the gash. "I just had a run-in with the Cityguard in the slave quarter. I need medical attention and a place to stay the night, maybe some help buying a horse and supplies. I will be gone first thing in the morning. I can't stay here long. They'll be looking for me."

A tense silence hung in the air for a moment. Jyson and Rose looked at one another, and Jyson shook his head in disbelief. Rose finally sniffed and gently took Caleb's left hand. "Come to the table. At least I can clean that up for you. Would you like some tea?"

"Thank you," he said as she led him to the table. He dropped his pack nearby and sat in one of the wooden chairs. He was soon sipping hot bitter tea while Rose took a bowl of water and a clean rag and washed out the cut on his forearm. She wrapped it again in dry cloth.

Jyson continued to glare at him from across the room, but he eventually walked over to the table and joined them. Rose set a cup of tea in front of him.

"Speaking of my Uncle," Caleb said. "When was the last you heard from him?"

Rose faltered, hesitating before she finished tying off the cloth around his wound, and then she sat next to him, pouring herself some tea. Jyson sighed and rubbed his beard, his eyes flicking to his wife. Rose blinked slowly.

"How long you been in the city?" Jyson asked.

Caleb looked from Rose back to Jyson. "Just got off the boat this afternoon."

"He don't know, Jy," Rose said.

"What don't I know?"

Jyson leaned forward over the small table. "Caleb, my boy, your Uncle Reyan's been captured and imprisoned by the Empire. They brought him here to the prison. He's at the Pyts."

—+—

Caleb sat quiet while Rose reached out and took her husband's hand.

"How long has he been in the prison?" Caleb asked.

"Three days, maybe," Jyson said.

Caleb breathed deeply. "Where did they find him?"

"They got him in Falya," Jyson said.

"Did someone betray him? Turn him in?" Caleb asked.

"Not know," Jyson said.

Caleb grunted. "Are they gonna execute him?"

"Not know that either," Jyson said. "But the Cryars keep saying that they gonna re-educate him."

The Moonguard or Bladeguard – Special Forces of the Kryan Empire - possessed all manner of means to get someone to talk, to twist their mind in unnatural ways. Kryus called this "re-education." Caleb knew full well what was in store for Reyan. He had been taught by some of the same Masters.

"I have to get him out of there," Caleb said.

A look of shock passed between Rose and Jyson. No one had ever escaped from the Pyts—at least not that anyone knew. "You know that's impossible," Rose said.

"Anything is possible with El," Caleb said, "wasn't that what he always taught?"

Jyson and Rose just looked at him.

"I'll need some help."

"We can't help," Rose said. "It's too dangerous."

"Too dangerous?" Caleb said. "We have to. Reyan knows where every pocket of resistance exists. Break it; he's responsible for starting most of them. And that includes the both of you. You're already crit deep in danger. All it would take is for Reyan to say your name in a moment of weakness. Then you and your kids would be hunted."

Jyson glowered at him. "Reyan wouldn't…"

"He wouldn't do it willingly, I know. But the elves have their ways."

The older couple gazed away from him. Rose chewed her lip. "How can we help?" Rose asked. She covered her mouth with her hand.

"Do you know anyone in the black market here in the city? Someone well connected?" Caleb said. "Someone we can trust. I'll need some supplies, off the books that the elves can't trace."

Jyson frowned at Caleb. "Don't ask for much do you? I know a man can get whatever you need, and he knows everyone, but…"

"Do you trust him?" Caleb pressed. "Will he betray us?"

"Freyd Fa'Yador owes me," Jyson said.

Rose looked away, shaking her head.

"He has no desire to come to the Empire's attention, nor give me up to them." Jyson scoffed. "But this man is not a man you want to deal with."

You don't know the kind of people I'm used to dealing with, Caleb thought. "You let me worry about that," Caleb said. "Can you get me a meeting with this man? Tonight?"

Jyson glowered at Caleb, the conflict evident in his face.

Caleb reached out and placed his hand on Jyson's arm. "I can do this, Jyson. Help me try."

A long moment passed as Jyson measured Caleb's gaze. "We leave in an hour," he said, and Rose groaned.

Caleb followed Jyson while they walked from the apartment to the Market Square to meet Freyd. Jyson explained how his position as stable master for the First Captain of the Cityguard had its advantages. The elves were comfortable around Jyson's constant quiet presence, and they let important information slip in his hearing, as they also believed humans were simple and stupid.

Freyd Fa'Yador ran the extensive, and lucrative, black market in Asya, and the main front for his operation was *The Singing Dragon*, a tavern. The Kryan Empire tolerated, or even encouraged, things like gambling and prostitution, as long as the taxes were paid. But the Empire kept firm control over the manufacture and trade of goods, however, setting prices and collecting profits and taxes. Those they caught usurping that control were punished severely.

Jyson was able to warn Freyd several times over the years of raids or other activity that threatened to expose the racketeer. In return, Freyd helped Jyson find a safe place for believers in El to meet or travelers to stay unnoticed, people like the Prophet.

Humans milled about or traveled through the Square, an octagonal area covered in cobblestones, well-lit with lamps and torches and surrounded by various shops. An imposing statue of Emperor Tanicus stood at its center.

The statue was made of pure gold, thirty mitres tall, depicting a perfect elf with long flowing hair and a robe draped over his body, his right hand reaching out to the west, pleading with the world of men. The statue's face shone with concern and wisdom. His left hand stretched down and grasped the golden human children, clamoring at his feet. Words were chiseled into the marble base of the statue: The Liberator.

Standing at the statue's base, one of the city's Cryars – a beautiful elven female with blond ringlets – called out the news and propaganda of the Empire as people walked by.

"Thank the Emperor Tanicus! He has captured the Prophet, and lies have been silenced!"

Caleb noticed that most of the citizens ignored her, but a few nodded or shook their heads as they passed. Leaflets and placards around the Square prominently displayed a Qadi-bol playoff game to be played the next night in the coliseum, but several posters publicized the heroic capture and imprisonment of the Prophet. Caleb gritted his teeth and followed silently behind Jyson.

Jyson led them left down Ceed street, and they stood before the opulent façade of *The Singing Dragon,* painted in red, green, and yellow with large torches burning in the mouths of iron dragons at either side of the open double doors that led into the tavern. Stringed music and clear singing could be heard as Caleb strode into the main room. The tavern was furnished with red padded chairs and round tables, all of it once painted to look expensive but it was now cheap and faded. Human patrons filled the place, most of them well dressed, some dancing, some singing along. Several men and women sat in a separate area where they smoked Sorcos, but the smell of the drug was minimized by perfumes and incense. Four women sat at the bar, dressed in red linen outfits that revealed almost every milimitre of skin. Known to the locals as crinkles, these women plied their bodies, whispering in the ears of the men who drank liquor and ale.

A beautiful woman entertained the room with a song. She was accompanied by a group of musicians – two with guitars, one with a mandolin, and the last played a fiddle. The woman sang about the encounter of two lovers who promised each other exaggerated and eternal affection; the lyrics of the song described the sexual intimacy in graphic, supernatural detail.

Jyson and Caleb walked through the room towards the back right corner where two large men guarded an arched doorway covered in a red curtain. Both men were a head taller than Caleb, thick with muscle, and wore red silk long-sleeved tunics, black loose trousers and boots. They looked past Jyson and regarded Caleb.

Caleb returned the stares, marking the way they stood, carried themselves, and shifted their weight. They possessed no real training or skill; strength was their one advantage, which was effective enough against most.

Jyson addressed the man on the right, a long scar across his chin. "Grat, I need to speak with Freyd."

Both men glared at Caleb. "Who is that?" Grat asked. The man on the left sneered with his pug nose. Caleb didn't move or respond.

"He's with me," Jyson said.

Grat frowned at Jyson, but he stepped aside. Pug Nose gave way, as well, but both men entered the back room behind Jyson and Caleb.

The dim back room was filled with more expensive items: gold and silver goblets, larger tables and chairs, and golden dragon lamps. Men and women lounged about the room, and in the far right corner sat a fat balding man with dark features. He was in his middle years, and he wore a long silk blue tunic gathered with a white sash over bright green trousers. He drank spiced wine from a goblet while sitting on a couch with a woman on either side of him – the women even more bare than the crinkles in the main room.

The large man looked up from his cup, his eyes smiling "Jyson!" he sputtered. "A rare visit. How are you?"

"I'm fine, Freyd," Jyson said, and Caleb felt Jyson's hand on his arm as they stopped five paces away from Freyd. "How are you?" The room quieted as Caleb and Jyson drew their attention.

"Can't complain," Freyd said, pulling the two women closer to him, and they giggled. "Settle down, ladies," Freyd told them, grinning. "We have a true believer in our midst." They silenced, smirking, but Freyd's tone lost its humor. "How are the kids?"

"Shel's still a stable master up in Falya," Jyson said. "And nothing new from Leni. She's well."

"Good to hear," Freyd murmured, and he waved at Caleb. "Who is this?"

Caleb stayed ready and alert, mindful of Grat and Pug Nose behind him.

"This is a friend," Jyson said, sighing. "And I need to call in a favor."

"Sure," Freyd said. "What can I do for you?"

Jyson glanced at the other humans in the room. "This is a big favor."

Freyd lifted his nose and sniffed, considering. "Everyone leave us alone for a moment," he said. The two ladies next to Freyd gave him a kiss before making their exit, and the room cleared. "You too," Freyd said. Grat grunted, but he and Pug Nose followed the rest.

"Sit," Freyd said. Caleb and Jyson pulled a chair from the middle of the room to face Freyd, who waited in silence.

Caleb assessed his options. Everything from threats to bribes crossed his thoughts, but he decided to leave those as a last resort. Jyson had a relationship with this man, and so Caleb would play that tablet first.

"My name is Caleb," he said. "And I need your help to break the Prophet out of the Pyts."

Freyd laughed heartily, his midsection jiggling. Then he caught Caleb's stare. "Wait. You're serious?" He turned to Jyson. "Your friend here is either insane or stupid." Freyd shot Caleb a mocking grin. "Shog a goat, boy, you know that's impossible. They're gonna do all they can to make an example of that poor soul, and I'm sorry for it, but how d'you expect me to help you?"

"Jyson tells me you're pretty connected. I'll need to get some things without the elves knowing about it," Caleb said. "And I'll need to find someone who has escaped from the Pyts."

"Like I said, impossible. No one has ever escaped from the Pyts." Freyd spoke too quickly.

Caleb sighed. "It is important to the Empire that people believe that, but you and I are men of the real world. We both know better, and if you know someone who can help me, I would like to meet him."

"You trying to start a riot? Crit on the Empire? They been huntin' that man for decades now. I've hid him myself in this city lots o' times. Elves'll be pretty piffed if they lose him now." Freyd had a tight grip on his goblet.

"Not trying to crit on anything," Caleb said. "Just trying to get him out of there." Caleb leaned forward, and his steel gray eyes held Freyd's gaze. "You're right. They'll try to make an example out of him, but first they'll bring in the best interrogators they have and try to make him talk. If he talks – and they are very good at making people talk – then they will get to your friend Jyson here. And if they get to Jyson ..."

Caleb let the words hang in the air, the logic not lost on Freyd. "So if you know someone that can help me ..." Caleb said.

Freyd's fingers began to fidget, and he put down his cup. "Big breakin' favor, Jyson. This could get us all shogged."

Caleb waited patiently. As Freyd knew, they might all be shogged anyway.

Freyd grunted. "I might know someone. Come back in the morning."

Caleb rose to leave, and Jyson stood with him.

"And Jyson," Freyd said before they left. "This favor? I do this for you, and we're even again, understand?"

Caleb watched Jyson nod somberly before they turned to leave.

Outside in the street, walking back towards the center of the city, Caleb asked, "What does he owe you?"

It took a moment before Jyson spoke, and Caleb thought he wouldn't get a response. But finally, Jyson growled, "I let his son marry my daughter."

The Dark Gate was concealed within the Kaleti Mountains, peaks that spread across the southwest region of the great continent of Ereland, also known as the land of Men on the world of Eres.

Thoros the Demilord stood before the Gate, waiting for it to open from within the mountain. It was dark but for the weak red light from the deep fiery caverns below, although his black eyes could see clearly. The scorching heat of the Underland wafted from behind him.

Known as the *Mahsaksa'ar* in the First Tongue, the Dark Gate was a curved arch of black stone, smooth and unnatural, and it was one of two portals to the Underland, or the *Heol Ra'eres*. The Dark Gate stood twenty mitres tall and ten mitres wide.

The Gate shuddered as it split, opening with a deafening sound, the gray stone doors swinging wide. Thoros rolled his muscular shoulders and stepped out from the Underland and into the world above. Storms raged upon the mountain and the surrounding region, the effects of the three moons of Eres coming into alignment – the green moon of Cynadi and the blue of Motali eclipsed by the red moon of Vysti. Black clouds gathered, tornadoes ripped through the foothills, and rain and hail laid waste to the countryside. Thick lightning accompanied by deafening thunder dug small craters into Maed and the plains to the north. The mountain trembled.

Thoros twisted at his waist to peer up at the arch. Written upon it was a script in a language older than even the First Tongue. Some once called it prophecy, others a curse, but more accurately it was a command from the Creator, the one responsible for its construction and the imprisonment of the demics into the Underland. The command inscribed in melted red gems stated that every five hundred and twenty-seven years, when the three moons of Eres fell into line in their orbit over the mountain of Maed, the Gate would open and allow a force of demics and one Demilord back into the world. The script placed the responsibility of defeating those monsters into the hands of humanity.

Thoros stood two and a half mitres tall. His dark red skin, hairless and thick as armor, had curses etched in black ink over his bare muscular torso and thick arms, each painful stroke a reminder of the dark power of the Underland; every excruciating phrase in his flesh had been earned as a reward from his Master. He wore a simple pair of loose black trousers that hung down below his knees. His eyes shone black and beady beneath a prominent forehead, and two large black horns curved up and outward from his temples to face forward. Two ebony tusks protruded from the bottom row of sharpened teeth in his mouth. He had pointed ears and a small nose. His hands and feet were three-fingered claws with long black talons at the end.

Thoros stood strong and immovable as the storm and gales beat at him. He took a breath of air, cold in contrast to the dark halls and caverns of the Underland, and his body adjusted to the chill. The night was bright to him, and he surveyed the northern vista from the face of Maed. He called his army of demics forth.

The common demics issued forth from the Dark Gate behind him in droves, a handful of them holding clubs fashioned from the stalagmites of the deep caves of the Underland, but most were weaponless; their talons and tusks would tear through any surface short of iron and steel. The demics looked much like Thoros but a third of his size and more simian with longer arms and shorter legs. The impish demics poured past Thoros, screaming in pain, a high pitched screeching sound, as the clean water and hail hit their red flesh, skin that had been scarred and tempered by the heat and dryness of the Underland.

The demics were not capable of much thought beyond destruction, hunger, anger and fear. Thoros commanded them with a telepathic link to continue through the Gate until as many demics as possible could make it. His orders were filled with implied threat in the face of the anguish from the hail and rain. They were created to obey, and he designed to drive them. He also promised them they would feed on the flesh of men.

Thoros felt the painful precipitation, as well, but his hide withstood it. The moon of Cynadi moved into the eastern sky and Vysti to the south; the storms lowered their intensity but still continued.

As the Gate finally closed, one demic was not quite fast enough, and the stone closed upon him and crushed the creature, black blood splattering on the stony ground. Other demics ran headlong into the shut barrier; Thoros could sense them in his mind. How many had made it through? Thoros guessed at least eight, perhaps, ten thousand.

Bana Sahat, the Lord of the Underland, had bred, trained, and tortured the Demilord for a millennium to come to the world of men and lead the demic horde for a single purpose: to find the Key that would free the demics and other creatures from the dark and fiery prison of the Underland.

The Lord of the Underland and the demics once lived in the world above, thousands of years ago, ruling the night and feeding on the flesh of the living. But Yosu and the warriors of El had driven the demics back after many years of war, banishing them into the deep chambers of the Underland where they starved or ate one another instead of the delicious flesh of human, elf, or dwarf. While the sun and rain would torture them, at least here they would feed. The demics were ravenous. So was Thoros, but he ate something far different and more powerful.

The same telepathic link that allowed him to communicate with the demics before him also helped him to locate the Key, the *Heol-caeg*. Thoros closed his black eyes and took a deep breath. North. Due north.

This was his hour, his time to do what none of the other fourteen Demilords before him could accomplish. He would teach the humans of this age the meaning of evil and hate and set his race free again to rule the night.

He opened his eyes again, and a smile spread on his face.

Thoros ran behind the demics, driving them north with an audible and mental roar, a demand to find the Key, and destroy and consume every living thing in their path.

CHAPTER 2

FROM THE PYTS

Laying on a pallet at Jyson and Rose's apartment, Caleb spent much of the night looking at the dark ceiling above him. He managed a couple hours of sleep before he woke and gathered his things. An uncomfortable silence dominated the apartment as Rose made a simple breakfast for him and Jyson.

After a few minutes eating, Jyson moved to the far corner of the main room, knelt down and pulled up a loose board. His hand came away with a set of parchments. He replaced the board, stood and came back to sit across from Caleb, staring at him. "You were away for a long time, and now you've returned."

Caleb nodded but wouldn't meet his eyes.

Jyson peered at the parchment. "The ancient scriptures contain a prophecy, a man who will return and lead humanity to freedom. The *Brendel*. Do you know it?"

Caleb didn't answer him.

Jyson began to read. Caleb wondered if that was his uncle's handwriting. "*He will be born in the land of men but travel far away. His return will be a sign that man will rise and claim their freedom from the chains of others and the bondage they place upon themselves …*"

"*He will be the rebirth of the Sohan-el,*" Caleb interrupted. Jyson and Rose fell still. "*The sword that gives him life will take his life. He will be inflicted with deep wounds, and those scars will follow him all his days. He is not a man, but a sword, and El will wield him as a sword, a blade to cut out the heart of those who enslave and oppress.*"

Caleb sniffed. "My father had a copy like that, translated by Uncle Reyan, and he used to sit and read it aloud, over and over, almost like a prayer. It haunts me every day."

"Great and mighty El," Jyson whispered. "Has it really begun?"

He pursed his lips. Believing an oracle to be true, to have hope in it, was one thing. Living it was a different matter. What kind of man does it take to embody a prophecy? Could he claim to be such a man? Before he could know for sure, he would need to travel west to find the Living Stone. If tested and found worthy, he would be given an unforged sword and become a *Sohan-el*, the first in hundreds of years.

"So you're going to the Stone?" Rose asked.

"As soon as I break Reyan out of the Pyts, yeah."

She covered her mouth with her hand, her eyes shining with tears.

He didn't want her pity, so Caleb stood and put the backpack over his shoulders. He moved to the door and Jyson followed.

"Sorry," Caleb said, facing him. "I'm going alone from here. This is where we say goodbye."

Jyson grabbed his right forearm, the one covered by the leather bracer, but Caleb wouldn't let him move the arm. Caleb met Jyson's eyes and set his jaw. "If I get him out tonight, we're leaving Asya and won't be back," he said. "If you see or hear anything suspicious, get out of the city and hide. You have a place to go, right? Arrangements for an emergency?"

Jyson nodded.

"Good, then don't hesitate," Caleb said. He wrenched his arm away from Jyson. "I know you trust this Freyd man, but the elves have their ways of getting information. You know the danger." He stepped into the hall. "Thank you both," he said. "I hope we meet again someday."

Jyson waited at the door, and Rose joined him. "We'll pray," she said.

Caleb nodded and left to meet with Freyd Fa'Yador alone. He would pray, too. He prayed what he was about to do wouldn't get them all killed. Or worse.

—⊢—

Still early, Caleb walked slowly down the street towards the Square, vendors setting up their booths. Once in the Square, Caleb noticed two Nican of Olinar, both dressed in long, flowing, blue silk robes down past their ankles. They wore short cloaks with roomy hoods made of a lighter blue, muttering prayers to the god of the ocean and dipping their hands into a crystal bowl before flicking drops of water as they asked for peace from the coming storm. Caleb lifted his head and noticed the clouds gathering on the horizon to the west. The storm would be upon them by evening.

The main temple of Ashinar, with the accompanying temples to the other eight Kryan gods, dominated the northern edge of the Square towards the Wealthy district where all the elves lived. The Temple was a cluster of nine high towers of white stone, trimmed in gold and silver.

Caleb wondered how the coming rain would aid or hinder his mission. Depending on the plan, probably both, and Caleb uttered a prayer to El, the Creator of all things.

The Singing Dragon was empty this morning, clean and spotless but eerily quiet. Grat and Pug Nose stood in front of the doorway to the back room again. They did not speak or move as he brushed past them to see Freyd.

A large round table was situated in the middle of the red carpet. The room was sparsely lit with oil lamps from the corners. Freyd reposed in a high back red velvet chair at the table, facing Caleb and drinking spiced tea. A pot of tea with porcelain cups and a plate of pastries sat before him. To Freyd's left, a small figure huddled in a smaller wooden chair, wrapped in a long hooded green cloak, the cowl up and casting a shadow across the face.

Caleb took the other empty chair that waited for him, plush and red like Freyd's. He removed his backpack and set it on the floor.

"Where's Jyson?" Freyd asked.

"I came alone," Caleb said. "Is that a problem?"

Freyd waved over the tea and pastries on the table. "Not with me. Please, help yourself."

"I already ate," Caleb said.

Freyd chuckled short. "Down to business, eh? A man after my own heart. But before we get to it, there have been some rumors of an incident yesterday at the docks."

Caleb raised an eyebrow.

"A man fitting your description seems to have struck an elf Captain of some boat," Freyd said. "My sources even say he killed a couple guard. The elves are very intent on finding this man."

"Interesting. You have a point?"

"This favor is even more dangerous than I thought. Attacking elves on the docks isn't my idea of a low profile."

"Are you saying you won't help me?"

Freyd shook his head. "I'll do what I can, but as a businessman, I have concerns that need protected."

"I understand," Caleb said. He leaned forward, facing the figure to his right. "Who is this?"

"A man such as you have requested," Freyd said. "The only person I have ever known to escape the Pyts, and I know this city better than anyone."

Caleb studied the shadows underneath the hood. "Let me see your face."

Freyd inclined his head. "As you may imagine, my friend here is nervous. The elves never advertised his escape – they might believe him dead – but if they knew …"

"Let me see your face," Caleb repeated.

The hooded head turned to Freyd, who nodded an encouragement. The figure faced Caleb, reached up with both hands, and lowered his hood, revealing a bone thin boy with a long, thin head and a beak of a nose, full lips and bulging dark eyes.

"You're a child," Caleb said.

The boy frowned at Caleb. "I'll be nineteen next month!"

Caleb raised his hands. "No offense." Caleb lowered his hands again. "What is your name?" he asked.

"Aden," the boy answered.

"My name is Caleb. Did Mr. Fa'Yador explain to you what I need?" Caleb asked.

"Yea, you wanna get someone out of the Pyts. Who?"

"His name is Reyan Be'Luthel, also known as the Prophet by some," Caleb said.

Aden froze, his eyes narrowing in either shock or fear or both. "You wanna free the Prophet from the Pyts?"

"That's right. Which means I need your help," Caleb said. "Did you escape?" The boy nodded. "How did you manage that?"

Aden took a deep breath, licking his lips. "Well," he began. "Like Mr. Fa'Yador say, I went in 'lil o'er a year ago. Been caught thievin'.'"

"He was a pickpocket and a courier of mine," Freyd interjected.

"So I was in 'bout nine full moons, and late full Daittle, I just couldn't take no more. One day, while they walk me 'round the yard, take me back to the cell, I figure I rather die than go back. So I jump down the crizzard pit."

Caleb blinked a few times. The Pyts was a prison of stone and iron, flat and spread out, built over three thousand years ago by men and now used by the elves. Prisoners were held within a hole, a pit fashioned into the floor. The opening of the hole was covered in iron bars. The crizzards lived underneath the complex, and they were large reptiles with six short legs, a long body, a prehensile tail with two bone spikes at the end, and a long snout with two rows of razor sharp teeth.

The "crizzard pit" was a hole where the guards periodically dropped prisoners below the prison for the crizzards to feed on fresh meat.

"You actually dropped down into the crizzard pit ... and survived?" Caleb asked.

"Well, crizzards be nocturnal, you know, so it was durin' th'day, and I ran and swam through the crit and mud as fast I could. They asleep, so by the time they up, I fast enough to find a tunnel that lead out to th'bay. A bar on the grate was loose and I could fit. Crizzards too big to follow. I swam out to the bay and hid under th'docks there." Aden cleared his throat. "After a few days, I made it to Mr. Fa'Yador. He help me."

Caleb shook his head through the whole story. "Great and mighty El," he said.

"Yeah, I was lucky," Aden said.

"I don't believe in luck," Caleb said. "Why don't you leave the city?"

"No got no money," Aden said. "Not enough to go nowhere. And not know where to go anyway. This the only place I know."

"He lives now in a back room I got in a store on the other side of the city," Freyd said. "Does odd jobs and cleans up late at night for room and board."

Caleb now turned to Freyd. "That is a kindness."

Freyd shrugged, as if caught. "Couldn't let the boy just die or go to the Pyts again," he said.

"You could, but you didn't," Caleb said, turning to Aden again. "Do you think you could show me that tunnel, help me get in the way you got out?"

"Yeah," Aden said.

"Do you think I could fit through the grate with the loose bar?" Caleb asked.

Aden's eyes narrowed and considered Caleb. "Dunno. Maybe. Prolly."

"Good. We go tonight," Caleb said.

Freyd put out his hands. "Hold on, racer," he said. "We haven't discussed payment."

"Payment?" Caleb said, leaning forward. "I thought you were doing Jyson a favor."

"Not payment for me," Freyd said. "For Aden. He don't owe Jyson – or you! – nothin'."

"Okay," Caleb said, turning to Aden. "What is your price?"

Aden met Caleb's glare. "Where you go after?"

"After?" Caleb repeated. "I don't understand."

"You know, after we break this Prophet out of the Pyts, where you gonna go?" Aden asked. "You not staying in the city. Where you gonna go?"

Caleb scowled at the young man. "Away. Far away."

"I figure. My price is that you take me with you where you go," Aden said.

Caleb scoffed as Freyd's eyes bulged. "Not possible," Caleb said. "Not going to happen."

Aden leaned back in the wooden chair and crossed his arms over his chest. "Then I not helpin'."

"Look," Caleb said. "I get it. You want out of the city, and I'll help you out of the city and give you money, enough to be comfortable anywhere. But my road is a dangerous one, more dangerous if the Prophet is with me. You won't be safe with us. Take the money."

Aden shook his head. "Don't want money or safety. Never had much o' either, and I come 'dis far. I wanna go with you and the Prophet. Thas the deal."

Caleb was dumbfounded. He sat back and grunted in anger, his gaze locked with Aden. This boy asked for the one thing he wasn't willing to give. Caleb didn't want to drag someone with them into the next city, not even his uncle, but he couldn't leave the old man there. And he needed the boy to find the tunnel, and the extra pair of hands to go with it. Caleb couldn't see a way around it. He could also discern when a person would not waver in their position, right or wrong. Aden was stone and ice.

"Okay," Caleb said. "You have a deal." He extended his hand.

"You and the Prophet take me where you go," Aden said, an eyebrow rising. "You give your word?"

Caleb sighed. "I give my word," he said.

Aden took Caleb's hand with a surprisingly strong grip and gave it a firm shake. "Deal."

Caleb released Aden's hand and turned to Freyd, who sat there with wide eyes. "Now, Mr. Fa'Yador, I need parchment and a stick of graphite. We'll need some things before Aden and I do the impossible tonight."

—┼—

Sitting back, Aden peered at the list on the parchment after Caleb left the room. The three of them had planned for over an hour, concocting a crazy plan, but this Caleb might be mad enough to pull it off. The plans written out before them included going to a priest of Olinar, an alchemist, for some acid and poison, and then going to the market for chickens, of all things. Caleb had gone to a local woodcutter for his own errand.

"If any of this gets back to me ..." Freyd trailed off. "All I'm sayin' is this is dangerous, and you don't have to do it. I don't know how much I trust that man." Freyd raised his hands in the air. "I still don't understand why he wouldn't take a sword. Did he kill those two Cityguard without a sword?"

Aden wasn't sure if he could trust Caleb, either. He unnerved Aden. The man was either absolutely insane, some religious zealot, or the only man of true courage and conviction Aden had ever met. Or all three. What Aden knew, however, without any reason but complete confidence, was that Aden's destiny rested with that man.

"You don't have to do this, you know," Freyd said.

Aden could have left the city of Asya at any time. After almost nineteen years of living on the streets and seedier places of the city, he was resourceful enough. But he had little motivation and no direction. He waited instead for something big to come along, and he had known the opportunity would come. When Freyd came late last night with Caleb's offer, Aden knew this was his turn of fate.

A golden dragon lamp transfixed Aden. A bright flame burned in its mouth. "I dunno, Mr. Fa'Yador. I think I do."

—┼—

Two hours after sunset, the air hung humid and thick. Dark clouds threatened rain and hid the three moons. Aden placed the last of the supplies on the deck of the small yacht, the *Happy Lamb*, docked at the end of a long pier close to the mouth of the River Tahan. A single lamp illuminated the work of the small group of men that included Aden, Caleb, and the three-man crew of the boat they hired. Aden knew the crew peripherally: Stash, Tym, and Chronch all worked for Freyd at various times. Stash, a short man thick with muscle and long black hair and beard, began to unfurl the main triangular sail.

"We're ready," Tym, said, a tall and thin man, bony but wiry, with bushy brown hair and a mustache that hid most of his mouth and muffled most of his speech. Chronch, a burly man of average height, didn't speak as he walked back to the rudder.

Aden joined Caleb on the starboard side of the boat. Caleb wore only a simple pair of tan linen breeches, leather moccasins, and that piece of leather wrapped around his right forearm. He was shirtless, and Aden winced as he saw horizontal scars on the man's back from shoulders to waist. Aden wore a similar outfit but with an added leather vest. Bags and packs sat on the deck nearby.

Freyd stood on the pier and faced Aden. "The Prophet is in cell three eighty-two. You know how to find that one?" he asked, and Aden nodded at him. Freyd reached out and extended his hand to Aden. "Gods be with you," he said.

Aden shook the hand gladly. "Thanks for your help," he said.

Freyd pursed his lips at Aden before his gaze moved to Caleb. "The boat is yours. The men will take you as far as you need to go. Pay them well at the end and you shouldn't have a problem."

"I will," Caleb said. He turned to the crew and said in a curt voice, "Let's go."

Freyd frowned and waved them on as he backed away. Tym untied the yacht from the pier and hopped back onto the deck with the heavy rope in his hand. Thunder rumbled in the distance as the boat sailed away from the dock. Aden held to the mast and kept his eyes on Freyd as long as he could, but Freyd faded into blackness. The *Happy Lamb* turned slowly and quietly to the right and southwest into the bay of Asya.

It started to rain.

A few big drops fell as a tease, and then the deluge drenched them all. Stash and Tym began to curse. The rain would only make controlling the craft in the darkness more difficult, which they had all warned Caleb about, but the man was undeterred. Chronch only grunted. Aden wondered if the first step of their plan was into action yet, albeit by other ignorant men.

———

The arena at Asya had been built three centuries ago by the elves, modeled after the great coliseum in Katriel. The immaculate circular field was more than two hundred mitres in diameter with a painted rectangular surface a hundred and fifty mitres long and seventy-five mitres wide. Quadi goals were erected on either end. With the storm, the field became a morass of mud. The rest of the arena was pure white stone, rising high in the air on every side. Tonight, thousands had come out for the game despite the rain. The violent game of Quadi-bol would be more captivating in the downpour. Someone might even die tonight.

Dozens of huge torches surrounded the edges of the field, torches designed by the alchemists of Olinar to withstand the rain and still burn bright as a small white sun. Mirrors were placed behind the torches to spread the light over the field.

Two men watched the game halfway up the stone stands on the western side among the fans of the visiting team, the Galya Bulls in blue. The home team, the Asya Griders, wore matching orange shirts. One of the Griders, on offense, struck one of the Bulls across the side of the face with his left paddle, shot and scored with his right paddle, knocking one of the two red balls through the upper half of the goal, scoring two points. The hometown crowd cheered at the score and the violence. Many cursed and raged. The goalie retrieved the red ball and put it back into play to one of his fellow Bulls.

Twenty-six total players ran around the field, thirteen on each side, a goalie, five defenders and seven offensive players each. Each individual player carried a paddle in both hands. Striking another player was as legal as striking one of the five balls in play, three green and two red.

The citizens of the Empire took the game very seriously, and even the poorest of the city would pay the money to attend a game. The wealthy got the best seats near the blood and brutality.

The first man was short and looked up at his companion with questioning eyes. The second man shrugged his narrow shoulders, and his eyebrows rose. The score was 53 to 50, in favor of the visiting team from Galya. The crowd grew anxious. Asya was supposed to have the better team. A man had paid these two friends a silver moon each earlier today while they had picked at their meager lunches on the docks – more money than they would see in a month, maybe two. Their instructions were to start a fight, a riot if they could. Riots were common at Qadi-bol games, so the men confidently said they could.

The shorter man nodded to his friend and regarded a group of men just below them who cursed the Griders for their foul play. Both men launched themselves forward and down on top of the group of men, their fists swinging, shouting, "Death to the Bulls!" The fans of the opposing team reacted violently, punching and yelling; a fight erupted and began to infect the crowd around them. A riot ensued.

The Cityguard would be busy tonight and the Empire's free clinics overcrowded in the morning.

—⊢—

Domitus, the Second Captain of the guard at the Pyts, hovered hear the thick iron gate to the main street, peering out from just inside the main entryway into the night, glad he was dry tonight. Beyond the entryway behind him, the Pyts housed over one thousand prisoners, spread out in fifteen hundred stone holes placed evenly in the floor. The Pyts stretched far and wide in an open enclosure with eight thick iron columns that supported a flat iron ceiling. The rain beat upon the roof and caused a constant rumble. The other guard behind him were in the midst of a game of Tablets; one even possessed a good hand, as Domitus looked over his shoulder – a priest, a warlord and two swords.

An elf new to the Cityguard came running through the street, splashing through gathering puddles to the gate. "A riot, Second Captain!" he said. "A riot at the game!"

This caught the attention of the small group of guard behind Domitus, light duty tonight already because of the game. The guard collected the Tablets strewn over the ground. Standing from their round of Tablets, they huddled closer to their Second Captain, looking eagerly at him. They couldn't all go, but they hoped to. It was an opportunity to bash some human heads or even use a gladus if it got particularly volatile. Domitus pointed to several of the guard and told them to go with the elf to the stadium. "The rest of you, stay here with me."

Domitus took out his large iron key and unlocked the gate, allowing the handful of prison guard to race out with Plinus into the street towards the arena. He locked the gate behind them again, and he smirked at the two who remained. Domitus pulled up a small wooden stool.

"Take a seat, gentlelves," Domitus said. "It will be a while before they return, and we'll be busy enough then. Get some rest." The Second Captain waved an arm out over the prisoners of the Pyts. "They're not going anywhere tonight."

—|—

Aden watched the crew throw an anchor over the side with a two-toned splash, and the *Happy Lamb* came to a stop a kilomitre out into the bay where the elven military ships were docked. He placed his bag across his shoulder, preparing to get into the water. Caleb looked back at the three-man crew, shouting above the storm, "Wait here for us!" They acknowledged him, and Caleb plunged into the cold water. Aden took a deep breath and dove in behind him.

Aden led the way, swimming through churning waves to the first pier. They paused underneath the dock holding on to wooden beams, and Caleb turned to Aden, his face a shadow. "You know the plan," Caleb said. "After you."

He mustered his courage, took a deep breath, released the underside of the pier, and swam again north. They swam from dock to dock, and Aden counted to the fifteenth pier, moving towards the rocky shore underneath. He paused for a breath, Caleb pacing him easily, and Aden swam towards a hole in the rock that led to the tunnel.

They tread their way slowly, and Aden could now see the grate at the edge. Both men were able to crawl into the rocky entrance. Covered in rust but still strong, the grate consisted of five iron bars, and Aden grabbed the second bar from the right and worked it back and forth. Caleb grabbed the bar and pulled. With Caleb's added strength, the bar came loose in a matter of seconds. He laid it carefully inside the tunnel.

Even through the wind and the storm, Aden could smell the stench from below the Pyts.

Caleb removed his heavy pack, handed it to Aden, and barely squeezed through the opening. He scraped through sideways, sucking in his breath. Aden handed him both packs and crept through after him. Caleb and Aden shouldered their respective bags again and trudged through waist high sludge towards a faint yellow light from the other end of the tunnel.

After reaching the end of the tunnel, they stopped, Aden squinting into the dark beneath the Pyts, hundreds of half spheres hanging from the floor of the prison overhead. He saw only two of the eight large iron pillars that continued up through the stone floor and to the ceiling above; the rest was lost in darkness. The rain rattled and rumbled.

The smell here caused his stomach to spasm, and the earlier dinner threatened to come back the way it entered. He glanced at Caleb, and the man grimaced in nausea, as well. At the bottom of each cell, an iron grate allowed the filth – urine, feces, and blood - to simply fall into the murk below, creating mitre high mounds of waste under each cell. Sewage and water ran between the mounds, the water bubbling and moving with the rain. Neither man retched, although they took a minute and breathed carefully through clenched teeth.

Pale light wafted through the grille at the bottom of each cell, and Aden observed Caleb traverse forward in knee high murk to the first round iron pillar, at least two mitres thick. Caleb opened his pack, reached in and pulled out a dead chicken, freshly killed and bloody. And poisoned. He heaved it out before him. Aden heard the splash but didn't see where it landed. Nine more chickens were spread out before Caleb. He hurried back to the opening of the tunnel and threw his pack across his shoulders awkwardly as he ran.

Aden and Caleb moved a short distance into the opening, close enough that they could see something approach but far enough that they could reach the bay again if a crizzard saw them. Caleb removed two more items from his pack, black wooden poles about a mitre long and sharpened at one end. Caleb adjusted his grip on them and swung each once.

After ten minutes, they heard movement, splashing near the pillar where Caleb threw the chickens. Low noises, almost groans, sounded and the splashing intensified. Crizzards possessed nocturnal eyes for hunting at night, but Aden was not so endowed. He could perceive dark shadows moving, and he caught a growl, a threatening tone. Another ten or fifteen minutes passed, an agonizing wait, both men still and silent, and the area beneath the Pyts echoed with a series of disturbing sounds, almost human grunts of pain that had Aden casting glances up above them. Could the guard hear? The crizzard sounds abated without incident, however.

Caleb waited until the only sound left was the distant rain, and he moved forward to the spot where he cast the dead chickens. He held the wooden poles before him defensively. Aden took slippery steps behind him. Soon enough, they came upon an area of floating dead bodies. Aden counted nine crizzard corpses in the shallow sewage belly up, all longer than a man was tall even before their tails.

"I hope that's all of them," Caleb whispered.

"Me too."

"We don't have time to wait," Caleb said. "Can you find the cell from here?"

Aden nodded and turned to trudge past the next pillar, and then he pointed up at the grille at the bottom of a cell. Measuring from the pillar and the wall to his right, this was eighty-two. Caleb approached the cell, climbing on the mound of sediment below the cell. He whispered through the grate. "Reyan?" Hardly audible, Caleb called again. "Reyan?"

Something, someone, moved over the grate, and Aden could hear a low grunt and scraping along the stone.

"Reyan!" Caleb called through another whisper.

A moment passed and a shadowed thin, wrinkled face appeared above them, framed by spare wisps of white hair. "What?" The voice was raspy and pained.

"Reyan, is that you?" Caleb asked.

"Who is it?" the old man asked as if speaking with sand in his throat.

"It's me. Caleb. I'm here."

The shadowed face above was still. "Caleb. Is that you? Really?"

Caleb's eyes brightened, his face beaming in the dim reflection from the yellow light above him. "Yes, it's me."

"Caleb, my boy," Reyan said, pressing closer to the grille, coughing and groaning. "I thought you were dead to us." Reyan had to take anguished breaths between words to speak.

"Not yet," Caleb said. "Move back, and take this!" Caleb handed Reyan a thin linen cloth from his pack, temporarily placing both poles in one hand. He pushed the cloth through the grille, and Reyan grabbed it with a gnarled hand. "Step back and put that over your mouth," Caleb continued. "Don't breathe in the fumes from the acid. And pray!"

"Acid? Of all the foolish …" Reyan muttered as he complied.

Aden now moved up to the mound, opening his pack in front of him, and Caleb slid down to the water below. Aden pulled out a linen cloth that he tied around his head and over his nose and mouth. He extracted one of the crystal vials of acid, taking a deep breath to calm his nerves.

The grille was small, and Aden doubted that a man could fit through it, but Aden's hands and arms were skinny enough to work through the bars. Aden barely reached high enough, though, but he was able to open the vial. A smell like sulfur hit him as he poured it around the stone of the grille. He heard a sizzling noise from the acid meeting stone, and he could distinguish smoke in the weak light. It took him several minutes, but he made it around two sides of the grate before the vial emptied.

Dropping the empty vial into the muck at his feet, he retrieved another vial and went through the same careful procedure. Aden finished covering the stone all around the grille with the acid, releasing the second vial to fall with the first. Grabbing the bars of the grille with both hands, he shook it. It moved, but not enough to fully remove it.

"Tryin' the chisel now," Aden whispered, he hoped loud enough for Caleb to hear. The steel chisel came easily from the bag to his hand along with the iron hammer. He placed the chisel against the stone between two bars and began to pound with the hammer. It made a dull scraping sound, and he hoped on his luck that the guards could not hear it. The stone chiseled away, and the bars all came loose in his hand. He dropped them to his feet.

The hole was open.

"Come on," he said to the old man in a hush. "We gonna try an' get you outta there." Caleb watched them anxiously.

The old man shuffled over and placed his feet through, then his knees, but he was too big. Aden pushed the man back into the cell. "Hole still too small," he called to Caleb. Sweat mixed with the saltwater on his body. Aden chiseled away at the stone again.

A distant and disturbing snarl froze him in mid motion.

"Aden. You have to hurry."

—┼—

Caleb adjusted his stance, shifting his feet a little farther apart and lowered into a crouch. The large shadow kept moving towards him, from Caleb's right as he faced away from Aden while the boy worked. Caleb hefted the two poles in front of him. Earlier, he had asked the carver for his stoutest Liorian wood to be cut into wooden stakes weighted like a gladus, the short sword used by most militan – Kryan soldiers - and Cityguard.

The crizzard snarled again, an unholy sound, and gloomy light through the grilles of other cells gave brief glimpses of dark green scales and glowing red eyes as the beast wandered its way toward them. It moved towards Caleb's left and the dead crizzards. Caleb got a better look at the size of the creature as it passed within ten mitres. It was more than twice as large as the others, both in length and girth. The six short muscular legs walked slow but deliberately. The spikes at the end of the tail were as long as the poles in his hands, and the tail swayed as the crizzard crept.

He now heard a loud sniffing noise, grumbles coming from the beast as it explored the area and found the corpses. Caleb also heard the desperate chipping and pounding of the chisel behind him, but he focused on the crizzard as it raised its head and turned to stare directly at Caleb.

It opened its mouth and sounded a furious bellow. It skulked quickly towards him.

Aden cursed loudly at his back, and Caleb did the one thing he could think to do. He charged the crizzard, both sharpened poles spinning in his hands.

He needed to protect Aden and Reyan. He assessed his environment: the sediment and sewage had its advantages and disadvantages. And he calculated the dangers: the two rows of sharp teeth, the spikes that could impale him on the tail, the claws on the short legs, and the sheer size of the beast.

The crizzard closed, and he got a full glimpse of the creature. A thought came to him as he noticed the size, girth, the darker scales, the ferocity and anger. "Oh, break me," he said under his breath. "You're the momma."

Throwing herself forward at him in one powerful lunge, the crizzard's jaws were open and forelegs extended. Caleb leapt to his left, pulling up his legs to clear the crizzard, and he made a slippery landing on the apex of the closest mound. Barely able to get his footing, he immediately launched into a flip over the back of the crizzard, stabbing downward with both poles.

It was to no effect. The wooden stakes bounced off the thick scales as if they were rock.

Caleb completed the turn, grateful to El that the poles hadn't snapped, and his feet found another mound of sediment. The crizzard's tail whipped toward him. Attempting to jump backwards and dodge, his feet slipped at the top of the mound. He fell back, the flat of the tail connecting with his torso and knocking him two mitres back into the muck. He managed to keep hold of the wooden weapons in his hands. As he scrambled to rise, a sharp pain lanced across his side. Ribs were broken.

He quickly climbed the nearest mound and set his feet as the crizzard's momentum carried her two or three mitres before twisting back towards him, splashing.

By this point, the other prisoners were awake and aware, crying out in fear, in anger, yelling for the guard in a chaotic din.

Caleb wondered if the underbelly might be softer, so he reached the top of this particular mound and crouched in readiness again. His heart racing, he sneered back at the crizzard as she lined up to attack him again. The crizzard spun with surprising quickness and strength to clear the mound where Caleb stood. He jumped this time to his right, down between two mounds and to the side. Caleb kicked out with his right foot, and the crizzard listed over just enough for Caleb to follow his attack with a double stab with the poles. Again, to no effect.

In his periphery, he scarcely saw the long thick tail sweep towards his head as the crizzard righted herself and scrambled down the mound, her body spinning away as the spikes of her tail aimed for him. Caleb dropped to his knees and bent backwards, and he watched the spikes clear his face by two or three centimitres.

Time ran short, the prisoners clamoring above him. Caleb took the risk of a quick glance towards Aden, and Reyan was still not free from the cell. The guards would be upon them any moment.

"Crit!" Caleb cried and ran towards the crizzard, ignoring the shooting pain in his side, his feet splashing as he raced straight at it. The crizzard hesitated but recovered fast enough to bound back at him. At the last possible instant, her jaws opened; Caleb jumped straight up, pulling his knees completely into his chest, and then kicked down with both feet on the crizzard's snout. He fell forward and stabbed down with both poles into her eye sockets. The poles went deep, but he kept his grip on them, tucking and rolling straight across her back, pulling the stakes with him as he did, blood and gore trailing his weapons.

The beast screeched in a deep tone, and as she gyrated in pain, she threw Caleb off to the side. He landed in water, keeping his head low and watching for the tail again, but the crizzard was in too much pain to be concerned with him.

Caleb scrambled to his feet, soaked with sewage and sweat, and he sprinted back to where Aden worked on the hole in the stone. "We have to get him out!" Caleb yelled.

Aden shook his head, looking up at the hole. "Still not big enough, but we can try."

The hole did look bigger, but it would be a tight fit. They didn't have the time for another failure. Caleb breathed heavily and faced the wounded crizzard, still alive and moving towards them. Even blinded, she lifted her snout to sniff the air, trying to find him, her head moving back and forth. Aden cursed loudly again.

"Get back to the other side of that pillar," Caleb said, pointing with a pole covered in bloody crizzard gore. As Aden moved, the hammer and chisel still in his hands, Caleb cried up into the cell above him, "Reyan! Get back!"

Caleb raised both arms and began to strike the wooden poles in a steady rhythm. Through the continuing but distant noise of the storm and the cacophony of the prisoners above him, the wooden clicks were clear and cut through all other sound. The crizzard turned towards him, the rhythm catching her attention.

"That's it," Caleb muttered "Come on girl."

Crawling in his direction, the crizzard covered the distance with increasing speed. Caleb kept striking the poles in his hands as loud as he could, next to the side of the stone cell behind him. The prisoners quieted.

The crizzard thrust forward in a desperate and powerful attack, blind and in immense pain. Holding his position until the last possible second, Caleb dove to the side as the crizzard jumped, and she collided head first into the side of Reyan's stone cell. The whole prison shook, iron and stone thousands of years old, the massive boom reverberating all around him. As the crizzard landed on top of the hill of sediment beneath Reyan's cell and slid down, unconscious, half the stone cell crumbled and fell with it, opening a hole large enough to fit two or three men through.

Standing quickly, he called out, "Reyan, are you okay?"

A faint, "Yes," was the response.

Aden was next to him as they pulled Reyan out of the cell, the old man leaning on the two of them. "Hand me the third vial," Caleb said to Aden. Aden frowned but reached into the bag and obeyed. Caleb let Aden take Reyan's weight as Aden took the Prophet to the tunnel.

Caleb placed the bloody poles back in his pack and walked over to where the crizzard lay, still breathing. He could see the shadowy faces of a few prisoners nearby looking through the grilles in the bottom of their cells, wide-eyed and open-mouthed. Caleb opened the vial, leaned over, and extended his arm as far as he could from himself and over the crizzard. He poured the vial of acid between the eyes of the creature. He stepped back quickly to avoid the fumes and threw the vial to the side. Caleb turned, hearing the sizzle behind him, and ran to join Aden in helping Reyan escape from the Pyts.

—+—

Domitus blinked awake, his mind scrambling to register the noise – a vicous roar. He sat up, rubbing his eyes, and heard another snarl from the crizzard, deep, dark and full. The mother? She hardly ever moved but to eat with her young once they made a kill.

The Second Captain had seen them feed more than once, and it had not been pleasant. The sight had caused a nightmare in which his own child had been thrown in that terrible hole, screaming at him to save her.

He sat up now, regular pounding sounds increasing in intensity, his mind trying to make sense of it all. The crizzard screamed in anguish, and the prisoners were crying out in fear, calling for the guard. In his confusion, Domitus frowned.

The two guard roused now, both standing. "What is it, Captain?" Quintus said.

Domitus rose and walked to the other end of the tunnel, looking over the torch lit prison, the other elves behind him. Nothing moved, but the clinking sounds and the mother crizzard roaring ...

The idea that was at once inconceivable yet fit the evidence fell into place in his head. Someone was trying to escape, or to free a prisoner. Not possible, but ...

His first impulse was to sound the alarm, but the Cityguard was engaged with a riot, he remembered. Another rhythm replaced the earlier metallic clanging, now a wooden sound. The Second Captain cursed and yelled at the two guard behind him. "Start checking on all the prisoners, all the cells. Move!" Their jaws had dropped at the implication to his orders.

Just as he and Quintus began to race into the Pyts, something exploded beneath them, a tremor vibrating throughout the whole prison. Quintus and Domitus both froze for a split second before continuing on at a full run.

"By the nine gods!" Domitus exclaimed as he sprinted towards the cell of the most important prisoner he had: cell 382. He pulled a torch from its housing on a pillar as he reached the cell, skidding to a kneeling halt just over it. He plunged the torch through the bars and cast light into the cell.

Half the stone bowl in the floor was gone, the stone blasted away somehow, and Domitus could see the dead matron crizzard, her head with a smoking gash between the eyes. But the one thing that stilled his heart and threw his mind into a panic was what he did not see.

The Prophet was gone.

Once they dragged the Prophet aboard the *Happy Lamb* amid the downpour, Aden and Caleb tore the wet and sodden tunic from the old man and wrapped the Prophet in a long cloak and blankets. The old man hardly breathed.

Caleb watched Aden collapse beside the old man, and he wished he could join him. It was exhausting work swimming in the violent waves, dragging the Prophet to the boat with them. His ribs screamed in pain. But they managed. Caleb knelt next to Reyan, and the three-man crew surrounded them. "You think we can make it back through the bay to the river?" Caleb asked the men. He held his right side.

The original plan had been to gather Reyan from the Pyts and sail back up through the bay and the River Tahan where they would stop at a town leagues away, perhaps Vicksburg, and catch the Asyan highway west.

Tym ran a hand through his soaked brown hair. "Dunno," he said. "Not fast, no. Not in this dark and storm."

A grunt came from the old man next to Aden, and Reyan began to speak beneath the heavy cloak and blankets. "No," he said. "Go south." Reyan coughed, a racking sound from deep in his chest.

Caleb leaned down, and Aden managed to get up on his elbow to face the old man. "South? Why?" Caleb asked.

"Galya," Reyan said forcefully. "To Galya."

"But I'm going west," Caleb said. "To the Living Stone."

Reyan froze for a moment; then he reached up with a bony white arm and grabbed Caleb's wrist. "Fool boy ... all the more reason. Listen!" He coughed again, and Caleb grimaced at the sound. "Go to Galya!"

Caleb frowned at Reyan, mostly in concern. "Always were a stubborn old man," he said. "Okay then," he reassured Reyan, "We'll go south to Galya."

CHAPTER 3

A REASON TO SPEAK

The *Happy Lamb* traveled out of the storm and into clear skies by morning, and Caleb watched as the horizon to his left began to grow a dim blue haze.

Once the rain stopped, everything calmed. One of the packs held dry clothes, and everyone changed. Aden helped Caleb dress Reyan, his body a mess of bruises and cuts. Reyan grunted, coughed, and moaned as they moved him, his eyes closed. Nothing seemed to be broken, but the man was suffering. After the new clothes, Caleb and Aden moved him to the bow and sat with him. Reyan lay still as death beneath dry blankets. The three-man crew hung back at the stern.

Caleb turned to watch the sleeping Reyan, and he was concerned. Had the elves gotten to him? Had they made him talk? The Reyan that Caleb once knew was strong, tall, and fit. Sixteen years ago, Reyan could have endured two days of cruelty, but this man was old and broken.

Reyan's hair had receded and whitened. His eyes were sunken and dark, even darker with dull brown eyes that had once been fiercely bright and wild. His white bushy eyebrows marked a pronounced forehead. His teeth had yellowed, a couple of them missing, sockets fresh and bloody wounds, his wide nose bulging from beatings. His cut and blistered mouth was small, covered by a full white beard. His right eye was swollen shut.

The old man stirred. Caleb reached out and shook the man. "Come on, Reyan," he said. "You should eat something." Reyan moaned and turned on his side. Caleb moved the old man's shoulder, and Reyan opened his eyes with a grunt.

He began to sit up, and Caleb had to assist him, handing the old man a soft pear. Reyan winced and grimaced at the pear in his trembling hands as he took a cautious bite. He glowered at Caleb.

Caleb watched in silence as Reyan finished the pear. He was unsure of what to say or how to begin. Despite a mountain of information they needed to share, the words were difficult to find after so long apart. But Caleb began anyway.

"What did they do?" Caleb asked, looking back at the crew. They were too far to hear their conversation. "Did the Moonguard or a Bladeguard get to you?"

Reyan coughed and nodded. "A Bladeguard. Name of Zarek," he said. "Came yesterday. Only beat me."

"He specializes in espionage and intelligence and interrogation." Caleb knew the elf's methods well. Zarek would have taken his time. "Did he make you talk?"

Reyan glared at Caleb. "I said nothing." Caleb nodded, somewhat relieved. If Zarek were on their trail, however, this would be more difficult than he thought.

"What happened to you in Landen?" the Prophet asked. "You went off by yourself and disappeared. We searched for days."

Caleb winced and glanced at Aden who sat nearby.

Reyan followed his gaze and scoffed. "He just helped you break me out of the Pyts. Can you get him in any more trouble?"

Caleb sighed and admitted to himself that Reyan was right, as usual. Stanks to be close to a Prophet again, Caleb thought.

"I did go off by myself that day. I snuck away and found a Sand-bol game on the other side of town. I played with them for most of the day."

Reyan shook his head. "Broke the rules for a game. Stupid."

"Maybe, but I was fourteen and loved to play Sand-bol. And I was pretty good at it. On the way home, I was attacked by an elf in a black robe with a black hood. I tried to fight him off, and I even got a good punch in across his jaw," Caleb grinned at the memory, "but he subdued me, bound me, and forced me to go with him."

"Did they capture you to get to me?" Reyan asked.

"That's what I thought at first. He took me to a mansion in the elven district of the city, untied me, and sat me down in a large dining room where a feast had been prepared. I was ready to lie or fight or die before giving any information about where my family was, but he sat across the table from me. He explained that he was offering me a unique opportunity.

"His name was Galen. He was the Master Bladeguard at the Citadel and he might want to train me."

"Train you for what?" Reyan asked.

Caleb leaned in and kept his voice low. "To be a Bladeguard."

Aden's eyes popped open and he sat up.

Of the Kryan Special Forces, the Bladeguard were the best; they were agents of the Empire and answered to the Emperor alone. Bladeguard were assassins, spies, and studied everything from strategy to philosophy. They were considered the ultimate in martial training, and only elves became Bladeguard. Until now.

"A human Bladeguard?" Reyan said.

"Crit on a frog," Aden said.

"Galen wanted to train a human Bladeguard because a man could infiltrate places an elf could not. But he needed to start the extensive training when the human was young. Galen was in Ereland in secret, looking. He came across the Sand-bol game and watched me most of the day, noting my physical strength and quickness as well as my competitiveness. He wanted to know if I was interested.

"He knew nothing of my connection with you, with the believers around Ereland. And I wish I could say that I saw this as some twist of fate or plan of El in that moment. But I remembered the death of my parents, how the Empire had taken them from me as a child, and I saw this as a stroke of luck. I would let them train me.

"Then I would kill them all.

"Before I was accepted as the candidate, however, Galen wanted to subject me to a series of difficult tests and trials, both academic and physical. We spent the next two days with these exams, and to his mind, I passed with flying colors, although I could barely stand or keep my eyes open after those two days. And that wasn't even the official training, yet.

"I asked to come say goodbye to my family, but he wouldn't allow it. He said that you needed to believe I was gone, and they couldn't know anything about what we were doing, for your own safety. I needed to leave everything behind.

"So we boarded a ship for the Citadel of Kryus in the city of Kohinar. And I began the training."

Reyan shook his head. "El works in darkness and gives light. How did you come back? Did you escape?"

"I didn't have to escape. I finished my training."

"And they just let you go?" Reyan asked.

Caleb took a deep breath, which caused a sharp pain in his right side. "Yes. Over time, as I was being trained, I realized two things. First, that this was not an opportunity for my own revenge but to return and help you and others fight back against Kryus. I could be a force for good. Second, that Galen was grooming me to do just that.

"Galen revealed to me his opposition to Emperor Tanicus, and that he believed the Kryan subjugation of man was an evil thing. Galen taught me martial arts and strategy and counter intelligence so that I could come back and begin a revolution. It was the ultimate in betrayal and treason to the Kryan Empire. Emperor Tanicus believed I was being sent back to find pockets of resistance to destroy them, but instead I was going to find them and organize them in an effective rebellion.

"So no, they did not let me go. Galen decided that I had finished my training. My Master sent me back with a bag of gold and a Bladeguard Letter of Regency."

Reyan's eyes were glistening. "Well, praise be to El, it is happening. After all this time." He swallowed hard and looked up at Caleb. "And I never thought it could be you. The *Brendel*. You were always asking questions and causing trouble. So bosaur-headed. Never wanted to listen. Reckless. Rebellious." Reyan smiled. "But it is you. We counted you as dead, and now you're back."

Caleb nodded.

"And you're going to the Living Stone?" Reyan asked.

"Yes. I was. Until you told us to go south."

"You still can. We need to get something there." Reyan coughed and grunted, frowning. He met Caleb's eyes again. "The Vow. Have you taken the Vow?"

"Yes. I took it with Galen before I left."

"No. Say it to me."

"But I already …"

"I want to hear it," Reyan interrupted, a tear falling from his left eye. "Say it again."

He looked at the Prophet, a man who spent his life traveling and teaching, sacrificing so much in a hope that men could one day be free. Perhaps he needed to hear it. Caleb sat up straight.

"Before the Light of El, the hand of Yosu, and the witness of the Living, I, Caleb De'Ador, dedicate my soul, my heart, and my life to find the Living Stone. I will defend the innocent, free the oppressed and spread light in dark places. I will keep my hands from any weapon of iron or steel until I prove myself worthy to be a Sohan-el and hold the sword that cannot be forged."

Reyan had closed his eyes, and another tear escaped as he opened them. He looked at Caleb's right arm. "You have the tattoo?"

Caleb nodded.

"Show me."

Caleb glanced back at the crew at the stern. "Not here."

Reyan looked sullen. "Fine."

"Now I have questions for you," Caleb said. "Carys and Earon. Where are they?"

Earon was Reyan's son, and for several years, Caleb, Carys, and Earon lived like siblings, sometimes fought like them, traveling with the Prophet and his wife, Aunt Kendra. Caleb counted Earon as a brother and a friend. It had been just as difficult to leave Earon and Kendra as it was his sister.

Reyan frowned. "Your Aunt Kendra …" he began.

"I heard," Caleb said. "I know she was caught and killed. I'm sorry."

Being close to Galen, the Blademaster of the Citadel, Caleb had access to information from time to time, and he would ask for any updates on his family. When Galen told him of Kendra's death, Caleb wanted to run out and begin the revolution right then and there, killing any elf who opposed him. The anger almost overpowered him, but he restrained himself as Galen spoke to him with reason. His day would come. Had it come now?

The Prophet sniffed. "Well, after she was gone, I was difficult to live with. So they left."

Caleb chuckled bitterly. Reyan was not an easy man before his wife's death, constantly running, hiding, sleeping in storerooms and barns, teaching and preaching when he could. Dragging a wife and children with him, Reyan was always about the next town, the next city, the next place to preach, the next message. And he never stayed in one place very long.

Kendra bore the responsibility of keeping the family together emotionally, her son Earon and Carys and Caleb. It was quite the burden, yet she handled it with grace and love. Caleb could imagine a difficult life with Reyan once she was gone.

"Do you know where they went?" Caleb asked.

Reyan sniffed. "They both left. Disappeared. Earon so hurt, and Carys so ... bosaur-headed. Like you."

Caleb nodded. He knew his sister well enough. One of the most compassionate yet stubborn of people, she was free-spirited. And Earon, strong in his own way, intelligent and sensitive; Caleb could understand what losing his mother would have done to him. The elves had killed his mother, too. "Do you know where they are now?"

"Carys, I don't know," Reyan said, and Caleb's heart dropped. "Earon I saw in Galya last year. He contacted me."

"Is that why we're going there?" Caleb asked, a flicker of hope within him. "To see Earon?"

Reyan shook his head. "No," he said. "Something I need to keep safe. Especially now." The Prophet tilted his head. "And maybe something for your journey."

"What are you talking about?" Caleb asked.

"You'll see," was all Reyan would say.

Caleb had one more important question. "How did they catch you? After years of moving and evading them, how did they find you?"

"Don't know," Reyan said. "I was in Falya, staying with this family. The Cityguard came in, killed the family, a man and his wife ... and his little girl. But they placed me in custody."

"Did someone talk? Betray you?"

Reyan shrugged. "Someone must have. But everyone who knew, I trust with my life. No reason to question. But the elves find a way. You know that. Better than anyone, now, I guess."

———

The sun continued to warm the day as the boat sailed south. Aden wore a thin tunic and his trousers, barefoot like the rest of the crew. A good breeze rose up close to noon, and the yacht began to cut through the water at a faster pace. Stash told the passengers they would make Galya by sunset.

The boat passed other ships on the trip, although most were larger trading vessels farther out in the great ocean. The boats sailed by the *Happy Lamb* without incident.

Aden had lived on the streets for most of his life. He assumed he was born there, but he didn't know for sure. And he suspected he never would. His earliest memory was of the man he knew only as Jo, an average sized man with thick muscular arms but a thin torso and short legs. Aden had heard others use the name; Jo never told him anything. When Aden would ask about the man's past, where he was from or what his full name was, he was ignored. At a question about his own past, his parents, any family, where he had been born, even his own name, Jo would frown at Aden with his weak chin, crooked nose and beady brown eyes then strike him across the back of the head and say some variation of, "Don't be idiot, boy. You nothin'. Born nothin' and always be nothin'." Aden stopped asking those questions.

Jo called him "boy." Aden didn't know his name. He didn't know if he ever had one. He was "boy" for the first seven years of his life. Other children roamed the Asyan streets, hundreds, maybe a thousand, sleeping and starving there. But they had names. Mostly. When he snuck into the theater and saw a musical about a woman who had five lovers but somehow kept them all ignorant of each other, he heard the name Aden, the name of the character she happened to love more than the rest. But he left her for a buxom beauty at the end of the second act. He remembered she had loved him for his good heart, even through graphic lyrics and gyrating scenes. Aden returned to the alley where he slept under Jo's protection and announced, "My name is Aden."

The man had laughed, a throaty, hollow sound. "You 'boy' and always be 'boy.' Stupid boy." And while Jo had continued to call him boy, Aden set in his mind his chosen name. Aden. He introduced himself as "Aden" to any who would listen.

Aden didn't talk very often growing up. Most of his energy was spent finding food, stealing it, and Jo only regarded Aden when they met at night and divvied up their spoils from the day. A rare day would give him a meal that filled his small belly. Most days he slept hungry. Jo taught Aden most things in silence: the best places to go to find scraps or booths in the market owned by vendors with poor eyesight, how to fight dirty, and their turf. That was most important. But Jo protected him and didn't expect Aden to do sexual things like other boys and girls had to do for protection. Aden considered himself lucky.

One night, Jo was drunk and Sorced. They had found some extra money and a stash of Sorcos. Jo had used half the money for ale, drank it, and smoked the Sorcos all in one night. He wouldn't let Aden have any. Jo was clear about the evils of Sorcos and ale, even though the man was as addicted to the drug as anyone, reeked of it, and loved his ale. "Not for kids," he said, but Aden had seen plenty his age, eleven by that time, drunk or Sorced. The drug and alcohol loosed Jo's tongue, though, for once, and he said something Aden knew was important at the time ... and knew he would never forget.

"There come times when a man be make an offer to you, and you need be take it," Jo had said, his dull eyes clearing for just a moment, as if even he understood the weight of the moment. "You just know you must take it," he continued. "And if you don't, boy, you regret you whole life. I know. I do." He leaned back among the refuse in the alley then, closing his eyes, preparing to sleep. "You take that offer and you not nothin' no more. And when you take that offer, follow to the end. To the end."

Eight months later, Jo disappeared. His things were gone one night. Aden still divided the spoils and hid Jo's share in the alley for a ninedays until he accepted the fact that Jo would not be returning. Aden filled his belly the next few nights but soon returned to his old habits. He was old enough. Other boys his age on the streets had no one to protect them. He took care of himself from that time on, working his way to odd jobs for Freyd Fa'Yador.

Four years after Jo left, Aden was in the square for an execution, attendance mandatory for all citizens. It had been a hot day, people sweaty and pressed close to him. Three "enemies of the Empire" were tied to tall wooden stakes naked. Their hands were bound and nailed together behind them, a heap of refuse piled at their feet. Aden almost didn't recognize Jo before he burned there in the square, the man so starved and beaten. And he wondered for the first time if that had been his father. He would never know now.

Caleb sat next to Aden at the bow of the *Happy Lamb*. He peered south, his hair tied behind him with a leather cord. Reyan was resting again.

"When we get to Galya," Caleb said to the boy. "I'll give you some money, maybe one of Reyan's contacts there can help find a place for you."

Aden turned on Caleb. "No," he said. "We had a deal. A deal!"

"Yeah, I know, and we took you with us," Caleb said. "But you heard us talking earlier. We're going a long way. And being with us is dangerous."

"I be alright. You won't have t'worry 'bout me. I help you," Aden said, the words coming from his lips in a rush. "Reyan an old man, sick and slow. I help 'im, take care of 'im where we go. I not slow you down."

Caleb scowled at him. "Who knows how long Reyan will travel with me ..."

"And I not eat much," Aden continued. "I give Reyan half o' my share. He get better. You see." Aden pointed at Caleb's chest. "You make deal!"

Caleb thought about the boy, a capable and strong young man. Aden knew better now what he was getting into. Could Caleb deny him the choice? "Why? Why do you want to go with me?"

"I see it to the end," Aden said. "To the end."

Caleb sighed. "Okay, but you do what I say, when I say. And if you slow me down one time, deal is off, hear?"

Aden nodded. "Yeah. Deal."

—

Chronch was a quiet man. Except when it came to money.

Freyd told the crew that this man – Caleb, Chronch caught the name; people tended to notice the quiet ones less – would pay them well. If Caleb could pay three men well, in Freyd's eyes, then he was over the mast with coin.

The three man crew, himself and Tym and Stash, all wore bland brown tunics, short tan breeches and went barefoot. They were all experienced sailors, all men in their thirties without a steady woman or children; at least that they were aware. After fishing the other men out of the bay last night, he thought he guessed who the man was they broke out of the Pyts, but he was so surprised that those lunatics had succeeded that it took him until midmorning to put it all together. By then it made sense. Who else would be so important that someone would go to such trouble to break the man out of the worst prison in the world? The shoggin' Prophet or he was full of crit.

By midmorning, Caleb, Aden and the Prophet largely ignored the three men huddled at the stern of the *Happy Lamb*.

That's when Chronch began to talk.

The other two men didn't listen at first. Caleb was going to pay them. Why be greedy and try for more? Chronch then explained who the Prophet was, the enemy of the Empire they had on the deck of their breakin' boat, and the fear emerged on their faces. They knew the trouble they could be in. They knew what happened to "enemies of the Empire." They knew well the screams of burning men.

Chronch then introduced another idea. A solution. What would happen if they turned the Prophet in? If they killed Caleb and Aden and turned the Prophet in to the authorities in Galya, they would get the boat, Caleb's coin, a reward from the Empire, and be heroes. They wouldn't have to work for anyone anymore, even though Freyd had been a good boss, he must admit. They would be set for life. They could go anywhere and travel free, maybe even join some pirates down south.

It took perhaps the better part of two hours before he had them convinced. They were men acquainted with violence and flexible morals, and now he had given them a cause and the motivation of money.

Noon passed and lunch was served. Let them have their last meal, Chronch thought. He had his dagger in the waist of his breeches at the small of his back, a simple and dull weapon of half-rusted steel. He would take care of Caleb first with the dagger, get the strongest out of the way. Tym and Stash would take the boy and choke him. The old man was going nowhere in his sick and beaten state.

Caleb, the Prophet, and Aden all sat in a small semi-circle toward the bow on the starboard side. Caleb settled facing away from the stern. Aden reposed toward the middle of the deck and the Prophet reclined on the other side close to the low wooden railing. Chronch and Tym walked from the stern. Stash snuck in from the side behind Aden. The boy happened to look over and caught just a glimpse of the dagger as Chronch pulled it free and went for the attack. Aden's eyes went wide in shock and his jaw dropped, preparing to cry some warning. It would be too breakin' late, Chronch thought.

He barely saw Caleb move, but one moment Caleb sat cross-legged on the deck of the boat and then the man was in a crouched position in the next heartbeat, his hands on the deck, his right leg supporting him and the other kicking out behind him.

Right into Chronch's calf, which snapped like a twig.

Chronch squealed. His face turned towards the sun in the sky, and his eyes rolled back in his head. He was aware of the dagger being taken from his hand, his wrist bent at an awkward angle that made it impossible to continue his grasp of the weapon. A punch struck him in the midsection, driving all breath from him, and he flew back two or three paces on his arse. The dagger clattered to the deck.

He heard Stash cry out, "Chronch! I got the …" and then go silent. Chronch managed to look to his left and see Stash leaning forward, holding his groin, his face turning beet red. As Stash's knees buckled and he collapsed, Aden brought a knee up into Stash's face, connecting with a dull crunch. Stash fell back, stumbling, and Aden rushed him, pushing Stash with both hands over the low railing into the ocean.

Caleb and Tym wrestled to his left. Chronch turned in time to see an elbow connect to the side of Tym's head, thick red hair shuddering with the impact, and soon Tym, dazed, was thrown headfirst over the port side and into the water.

Chronch panted and rose up on his elbows to see Caleb standing above him; the man's eyes narrowed and mouth twisted into a sneer. "I – I …" And that's all he had time to say.

Awaking to pain, Chronch's eyes fluttered open to a late afternoon sun, lower in the west, the wind tugging on his long black beard. He gasped and cried out as he tried to sit up, but he couldn't. His arms were tied behind him and lashed to the railing on the starboard side. He saw the Prophet staring at him across the deck. Chronch wanted to look away but his eyes were held there in that moment as surely as ropes bound his arms. He heard the boy say, "Caleb, he's wakin' up."

Chronch noticed Aden to his right with his hands on the rudder. Caleb rose from beside the boy and walked towards Chronch and leaned against the mast.

"You're fortunate," Caleb said. "We're not very good sailors." He pointed behind him to the Prophet. "He's probably the most experienced, but he's not in the best shape. The boy is sharp enough to steer us and keep us somewhat close to the coast." Chronch took another look at the sun. They were sailing more southwest now. Galya was close. "El will help us either way, but you seem a pretty good man with a boat. I know you're quiet, but maybe you would help us when we get closer to the shore, hmn? I'm pretty spry and a fast learner. And Reyan here will keep you honest."

Chronch tried to talk, to explain, "I – I'm sorry. I'm so sorry ..."

"Just a yes or no will do for now."

"Yes."

Caleb smiled, but it didn't touch his eyes. "Good. Which means I'm going to have to set this leg and dress the wound if we're not going to just throw you overboard with your friends. Seems like the decent thing to do." Caleb knelt down over Chronch's broken leg. Chronch could see a bone sticking out from the skin. Caleb grabbed Chronch's foot. "Now, try to hold still. It'll hurt worse if you move." Caleb looked up at Chronch and showed his teeth. "I wanted to set this while you were still awake."

Chapter 4

The Sound of Warning

Peliver Se'Chor perched atop the iron tower wearing his thin woolen cloak. The moonlit night was still warm enough, but the breeze could chill. His long blond curls stirred in the wind as he leaned back against the side of the perch at the top of a watchtower that was built on a low, flat hill two hundred mitres south of the town of Campton.

Campton marked the end of the Manahem road, the road that shot almost straight south from Ketan, the capital of Manahem, across the flat lands of the Julan plains. The center town boasted a few main buildings, made of stones, straddling the wide Manahem road. Small structures housed skilled labor, like the blacksmith. An open area with a semicircle of stone tables and platforms was the common market. Campton used one building, a long rectangular stone hall, for community gatherings, weddings, and other celebrations. They said that the building used to be a temple of some sort, but Pel didn't know for which god. Didn't matter anyway. No one in Campton – or southern Manahem – worshipped any god.

The people of the towns of the western Julan plains worked at two main professions: farming and herding. Leagues of grains and corn covered the landscape, fields marked with low stone walls. In other areas, herds of sheep or cattle could be seen across the countryside. Most of the houses sat within a kilomitre or two of the town. The towns got larger as the Manahem road moved north and closer to the ancient city of Ketan, the only place in Manahem with any real elven presence. The towns of the plains remained self-sufficient and isolated. And the men and women there preferred it that way.

The watchtower had been built more than four thousand years ago, and the men of Campton had always had a man upon the tower. The tower rose fifteen mitres high on four stone pillars and was topped with a square stone enclosure that looked like a battlement from an old fire tale. A massive horn began on the southern side, twisted around on the east, growing wider as it wound its way to point to the north. The horn was made of steel, a type of tempered steel that didn't rust, and the knowledge of how the Old Men forged such a thing was long forgotten.

What the watchtower had been built for, no one knew. Some thought maybe the old armies of Lior had once invaded from the south. Others told stories of men made of sand that could escape the desert of Gajens to eat crops and spread the boundaries of that dangerous wasteland. But those were tales meant to scare children. People rarely discussed it nor did they care.

Man is a strange creature, Pel thought. Traditions are followed even when the reason is no longer known, and the tradition itself becomes a hallmark of safety to the ignorant. Someone sat on that watchtower every night and they were safe, even if they didn't know why.

The horn was blown for special events in the town. It had been blown once at night when Pel was a child, but his friend Sal, thirteen at the time, had done it on a dare. Sal couldn't sit for a week, but the kids in town had laughed. The adults probably, too, but Pel had never seen them.

It was Pel's ninedays to sit the tower. He didn't mind it too much. Pel looked out and could see the dark peaks of Kaleti far to the southeast. He turned and could see the summits of southern Gatehm Mountains to his right. He gazed at the three moons, the red moon of Vysti three-quarters full and looming large overhead. For a moment, Pel felt peace in the still and quiet, as if all would be right with the world.

The rumble began almost at midnight. Barely perceptible, Pel wondered if it was distant thunder, and remembering the violent storm and earthquake from a few nights before, he leaned forward against the stone of the perch and squinted at the southern horizon. But it wasn't thunder. The rumble was constant. And it grew louder. Pel sucked in breath through his nose. Didn't smell like rain. The wind was brisk but dry.

Far to the south, Pel could see something black covering the plains. Still more than a kilomitre away, a black wave blanketed the once night-gray plains, spreading straight toward him. Both hands upon the edge of the perch, he leaned as far forward as he dared, focusing on the landscape to the south. The sound turned to something more familiar. The rumbling grew and resonated like a stampede. How many animals would it take to cover such an area? Were they animals? Men? Whatever they were, thousands of them ran toward him and the town of Campton.

Willing himself from his awestruck daze, Pel attempted to do one heroic thing in his life. He covered the puckered mouthpiece of the warning horn with his lips and blew as hard as he could.

Which proceeded to produce a sad, flatulent squeak.

He cursed, glancing over the iron horn again. The massive black wave grew closer. Was it moving faster, too?

Pel had never blown the horn before and had never been taught how. No one ever found it important. After a few attempts, though, he managed to do the one thing he was there to do. He compressed his lips this last time, curving his tongue, and blew more directly into the mouthpiece. The peal echoed loud and clear throughout the plains. He was able to sound the warning a total of four times before he was eaten alive.

The first warning of the horn woke Eshlyn Se'Matan from her sleep. She had a four-month child in a cradle to her right at the side of the bed. She was amazed at how fast she could wake, even from a dead sleep, after the baby had been born. She sat up on the mattress of hay and feathers, pushing the wool blanket off of her. Wearing her nightdress, she rubbed her big green eyes. The baby was asleep in the cradle, a bundled shadow in the moonlight coming through the window. Eshlyn frowned as the watchtower horn sounded again.

She turned to her husband, Kenric, who already sat upright in the bed, his feet over the side, facing south. "Was that the watchtower horn?" Eshlyn asked.

Kenric, a handsome man with shoulder length black hair, intelligent blue eyes, and a close-cut black beard over his square jaw, grunted assent.

Their one room house was sturdy and well furnished, situated at the southern edge of their farm just north of the town of Campton, land that Kenric's family had owned for generations. A low fire burned in the hearth in the middle of the room. Kenric stood, wearing only short linen breeches, and stretched his wide muscular shoulders. He was the "guardian" of the town, a title that sounded more dramatic than it was. Kenric's duties consisted of getting neighbors to talk and compromise. Campton never had any serious crime or conflicts that necessitated violence. But she knew her husband better than anyone, and his sense of responsibility gnawed at him.

The alarm sounded again. Eshlyn swore she could discern panic even in that tone, a hysterical desperation. It chilled her even in the warm room.

"Esh," Kenric said. "Get dressed. Get the baby packed up." Without even glancing to see if she complied, he pulled clothes from the trunk at the side of his bed and dressed himself in leather pants, a blue wool tunic and his leather boots.

Eshlyn was worried now. "What is it?" she asked as she pulled off her nightdress and began to don a long green wool gown with long sleeves.

"I don't know, but the town is in danger," Kenric murmured as he began to gather other items: a half-eaten loaf of bread and a block of yellow cheese from the small wooden table in the corner, the small purse of money for emergencies. He filled the leather water bag with the bucket near the hearth.

The alarm sounded a fourth time.

Eshlyn had on her own short leather boots and began to gather up the baby, who began to wake, whimpering. "What could it be?" she asked, fear in her voice. "What could be out there?"

Kenric shook his head. "Come on, we're going to the barn," he said. Eshlyn had the baby wrapped up in gray wool blankets. "Get a cloak," he told her as he opened the plank wooden door and headed out into the night. She grabbed a long brown cloak and the sling for the baby and followed him.

Noise carried well from the town, especially on a night when the wind blew up from the south. So they both heard the screams from the center of town. Human screams.

Eshlyn stumbled and almost fell, gathering her crying baby closer to her chest. Kenric paused for a split second, staring again to the south, and he ran to the barn. "Come on!" he shouted.

She ran with him, across the gravel path between the small house and the barn that held Silly the ox, a few chickens, the plow, various farm supplies and feed, and Blackie the mare. Kenric threw open the double doors and began to saddle the horse. A good strong horse for riding and traveling, Blackie's eyes bulged and darted, and she stepped nervously as Kenric pulled the bridle over her head.

Kenric turned to Eshlyn, holding out his hands to the side of the horse. "Give me the baby and get on," he said. She hurried to do as he said and soon sat in the worn leather saddle with her son. Javyn was in her lap in the next breath, and Eshlyn fumbled with the sling. Setting it, she placed the baby within.

Looking up, her husband had raced to the far corner of the barn, digging beneath the hay, and stood again with a long gleaming sword in his hand.

"Ken!" she shrieked. "Where did you get a sword?"

Looking up at her with a steady gaze, Kenric walked back to the horse, grabbed the reins, placed the scrip of items gathered from the house onto her lap, led her out of the barn. "Listen carefully to me," he said. "My ancestor was the last king of Manahem, King Judai."

"What?" Had the most pragmatic and grounded man she ever knew gone full maddy?

"Just listen!" Kenric took a deep breath. "He gave his grandson this sword and commanded him to move far to the south and continue the line. That grandson dressed as a pauper with nothing to his name and moved here to Campton almost four hundred years ago. He passed it on to his son, and his son to his son, and so on. Our son, Javyn, is the rightful king and heir to Manahem."

He led the horse out to the Manahem road, a short distance from their house. "I want you to ride as hard and as fast as you can and warn people. Get to the city of Ketan. Get people behind the walls of Ketan."

Eshlyn twisted violently in the saddle. "No!" she screamed. Why was he talking like this? What was he saying? "You're coming with us!"

"I can't," Kenric said. "I have to see what is going on in the town, if I can help."

"Then I'm staying with you!" She began to weep and tried to slide off the horse.

Kenric's strong arms kept her where she sat.

"I can't leave you here. I can't go without you!"

More screams met their ears, and they both turned south. The cries of horror were mixed with snarls and growls of something inhuman and violent.

"I love you," Kenric said. "And I love Javyn." Kenric placed his right hand on the child. "He is more important now. I need to know that you both are safe. Please. Go."

She shook her head. "No, no."

"If this is what I think it is," he said, "then tell them all to run to Ketan. And when you get there, try to find the Key."

She still shook her head, her heart denying his words.

"The Key, Eshlyn," he said, firm and deep. "That's what they're after, I think. That's all my father told me." He smiled at her one last time, his eyes brimming with water. "And keep singing my lullaby to him for me, please."

Gaping at her husband, she knew she should speak to him, argue with him, but for once in her life she was speechless. Torn between wanting to stay with the man she loved and her child, and overcome by fear, all she could produce was a weak whimper. Ken pulled her down and kissed her full on the lips. She closed her mouth and clutched the baby to keep him from spilling from the sling. Pushing her back up, Ken whispered, "I love you."

Eshlyn groaned as he slapped Blackie's back, and the horse galloped off to the north. After a few minutes, only the noise of the wind filled her ears, and she kicked the mare to her top speed.

Then she realized as she wept and raced into the night: she'd never told her husband goodbye.

———

Kenric watched his wife and son ride off into the night. But he didn't have the luxury to watch for long.

He turned and sprinted towards the town down the Manahem road with the sword in his hand. His father had shown him the sword when he was twelve, when he was big enough to hold it in two hands, and the sword brought back memories, warm and clear as his heart raced with fear. He remembered secret moments working with his father, learning basic slashes and cuts with the blade, hearing tales of ancient kings and heroes and his own heritage. Kenric's parents both died from a sickness two years ago, just after his wedding to Eshlyn. He had hoped to have those same secret times with his own son. But that was not meant to be.

Just outside of town, the scene was chaos. Small, dark man-shaped figures darted back and forth, screeching and snarling. As he got closer, his fears were realized.

Demics.

When his father had told him of the demics almost two decades ago, Kenric was sure none of it could be real. Like the tales of dragonmen – children of dragons and women that hid in dark places and under beds to eat children – Kenric believed that his father's tales of the demics sprang from some ancient myth that had taken on a life of its own over the centuries, used as entertaining hearth tales.

Could there really be demon beings from the Underland searching for a Key that would free the whole of *Heol* and inflict the world with terror and death? It all seemed fantasy to a boy who knew grain, hard work, and a clear open sky.

But here the fantasy was real, and he was glad he had told Eshlyn about the key. Maybe his death would mean something. Maybe his son would live, and one day Manahem would rise again.

A demic, small and red-skinned with black eyes, crawled nearby. Kenric ran to place himself in its path and swung the sword with all his might, cleaving the demic in two like a plow through a soft field. The sword never even slowed as he killed the thing. Others randomly ran about him, and he slew three more before they began to take notice of him.

Kenric's father told him that the sword was special, an unforged sword, whatever that meant, that it was stronger and more powerful than other swords. Kenric had considered that part of the fantasy: a holy sword, a demon horde. Silliness, but he had loved to hear his father tell secret stories and share things with him, so he remembered it all in detail.

But as he put it to work he began to believe the sword was special. He swung it with dexterity he didn't know he possessed, back and forth, spinning with forms he didn't remember to connect perfect killing blows upon the demics that began to surround him. He hacked and struck, stabbed and slashed, striding through the sea of demics. But the combat only drew the bloodthirsty demics to him, and they moved closer with sharp claws and teeth, wave upon wave.

He fell underneath the mass of demics, and one of the creatures bit into his right wrist and tore off the sword hand. Kenric cried out and found himself on his back, another demic ripping flesh from his leg.

He didn't know how long he was able to fight them off, but it didn't seem like enough time. He prayed to El, a god he only knew by name from his father, a god his distant ancestor – a king – had served, and he hoped that his wife and son were safe.

"*Stop.*" He heard a voice, deep and loud, reverberating through the night and the ground beneath him. The demics pulled away from him, many with his skin or muscle in their teeth or claws, and they looked up. Kenric's vision faded, but not before he saw a massive figure standing over him.

———

Caleb guessed that Reyan was leading them to the ancient and forbidden ruins of Debir across the river from the city of Galya. They reached it three hours after sunset.

Earlier, they managed to navigate themselves to a little inlet off the coast on the southern edge of the river Moriel. Galya's white and smooth stone walls shone yellow and red in the twilight on the northern border of the river. Caleb threw out the anchor in an area hidden from the ships that would pass journeying south from Galya to Landen or back again.

The three of them – Aden, Caleb, and Reyan – had a quick dinner on the deck before he and Aden brought the bags of supplies to the shore, carrying Reyan to the beach last. All men knew this area was forbidden, and Chronch watched them prepare with a constant wince. But they left him, still tied to the railing.

They piled their supplies at the base of a big tree underneath some brush at the bank. They were not worried about anyone finding or stealing it. Caleb did sling one bag across his shoulders, however. Caleb and Aden supported Reyan on either side, and the three of them walked westward to the ruins. They came to an open field of tall grass. Caleb could feel the ancient memories in the very air around them, the ground.

"What's this place?" Aden asked.

"Once, long ago, before the War of Liberation, this whole area was a Temple to El," Caleb said. "The Creator of all things."

"Nothin' here now," Aden said, glancing around.

"It was once a great complex," Caleb said. "With walls five kilomitres around and ten mitres high, covered with gold and silver, and eight silver spires were regularly spaced around the walls. There was a single entrance with no gate or door. All were free to enter. People from all the lands of men would come to worship.

"At the center of the complex was the Dror, the sacred place. It had no walls, only marble pillars that supported a golden dome. There was an altar there, not made of precious metal or stone, just a simple pile of rocks. It was said El would make precious the heart that humbled itself at that altar. Kings, rulers, peasants, criminals—they were all welcome and equal there."

"What happened to it?"

"After Asya, Galya was the next city to fall in the Kryan War of Liberation. Galya was a place known for peace. It fell without a fight. The

Temple complex had fallen into disrepair by that point as faith in El waned and man became more corrupt. Nevertheless, the elves stripped Debir of its precious metal and stone and razed it to the ground. Some say it burned for a month."

Caleb peered about them in the dark as they walked. The vast field of tall grass was all that remained.

"What was here?" Aden asked.

"The Dror," Caleb said. "The altar of humility, exaltation and equality."

"And something for those even more humble to remember," Reyan said, finding purchase in the dirt with his gnarled hands. "Here. Pull. I can't." He sat back, overcome by a racking cough.

Caleb and Aden stepped forward and reached down to where his hands had been, and they found an iron handle. Caleb nodded as Aden glanced his way with a raised eyebrow. They pulled upwards, and a heavy stone door, covered with sod and tall grass, rose up like a lid.

In the moonlight, Caleb saw the stone stairs that led to the underground room. He held the door open while Aden lifted two iron poles from the stairs below to hold it in place. The two men then reached down and helped Reyan stand. The three descended the long winding stairs several mitres. Once at the bottom of the steps, Caleb stuck out his hand to his left and grabbed an unlit torch. He took his flint and struck a fire to light it. The yellow glow extended halfway into the large room below, and Reyan urged them straight to the other end of the room.

"What's this room?" Aden asked.

"Centuries before the siege of Asya, the caretakers of the temple here knew that man would fall," Caleb said. "The prophecies were clear to the caretakers even as man denied their own fall. So they dug this room under the cover of night and in secret."

"The elves never find it?" Aden said.

"No," Caleb said. "The knowledge of this place was unimportant to humanity and lost to them long before the War of Liberation. The elves never even knew to look, and so it survived." The room was an approximate fifteen mitres square, covered in stone with murals painted around the walls, faint shadows in the dim torchlight now they were in the middle of the room. A long stone table rested against the far wall.

"And how you know 'bout it?" Aden asked.

"A select few kept the secret and still lived in Erelon," Caleb answered. "That secret passed to Reyan's father, who passed it to him." Caleb shrugged. "And me and Earon and Carys, too, I suppose."

"And why're we here?" Aden questioned.

"I think we're about to find out," Caleb said. "Reyan?"

"There," Reyan said, pointing to the stone table.

A large leather bag lay upon it. Leaning against the table was a long wooden staff. Aden and Caleb sat Reyan on the table next to the leather bag. Caleb opened it for him. Within the bag were four leather bound books, two of them very old, and a small wooden box with a dragon etched in the top. He recognized those old volumes. The other two books were bound with fresh leather and crisp, white paper.

He turned to Reyan. "Did you do it?" Caleb asked the old man, running his fingers along the leather with a light touch.

Reyan nodded. "It took me twenty years, but I translated the scriptures and the testimony from the First Tongue to the common."

Caleb chuckled. "And let me guess," he said. "These are the only copies."

"For now," Reyan said.

"Of course," Caleb said, rolling his eyes. As if I don't have enough to worry about, he thought. Caleb noticed Aden's quiet questioning face in the yellow glare. "The testimony speaks of the creation of the world, the history of the first race, the division of the three races, and the First Men." Caleb pointed to the thinner volume. "The scriptures are the teachings and prophecies of the first men; at least the ones they recorded." Caleb turned now to Reyan. "And you want to take these with us?"

"The time has come. We need them."

"What's in th'box?" Aden asked.

Caleb exchanged a glance with Reyan. "The very reason why they built this room," Caleb said. "The dracolet. It's an amulet forged by the First Men and it gives the bearer great power."

"What's it do?" Aden whispered as if someone might overhear.

Caleb shook his head. "Power to rule the lands of men again, to drive away any invaders. And that is why, when men lost their faith and became corrupt, the caretakers of Debir knew they had to hide it. Humanity lost their faith and became slaves to the elves, but the caretakers hoped that one day man would be worthy enough to be free again." Caleb frowned at Reyan. "And you want me to take this, too? You know it's not for me. Can't be."

"Yes," Reyan said, taking the box from the table. "We take it. But no, not for you." Reyan pointed to the staff. "That is for you."

This time Caleb was ignorant. "I don't know what this is," he said.

"That is the Kingstaff of El," Reyan said. "An ancient elven king carved and fashioned that staff and gave it to the king of Erelon as a gift over a three thousand years ago."

"Ah, yes," Caleb said. "I remember now. Where did you find it?"

"In a cellar in the city of Oshra," Reyan said.

The Kingstaff of El was legend. Made of dark, smooth brown wood, the staff came up to his shoulder, straight and blunted at the ends. It was a simple length of wood marked with an ancient inscription along the side. Caleb read the flowing black script, written in the First Tongue. Loosely translated: *To lead with compassion, justice, and strength*. It was light but felt strong as he stepped back, picking it up and swinging it around himself.

"It's special or somethin'?" Aden asked.

"Supposedly," Caleb said, watching Reyan for confirmation. "The Kingstaff of El was taken from a tree deep in the First Forest by the elves of the Kingdom of Faltiel. It is supposed to be as strong as steel. The elves there made this and gave it to the king of Erelon at the time. Don't remember his name."

"Whevel," Reyan said.

"Strong as steel? It's made from magic?" Aden asked in fear.

Magic – the manipulation of the forces of nature – was once widely practiced by the elves, but that magic proved destructive and dangerous. The kingdoms of men and elves had outlawed magic thousands of years ago. Things made with magic caused awe and terror. But the Kingstaff had been made long before magic was made illegal.

Caleb looked to Reyan again, who shrugged as if it didn't matter. "Don't know," Caleb answered. "I do know that the elves of Faltiel have skills when it comes to woodworking that are beyond our understanding but also do not take magic to complete. Either way, this is an amazing find." Caleb began to eye the staff itself. "The ancient ways are being found again."

"For you," Reyan said. "Until you get your sword."

Caleb nodded. "So you just hid all this stuff down here? You were caught and might have died in the Pyts. What would have happened then?"

Reyan coughed. "El finds a way, and Earon knows. He knew what to do."

"I would love to see him again," Caleb said.

Reyan grinned. "You can leave him a message. Tomorrow."

Caleb grinned back at Reyan. He looked over at Aden, smiling. The boy looked confused, an infinite amount of questions on his face. So much to explain. So much knowledge lost. "Go give Chronch something to eat and bring the rest of our supplies back, Aden," Caleb said. "We're spending the night here tonight."

—

Thoros stood over the dying man on the ground as the demics made room for him. He reached down and picked up the sword, tearing the man's bloody hand from the hilt. He couldn't believe his black eyes. An unforged sword. Could this be a *Sohan-el*?

In order for the Key to work, to open the Dark Gate and allow the Lord and the races of the Underland to live upon Eres again, the Demilord would need to defeat and feed upon a Sohan-el. And only Sohan-el were worthy to carry an unforged sword.

The man twitched, life and blood flowing from him and soaking the soil underneath. Ragged and random breaths racked the body as it attempted to survive one last moment. The man's eyes stared off into nothing.

Thoros peered down at the man's right forearm that ended in a chewed and bloody stump. Warriors of El were marked with a tattoo on their arm, a tree growing from a stone. This man had none.

The man may not be a *Sohan-el*, but Thoros would still feed upon him. The Demilord had to hurry before the man passed into the Everworld and beyond his reach.

Demics fed on the flesh of the living. Demilords, however, ate something that did not exist in the Underland: the souls of the living.

Thoros pressed his three-fingered claw upon the man's chest. He spoke an incantation in a language older than the division of the three races. Thoros was blind with pleasure, his head tilting back with a smile. Then he consumed the soul of the man, and it nourished the Demilord.

The soul told him all he needed to know. The man had not been a *Sohan-el*. But he tasted rich and strong just the same.

Chapter 5

A Message

Chronch was shaken awake just before dawn. His whole body ached, but as he stirred, he noticed he was no longer bound to the boat. His broken calf was bound in linens to a firm branch. Caleb knelt before him with a small bag in his right hand and a long wooden staff in his left.

"Good morning," Caleb said.

Chronch did not answer but sat up straight, backing away as far as he could, wary of the man. There was murder in his eyes.

"I'm going to tell you how this will work, now, okay?" Caleb asked.

Chronch nodded.

"After I leave this boat, you will sail past the border of Erelon and go all the way to Landen or farther," Caleb said. "You get to keep the boat. We won't need it from here. That will be your payment and we'll call it even. Everything in me says to kill you, but I'm showing a kindness instead. Hopefully you won't prove me a fool for doing so." Caleb lifted the bag in his hand. "This is enough food for a few days. I suggest being frugal."

He threw the bag at Chronch's feet. Chronch watched in stillness as Caleb turned and left him, wading back through the inlet to the coast and walking away.

Within minutes, he had raised the anchor and was sailing south, limping around the deck. Maybe he would stop at Landen, but he thought Oshra was a better idea. Oshra was a thousand kilomitres farther than Landen.

———

By the time Aden awoke, Caleb was gone. The fire they built the night before burned low in the middle of the underground room. He added a few dry branches to the fire as Reyan stirred on blankets on the stone floor. Aden stretched and pulled on a shirt before breaking out some food for breakfast: spicy mutton jerky, dried apples and small hard biscuits. He and Reyan shared the food in silence while they drank fresh water from the river Moriel out of their canteens. Sunlight had just begun to peek through the door to the hidden room where they were from the ruins above.

Licking the crumbs from his hands and drying them on the seat of his breeches, he stood. Three walls of the underground chamber had murals painted upon the plaster. He lit a torch from the fire and began to examine them. He first walked towards the mural behind the stone table, where the items within the leather bag had been last night and were now joined by a couple of bags of their supplies. Aden moved the torch closer to the plaster wall to study the illustration.

The painting there showed a handsome man with shoulder length dark hair and dark eyes and a thick beard. It revealed the man from the waist up, and he wore a white robe that billowed about him. His head bowed down, and he held a long and powerful sword upright before him.

"Yosu," Reyan said. "The First Man." Aden twisted at his waist and saw Reyan sitting cross-legged on the floor, eyeing Aden and the mural behind him. "The man El sent to show us how to live," Reyan continued as Aden turned back to face the mural. "To be like Yosu is to be who we were created to be." A light shone in Reyan's eyes, a life within.

Aden turned to the wall on his left, and he cast the torchlight on the mural there. It displayed ten men and two women all riding horses away from a bright horizon behind them, the humans all from different nations, their horses a myriad of colors. All twelve wore long white robes and raised long bright, blazing swords before them as if riding off to battle.

"The first *Sohan-el*," Reyan explained. "The first twelve warrior-leaders of El. They were trained and commissioned by Yosu himself. They passed down their discipline for more than eight thousand years to hundreds of others."

"What happened to them?" Aden asked, still looking at each unique face.

"The first twelve died out, but they taught others. Their numbers grew, and man made some of them kings. Men rely too much on a king. And kings are sometimes tempted by more than they can bear," Reyan said.

"How's a king different from a warrior-leader?"

"They just are." And that's all Reyan would say on that subject.

"So they n't no more?" Aden asked.

"There was only one *Sohan-el* left when the elves conquered men," Reyan said. "In Manahem. There hasn't been a *Sohan-el* in four centuries." Reyan grunted. "But the elves took that for themselves, too, perverted it. They call them the Bladeguard now."

Aden turned to Reyan again. Everyone knew the story of the last king of Manahem. But from what he could remember from the rare times he made it to the Ministry of Education's public school in Asya, and the recitals by the Cryars, the last king of Manahem had been the pretender, masquerading as a Bladeguard. Tanicus called him an enemy of the Kryan Empire and corrupter of men. The Emperor led the army that sieged Manahem himself and had beaten the king on the battlefield, the last battle of the War of Liberation. It was famous.

Aden's brow furrowed at the old man. "The Bladeguard are the *Sohan-el*? They the same?"

Reyan shook his head. "No. Not the same. The *Sohan-el* would rise when men needed them and serve others. But the Bladeguard are instruments of Kryan control."

Aden spun on his heel and walked across the room and toward the third and final mural. His breath caught for a moment, looking at it, though he didn't know why.

The painting exhibited a huge dragon in profile flying through a twilight sky, a dragon of blood red scales and black wings, fearsome and breathing bright yellow flame from its throat, its eyes small white stars. Upon the back of the dragon, two figures sat, one man and a woman behind him, their arms flung high in an expression of exultation, pure joy, as they rode the ferocious beast. Aden waited for a moment for another explanation that never came. He looked to Reyan, and Reyan had turned back to the flame.

"Reyan?" Aden said. "What's this?"

Reyan took a drink from his canteen and sighed. "Don't know. The testimony speaks of a day when dragons lived and served men and El. Only mentions briefly. Maybe true," Reyan said. "Maybe symbolic of something else. Don't know. But the stewards of this place believed that when man was worthy the dragons would return to us." Reyan sucked air in through his nose. "Maybe they were crazy."

Turning back to the mural, Aden could not take his stare from the dragon and the people riding on the back of the wyrm. He shook his head. How could they be so full of joy? Riding on such a horrible creature would terrify him. "Why did they believe?" Aden asked.

"Prophecy sometimes makes people believe and do crazy things," Reyan said. And that was all he would say about it.

—✛—

Crossing the bridge over the river Moriel, Caleb entered the western gate of Galya. The season for heavy traveling was the late fall, after the great harvests in the west and north. Few people used the gate today. As he made his way through a side street to come at the Food Market from the north, he passed by one of the Ministry of Health's free clinics.

A line of six women with newborn babies in their arms stood outside the clinic there this morning. A couple of them stood hunched with pained and teary eyes; the rest waited with dull and lifeless, Sorced eyes. It was Yodae, the last day of the week, the day they could have the Empire kill their children without an extra population tax. The infanti.

The Kryan Empire was worried about overpopulation. Humans bred without restraint, and so it was in everyone's best interest to restrain the growth of humanity. At least, that was the Empire's position and stated platform. The infanti was their solution. People like Jyson and Rose back in Asya, and Caleb's own parents, needed to scrimp and save to pay the fine for a second child.

Caleb saw a woman leave the clinic in a daze, her arms hanging limp and empty. He could hear the screams of a baby inside. Angry, he forced himself forward and through to the Food Market.

While not as large as the square in Asya, the Food Market in Galya stretched far and was in the shape of a square. He had no trouble finding the haberdasher, Ezmelda.

Just as Reyan had claimed, her voice carried shrill and loud over the crowd. She could be heard all around the square, and Caleb followed the sound of her calling. "Hats! Hats of all size and shape. You know you want a hat! Get your hat here. Hats like no one else." Ezmelda was a large woman, tall and round with a pronounced bosom in a tight silk dress. Her own hat sat more than half a meter high on her head, also bright red and decorated with silk flowers of various bright orange and yellow. As Caleb neared her, he noticed her kind eyes, blond curly hair and full lips painted a bright red. A constant smile covered her face.

As he approached her booth, she regarded him and smiled even wider, if that were possible. "Yes, honey," she said to him as he stood just in front of her. Dozens of hats were displayed behind her, each of them unique and flamboyant. "What can Ezmy do for ya?" She spread her arms wide as if to embrace a long lost son.

He couldn't help himself but to return her smile. "I would like a hat for my favorite cousin in Oshra." He spoke the exact words Reyan taught him. "Her name is Harriet, and her favorite color is red."

Ezmelda's eyes narrowed for a moment, but the rest of her expression never changed. "Oh, honey, Harriet will get herself a hat, to be sure." She put her hands on her hips. "You got the money, honey?"

Caleb produced a silver moon from the purse at his waist.

"Good, honey," Ezmelda said, her tone and volume never changing. Anyone within ten paces could make out every word, despite the din in the square. "Now, I need her hat size." She pushed a stick of graphite and a small thin parchment across the counter of her booth at him. "Write that down for me."

"Yes, ma'am," Caleb said. He bent down and wrote on the parchment: Father with me. Meet us in Biram. Caleb. He folded the parchment and put it in her palm. She deftly stuck it between her breasts. "Thank you."

"This hat take a day or two, okay?" Ezmelda said.

"Yes, ma'am," Caleb affirmed his understanding. Earon would get the message in a day or two.

"Anything else I can help you with, honey?" Ezmelda asked.

"Yes," Caleb said. This was now off script. "I need to buy some good horses for riding, traveling. You have any recommendations?"

"Oh, honey," Ezmelda said. "Yes! You go see Jodi in the Food Market. He got the best horses, I say. You tell him Ezmy sent you."

Caleb bowed. "I appreciate it. Thank you."

Ezmelda leaned forward and held his gaze with her eyes, the smile on her face continuing to beam. "You ride careful, you hear, honey? You ride safe."

"Yes, ma'am. I will."

—┼—

Eshlyn rode Blackie at a gallop for a couple of hours before slowing the mare to a trot, after getting a handle on her fear and realizing that in another few hours she might kill the horse at that pace. An hour after sunrise, tears still streaming down her cheek, she slowed Blackie at a fast walk.

What had she done? Why had she just gone? Her mind had cleared, and as she ran over events from the night before, she felt a deep shame. She hadn't told the man she loved goodbye. She didn't kiss him. She didn't even tell him she loved him. And then she left him to whatever ravaged the town and for all she knew, his death.

The Manahem road stretched out for kilomitres before her over low rolling hills of high grasses and sparse trees or shrubs. Soon, the sun was hot overhead, getting close to noon. She wiped sweat from her face. Should she go back? Could she really carry her son back into whatever attacked the town? Should she sit somewhere and just wait for Kenric?

She knew, though, that her husband was dead. Even though he carried a sword, she had heard those unnatural growls and screams of the dying men and women that left her no hope.

And where had the man gotten a sword? Break it all, what was the man rambling about as he made her leave him? A king? Kenric? Javyn? The man had been talking maddy.

But no, his eyes had been calm, his voice firm. He had been telling her the truth, at least a truth he believed in his soul. She must believe it now, for him.

The road passed near a tree, and the baby wailed with hunger. In her haste, she missed the morning feeding. She should be hungry, too, but she felt nothing. Letting Blackie graze, she stopped at a tree and sat down in the shade. Eshlyn nursed her baby boy, and he guzzled milk from her breast. She began to cry when she looked down at him, his desperate eyes looking back up at her, so she looked off in the distance towards the south instead.

Should she return? Should she get back in the saddle and race towards her home and husband again? Just to make sure, so she would know? Part of her wanted to; the rest of her was afraid, but she would steel herself and do what must be done. But no, Kenric had told her to get Javyn to safety and warn as many people as she could while she traveled to the protection of the walls of Ketan.

Eshlyn broke open the scrip and nibbled on hard bread and cheese, but she couldn't eat much. She felt nauseous at the thought. She drank a good amount of the water instead, knowing she would need the fluid to feed the baby and withstand the heat of the day. The baby had finished nursing, settled, and was soon sleeping in her arms. She gathered the scrip again, stood, and then took Blackie's reins. After tying the scrip to the saddle, she hoisted herself up on the horse with Javyn in the sling, and Eshlyn began to ride north again towards the town of Pontus.

———

Aden had never ridden a horse before, and so Caleb gave him quick instructions on the way through the forest to the main road. Caleb and his horse were in the lead, and Aden rode next to Reyan behind him. They waited in the forest to be sure they were not seen coming from the ruins of Debir, and by early afternoon they were well on their way west.

Every hour or so, they passed someone on the road to Galya, but other travelers inclined their head in greeting.

Caleb said that there wasn't a chance that news had spread about their escape a few nights before. The wheels of a large bureaucracy crawled, especially in a situation where the Empire would want to take time to decide how they would be able to spin it. They were safe from any humans, or even elves, they would see on the road.

Aden stayed atop his horse, a white mare with a black mane and tail, but within two hours, his buttocks were raw and chafed. Light vegetation clustered at either side of them, the river Moriel to their right. Soon, however, the river swung more to the north but the road kept west.

Reyan sat hunched in the saddle of a gray gelding, riding in the front of their group, but he looked and sounded stronger than he did yesterday. With some sleep and good food, Reyan's health seemed to be improving. The old man might make it yet.

Aden looked over at Caleb sitting on his horse, a brown stallion with a white star on his forehead. They appeared good, strong horses to Aden, but he had to admit he knew nothing of them. Just the thought of owning one was beyond his comprehension. And here he was on one of the large animals, getting sore muscles from trying to keep his balance.

Aden didn't mind the silence, but he needed something to distract him. And he had questions.

"So what's this about a prophecy," Aden began, turning to Caleb, who blinked back at him. "I hear you an' the old man speakin' of it couple times. What prophecy?"

Caleb scratched at his beard, keeping his face straight ahead. "In the scriptures, one of the first *Sohan-el* prophesied that one day man would grow weak from within, that the nations of men would grow corrupt and become enslaved to a foreign power."

"The elves?" Aden asked.

"He didn't say the elves, but it seems likely," Caleb said. "And once the men were enslaved, they would come to a dark time for many generations. But one day, a man would return to the land of men and lead them back to freedom and throw off the chains of their oppressors. The Fyrwrit calls him the *Brend-el*."

"And you're this man?"

Caleb's frown deepened. "Again, it is always difficult to know with prophecy, but the prophecy says, '*He will be born in the land of men but travel far away.*' I left home at a young age, sent over to Kryus. I have now returned. It could be."

"Seems like a lot of 'maybe' to me," Aden said.

"Yeah, me too," Caleb said. "But Reyan has been preaching and teaching, in secret, for years now. Decades. He believes that it is time. We'll see. I have to find the Living Stone first. Only a *Sohan-el*, trusted with an unforged sword from the Living Stone, can fulfill that oracle."

"You'll fight the elves?" Aden asked.

"I've seen their power, their strength," Caleb said. "I'd rather it not come to a fight. But it might have to."

"You got an army somewhere?" Aden asked with a chuckle. "A lotta soldiers somewhere?"

Caleb shook his head. "Not really. I'm sure there are people ready to fight, to be free, but they are few and far between. And most have no weapons, no training. If it came to a fight now ... it wouldn't be much of one. But given time we can organize and train."

"How much time?"

"I'm sure it will be a few years, at the least," Caleb said. "To make the contacts, to gather the right people, train them to fight, that all takes a while."

"How you get an army without elves knowin'?" Aden asked.

"There are ways," Caleb said.

"And you'll take on the elves?" Aden scoffed. "Bladeguard? Moonguard? Maybe Tanicus? You crazy."

"It seems crazy to imagine something you've never seen before or thought possible," Caleb said. "But someone has to try. It will be difficult.

It isn't as simple as just getting rid of the elves. That is easy compared to making sure humanity is truly free.

"Humanity fell long before Tanicus and Kryus hit our shores with their armies and wealth and power. We made men kings when they were meant to be our servants. We gave them power over us, and that power corrupted them. Over time, mankind handed over their freedom in exchange for safety and provision. We became corrupt and violent. The nations of men fought each other for generations. We were divided and fragile."

"So the elves're right?" Aden said. "Man need elves to protect and keep peace?"

Caleb shook his head. "It is a fake peace," Caleb said. "It is a peace from violence, control and force; from without, not within. The elves call it liberation and peace, but it increases the evil within. Remember those men on the boat? They were going to slit our throats and turn the Prophet in for money." Caleb scoffed. "But how are they to know any different? It is how they've been treated; like animals. They must be reminded and inspired to do the impossible. We must find a way."

"What impossible?" Aden asked.

"To trade their safety and provision for freedom again. It will cost more than they are willing to pay, but the price is what it is. You cannot cheapen it. My hope – our hope – is that then mankind will again be strong enough to be worthy of freedom."

Aden watched Caleb in silence, studying him. Caleb was right. Between the power and safety of the Empire, the drugs and the reign of Tanicus, he couldn't see many making that trade. But if they could … what kind of world would that be?

"Don't do that," Caleb snapped.

"Do what?" Aden asked.

"Look at me like I'm some sort of hero," Caleb grumbled. "Even if it is done, even if I can begin this revolution, most will curse me before the end."

—+—

The sun set, and Eshlyn left the road a short distance to a grassy hill with a small tree at its apex. She tied Blackie to a low branch with enough slack that the horse could graze if she chose. Eshlyn nursed her son once again, and she managed to eat more than a few bites of the cheese and hard bread. She drank again from the water bag, doing her best to leave herself some water for tomorrow. She might reach Pontus the next night.

Eshlyn found the softest part of the ground that she could and huddled beneath her cloak with her son clutched to her chest. He slumbered, appearing at absolute peace, and Eshlyn envied him. As exhausted as she was, she didn't know if she would be able to sleep, but after an hour of tossing, she closed her eyes and cried until she dreamed.

She awoke in a sweat with the three moons still overhead, the green moon of Cynadi full in the west. All she remembered from the dream was Kenric locked in a dungeon, covered in flames, reaching out and begging her to set him free.

CHAPTER 6

UNDER THE STARS

The morning air carried a slight chill, the dew dampening the hard ground. Aden was glad for his woolen blanket and the nearby fire that still radiated warmth although it had died down from the night before. He turned to see Reyan slumbering on the other side of the fire. The old man snored. Loudly. But Aden could sleep through some noise in the middle of the night. Caleb was absent. Aden sat up, stretched, and stood.

His lower back, legs and hips were stiff, and he cried out as he stumbled. He extended his legs and stretched them as made his way upright. A distant bird called as he walked around the campfire. He felt older than the man who was still sleeping next to the fire. Cursing a few more times, he stretched and felt his body begin to loosen. How would he feel after another day in the saddle? A week?

Aden continued to walk. It seemed to help the stiffness in his muscles and joints. By the time he rounded a low grassy hill, he could walk without much discomfort. Caleb was there on the other side of the hill, practicing with the staff, a mist covering the ground about ankle high. Barefoot, Caleb wore his leather pants and long sleeved white cotton shirt, his hair tied behind him with a leather cord. Aden stopped and watched him.

Caleb moved at a measured pace, the staff spinning as he stepped forward and back, the staff turning and twisting. Caleb's eyes were closed, but his hands were always in perfect position to grab the staff as it rounded his waist or his shoulders. Sometimes neither hand touched the staff, and the staff itself appeared to have a mind of its own, obeying a master.

In Asya, Aden would often sneak into the theater or find a place to catch a glimpse of an outdoor pavilion play. One time an elven circus came through town, and the performance had been in an outdoor amphitheater in the wealthy district. Even though outside his "turf," Aden had been curious and found his way to see the acrobats. The control of their bodies, perfect command of their movements and exercises through positions and stunts that seemed impossible; it all came to mind as he breathed the morning air and observed Caleb with the staff.

Caleb picked up the pace, and within a couple minutes, the staff was a blur. He executed the same forms, now at blinding speed. His breathing, however, never quickened, and his eyes never opened.

The whole routine then ceased in an instant, and he halted, frozen in a crouched position, leaning over with a forward strike head-high, his back to Aden. Caleb stood.

"Make sure you don't bounce too much when you ride," Caleb said, turning to Aden, his eyes now open. "Relax and move with the horse. You ride too tense. You might need more padding in the saddle to start with. You could develop some serious saddle sores if you're not careful. We have a long way to go."

Aden was startled for a second, but recovered and said, "It gets better? I never rode a horse before."

Caleb grinned as he wiped a sheen of sweat from his brow with the leather on his forearm and walked towards him. "It gets better. Get to know the horse. What did you call him?"

"Robby," he said.

"Good. Talk to the horse. You're going to be spending a lot of time together." Caleb was standing in front of Aden now. "Your body will hurt for a couple days, but you seem like a fast learner. Learn to ride with Robby and you'll be fine."

Aden nodded. "You ride a lot?"

Caleb chuckled. "Used to. When I was younger. Spent a lot of time on the road, especially with Reyan. So yeah. Rode with my sister most of the time. We were young and small enough to share."

"You miss your sister?" Aden asked.

"I haven't seen her in a long time," Caleb said. "We were very close. I miss her more than anything."

"You knowin' how to find her?"

Caleb shook his head. "We traveled a lot in those days. She knew every town and city like I did. Maybe better. She could be hiding out anywhere." Caleb's eyebrows rose. "Great and mighty El, she could be married by now. She's old enough." He smiled at Aden. "Carys has a part to play in this, too, I think. El will bring her to me again when it is time."

Aden was silent for a moment. "You keep speak of this El," Aden said, squinting at Caleb. "You believe in this big god who create everything? You believe he wants to help us? To be free?"

Caleb cocked his head. "Yes. I do. What do you believe in?" Caleb stepped closer.

Laughing, Aden said, "Believe? Me? Nothin'. No nothin' to believe when just I just try to eat every day."

"I don't think that's true," Caleb said. "You believe in something, or else you wouldn't be here with us."

"No. Nothin'."

Caleb grunted. "Okay," Caleb said, his gray eyes knowing and searching. "If you say so."

———

Eshlyn had met Kenric at seventeen. He had just turned thirty. He was dark and handsome, but that did not impress Eshlyn. She had seen handsome men. Kenric's eyes lingered on her in her father's store for a moment. Most men did that.

Several had been courting her since she was young. She was not only beautiful; her father was a wealthy rancher, the head elder in Delaton, and owned the general store.

Good Mr. Naman approached her father when she was fourteen years old. A fifty-two year old blacksmith in Delaton, Naman was a kind man with several teeth missing, and he searched for someone to care for his two younger children after his wife's tragic death two years earlier, and a pretty face to warm his bed in his old age.

But Eshlyn had bigger plans for herself than that, even at fourteen. She already helped her father run the general store, more than her brother or mother. She loved numbers, making a good trade, and an honest profit. Seeing her father's face beam with pride was a treasure. Eshlyn planned to either take over the family business or start one of her own.

So Mr. Naman was turned down. But the suitors continued unabated. One after another they came to her father. Men and boys proposed to her over the next few years, but they were all refused. They spoke of her beauty and her father's wealth, but she wanted a man who saw past what would fade and see what would last: her mind, her strength, her courage. Eshlyn's father, Eliot Te'Lyan, saw all of that and celebrated it. That was her standard.

Over the years, Eliot gave Eshlyn more responsibility at the ranch and the store, even as her younger brother grew into manhood. It was tradition to hand the business over to the boy in the family, but her father saw her value and made use of it. Her brother was never interested in learning much about the ranch or the store, anyway.

She gained a reputation as a shrewd businesswoman. But the town did not see her as kind. Some even called her cruel and opinionated. She didn't care. Or she tried not to care. Her mother, Morgan, wondered if Eshlyn would ever find a husband.

Morgan did not need to worry about waning interest, however. The suitors showed up unabated, and Eshlyn lost track of them. They came from Pontus and Roseborough. One even came from Biram, a large town far to the north. He claimed to have heard of her beauty from afar, descriptions he said paled in comparison to the true vision before him. He gave her pink lilies and read her poetry he had written for her. She was eighteen and showed him the door like the others.

People in her town thought her arrogant and ungrateful. Most girls would have cried for joy at some of the men paraded before her, so they could not understand her rejection of a husband. The target of gossip and scorn, she tried not to let it bother her, but late at night she struggled with fears of being alone. She threw herself into her work; it distracted her.

When Kenric came in the store the next year, she recognized him as a man from a town to the south. He was quiet and calm.

Eshlyn's friend Sirah took a long minute to regard Kenric as he perused the store. He was oblivious to Sirah's lustfully critical eye. Sirah, a red haired girl with an under-bite and bright blue eyes, made a short grunting sound and shook her head. "Such a shame," she whispered to Eshlyn.

Eshlyn noticed she had been staring at him, too, and looked back at the leather bound record book in her hand at the counter. "Oh," she said, her own voice low. "What shame?"

"To be sure, that man needs a wife," Sirah said. "How can a man so pretty still be without one?" Sirah leaned in closer to Eshlyn. "They say he odd. Odd."

"Odd how?" Eshlyn asked.

"Well, plenty girls be proposed to him, and some pretty as can be," Sirah said. "And he turn them all down."

Eshlyn looked over at Kenric again and caught him watching her. He averted his eyes to examine a set of shears. She smirked.

"Maybe he's just picky."

Sirah scoffed. "Ain't no man that picky, to the real. Not if he like girls."

Kenric soon had his things in his hand and came to the counter. He paid and thanked her as he left with his things in a leather sack. He had such a warm smile. "Odd," was all Sirah had said as he walked back out into the main street.

Over the next year, Eshlyn asked around about the man. A few of her father's business partners, men who now dealt with her almost as much as Eliot, had heard of him. A couple even dealt with Kenric. He was a loner, they said, but a good man. A fair man. A hard worker. A leader in Campton, a peacemaker in that small town; the guardian there.

Next season, she stood alone near her father's small paddock at the market near the center of town, keeping watch over the stock her father had for sale and reading a book. A few animals were still in the pen, a fine horse and two oxen, but the town avoided negotiating with Eshlyn, notorious for driving a hard bargain.

Turning a page and engrossed in the book – Navicus' Treatise on Business Ethics – she didn't notice Kenric until he leaned against the wooden fence and began to give the black filly a critical eye.

She raised a brow at him, but he didn't respond, his face blank, his gaze squinting into the setting sun.

"She's a fine horse," Eshlyn said, trying to appear conversational and nonchalant. "Well bred."

Kenric winced. "I'd have to disagree," he said. "Average, I'd say." Not cruel or argumentative. Just stating an opinion.

"You've seen better?" she asked.

"I have," he said.

She grunted, closing her book and holding it to her side, her finger marking her place. "Not around here," she said.

"Oh, no." The man grinned and stood straight, turning towards her but still leaning against the fence. "That is a fine filly for such a town as Delaton. But down in Campton, we raise strong and hearty horses. Only by necessity, to be sure." He motioned over his shoulder at a scrawny nag a few paces behind him. "Now she's a quality animal. Best there is in Manahem."

"That your horse?" she asked. He nodded with pride. "I believe I could outrun that tragic excuse of a horse."

"Don't insult Beatriz, now," he said. "She's practically part of the family, and can still do more than most horses." He shrugged. "But she is getting older, and my da needs something younger for traveling."

"Well, why don't you just buy a horse from your great town of Campton?"

"Ah, I would. I would." He shook his head. "But no one wants to part with their horses down there. Hate to go home empty handed – promised my da and all. This filly should be satisfactory."

"Satisfactory?" She laughed. "I don't know if I can sell a man a horse doesn't know its worth."

"Come now, show some kindness." He turned back to the filly and frowned. "I'll give you thirty bronze stones for her."

"Are you mad out of mind? She's worth a silver moon if she's worth a copper drop."

"A silver moon? I suppose of you threw in a private audience with the Emperor, I could give you such a treasure. But far too much for the filly. She got a name?"

"Her name is Blackie."

"Fine name." He crossed his arms, raising his right hand to scratch the short beard on his chin. "Tell you what. With a name like that, I could see forty bronze."

By the sky, he had nice eyes. "You learn haggling from your nag? I might go to 90."

"90? Not even for three of her, I say. But it is a beautiful day, sun nice and warm but not too hot. I'll give you 50."

Eshlyn threw up her hands. "Hopeless. She's the finest filly we've seen in a generation, bred from the finest stock you've ever seen." Sighing, she stared at the man, and she swore she saw a hint of a smile, like he was enjoying this. She put her hands on her hips. It would be nice to tell her father she sold Blackie while he was gone. "I'll go down to 75. No more."

Lowering his head, Kenric clasped his hands behind his back. He rocked back and forth. He looked up with a nod. "My final offer. I'll give you 70 bronze stone and you have dinner with me this fine evening."

Her jaw dropped. "What?" She took a step back and held the wooden post of the fence. "You are a madder. Why would you want to have dinner with me?"

He chuckled at her. "Because you're looking mighty beautiful in the orange glow of the sunset? Because this is the most fun I've had all day and would love to continue?" He glanced at the book in her hand. "Maybe I'd like to hear your thoughts on Navicus' third tenet of remuneration."

She raised the book to her chest. "You've read this book?"

"Aye," he said. "My da makes me read all the time." His head tilted at her. "We have a deal?"

"Well, I … uh …" She gathered herself, brushing a hand across her skirts. "For the dinner, you'd have to ask my father's permission."

"Then, depending upon your father's kind permission, we have a deal?" He extended his hand.

"We do," she said and shook his hand. He gave her a firm shake, not delicate with her as other men.

Kenric smiled and looked over at Blackie. "Finest animal I ever saw."

Her father returned soon, and she threatened the poor man to give his consent. Eliot was so flustered and surprised that he was barely able to speak to Kenric when he did come back to the paddock with his nag and 70 stone, yet that night she and Kenric sat at the main inn in Delaton, the *Lovely Loaf*, eating dinner together in the common room. They did discuss Novicus' third tenet of remuneration. He argued it was too self-serving for his taste, and she responded with her strong opinion that it was flexible enough to allow for compassion when necessary. But business was about making a profit, after all.

Kenric asked her to walk with him after supper, and she did. And then Kenric asked a simple question. "So, Eshlyn, what do you want to do with your life?"

That opened the floodgates, and she told him of her love of business and her dreams of operating one she owned. She spoke for several minutes while they walked, and he listened. She fell silent, aware she had been rambling, and he stopped in the middle of the road on the southern edge of town. He pointed up at the sky. "Do you see that star?"

She followed his gesture in the southern sky and nodded as she noticed the brightest star of the night.

"That bright light is two stars, together. The old men used to call them the warrior and the lover. Later they called them other things, the king and queen, I think, but that was their original name." He lowered his hand and crossed his arms at his chest but still stared up at the sky. "The old men, the First Men, believed that there was one star at first, and it shone bright, but not near so bright as now. Eventually, another star, a beautiful star in her own right, came and joined him. And together, they shone brighter than any other star, brighter than they could have alone."

He turned to her then, and he held her eyes with his own. "You were born to be a queen, Eshlyn. You were born to rule the land as a queen with her king, as those stars, together, rule the sky and shine brighter than other stars. You were born for something great and good." He smiled and looked back up at the sky. "I was wondering," he said. "Could I call upon you again?"

Silent, she nodded her head, the first time he had rendered her speechless.

"Thank you," he said. "I shall."

Yes. She could believe that man was a king.

—┼—

Thoros watched the sun set in the west and move behind the peaks of the Gatehm Mountains. He was impatient. The man's soul had satisfied him, but the Key called to him from the north, a faint pulsing signal.

Night settled across the land, and he watched as the demics emerged from their different hiding places. The demics had fed upon all that lived in the town and surrounding area until nothing was left. Their bellies were full, but they had far to go. Once the demics became hungry again, they would start eating one another, beginning with the weakest and smallest among them, as it should be. But these were his tools, and he wanted to have all the fodder possible to meet any challenge ahead.

He could still feel the soul of the man within him, giving the Demilord energy and power. It had been a strong soul, a feast for his first meal. Thoros looked down at the supernatural blade in his claw, turning it over. The sword intrigued him – bright steel, flawless. At times, he felt he could see faint etchings in the sword, but as he focused, they would disappear. A perfect and immortal weapon of destruction from the hand of the Creator. Curious.

Thoros sent out a telepathic message, a command to gather. The demics obeyed. His command carried an inherent threat, and the creatures responded out of fear. After they gathered, he ordered them forward, north. They began to walk, and he urged them to a run. He followed them with the unforged sword in his hand.

—┼—

Venys De'Ban had just finished feeding her five kids. Her husband Olver sat near the hearth, smoking his pipe as she wrangled and wrestled their children into the big hay bed on the other side of the large one room house. He sat rocking in the wooden chair, blowing smoke out of the side of his mouth, staring pensively down at the hearth in the middle of the room, as if he didn't or couldn't hear the screaming of the children as they complained and fought their way to bed with a healthy amount of help from Venys, her cursing, and a wooden spoon.

Her house smelled of cornbread and corn chowder. Her house always smelled of some corn recipe. She tried to be creative, but there were only so many things one could make with corn. She had never minded corn before. But then she married a corn farmer who lived on the other side of Pontus when she was sixteen. And after five kids and ten years, she despised it. She would say she had it coming out of her ears, but people laughed at that as if it were a joke. And it wasn't funny.

The hearth blazed low, the house in comfortable shadow, and the children were quiet when she fell into her own rocking chair next to her husband, exhausted, the wooden spoon still in her hand, ready for use. Olver reached over with his left hand and touched her knee. She leaned back and closed her own eyes after a long day.

The knock came at the door, and she cursed under her breath. Her husband arched an eyebrow at her as she cursed again and made it to the wooden door of their house. She opened the door and had to wait for her eyes to adjust to the figure out in the dark. Tall woman, long dark hair, child in her arms, horse tied to the post a few meters behind her ...

"Eshlyn?" Venys said. "Is that you?" She pulled the woman into the house, noticing her puffy eyes, dirt and grass stains on her nice brown cloak.

"Yes," Eshlyn said, her voice worn and strained.

"What happened?" Venys asked.

Olver was next to her in an instant. "Where's Kenric?" he asked.

Eshlyn's eyes glistened with tears. "Kenric?" she repeated. She began to sob as she continued. "He's dead. The whole town is dead."

———

Caleb unsaddled the horses as they stopped in a low grassy field twelve mitres from the road while Aden went to gather dry dead branches for some firewood. The ground was soft and flat. Tying the horses to a nearby bush, Caleb began to gather some stones for their fire. They'd traveled a good distance today, in silence most of the way, and Caleb decided that they could make camp just after sunset.

Reyan already sat underneath some blankets at the campsite. The old man had improved. He coughed less and could speak in longer phrases without having to pause to breathe or gather his strength. His color had improved through the day, and the man could now get on and off the horse and walk without any help.

Caleb brought the saddlebags to the campsite and began to prepare the evening meal.

Reyan spoke after a silence. "I like the boy."

"I like the boy, too," Caleb said. "But he asks a lot of questions."

"Sounds like someone else I used to know," Reyan said, grinning.

Caleb chuckled. "I wasn't that bad," he said.

Reyan scoffed. "Worse."

"I didn't always like the answers," Caleb said. "So I would ask more questions."

"More questions don't change the answers," Reyan said.

Caleb squatted still for a moment, nodding. "Yeah, I figured that out."

"He will, too," Reyan said, turning as Aden came back with an armload of twigs. "Give him time. He will, too."

ChAptER 7

To CALL A MuStER

Eshlyn sat at breakfast with Venys and Olver over cornmeal cereal and cornbread around the long wooden table against the wall opposite the children's bed, all of them eating in silence. The children had been excused some time ago to play outside, and Javyn lay content on a blanket nearby. Venys was a short woman with narrow shoulders and hips that had thickened after five children. She sat chewing her cereal with a frown on her long, narrow face that wasn't improved by her buckteeth.

Olver, a wide man with powerful legs and arms protruding from a wide midsection, picked at his food, watching Eshlyn with his brown eyes set in a chubby bearded face. She ignored his pity as much as she could. Olver and Kenric had been friends, sharing a pipe or mug together when Ken passed through town.

Eshlyn looked from Olver to Venys. "Thank you so much for letting me stay here," she said. "I need to get on into town and speak with the elders. They need to know what happened."

Venys wore a blank expression. Her husband frowned and nodded.

Eshlyn turned to Olver. "I need to find Yal," she said. Yal was the head elder of Pontus. "Do you know where I can find him this morning?" Yal was a stonemason; he could be working anywhere today.

Olver sighed. "I think he's in town today. Should be easy to find, ask around."

Venys glowered at her husband.

"I'll go with you," he continued, leaning forward. "I'll help you."

Venys turned to Eshlyn with a forced calm and reassurance. "Leave the baby here with me," Venys said. "You come back after you speak with Yal. You can borrow some of my combs and a brooch."

Eshlyn nodded. "I'll nurse before I leave, be back by lunch."

"Don't you worry, to be sure," Venys said. "I've got five of my own and one more don't make no difference."

Once that was settled, Eshlyn and Olver prepared to go. She nursed the baby and washed herself as best she could in the washstand. She had been wearing the same dress for more than two days now, and while her hair looked neat and her face and hands clean, she sighed back at herself in the glass. Lifting her arm, she ran her fingers over the golden marriage bracelet Kenric had given her on their wedding day.

Olver had his mare and Blackie both saddled by the time she got out to the front of the house. He had put Blackie up in his barn the night before while Eshlyn and the baby had gone to bed. He was a kind man, and he remained quiet as they rode the narrow side road that led to the main part of town.

Pontus was a larger town than Campton, although that was not a high mark. Perhaps twice the population, Pontus also boasted a larger gathering hall. More houses dwelt on the outskirts, and the center of town usually had some people milling about. Eshlyn and Olver rode down the main road, and they approached two men standing at the inn.

Yal leaned against the wall of the small inn, smoking his pipe and conversing with Meuthel, the owner of the inn. They called it an inn, but it was more of a boarding house. Meuthel and his wife lived in the house, and it had two extra rooms upstairs.

A tall man, Yal appeared even taller because of his thin, narrow frame. Notorious for eating a whole side of beef in one sitting at a wedding some years ago, the man was still fit and strong. Yal could be considered handsome, but Eshlyn always thought his face plain and ordinary with a balding head. He was quick with a joke and quicker with a jab of his tongue, but he had a sharp mind, for the most part. Eshlyn's father always held Yal in fair regard.

The head elder of Pontus frowned as he saw them riding towards him. He paid half his attention to Meuthel, a square, squat man with a black handlebar mustache and a hat two sizes too small on his head. Meuthel rambled as he relayed some story, and he sputtered to a halt when he turned to see Eshlyn and Olver dismount and walk their horses the remaining paces to the two men.

Yal stood straight now, his arms crossed over his narrow chest, his pipe trailing a vapor to the side. The men acknowledged one another with curt nods of the head. "Olver," Yal said, and Meuthel repeated the name.

"Yal," Olver said. "Meuthel. You know Eshlyn?"

"Kenric's wife?" Yal asked. "And Eliot Te'Lyan's daughter, too, I believe."

"Yeah," Olver said.

Both men noticed the tension, finally, glancing at Eshlyn and her dirty clothes, and they straightened. "What can we do you?" Yal said.

Eshlyn stepped in front of Olver. She peered at Yal and Meuthel. "Kenric is dead. The whole town is dead," she said.

Meuthel's eyebrows rose, and Yal held up a palm. "Whoa there," he said. "What is this?"

"Something ... attacked Campton two nights ago," Eshlyn said. "People were screaming, and Kenric went back to help ... and I ran. Break it all, I ran, but I had the baby and he needed to be safe, and Kenric had a sword and –"

"Okay, okay," Yal broke in. "Kenric had a sword?" Even this far from the control of elves, no one had a sword.

"Yes," Eshlyn said. "I'm telling you, the town was dying. We could hear the screaming people and the animal sounds, growls or something, and he went back with a sword – I don't know where he got a sword – and he went back to try to help and told me to come and warn you, to warn everyone to go to Ketan, to run and escape to Ketan and get behind the walls."

"Now, wait just a moment," Yal said, casting a knowing and suspicious glance over at Meuthel, who returned the look and let Yal continue to take the lead. "Did you see what was attacking the town?"

"No, I didn't," she said, exasperated. "You don't understand –"

"Could have been a cattle stampede," Meuthel interjected, taking his cue from Yal. "I know I'd be frightened if a stampede came through town in the middle of the night and woke me up!" Yal nodded as if this made perfect sense.

"It weren't cows," Eshlyn rolled her eyes at them. "We know cows; it weren't shoggin' cows!"

"Or sheep," Yal added. "Could have been sheep." His brows rose as another idea hit him. "Or a random herd of wild horses. I hear maybe there be some of them down south of Campton." Meuthel nodded back to encourage the notion.

"There aren't any wild horses south of Campton," she said, as patient as she could manage. But she didn't manage well. Her hands and arms began to wave while she spoke. "And we wouldn't be afraid of a shoggin' stampede of breakin' sheep."

"Well, language like that ain't gonna help us right now, little woman," Yal said. She hated that tone, that condescending tone that men used with women as if talking to a child. Eshlyn was tall for a woman, as tall as most men, and it took all her self-control not to punch him dead in the face. If Yal called her "little woman" one more time, she would. "I'm sure that you just overreacted. And I'm sure it was a frightening night, but everything will be to the fine, to be sure." He reached out and patted her arm. "We'll send someone down tomorrow, to check, okay?" Yal thought that would end the conversation, and he moved to enter the boardinghouse, Meuthel on his heels.

"Yal," Eshlyn said, her voice soft. "You know Kenric."

Yal paused in the doorway. "Yeah. Good man," he said. Meuthel nodded again in agreement. Did the man have an original thought? She might knock the hat off his head for good measure, too.

"Is he the type of man who would overreact?" she asked him. "Is he the type of man to take something like a stampede of sheep and blow it out of the boundary?"

"No," Yal said. "But his wife might."

As they turned again to enter the house, Eshlyn said, "I call an emergency Muster."

Both men froze. "What did you say?" Yal asked.

"I call an emergency Muster!" she said, and she was faintly aware of Olver's hand gentle on her arm, pulling her back. She shrugged it off.

Yal laughed. Meuthel chuckled. "You can't do that," Yal said. "That's only for times of war and crisis. You don't have the right. For one, you're not a citizen of this town, and for two, you're a woman. It takes a man to call an emergency Muster."

Eshlyn turned to Olver, her eyes pleading with him. He looked like a rabbit caught in a hunterhole. She begged him without a word as the men began to enter the house.

"Yal, wait a moment," Olver muttered. The men turned back to him. Yal scowled. "I ... call an emergency Muster." He sounded resigned to his own execution. He might have just saved their life instead, she thought.

"Olver ..." Yal began with annoyance.

"He called it, Yal," Eshlyn said, facing the head elder again. "And it's before noon, so we – you – need to have it before sundown. It's the law."

Yal shook his head. "Okay, little woman. Olver, meet the town in the gathering hall suppertime. You'll have your Muster."

Eshlyn had to clasp her hands in front of her to keep from smacking the back of their heads as they turned and went inside the boardinghouse.

Yal had been correct. An emergency Muster was an old tradition, an old law from even before the time of the elves, and it was called in times of great distress and crisis. And to Eshlyn, this was a crisis. Now she stood in the gathering hall, a long rectangular building with walls of stone and a tiled clay roof. All the men of the town that had been called from their busy lives, their jobs, their farms, and their herds, and they were not happy about it. Evening began to fall outside. She was the lone woman, standing up at the front with Olver, who looked as though he would rather be anywhere else but there.

The other elders stood up front with Olver and Eshlyn. She knew most of them by name. She still hoped to one day knock that hat off of Meuthel's head. Yal congregated among them, talking with them, apologizing for the inconvenience. The whole room buzzed with easy conversation; as annoyed as they were, they were men in a community, good friends and a few favorite enemies. They were strong and independent men with women and children at home.

She needed to convince them.

Yal whistled through his teeth, and the room quieted. "Let's get this over with so we can get you all home," he said. "Night ain't getting younger." He turned to Olver. "You called this Muster. You have the floor."

Olver glanced sheepishly around the room, his head down and his shoulders hunched. He wrung his hands before him and spoke in a low tone. "I ... well, uh, you know Kenric Se'Matan," he began. Men nodded at him, and a couple murmured, "Good man." Olver collected himself and continued. "Well, uh, you see, this be ... uh, Eshlyn, his wife and mother o' his boy, Javyn. She ... uh," he coughed in his hand, "she got something to say to everybody." He stepped back and stared down at his toes.

It was her time to speak. She had meditated all afternoon on what she would say. But looking in the faces of those men, she drew a blank. She took a deep breath and reminded herself that she was here to save their lives, and she began.

"Two nights ago, the great horn was sounded at the watchtower, and we were awoken," Eshlyn began. "We heard screams and some sort of ... animal sound. Growls. People were dying. We could hear it. Kenric went back to the town to help. Maybe fight whatever it was," she bit her lip. "And before Ken packed me and Javyn up and put us on our horse, he told me to warn you. To warn all of you. To tell you to run. To run north and get behind the walls of Ketan for safety." She met the silent frowns of the men before her, most she didn't know very well, some not at all. "So I'm here, as he asked me, to warn you and ask you come with me north to Ketan."

Men around the room shifted on their feet. She had rehearsed a long speech, a speech about the strength of men and how the ancient men must have put that watchtower there for a reason. They could honor the ancients, prove they were strong like the men of old if they could move to the safety of the city, heed the warning. But she hadn't said all of that. Her actual words had taken a few seconds. She didn't feel it was enough.

She heard Yal's voice from her right as he stepped forward to stand next to her. "But you didn't see what it was," he said. "You didn't see what was actually happening in the town." He looked at her but spoke for the benefit of the men.

"No, I didn't see. I had to ride, to come and warn you and keep my son safe," she said. "If I'm right, then you're all in danger." She turned from Yal's skepticism to the faces of the other men. "Please. Come with me."

Men shook their heads. She turned from side to side, and no one would meet her eyes. No one but Yal. Olver studied the tips of his boots. She heard men: "Leave the farm?" "Leave the shop?" "Just pack up and go?"

She was failing, and she didn't know what to do.

"Vern," she said, turning to her left. "You know Kenric. He helped you build a shed last year." She reached beyond him. "Nuvom, you always shared your hearth with him, a pipe Kenric always said was good and warm and to the fine." She turned all the way around her, grabbing a wrist. "Eilner. You tried to marry your daughter off to Kenric! Would you try to give your Kali to a dishonorable man? You know him." She faced the bulk of the men again. "All of you, you've heard of the guardian at Campton and the good man he is. I know you have. We heard all the way up in Delaton. Please believe me. Please listen to his counsel. Come with me to the city. We'll be safe there."

The men still avoided her gaze, and an awkward silence stretched. "But you don't know for sure what happened to Kenric or to the town," Yal said again, standing closer. Eshlyn closed her eyes. "We have farms and ranches and jobs to think about," Yal continued. He sighed, and as she opened her eyes, she saw the men in the large room looking to Yal for direction. "All right, men," Yal said to them. "Let's see what we think. Anyone think we should pack up and go north all the way to Ketan? Show of hands."

No one raised a hand.

"All right, then," Yal said. "I propose we send someone down to Campton to see just what is going on and come back to report to us."

"I've got a fast horse," Heaf announced, a man just a year or two older than Kenric. Men nodded in confirmation. Heaf looked at Eshlyn, his brown eyes kind and compassionate, almost apologetic. "I'll go and see what happened."

"Thank you, Heaf," Yal said. "So Heaf will go and report back to us what has happened in Campton. And we will have another Muster when Heaf returns. All in favor of that plan? Show of hands, please."

One by one, every man in the room raised his right hand. Olver was last.

Eshlyn's heart dropped. They were all good men. But they hadn't heard those screams. How could she convince them when all she had was her own conviction? "Heaf won't return," she said.

Yal turned to Eshlyn, shaking his head. As angry as she had been at him earlier, he was trying tried to be a comfort. "Eshlyn. You're more than welcome to stay with us in town until Heaf returns. I'll pay for you to stay at the inn. Please."

She shook her head. "I'll stay with Olver and Venys tonight and leave in the morning. Any are welcome to come with me to my parents in Delaton." Maybe her father would listen. She prayed to whatever god could hear that he would.

"We will wait for Heaf to return," Yal said in a firm voice. "And we wish you well on your journey. I'm sure Eliot will be happy to see his fair daughter and his grandson."

She nodded and walked out of the gathering hall, the men politely parting for her as she left. The sun was setting behind the mountains to the west as she stepped through the thick wooden door. Olver joined her, and they rode back to his house in silence.

—+—

Caleb's parents had died in Anneton.

It was a sprawling town that boasted an elven Steward. Other villages and towns died out as men were forced to rely more and more upon the lacking provisions of the Kryan Empire. Farms were abandoned to the larger Kryan landowners and people moved to places like Anneton. Now those abandoned villages and towns were memory and ruin.

Caleb explained these things to Aden as they passed two places where crumbled foundations and rotting boards strewn about were all that was left of those small communities. Encouraged by how far they traveled over the last couple days, Caleb looked forward to a fresh cooked meal and a night in an actual bed, even though it was Anneton.

They rode into the large town that afternoon. Wooden buildings with four or five stories rose on both sides of the main road. Some were tenements, others shops. They reached the center of the town and the road widened to an open circular area, a plaza that was used for market days or public gatherings. This was the place his parents were burned at the stake.

On their right was the main inn of Anneton, the Rambling Lady, a long rectangular building three stories tall. The main administration building was across the plaza from the inn. The other two buildings around the plaza were the Ministry of Health and the school.

It was eerily quiet tonight, but Caleb didn't know if he discerned the mood of the town or his own sobriety as they passed through the very area where his parents had been bound to a stake and burned to death.

Caleb led the three of them into the Rambling Lady to pay for their rooms as Aden and Reyan sat at a corner table in the dim common room and ordered a simple meal. After stabling the horses, Caleb joined them to eat the lukewarm soup of pork and overcooked vegetables. He eyed the old man and noticed Reyan continued to improve. Finishing the meal and watered-down ale, they took their packs and saddlebags up to their room, the largest on the third floor. It had four beds with thin mattresses and worn sheets, but it was clean. A wide window with a view over the plaza dominated the wall.

Standing at the window, Caleb took a deep breath.

"I was born near here," Caleb said. Aden raised an eyebrow at him, and Reyan's expression didn't change. "A few kilomitres south of here, in the foothills of the Ehan Mountains." Caleb rubbed his short beard.

"There's a farm and small cabin there. Or was. Good place. We've been making good time. Maybe tomorrow we'll ride down and see the old place. Reyan, we could try to contact some of the believers here in town." Reyan grunted but didn't say anything.

Even if he had to go alone, Caleb thought it would be good to see the small cabin hidden away to the south, to see what had happened to one of the few places in his past that contained good memories, happy memories.

Moving from the window, Caleb remained in his long sleeved shirt and underbreeches, and lay on a soft, comfortable mattress under white linen sheets. Aden was asleep seconds after putting out the lamp, and within another few minutes, Reyan's breathing became a snore. Caleb lay back with arms crossed behind his head, looking up into the dark.

It took him over an hour to get some sleep. The plaza outside his window burned in his mind every time he closed his eyes.

Chapter 8

While Others Burn

The morning air felt cool even this late in summer. The day would warm, Eshlyn knew. Olver helped Eshlyn saddle Blackie and gave her an old saddlebag, which Venys had filled with cornbread, cold cornmush, and a slice of ham. The couple tried to give Eshlyn more money—some of their savings—for the journey, but Eshlyn would be with her father in a few days. The supplies were enough to get to her hometown: Delaton.

Her clothes were clean, and an extra linen blanket swaddled her son who was awake but lay quiet and content in the sling that hung from her shoulders. Eshlyn sat on the mare and looked down at Olver and Venys. "Thank you for your kindness," she said. "I wish you would come with me."

Olver put his arm around his wife. "We'll see what Heaf has to say when he comes back," Venys said. "And we wish we could do more. You're welcome to stay."

"No," Eshlyn said, turning the horse to the narrow path towards the main road. "I'll be with my family in another few days. I need to warn them." Her sight blurred as she looked at Olver and Venys and the children playing in the far field. "I wish you well."

"We do wish you well, to be sure," Venys said.

Eshlyn forced a smile, as did they, and then she spurred the horse to trot from Pontus to Delaton.

—

Caleb was immediately awake and on his feet. It had been a few years, but one never forgot the sound of men screaming as they burned.

He had already donned his leather pants by the time Aden sat up. Reyan also woke, but he didn't yet move. Aden, in his underbreeches, walked to the window. "Well, breakit," Aden said. "An execution."

He joined Aden at the window. The plaza below was filled with people facing the Administration building, their backs to the inn. On the far side, two stakes had been erected—thick wooden poles three mitres tall—with other wood and refuse gathered at the base. A figure was bound to each pole. One person was already burning.

Nine elven guard and two elven officials stood between the stakes and the crowd, one of the officials with a torch in his hand, waiting to light the other pile while the first burned to death, the figure in the throes of pain as the flames covered his naked body. The other screams were from the person tied to the other stake, higher pitched and pleading. The other figure was a woman.

His memory stirred, and he recalled the sound of his sister weeping, terrified, as he held her in his arms in a cave not far from here. His mother had been screaming.

Turning back to his clotes, he rushed to finish dressing; his boots, his leather vest, his coat. He began barking orders. "Aden. Get dressed. Go get the horses. Get money out of that purse and give coin to anyone left in the stable, if there is anyone, and see if they will help you saddle horses."

"But what if no one's there?" Aden asked as he complied, also dressing. "I dunno how to …"

"You'll figure it out. Take the saddlebags with you," Caleb said.

Reyan sat on the edge of his bed, shaking his head at Caleb. "What are you doing?"

Caleb grabbed the staff that leaned against the corner of the room.

"What does it look like I'm doing? I'm going out there." He helped Aden finish gathering their things into the saddlebags.

Reyan sighed. "They could be real criminals."

"That doesn't make it right," Caleb said.

"You can't save everyone, Caleb," Reyan whispered.

Caleb turned on the old man with a snarl. "I can save this one!" Caleb opened the door and started to walk into the hall.

"Reckless," Reyan said. "Just like your father."

Caleb froze at that, his right hand tightening on the staff with a crushing grip, glad the wood was stronger than steel. His hands covered the script written there: To lead with compassion, justice, and strength. He repeated words of the Vow in his mind – defend the innocent, free the oppressed, and spread light in dark places.

"Break you, old man," he said in a dangerous tone. "I will not run while others burn. Get dressed and help Aden if you don't want to get left behind." Caleb slammed the door behind him.

He raced down the hall, down the stairs, and through the common room. Bursting through the front door of the inn, he leapt the five stairs down to the street and ran across the plaza.

A few citizens glanced over their shoulders as he neared. The crowd was sparse at the edges, but as he entered its center and brushed past the few that did not part as he ran, a man sprawled with a cry as Caleb elbowed past. The elves watched him then, the nine Cityguard hefting their gladi in their hands as they strained to see Caleb through the crowd. He broke through the throng of humans to face the elves. The elven official with the torch stepped forward and away from the woman.

She was a diminutive woman with brown skin and long black hair, weeping as she turned to observe Caleb emerge from the throng of people to face the elves. The man on the other stake was already dead, the charred body continued burning but hung still.

Caleb sneered at the elves. The scars on his back began to itch.

The mass of humans behind him stepped back a few paces.

The elven official not holding the torch wore a long, flowing red robe with full sleeves, embroidered in golden roses. The sash across his chest marked him as the Steward of Anneton. His sleeves billowed out as he moved to confront Caleb. He was average height for an elf, with short blond hair; athletic and quick, martially trained. A scimitar hung at his side. "What ..."

"Let her go," Caleb said, holding the staff out in front of him.

"Get back and away," the Steward said. The nine Cityguard, all dressed in light silver mail under shorter gray tunics, flanked the steward. "You interrupt a legal execution under the authority of the Kryan Empire. You will stand down and be arrested."

Caleb wondered if this was the same Steward who had murdered his parents. The wind shifted. He got the full scent of burning flesh and grimaced.

Everyone was still: the elves, the crowd behind him, even the woman on the stake quieted to whimpering now, her head down. Caleb reached over with his left hand and began to roll up the right sleeve of his white cotton shirt to the elbow and removed the leather bracer on his forearm, revealing the tattoo on the inside of his right forearm: a tree growing out of a large, round stone, with intricate detail.

The mark of the Bladeguard was immediately recognized by the elves arrayed before him. It was a tattoo once meant to signify one of the ancient warriors of El, the *Sohan-el*. Caleb would show them the difference.

A collective gasp emitted from the elves, and the guard bent to a fighting position, their gladi extended before them. Every eye was wide.

"Let her go," Caleb repeated.

"Impossible!" the elven Steward said once he recovered from his shock. The other official in the white robe glided forward, dropping the torch to his left, away from the second stake, but halted just behind the guards. His white robe was embroidered in golden roses. "You are not a Bladeguard." The crowd behind Caleb now reacted at the title, but Caleb didn't turn around. His stare was fixed upon the Steward, although he marked the position of everyone around him with his peripheral vision. "You cannot be." Fear laced his voice even through the denial.

Caleb hefted the Kingstaff in front of himself, crouching in a low guard. His long hair fell in his eyes as he lowered his head. "Only one way to find out."

The steward glowered at him. "Kill this fraud."

He did not move as the elven Cityguard moved between himself and the Steward. They started to surround him. He waited until they arrayed themselves in a half circle. He could hear the humans behind him shuffling further away. The sneer on his face turned into a murderous grin.

With a yell, Caleb sprinted forward and he spun the staff before him. He moved on instinct as he attacked the two elven guard just in front of him. Striking one on his right in the middle of the chest, he knocked another across the side of the head. Both were down before the rest reacted, seven guard attempting to box him in. The Steward and the other official stumbled backwards and away from the battle.

Caleb took three steps to his right, the staff a blur in his hands above his head., He brought it down to disarm one guard; he spun his body away from a thrust of a gladus from his left, the staff laid square against the back of that guard's head and dropped him to the dirt with a sickening thud. Caleb reversed and drove the staff down on the guard he had just disarmed. The elf managed to shift to the side to avoid catching the strike on the top of his head, but his shoulder shattered under the power of the staff instead. He screamed in pain.

Two elves were now behind him, the others rushing him, and Caleb ducked under a flashing blade, grabbing the screaming elf with a crushed shoulder and tossing him towards those at his back. He wheeled around and swept the staff at the nearest elf, who awkwardly blocked; Caleb kicked out with his right leg and caught him in the face, his head snapping backwards, the rest of his body following. Without hesitation, Caleb struck low with the other end of the staff and caught the other nearest Cityguard behind the left knee, upending him. Caleb reversed the staff again and plunged the other end into the guard's face.

Taking a few steps back, he distanced himself from the three remaining guard. The Steward and the other official were to his left now, between him and the woman on the stake. She watched him with a confused frown, squinting at him.

The guards spaced themselves before him, a pace apart, their eyes darting to the six others that now littered the end of the plaza. Cityguard training, Caleb thought with derision as he took a calming breath.

Rushing them with a spinning staff, Caleb pressed forward and isolated the elf on his right from the other two, even as they were able to parry the speed of his strikes. The isolated elf was disarmed within a moment, his wrist snapping and hanging at an odd angle. He cried out, but a blunt blow to his windpipe silenced him.

Caleb rotated his body away from another thrust from behind him and laid the staff across the shoulders of the elf to his right, who fell forward between Caleb and the other guard, who couldn't get a good stab around or over his companion. The staff, however, was long and hard as steel, and Caleb felt it hum with the impact to the face of the guard. Down. Caleb leapt away as the other elf, still falling from the strike to his back, caught himself and flailed behind him with a shout. One easy blow to the extended sword arm and another to the face finished the last of the guard.

The Steward advanced with the fine sword in a low thrust. The official in the white robe hopped and ran in fear towards the Administration building. Caleb hefted the staff like a spear and launched it at the white-robed official. Just as the staff left his right hand, Caleb blocked the thrust from the Steward with his left, spinning with all of his strength and speed, grabbing the Steward's right hand and pulling him past.

Caleb heard the white-robed official cry out as the staff landed at the small of his back, sending him sprawling to his face on the marble steps of the Administration building, his head popping back. Caleb attempted to strike the back of the Steward's head with his right elbow, but the the elf had been well trained and ducked the strike, twisting his wrist from Caleb's hand.

Master's training, Caleb thought. *Not that Cityguard crit.*

He kicked out with his left foot, connecting with the Steward's right forearm, breaking it cleanly. The sword dropped, and the elf hesitated with the pain, although he made no noise. Caleb was impressed.

But the hesitation cost the Steward. Caleb swung back with his left arm, the back of his fist catching the Steward across the nose with a crunch. He stumbled, sputtering, and Caleb caught the elf's head, snapping his neck with a savage twist as he fell.

Caleb stood over the dead elf for a moment, his hands in a defensive position to either side of him, breathing through clenched teeth, and he surveyed the plaza. The human crowd was mitres away now, although they watched him with fear-filled eyes and slack jaws. Men, women, children. Doing nothing. He turned to retrieve the staff, lying against the steps next to a groaning elven official. His nose and mouth bled. The elf turned over on his back, dazed, his eyes rolling up into his head. Caleb picked up the Kingstaff and crushed his skull against the stone steps.

A select few of the guard in the plaza still moved as they could, one crawling away, asking the human crowd for help. The people the elves had under the control of fear and force wouldn't help, either. Many of the elves were dead, but Caleb found the ones that still drew breath and rectified that.

Aden and Reyan, mounted on their horses, made their way around the crowd. Aden held the reins of Caleb's stallion.

Walking forward to the people in front of him, he pointed the staff at two young men in the front of the crowd. They were both lanky and thin. "You. Go get buckets of water. As much as you can carry," he said in a firm tone.. Some women and children in the crowd wept with fear. "And put out that man. He's still burning." They didn't move, as if a ghost spoke to them. "Go!" Caleb snapped at them through clenched teeth. They jumped and ran in compliance. He hoped.

Aden and Reyan rode up to Caleb now, but he turned from them and went to where the dead Steward lay. He tore the long red robe from the elf's body, distant gasps from the people meeting his ears. With the red robe in his hand and the dead, naked steward behind him, he moved to the other elven official and tore his white robe off of him. By this time, the two men returned with water, two buckets each. They paused a few paces away from the man still smoldering on the stake. One wordless gaze from Caleb, and they doused the burning dead man.

"Get down here, Aden," Caleb said now that the horses were close. Aden started and swung down from the saddle, laying the reins of Caleb's stallion across the pommel. "Grab one of these swords and cut her down," Caleb said as Aden jogged towards him.

He heard the boy gulp, but he did as he was told, stooping down, grabbing a gladus, and running towards the dark skinned woman, who was looking over at the dead burned man now soaked with water. "Are her hands nailed to the stake?" Caleb asked.

"Uh," Aden peered at her hands bound behind her. "No."

Thanks to El, he thought. "Good. Cut her down and give her the white robe to wear."

The men who had doused the dead man at the stake still stood close with the buckets in their hands, in shock. He pointed at them again. "You two, get one of these swords and cut that body down and wrap it in the red robe," he told them. They grimaced at him in disgust. "Go on," Caleb said.

They did. He heard retching sounds as he walked to the saddlebags on his horse. He opened one and pulled out a small purse. Reyan glared at him but sat still and said nothing. He glared back.

Caleb walked over to the two men that now had the body wrapped in the red steward's robe. He handed them each a golden sun. Their hands were black and red from handling the charred flesh. "Did you know this man?" he asked them.

The two men nodded.

"What was his name?" Caleb asked them.

"Berran," the man with the long straggly beard said. The other man had vomit down the front of his tunic.

"I want you to take his body outside of town and give him a proper burial. Do you understand?"

They nodded again.

He heard steps from behind him, and he turned to see the dark skinned woman, covered in the white robe that dragged on in the dirt since it was too big for her. She walked past him and knelt in front of the body. The two men stepped back. Aden stood next to Caleb, his eyes drawn towards the tattoo. She reached out her right hand and placed it upon the red cloth.

"I'm sorry, my love," she said with a strained whimper. "I'm so, so sorry."

Caleb let her cry there for a minute, but he laid a hand on her shoulder. "Come on," he said. "We have to go."

She shook her head. "I've nowhere to go," she said. "He was ..."

Your husband, Caleb wanted to finish for her, but he didn't.

Caleb glanced again at the crowd, huddled together in fear. Not simply fear of him, he knew, although there was a fair amount of that. But also fear of what the elves would do to the town when news of this spread.

"You stay here, you die," Caleb said. "They'll turn you in out of fear. And more elves will return. Come with us and I promise I'll find a place for you where you'll be safe. Or as safe as you can be."

The woman was quiet for a long time. As she bowed her head low, her hair fell and revealed her ears. They were elven ears. She was half-elf.

"Will you teach me to fight as you did?" she asked. "To kill them as you did?"

His heart fell within his chest. "I can't promise that," he said. "But I'll do what I can."

She rose then, gathering the robe about her with two hands. She looked back at Reyan with tear-filled, but cold, eyes. "I'll go."

"Let's go, then," Caleb said, meeting her stare for a short pause before striding back towards his horse. "Aden, take that gladus with you and get another one for Reyan," he said over his shoulder. "And another one for her. I have a feeling we're going to need them."

"What about you?" Aden called to his back.

He shook his head as he got up in his saddle. "Don't need one of those," he said. "The woman rides with you."

———

The half-elf woman rode in the saddle with Aden, in front of him, as they rode through the morning at a decent trot, but by lunch, the horses were walking again. His buttocks hurt like never before, but he barely noticed the pain. None of them had breakfast, and they skipped lunch. No one spoke. Hunger was distant. Aden had been hungry before.

Aden could not get the image out of his mind. Riding up and seeing Caleb standing, little sign of sweat on his body, with the dead and broken bodies of elven Cityguard all around him with a staff in his hand.

Giving strict orders for silence, Caleb wanted to make sure he could hear any pursuit, but the woman continued to sniff as she cried. Aden wanted to ask her questions, talk to her, comfort her, something, but he couldn't. Not now, at least.

Caleb made the whole group of them pull off the road when he heard noises coming up ahead of them. That happened twice. Once a woman and her daughter on a bony brown mare passed them, next a grinning old man with no teeth in a short wagon carrying different colors of linen cloth. He saluted them while Aden and Caleb pretended to give a rest for the horses, letting them graze a bit, and they waved in return with calm smiles. Reyan shielded the half-elf woman.

Aden also stayed quiet due to the tension between Caleb and Reyan. Not that either were the warmest of people he had ever met anyway, but Aden felt he would get his head lopped off if he made a sound. Their exchange back at the inn in Anneton still hung over both of them.

Night fell, and they still rode for another hour. Aden began to fall asleep in the saddle before Caleb pulled aside to the left of the road, winding through some brush for a half-kilometer and finding a grassy knoll. Caleb dismounted.

"Aden, start setting up camp and gather some firewood," Caleb said, holding the staff in the dark. "But keep the fire low. Reyan, help as you can. Stay with her. Keep the horses saddled but get them watered and fed. I'll help when I get back."

"Where you goin'?" Aden asked.

"I'm going to cover our tracks as fast as I can. I'll be back," was all Caleb said and went off into the dark alone with the Kingstaff.

———

Finding an old abandoned farmhouse a hundred mitres from the road, Eshlyn rested there for the night. She saw it first in the late afternoon, and it was evening by the time she reached it. It no longer had a roof and the dirt floor was now grass, but it protected her from the night wind and allowed her to feel as if she was hidden from the road, from the awful things that she knew chased her. She settled Blackie, nursed Javyn, and ate a meager meal. She drank just a little water, saving as much as she could.

All that day, every moment as she rode, she couldn't escape the feeling of failure, the crushing defeat and depression that accompanied the vision of the men in the gathering hall and Olver and Venys and their five children. Three things kept her going, kept her from giving up and lying down to wait for whatever killed Campton to sweep down upon her and finish her, too. First, the safety of her son. If she had lost Javyn ... she didn't let her mind wander there. Second, her promise to Kenric. The man had been talking maddy, but the more she rode, the more she meditated on that last night in Campton, the more she believed his words. She had gone over them so many times in her mind; she could quote them verbatim.

Third, and last, the hope of seeing her family: her brother, her parents, even her hometown of Delaton. She had to warn them. She had to make them see. But how?

She had no answers as she drifted off into another nightmare. Kenric was in a dark dungeon, the bars made of black iron, and he suffered in flames like before. But this time, his face was set and angry. His arm reached out between the bars and held a bright sword in his hand, that sword from the night in Campton. His father's sword. He gripped it with all his might. His eyes blazed.

Eshlyn awoke and slept in fits after that.

Chapter 9

To Learn the Sword

As promised, Caleb had the group up, on the horses, and riding west again as the sun rose. He slept a few hours after covering their tracks and finding a nearby pond to refill water bags and canteens. With the addition of another person, they would need more supplies soon. He would need to hunt.

Caleb's actions had put the group in greater danger. He would lead them away from the main road soon, avoiding any people as much as possible. Word of what happened in Anneton would get back to the Masters in the Citadel, even the Emperor himself. It would ultimately expose Galen.

Galen had taught him to never enter a fight he couldn't win. Assess the threat; see the solution. Extensive training and youth cause pride, Galen said, make an elf or man feel invincible. But no one is invincible. No matter how many times a warrior wins the battle, or the ease, there is always someone better trained, faster, stronger. A great warrior also understands the battles he cannot win.

So was it hypocritical for Galen to send Caleb to begin a revolution? Humanity was beaten, weak, emasculated. They forgot the meaning and beauty of freedom long ago and learned instead the easy road of fear and powerlessness. Was this a battle he could win?

And what did it mean to win? Or lose?

Caleb remembered his father sitting by the hearth, pulling Caleb close and sharing stories from the First Men from the testimony, the Ydu. He read to Caleb in the First Tongue but translated as he went, explaining. He could still see his father running his hands along the parchment as he read the translation of the prophecy of the *Brendel*, like it was a precious thing, a treasure.

The words of the Vow echoed in his mind. Defend the innocent, free the oppressed, and spread light in dark places. Was that what it meant to win, standing for truth and doing what was right, regardless of the consequences? Perhaps that was freedom.

He felt blind like a grider – a creature the Kryan Empire trained into a fierce killer; but a grider could not see. A creature of the dark, it did not have eyes. It needed to hunt with other heightened senses. Yes, Caleb thought, I'm like a grider.

Caleb was not a priest or philosopher. His cousin Earon had always been gifted in those areas. Caleb was a fighter, a warrior, and he would put those skills to use according to his convictions. He wasn't much of a leader - yet he kept accumulating more people along his quest. They were all here as a result of his action. Was it right that they suffer the consequences of his convictions? They were free, and he had to allow them that choice.

He realized, however, that if he was to begin a rebellion among men, against the Kryan Empire, he would place a whole race of people in even greater danger than this.

———

As they mounted for their travels, Aden turned to the woman. "We don't know your name," he said. "What is your name?"

"Tamya," she said.

"Well, my name is Aden –" he began, but she spun away from him.

"Leave her be," Reyan said to Aden under his breath as he passed close by. "She'll talk when she's ready." Reyan raised his voice louder to Caleb and said, "The woman rides with me today." Caleb did not answer and wouldn't look the Prophet in the eye.

Aden gave the woman some of his clothes to wear. They fit her loosely, but they were sufficient. She did not talk, look at or acknowledge anyone, and she wept again once that morning. She threw the red silk robe in the fire when they left, and they let it burn.

Caleb and Aden rode side by side at a brisk walk. Reyan and the woman rode together behind them.

"What does the tattoo mean?" Aden asked.

Peering down at his forearm, he hesitated before he rolled up the sleeve of his white shirt and turned the tattoo towards Aden. He pointed to the stone. "This is the *Ebenelif*, the Living Stone. The tree growing from it is the Living Tree of El, the *Aes-elif*." Caleb rested his hands in his lap again. "The *Sohan-el* would train for years, rigorous training that covered all subjects and disciplines. Foremost, however, they were masters of the sword.

"When they felt ready, they would take a pilgrimage to the Mountain of El, called Elarus, far to the west. They would climb that mountain, and there near the peak they would find the Living Stone and Tree. If the Stone found them worthy, it would give them a sword, an unforged sword, called a barabrend. These unforged swords were indestructible and the *Sohan-el*'s most prized possession."

Aden spoke after some consideration. "So the Bladeguard, they go this mountain and get one o' those swords?"

Caleb shook his head. "Not anymore. Galen told me that any who ever tried to climb the mountain never returned. They continued wearing the tattoo to keep up the ruse that the Bladeguard are the same, or better, than the *Sohan-el*. It is more tradition now."

"If they don't go to the mountain, where do they get their swords?" Aden asked.

"Galen told me they get them now in the city of Ketan, at a secret forge," Caleb answered.

Aden grunted. "If these swords're indestructible, as you say, and *Sohan-el* were around, where did all the swords go?"

"Galen didn't know that," Caleb said. "I don't think anyone knows the answer. Maybe going to the Living Stone will tell me."

"You gonna climb that mountain, then," Aden said.

"I'm going to try, yeah," Caleb said. "I've come this far."

"And you really not gonna use a sword until you get this magic one?"

"Not really magic," Caleb corrected. "But yes, that's the idea. To prove myself worthy without one, someone who will fight for what is right without the power, then I can be trusted with it."

They rode in silence until the road made a turn to the southwest. "I want you t'train me," Aden said. "Train me to use the sword."

Caleb sniffed and scowled. "I don't think so."

"Why?" Aden asked. "We got time. We got a long way to go to th'mountains of Gatehm." Aden pointed at the saddlebags behind Caleb. "And we got swords, gladi. You got those wooden poles from when we fight the crizzard."

One of Caleb's brows rose. "We?"

"Y'know what I mean. You say the poles weighted like gladus, perfect to train. I want to learn."

"Teach the boy," Reyan said from behind them. "Why did you have him pick up swords back in town if you won't teach him? What good is a sword if you don't know how to use one?"

Caleb sighed and said, "Fine. I'll teach you."

Aden heard a female voice speak from the rear. "And me, too."

⊢—

Caleb rode them past sunset again, and they set up a hurried camp. They passed a handful of people on the road, but Caleb explained they would have to travel along the foothills and off the road soon. There were more elves in Anneton, and one of them there would have questioned the humans that had witnessed the event and found the direction the four of them headed, west towards the town of Botan. They would send a pigeon to the elves in Botan, and the city Galya as well, for good measure. It was only a matter of time before more Cityguard or others were racing up behind them. And if any official put two and two together and connected this with the escape from Pyts, they would have a team of Wraithguard or a Bladeguard after them.

Earlier that day, during the quick stop for midday meal, Caleb caught a couple of rabbits. They cleaned the animals while the campfire blazed, and the group sat around the flame and ate their evening meal. After finishing the meal, Tamya wrapped herself in Caleb's cloak and Aden's blanket, turned away from the fire and lay still. Aden huddled in his own cloak, sitting up.

Caleb looked at Reyan. "What happened to my parents?" he asked. "I want you to tell me how they died."

"You know how they died," Reyan said.

Aden peered over the edge of his cloak. Caleb didn't care.

"No. I know what you told me when I was seven years old," Caleb corrected. "Only that the elves arrested and executed them for harboring the enemies of the Empire."

Reyan glowered at him. "Isn't that enough?"

"No, not anymore. Not now. Not really then, either." Caleb brought his knees up and rested his arms on them. "I've thought my whole life, wanting more details on how they died. You said, 'Just like your father,' yesterday. I want you to tell me about how they died. And why you said that to me."

"You know what your father was doing. You remember that day."

Caleb's father, Mac, had become a believer in El and then a disciple of Reyan's father as a young man. Mac met Sheron, Reyan's sister, and they fell in love. They got married, and she was soon pregnant with Caleb.

Mac and Sheron moved from northern Erelon to the southern foothills of Ehan to a cabin there to settle down. Somewhat. They were caretakers of the cabin as a haven for "enemies of the Empire" – believers in El – to hide and then relocate them elsewhere in another colony within the land of men. The cabin was also a small tenant farm they rented from an elven landowner, and they raised various animals.

Caleb was seven and Carys three years old when the Cityguard came to the house. His father had been away that day to help a believer reach the next town. His mother managed to send her children to hide in the woods before the Cityguard arrived. Caleb carried his sister into the trees to the hidden cave they were meant to use in such an event. He comforted Carys while they heard their mother's distant screams. After living on the meager provisions in the cave for five days, Uncle Reyan came to get them. They already knew him to be a hard man, and the simple explanation they received confirmed what they accepted after those five days without a sign of their parents: Mac and Sheron De'Ador were dead. "I know what my father was doing. And I remember that day as well as anyone," Caleb said. "But I asked you questions over the next few years that never got answered. And I want you to answer them now. Why didn't my mother run with us to the cave?"

Reyan's shoulders sagged. "To protect you. She knew that if they came and found no one, then they would begin searching around the cabin. She gave them what they wanted: a prisoner, someone to make an example of, and so they were satisfied and wouldn't search the surrounding area enough to find her children."

"Did they already have my father? Had they caught him first?"

"No," Reyan said. "Your father …" Reyan paused and met Caleb's gaze in the firelight, his own eyes glistening with anger. "Your father went to save her from the prison at the Administration building in Anneton. And they caught him, too."

"And you're angry at him for that?"

"He was stupid," Reyan spat. "They were probably holding her just to get to him anyway, as bait. He knew how the Empire worked. And he went anyway, against all we had taught him. He was reckless and emotional. And so he got caught. And you lost your mother and your father as well." Reyan spoke through a clenched jaw. "They made your father watch first." Reyan's voice cracked, and he waited before he could continue. "They made him watch her burn to the bone before they set him afire."

Caleb closed his eyes and tears fell down his face. "Well, I'm sorry he left you to take care of his annoying kids," Caleb said, his voice full of derision. "How dare he."

Reyan tilted his head at Caleb. "I never felt that way about you or Carys."

"Crit and piff," Caleb said. "You never wanted us around."

Reyan groaned. "Every time I saw you and Carys, I saw one of my best friends and my sister looking back at me. You have her eyes and look just like your father. Carys looks just like Sheron, only shorter. There were some days I could barely look at you and still go on. I loved you like my own children, but I hated what you reminded me of every day. It wasn't your fault, but that's the truth." Reyan grimaced. "They tried the same trick with my wife, and I didn't try to save her. They were after me, not her. I was the endgame. And after she died and Earon and Carys left, I admit I was relieved. They were safer away from me."

Caleb rubbed his eyes. He understood how the Prophet felt.

CHAPTER 10

The Dark of Night

Heaf Mo'Kel had the prettiest girl in town, two daughters, a turnip farm, and the fastest horse in Manahem.

Thunderhoof was a beast of a horse. Long and muscular, he had won the race at the festival in Roseborough for the last three years. A feisty stallion, Thunderhoof was black with gray mane and tail, and his lower right leg looked like it had been painted white. Heaf rode him exclusively, and he even toyed with the idea of taking him up to Ketan for one of the races there. Might be some real money in it.

But overall, Heaf wasn't a greedy man. He had pride in his horse, to the sure, but more than anything, he considered his wife and two daughters, Odyssa and Clyssa, eight and ten, the most precious treasure in the world.

He walked Thunderhoof southward on the Manahem road. The sun was bright and hot, and he knew he had a good distance to go to make it to Campton. Despite the joy he felt riding the horse at a full gallop, it was a good two-day ride, and he didn't want to exhaust the horse on the way there.

He wasn't sure what Eshlyn had experienced, but she had been plenty afraid. Kenric was an old friend, a good man to share a pint with. The man didn't ask many questions, nor did he ramble on about farming. Every now and then he would tell an old story about some legend or other. Heaf never understood them all, but some made him smile, gave him hope maybe life could be a little better, a little brighter.

In the noonday sun, the single sound for kilomitres was the clopping of hooves on the wide dirt road and the wind, but he heard a skittering sound to his right. He looked around him, into the tall grass, and he could see small red shapes there. He slowed Thunderhoof and walked him to the edge of the road to his right. As He peered down from the horse, the shapes looked like little red children, and his breath caught with a choking sound. They were grotesque little creatures curled up into a ball, and as he stared out over the kilomitres of tall grass as far as he could see, there were thousands of them lying in the grass.

His curiosity became confusion and then terror as something stood up in the grass about a hundred mitres to the south. Huge, it stood and looked something like a man, but it had red skin with black markings all over it, long black horns on its head, and it held a long shimmering sword.

And it looked right at him. And it smiled, its teeth black and pointed.

All at once, the creatures around him – one just a few paces away – began to make horrid screeching sounds, sounds of pain and fear. But they began to stir, and at that point, Thunderhoof began to panic.

Heaf had known the horse all his life, and without that familiarity, without over six years of caring for the animal and becoming a fine horseman of his own, Thunderhoof would have thrown the man and raced off in terror. Not that Heaf was against the horse running off in terror; he wanted the horse to run north … just not without him.

As they took off at a full speed and Heaf glanced under his arm behind, he could see the creatures, terrible things, standing up in the grass, making that screeching sound, their hands and arms over closed eyes, but they faced north and ran after him. And they were fast.

He built a good distance from them, however, Thunderhoof at a full gallop. He cursed the flat plains of Manahem for carrying the painful cries of those creatures like they were at his shoulder. He cursed the creatures, whatever they were. And he cursed the men of Pontus for not listening to Eshlyn. She had been right to warn them. But how could they have known? He cursed them again anyway.

—|—

Tamya focused on the lessons from Caleb, taking it all in silently. He taught her and Aden basic stabs and slashes, urging them to attack while he parried with that staff that felt like wood but was stronger than steel.

Every move of her body ached, but she blocked out the pain. She was getting good at that. Her arms and shoulders burned from swinging the short sword then holding it firm and still. Her hips and legs throbbed from the balance and the constant crouching; her knees felt as if they might buckle at any point. She pushed all the pain in the back of her mind, using her bitterness and anger and hate like a small sun in the center of her being, continuing to push herself, to learn, to train her mind and body to kill other beings with a weapon.

Aden was fast, faster and stronger than she, but he was sloppy. He was a quick learner, though, and Tamya used the competition to push herself.

She found it difficult to sleep at night, and that compounded her exhaustion. She dreaded waking in the morning, waking and for a moment forgetting that she had lost her husband and baby, the one good thing she had ever known. That moment where the realization of their death, their brutal murder by the hands of the Empire, came back into memory was like reliving it all over again. So every morning she was motivated anew to train with this Caleb, this human Bladeguard with delusions of grandeur. She didn't care as long as he taught her how to fight, to protect herself, and to kill.

Tamya still couldn't believe that she had allowed Berran to convince her to run away with him. She didn't enjoy her life as a slave in the Steward's house in Oshra; she hated it with every fiber of her being. But a person learned how to endure certain pains and horrors, with the mocking and condescension, the abuse. Berran came to her with his idealistic notions, and fool she was, she had believed him. For some reason she still couldn't fathom, when he looked into her eyes and told her it would all be okay, she had trusted him. She trusted that something good could exist in this world.

She vowed to never believe it again.

And proving that fate was cruel, she found herself rescued by men who conversed often about a good god and the redemption of men. She couldn't listen to it without wanting to either vomit or rail at them … or both. It reminded her too much of the foolishness her husband believed.

But she did believe that one day they would help her fight elves, where she would get to stick a weapon into the gut of an elf. So she was patient. She needed them. For now.

She was conscious of her half-elf status. She had been well aware of it even as Berran wooed her and made her fall in love with him. Fool man. She knew in the back of her mind what it could cost them, and she ignored the truth of this ugly world in the name of empty words like love and hope. The baby had made it easier to dismiss the savagery she learned so well before meeting Berran. She would know better next time. Next time she wouldn't allow some idealist or fanatic to get in her head. However, fate had also allowed her to know the source of Berran's idealism.

Aden and Tamya both worked up a sweat by the end of the lesson. Caleb took Aden with him to scout the area back towards the road, and Tamya came back to sit at the fire that Reyan now had roaring.

Taking a water bag, she drank, the gladus still in her right hand, eyeing Reyan the whole time. After a few minutes of silence, she said, "I know who you are."

Reyan grunted at her.

"You that Prophet," she said, almost an accusation. "Berran spoke of you. He knew you."

"I thought I recognized the name," Reyan said. "He was one of my contacts in Anneton. I'm sorry."

She took another drink. Berran had talked about this man, this Prophet, like he was some hero from a fable. The reality left a little to be desired.

"Was there a baby?" Reyan asked.

She squinted her eyes at him. An easy guess. The Kryan Empire had a strict policy against interbreeding between humans and elves. An elven male could have a child with a human female, but an elven female, even a half breed, could not have a child by a human male. The child and the man were both killed, as a rule. And since she was a half-elf, her life mattered less. She and Berran had been married, and that was enough for the Steward in Anneton to make an example. And Berran couldn't keep his mouth shut about El and faith and redemption. That sealed their fate. And her baby's.

Tamya nodded. "Three months old," she answered, anger and bitterness dripping from her voice. "Bashed he head against a stone."

"I'm sorry," Reyan said.

"Berran say you were a great man, and that El was this great god," she said. "You look be tired and weak. And what god lets be what is? No good god, to the sure."

Reyan settled in, crossing his legs, nodding his understanding. And he began to sing. He didn't have a good voice. It was like listening to a Bosaur give birth. But he kept singing, looking off into the trees to their right, away from the road. It was a simple song.

When I am afraid, when I am alone
There is one thing that I know
The Creator of all
Loves the world even when we fall
He will return us again
To a world without sin
If we will only believe
Live for the truth and the blind will see
Even while surrounded by the dark of night
Yea, my love for the Creator will give me light

He finished the song, his voice a grating monotone, and Tamya shook her head in disgust. The singing didn't annoy her, though. She rose without a word and went back to the clearing where Caleb taught them earlier. Slashing and cutting the breeze, she imagined killing more than air.

—

Thoros stood at the edge of town, the unforged sword in his hand, leaning against it as he surveyed the destruction and chaos before him. He reveled in the death, in the blood, in the pain as he felt himself connected to the frenzy of the demic collective. This wasn't even a real battle or a city. What would that feel like? He drew in a deep breath of satisfaction and lust.

But he didn't have any telepathic response from the demics about the man on the horse that had roused them earlier that day. He knew they had been close to some human population. He could smell the blood of men and animals. The demics didn't run very fast under the sunlight, but once the moons rose, their pace quickened and they began to close the gap between themselves and the man on the magnificent horse that ran to warn the other humans of their coming. Thoros wanted to taste that animal's blood, so he sent a query through the simple telepathic link, more of a visual representation of what he sought. He urged the demics to continue to search and find that man.

———

Riding straight through Pontus, the monsters were at his heels. Heaf screamed as he passed Meuthel standing at the door of the inn in his nightdress and that little hat on his head. Heaf saw the hat fall from the man's head as the exhausted and dying horse blew by him.

Thunderhoof collapsed to the ground, panting, mere seconds after Heaf arrived at his home. He thanked the horse, but he didn't have time to mourn or grieve. He opened the door to the one room house and yelled at his wife and family. "Get up! Get up! We have to go!"

The hearth gave a little light to the room, and his wife and daughters sat up in their beds. Clyssa screamed, but then comforted her sister as she recognized her father. "Glyn!" he said. "Get some food and blankets and meet me outside!"

"Heaf," his wife said, her hair a dirty mop on her head. "Are you maddy? It's the middle of the night."

"Do what I say, woman," he said. "Get the food and water and blankets."

"We're not dressed," she said.

"Don't get dressed; we're leaving as soon as I can get the wagon ready to go," he said and ran out the door.

Heaf heard mutters and crying behind him, but he ignored them, hoping they were doing as he asked. Making his way to the barn, Heaf grabbed his other horse, Fetch, a big, strong brown workhorse. The gelding was awake and skittish, but Fetch hadn't gone into a full panic yet. He hitched the horse to the wagon and was almost done when his wife and daughters wandered out to the yard between the house and the barn.

"Thunderhoof?" Odyssa, his older daughter, cried and ran to kneel beside the horse. Heaf cursed. She loved that horse.

"What happened to Thunderhoof?" Glyn said with gravity, a sheet full of bread and water bags awkward in her hands.

"I ran him all day," Heaf said. He didn't mention how he beat the horse to keep running far past exhaustion, how he had pummeled a horse he loved to save the family he loved even more. He would never be proud of it. "We had to get here." He moved to grab his daughter, now shivering in her yellow nightdress. She wept over the dying horse. "Come, love," Heaf said, his hand on her upper arm. "Get in the wagon."

He hurried his daughters in the back of the uncovered wagon, both of them crying now, asking questions he ignored. Odyssa and Clyssa huddled there in blankets as Glyn gave over the sheet of food for them to keep. Glyn sat next to him on the bench in the jockey box of the wagon. Gathering the reins, he slapped them against Fetch, who lurched forward.

Heaf didn't follow the path to the main road; it went too far back south. So he guided the wagon through the upper field, tearing through the crops they were to harvest in a few months. He gave the crops no thought as turnips flew in the air behind the horse and the wagon. He was far more concerned about Fetch and the wagon – the uneven ground might break a horse's leg, and it was an old wagon; those axles were rusty. He had been meaning to replace them.

They met up with the road without mishap, however, and soon they were racing north on the Manahem road. Even with the noise of the wind and the galloping horse and the crying girls in the wagon, he heard the sound of those creatures behind him, snarls and screeches.

Heaf cursed and urged Fetch on with the reins and his voice and his very will. But Fetch already galloped forward at full frantic speed. He wasn't getting any more out of that animal.

"Daddy!" Clyssa shrieked from the back of the wagon.

Twisiting in the seat, Heaf looked behind him and saw figures in the dark running up the Manahem road. And gaining on them. Glyn turned, as well, her hair surrounding her face in the wind. "Heaf! What is that!"

"Hahh!" he cried at Fetch.

Within minutes, he could hear the creatures close. The girls screamed and huddled as far forward in the wagon as they could. When he turned to look again, the monsters were almost to the back of the wagon. "Glyn," he said to his wife, her face grimacing in terror. "Take the reins!" Those nightmares would be upon them at any moment.

He cursed himself for not bringing a weapon of any type with him in the wagon. He had been so frenzied, he had his family grab what food and water they could. It would have been ironic to escape the creatures and then starve or fall from dehydration. If they would escape now, anyway.

Heaf climbed over the jockey box and his daughters to the back of the wagon. It rocked, and he stumbled. But he stood again and moved between his daughters and the creatures groping for the wagon. He could better see the numbers now, maybe a hundred of them. One jumped to grab the back of the wagon, but it fell and was trampled. Another jumped and missed, trampled by the others without a thought, but the others learned from those and soon a red imp had latched on to the back of the wagon with its black claws. Heaf punched the monster in the face and watched it fall back into the horde that chased them. A few dodged it and recovered to catch the wagon. Two leapt for the wagon, reached it, and one received a fist to the jaw and the other a kick to the side of the head.

More were upon the wagon, however, and soon four were on the back. One ran up along the side and tried from that vantage. He struck with fists and elbows and feet and knees, furious and frightened. The creatures were running on both sides of the wagon now. "Back and forth!" Heaf said. "Steer the wagon back and forth!"

They ran over a few of the monsters that way, but the creatures learned to stay wide and at the edges of the road, out even into the grasses, after a dozen or so ate the dirt of the road to their deaths beneath the wheels of the wagon. Heaf looked and could see a few running alongside the horse. Between blows he called his wife's name as he saw two monsters leap up and latch themselves with long black claws to Fetch's hide. At the same time, black tusks clamped upon his left arm. "No!" he cried.

More creatures sprung to Fetch's back. The horse squealed and tumbled and fell. The wagon suddenly flipped in the air and threw the humans forward to land sprawling on the road, their bodies bouncing as the monsters leapt upon them. He heard his daughters scream as creatures tore into their bodies.

Then there was a voice, a rumbling sound that came from the darkness around him and the ground beneath him.

"*Stop.*"

CHAPTER 11

THE NATURE OF TRUTH

Aden and Tamya rose with Caleb, just before first light, to run through the sword forms again. Caleb claimed the forms were from an ancient martial discipline. He taught them position, balance, movement, everything to put power and precision behind the attack.

Aden was still sore from yesterday when they had two lessons: one in the morning and one in the evening. Between the sword lessons and riding all day, he wondered if his body would ever feel normal again. If the journey took them all the way to Ketan so Caleb could climb some mountain, he supposed not for a long time.

"Faster now," Caleb demanded. "The forms are simple, but in the middle of a real fight, you don't have time to think. They must be as natural as breathing."

It pained Aden to go over them again at all, and moving faster exacerbated the discomfort. But he pushed through and finished the lesson while Reyan gathered their things into the saddlebags. Once finished with the morning lesson, Caleb and Aden saddled the horses. Tamya would be riding with Aden again today.

As Aden placed the saddle on Robby's back, he looked at the leather bag behind Reyan's saddle that held the books from the room underneath the ruins at Debir. Reyan noticed him eyeing the bag and turned a questioning brow up at him.

"I was wonderin'," Aden said. "Could I try to read them?"

Reyan mounted his horse. "You know how to read?"

Aden shrugged. "I not go to school much," Aden said. "But I learn little bit."

Reyan nodded. "You can read them, sure. That's what they're for," the Prophet said. "Maybe tonight, if we get to have a campfire. Don't read in the saddle while we're riding through the brush. You're not an experienced rider and … well, just not a good idea." Reyan turned and opened the leather bag while Aden mounted Robby. "They are my only copies in common tongue, so you must promise to be careful. Which one would you like? The Ydu or the Fyrwrit?"

Aden thought for a moment. He pulled Tamya up on the horse behind him. She wrapped her arms around his waist. "I promise t'be careful. Which's the one have th'prophecy you keep talking about? About the *Brendel* and man bein' free again."

Reyan reached in and grabbed the thinner volume. "The Fyrwrit, the scriptures. Teachings from the first *Sohan-el*. You can find most of it in the second letter of Mychal." Their horses began moving through the brush back to the road together, and Reyan reached out and gave Aden the book. "You will figure it out."

Aden took it from the man and placed it in his lap while they rode. The leather binding felt warm in his hands as he ran them across the cover. "Thank you," Aden said. "I maybe could ask you questions? As I read?"

Chuckling, the Prophet grinned at Aden. "I'll answer the questions that I can," he said. "I've been reading and studying those books my whole life, and just when I think I have a good hold on it, something comes up and I have to study some passages all over again from a fresh perspective. It is the nature of truth. It is bigger than us, but I'll help if I can."

—<del></del>—

Heaf opened his eyes and knew agony in the first instant.

The last thing he remembered was a tall figure standing over him, the same massive being he saw yesterday. Was it yesterday? What day was today? While his wife and daughters screamed, the hulking creature struck him across the face, and Heaf was sure he was dead.

The place was dark, a barn, but it was daylight outside. He could see the sun between the wooden boards of the wall and ceiling, enough light to give shadows shape. He sat against the wall of the barn and felt intense pain in his arms. Lifting his head, he turned to see that long iron spikes were driven through his arms, spread to either side of him. Blood ran down his arms and pooled on the floor underneath him.

He wanted to scream but groaned instead. As his eyes adjusted to the light, he could make out more shapes in the dark. A woman was in the corner of the barn, two or three mitres from him. Her arms were also spread to the side, fastened to the wooden wall behind her as he was. Blond hair caught a sliver of sunlight.

"Glyn," he said. He tried to yell, but all that came out was a whisper. He said her name again. Her head was down, and she didn't respond to him.

Something moved on the other side of the barn, something too big for him to recognize as real for a moment. He turned his head back the other way, grunting in pain, and he squinted, trying to focus. Then he heard the voice.

"Do you know why you are weak?"

The walls of the barn shook when he spoke, dust falling from the ceiling and through the fragmented sunlight. The figure walked closer and knelt before Heaf. He carried a sword.

When Heaf had been thirteen years old, his father took him east of town out to find a cow that had wandered through an open gate. Heaf had left the gate open, and so his father meant to teach him a lesson, take responsibility and help track the cow down. It took them all day, but they found her at twilight. It had fallen into a ravine and broken its neck the night before. The cow lay there dead all day, baking in the hot sun. Its body was bloated with death and covered in vultures.

The smell was so terrible, he retched. He never left the gate open again.

When the monster knelt close to him in the darkened barn, the stench made Heaf feel thirteen years old again, and he vomited as he did then. As his body heaved, his arms pulled against the spikes in his arms. This time he did scream.

"Do you know why you are weak?" the beast repeated.

Heaf caught his breath and looked up at the monster.

The monster looked over at Glyn and then back. "Love. You care for one another. That makes you weak. Strength comes from hate, from fear, anger." He raised a claw and made a three-fingered fist. "Pain makes you strong. Perhaps because you humans live such short lives, you cling to love. But living with hate, fear, anger, for millennia teaches you. You learn what makes you strong."

The monster stood. He walked over to the corner, and Heaf thought for a moment how graceful he walked despite its size. "You will learn to embrace the hate and fear. We will teach you." It knelt before Glyn.

"No," Heaf moaned.

The beast opened his claw and pressed it against her chest. "Wake up."

Glyn roused now, raising her head, disoriented as he had been. She groaned, and as she lifted her head, she opened her eyes. It took her a moment, but she looked into the face of the nightmare before her.

She found the power to scream the first time. She had always been stronger than him. Her eyes bulged and her mouth grew wide. She tried to move away from the beast, but she pressed against the wall behind her.

The monster turned to him again, the claw still on Glyn's chest. "Do you know where I can find the *Sohan-el*?"

"What?" Heaf said.

The creature grinned and squeezed against her chest, its talons digging into her flesh. Glyn turned her head and cried out.

"No," Heaf said. "I don't know …"

The beast showed him the sword. "I am looking for the *Sohan-el*. Tell me where I can find him."

"Please. I-I don't know what you're talking about."

"You don't know the *Sohan-el*? Perhaps they have a different name. The warriors of El. This is one of their swords. They must be close."

"W-warriors?" Heaf said. "Swords? Humans a-aren't allowed to have swords."

The monster clutched at Glyn's chest again, and blood flowed from the punctures. She thrashed in pain, screaming. "You lie. One did have a sword."

Wait, Heaf thought, didn't Eshlyn say something about a sword? "Kenric? N-no. He's no warrior. H-he's just a man." He leaned his head back against the wall of the barn. "Just a man. I don't know where he got that sword."

The monster stared at him with those black eyes for a long minute. "I believe you," he said.

Then he began to chant in some gutteral language. Each word sounded like an angry curse. Glyn's body shook, and her breath caught, her eyes searched the room and found his. She mouthed his name, her eyes glistening. *Heaf.*

Her body continued to spasm, and a mist appeared from the pores of her skin. She paled and turned gray and her cheeks became hollow. The creature tilted his head back and his black eyes turned white. The mist from her body drifted into the monster's open mouth. Hearing his own voice crying out in anguish, he said her name over and over, and then it was done. Everything was still. Glyn's eyes were dead, her face frozen in pain.

The monster stood up, moaning in something like pleasure, and he turned to Heaf. His eyes were black again.

"I drank her soul. It is now mine." He walked over and knelt down again, leaning close with that overpowering stink of death. "You too will know how it feels."

———

Eshlyn had never been more relieved to see her hometown and never so full of grief.

Javyn wiggled in the sling, anxious from having to lay in it over such a long ride. She murmured. "Shush. You'll see Granda and Granma soon. Soon."

The town of Delaton rose before her in the pre-evening light. The sun hung low and bright to her left, just over the peaks of the Gatehm Mountains. She approached from the south, and soon two roads split off to her right and left. The one to the right was the Saten road, and it led east to the farms that extended to the western edge of the Forest of Saten. The road to the left was the Me'Bako road, winding southwest to the large Me'Bako farm that covered acres and acres all the way to the foothills of the mountains.

The center of town welcomed her after the two roads split away. A few buildings and homes clustered together on either side before the official center of town began, marked with the *Lovely Loaf* on the left and her father's store, the Te'Lyan General Store, on the right. Blackie slowed her walk as they passed the store. A young man stood just inside the main door, talking with his friend, waiting to lock up.

Her younger brother, Xander, was laughing at some joke told by his friend – assuming a crude joke since she could see it was Joob, a short, thick young man with a thicker brain – but then his eyes caught the sight of Eshlyn riding by on Blackie with Javyn in her arms. He froze, his smile melting as recognition crossed his face. She heard him curse and watched him push past Joob, who also cursed with annoyance. Xander jogged out to the middle of the road as Eshlyn pulled Blackie to a stop. His face was full of concern.

Her brother was tall, almost two mitres, and dark and handsome. He and Eshlyn had the same basic features, the full dark hair, green eyes, long nose, oval face, but his skin was more olive than fair. He was three years younger than Eshlyn, nineteen now, and his beard was just coming in. Soon he would be a man of the town, if he ever chose to grow up, she thought in that moment.

"Hey, Esh," Xander said. "What –" he looked at Javyn and back up at her. "What you doin' here?" Joob walked up beside Xander now, his own face a smirk. Xander, however, caught her eyes again, saw something there, and frowned, turning even more serious. Maybe he was becoming more of a man. "Where is Ken?" he asked in a slow voice.

She almost wept, broke into tears just then, but she wouldn't give Joob the satisfaction. Her face turned to a grimace despite her effort, and even Joob the Boob began to frown in concern. Eshlyn shook her head, unable to speak. She knew once the words began, she wouldn't be able to stop the sobbing that would accompany them.

"Okay," Xander said. "You goin' home?"

She nodded, her eyes looking up the street.

Xander moved closer and laid a hand on her thigh. "Just wait a minute while I lock up and get Yaysay from the stable," he said. He turned and grabbed Joob's elbow. "Come on," he told his friend. "Help me."

Joob complied, and after two or three minutes, Xander rode from behind the store on his horse, Yaysay, a dapple stallion. Eshlyn watched Joob walk off to the south with a nervous wave, his wide brimmed hat skewed to the side. Eshlyn didn't wave back.

Xander rode Yaysay up next to Blackie. His horse nipped playfully at Blackie, but the mare was tired and turned away, ignoring the stallion. "Let's go," Xander said, and they rode together through the town making little noise. Xander's eyes continued to glance at her with concern. "You okay, Esh?" he asked.

She shook her head.

"You wanna talk?"

She turned away with another grimace.

"Alright, it's to the fine," he said. "Let's get to the house."

Delaton was quiet in the evening. Most people had gone home or were on their way there for dinner. Eshlyn and Xander rode in silence past the large open field used for market days on their right, just next to the general store. Adjacent to the field, the gathering hall appeared, three or four times the size of the one in Campton.

The gathering hall carried so many memories for Eshlyn, still and empty now, but one was first and foremost in her mind. When she closed her eyes, she could see the flowers everywhere, the people dancing, even hear the music beating through the town as people celebrated. She tried not to close her eyes. But even with her eyes open, the memories invaded her thoughts.

After Kenric courted her for a full season, Eliot had thrown the wedding of the century. Eshlyn wore her grandmother's dress in early Febmo, and Kenric stood like a hero from a firetale in his lime green silk tunic, embroidered with leaves and lilies. The tunic hung over new leather pants and high boots. They kissed in sight of heaven and earth after giving her the golden marriage bracelet. Men and women had cheered. The ale flowed and people danced late into the night. Eshlyn and Kenric spent their first night at the *Lovely Loaf*. And she would later tell Sirah that he did, in fact, like girls. Three times that night, in fact.

Eshlyn bent over in her saddle in grief, a moan escaping her lips, holding the golden band upon her wrist. Why did thinking of happy things cause such pain?

"Esh, are you okay?" Xander asked. She didn't answer him.

After the gathering hall, more houses clustered to the left and right. At the outskirts of the town, two roads split off again. The road to the left was called the Upper Road and led to the many farms to the northeast of Delaton. Her one good friend through childhood lived there now, married. Sirah. Eshlyn and Xander, however, took the road to the right to the Te'Lyan Ranch, aptly named the Te'Lyan road.

Within a few minutes, even as the sky began to darken, she could see the wide arch over the road and the sprawling house made of stone and wood beyond the arch with their family name burned into the board at the top. Yaysay began high-stepping as they neared the house.

They halted their horses at the main dwelling, tying both horses to a post. Xander helped his sister down, and they walked up to the front door of the house together. Xander carried her bag from Blackie's saddle.

Taking a deep breath, she opened the door to the home she grew up in, the home of so many good times, so much learning and working. It seemed bigger and warmer now than ever before. And she had to convince them to leave it all.

Her parents both sat in the great front room, her mother mending a hole in her father's fine linen cloak. Her father went over the books, just next to the hearth of the fire. Lamps lit the room well, but Eliot had always loved the rocking chair there next to the hearth, his own father's chair, worn and comfortable. Her mother, Morgan, a woman with full lips, kind brown eyes, and reddish yellow hair that had begun to gray, was dressed in her long linen green dress that hugged her still fine figure even at her age. Morgan looked up first, taking a moment to register her daughter's presence. "Eshlyn?"

At her name, Eliot looked up from the record book in his hand with an immediate smile that faded when he saw her. Eshlyn and Xander got their dark hair and long faces from him, and he was still strong and able, well-built and athletic, although the top of his head was bereft of hair and the little he had over his ears grayed. Eliot's full beard hung down to his chest. He set down the record book on the small table next to the hearth and leapt to his feet.

Eshlyn turned and her mother stood before her, staring deep into her eyes. "What is it, my love?" Morgan said. "Are you all right?"

Eshlyn managed two steps into the room, and as she saw her father moving towards her, she collapsed on the nice wooden floor to her knees, sobbing. Her family surrounded her, also on their knees, calling out her name, touching her shoulders, her arms, careful of the baby now also crying in the midst of them still in the sling. She managed to look up and meet her mother's eyes.

"I left him," she said through tears. "I just left him to die. Oh, Ma, I didn't even kiss him! I didn't kiss my husband goodbye."

—•—

Over the next hour, Eshlyn found herself in a cushioned chair next to the hearth, her family seated around her, Xander's eyes wide with fear as she began to tell the story about that last night in Campton. Morgan held the baby after Eshlyn nursed him, rocking him as they listened. Eshlyn told them of her ride to Pontus and the emergency Muster there, how no one believed her enough to leave. She had stopped crying, although those emotions were always there, threatening, as she looked to her father in particular, who frowned and looked dark and serious, more serious than she had ever seen him, his pipe smoking in his right hand.

Turning to her father, the man who had forever made her feel safe and loved, the greatest man she had ever known save for Kenric, she leaned forward with pleading eyes. "You have to call an emergency Muster tomorrow," she said. "Kenric told me to warn everyone and get them to go north to the city. He said we'd be safe behind the walls. Please, Da. Please."

Eliot leaned back in the rocking chair. He took a draw on his pipe, gazing into the hearth to his left. He looked back at her with his own green eyes. "Bain will stand agin' it," he said.

Bain Me'Bako was the mayor of Delaton. The town also had a council of elders, and Eliot was the head elder. Bain and Eliot were old enemies.

Bain had the largest farm to the southeast, what he called a plantation, a term taken from the elves, and the Me'Bako family owned the town inn. Eliot owned the largest ranch and facilitated a great deal of trade through Delaton. Bain was powerful and manipulative, and the single man strong and influential enough to stand against him was Eliot. Unfortunately, this divided the down along lines of who was loyal to whom. Eliot did as much as he could to keep peace, but his own convictions for the good of the town often caused conflict. What Eliot meant, therefore, was that Bain would try to derail anything Eliot would suggest, out of general principle.

"But he can't," Eshlyn said. "If you call an emergency Muster, as a citizen of the town, the men are obliged to come. It is ancient tradition."

Eliot scoffed. "Bain doesn't cater to ancient tradition. He is more of the elf sometimes than the man."

She remembered one town meeting where Eliot had gotten passionate and more than implied Bain's likeness to Emperor Tanicus. There had almost been a brawl right there. That only further divided the town, and Eliot had regretted it. But Bain did openly express his desire that their town be more like the larger Biram and receive Kryan support and provision, which always came with Kryan control. It hadn't been a bogus claim, despite the incendiary words.

Eliot met her eyes. "He won't believe you."

Eshlyn swallowed hard. "You believe me, Da?"

Eliot sighed, a sad sound. "I believe you, Esh," he said, and her heart settled within her chest. She might have lost all hope had her Da disbelieved her. "I don't know what happened down there in Campton, but that watchtower was there for centuries for a reason, built by the old men for a reason, to be sure. And Kenric was a good man, a prag man, not likely to madness. I believe you."

Eshlyn let out a breath and smiled at her father, then her brother and mother. Sitting on the edge of his seat, Xander looked ready for a fight right there. Morgan held the baby, rocking him still, tears running down her face. "Thank you," Eshlyn said. "And will you come with me to Roseborough? Will you leave with me north to the walls of Ketan?"

She knew what she asked of him. Her father was a generous man, never motivated by coin, despite Bain's continual accusations of his greed. But he was also a good businessman. She was asking him to leave his livelihood – herds of cattle and sheep, and even a small herd of fine horses – behind on the word of his daughter, who hadn't seen anything, and a man he knew to be an upstanding man, but a man who might be dead or alive in anyone's honest estimation.

Eliot nodded, and Morgan began to cry. "We have the Muster tomorrow, see what we can do. But one way or the other we go with you north to Ketan."

"For the real?" Eshlyn asked.

He blinked and said, "For the real."

———

Aden couldn't read while navigating the hills rock and brush with Tamya holding onto him close behind. Reyan was right: Aden put the book away.

Caleb brought them to a halt at a clearing near a small rocky overhang.

"We're about three, maybe four, kilomitres from Botan as the pigeon flies," Caleb said. "That overhang should allow us to make a fire for the night." He dismounted, glancing around. "It's a good place to stop. We'll set up camp. Tomorrow we should make it to the forest."

The four of them were quick and efficient at setting up camp. Even Tamya did her part, as quiet and brooding as she remained. Tamya was a beautiful woman with her dark skin and brown eyes. The elven mixed with her obvious Liorian heritage made her striking.

Aden tried several times to talk to her, to no avail. He received sharp looks and scowls in return for his attempts to get more information out of her. Where had she been born? How old was she? Aden guessed his own age, but with those elven features it was difficult to tell. From her, though, he got nothing. She was a mystery.

However, she make sure she was ready with her gladus in her hand to do the forms with Caleb, a quick and easy learner, almost as much as Aden. Her stances and balance were better, but Caleb noted that Aden was faster. If Tamya experienced any soreness at all from their grueling lessons, she never expressed it or showed it in any way. Aden had to stretch for a few minutes before and after each time with Caleb. Her stoicism made him feel weak.

He noticed that Caleb walked a little slower tonight. The man had spared few hours of sleep in the days since Anneton. He kept them moving all day and kept watch all night while they slept. But as skilled and trained as he might be, the man was still human and would need sleep.

As they settled in for the night, Aden sat next to Caleb. "Let me be the watch tonight," he said. "I can do it."

Caleb peered at him, eyes red and bloodshot. "Not tonight. Maybe tomorrow night. We need to get to the forest first."

Reyan turned over under his blanket. "Let the boy watch tonight, Caleb," Reyan chided. "You need to sleep."

Caleb shook his head. "They could be searching tonight," he said.

Reyan coughed. "They'll be searching tomorrow, too."

"I can do it," Aden said. "I grow up on the street. I hear good. Need fine ears to survive the streets."

Caleb looked at him. Tamya, as usual, was silent on the issue, laying down and facing away from the group as they talked. "Okay, then," Caleb said. He pointed his finger into Aden's chest. "But you wake me. I'll only need a few hours." The man needed more than a few hours, they all knew, but Aden nodded his assent. Caleb glared at him one last time and prepared his blankets for the night.

Bringing out the book Reyan had given him that morning, he opened it. He sat next to the fire. Between the light of the fire and the bright moonlight, he could make out the words. Reyan didn't even look his way as he spoke. "Be careful next to the fire, Aden." His gravelly voice was soft but clear. "That's my only copy."

Nervous, Aden began to read. It was difficult. Some words he didn't understand, but many he did. It was rare when he made it to the school, and it had never helped much anyway. Jo didn't want Aden going to the school, said the elves would get suspicious and look for Aden's birth papers or his parents. Aden didn't have any, although he never knew why. And the Ministry school was a great place to get hooked on Sorcos, which Jo also opposed, even though Jo himself was as addicted as anyone Aden had ever seen. The Ministry gave out the Sorcos at school to help control the students. So most of Aden's literacy came from his own initiative, and he had even impressed Jo with his ability to sound out the words and understand them. Jo didn't say he was impressed, but he took advantage of Aden's literacy.

This was the first time, however, that Aden had held a real book. He had pamphlets and other smaller materials in his hands, things others threw away, materials distributed by the Kryan Empire to its citizens, written with easy and small words. Real books were rare among the Asyan poor. Theater and Qadi-bol was available to everyone. So Aden cherished the volume in his hand as he sat near the fire with great care.

Soon Aden could hear Reyan's snores and Tamya's rhythmic breathing. Even Caleb was in deep slumber within minutes, although the man was still enough to be dead. Aden sat cross-legged and laid the book in his lap as he read, focused and engrossed. He never woke Caleb. He read until the sun came up.

CHAPTER 12

THE BOOK OF THORNS

Bain Me'Bako woke up that morning, but not in his house.

A man of average height, he was almost sixty years old with a full head of gray hair, cut short in the elven style, and a clean-shaven gaunt face. He had big, blue eyes that people seemed to trust, or be intimidated by, whichever. Sometimes both. He was the most powerful man in town, and he knew it.

That didn't mean he got whatever he wanted. No, some people couldn't appreciate the good he tried to do and opposed him. Most of it was due to that Te'Lyan man, selfish and stubborn like his father before him. The man couldn't see how Bain tried to bring Delaton into a new age of progress. Eliot Te'Lyan kept referring back to the old traditions, the old ways of the old men. Most of the stories of the old men were legend and tale, anyway. No educated man would believe such drivel.

Bain's father had sent him to Ketan for three seasons to be tutored by an elven cleric. The traditions that weren't based on legend were proven wrong the day Manahem had been handed over to the elves, surrendered by a weak king of a weak nation. And that king had been the strongest the men had to offer. Who would try to honor traditions from a failed race? But most of the town trusted and needed Te'Lyan. His contacts with others, in Roseborough and Pontus, kept trade alive that people enjoyed. And most of the town knew it. He couldn't get rid of the man; he could only try to contain him as best he could.

He wanted so much more for the town, if he could get them to see it and let go of the old ways, ways like the old rules on marriage and fidelity. The elves were a much more enlightened race. They lived for thousands of years and had a much better perspective; how could they not? They married several times over their long life, which Bain understood – he got bored with a woman after a few years himself; he couldn't imagine centuries with just one woman. The elves understood that sexuality was meant to be explored and with several partners.

Syan lay next to him in the big feather bed in her house on the northern edge of the town. She stirred and ran her long nails through the gray hair on his narrow chest. A pretty enough woman, Syan stretched her arms and sat up in the bed. Bain smirked at her. "Top morn," he said.

She smiled back at him. "Top morn back to you," she said.

Bain rose from the bed, naked, and gathered his clothes from the night before. His wife, Suse, would not ask where he had been. She had stopped asking decades ago.

"Oh," Syan said, frowning at him with a hint of a grin. "Do you have to go for the real? Jaim doesn't come back from Roseborough 'til the morrow."

"Need to get back to the farm after I check on at the inn," Bain muttered. "Always more work to do, for the sure. That is, unless I can get the elves to support the town. Maybe I could be a mayor for the real then. Not have to work, just get coin to run the town."

Syan rolled her eyes at him. "You run the town now," she said. "At least you and your kids."

Bain had five children by his wife, Suse. She had always been a hearty woman, and her father had owned the inn. It had been a good and profitable marriage and gave him even more leverage among the citizens of Delaton. She had also been fertile. He had other children in the town, though, but he never publicly acknowledged those. He couldn't do so without being forced to have difficult conversations with married men who wouldn't understand, men still bound by those old ways. He had also made promises to Suse that he would claim her children as his own but never any from another.

Unfortunately, the infanti wasn't available here in Delaton like it was in Ketan or even Biram. That had saved him some headaches back in the city and would've saved him more headaches here in town. Most of his children were competent enough, but one or two had caused him some serious coin with their indiscretions themselves.

"You know what I mean," Bain said. He didn't get paid to run the town. Syan quieted and pulled the linen sheet over her body.

He finished dressing, pulling on his expensive crizzard-skin boots, and a knock came at the door to Syan's house.

He glanced at Syan, and she got the hint, rising and hastening put on her wool dress. The bedroom was in the back of the house, and she closed the wooden door behind her as she walked barefoot to the front to answer the continuous knocking. "Hello?" Bain heard her say as she opened the door.

"I need to speak with my Da," he heard the voice say. One of his sons. "Quickly, woman, get the man!" His second eldest son, Comy, one of the few he trusted.

"He … he's not here," Syan stammered, but she looked a fool when Bain came out of the bedroom and stood behind her. The shame on her face showed as she moved aside.

"What is it, Comy?" Bain said, straightening his silk shirt.

"Eliot Te'Lyan called an emergency Muster," Comy said. "For today at noon."

"Shoggit," Bain said. "He what?"

"I say he call an emer – "

"I hear what you say," Bain said. He heard the door to the bedroom close again behind him as he moved outside, Syan back into her bedroom alone. Bain closed the door to the house, looking up and down the street. Some people milled outside, but not many. Not that he cared about his reputation too much. Most people suspected his activities. But Syan would care about her reputation, and gossip getting back to her husband. She would not be pleased. Not that he cared for her pleasure, but he might have to find another mistress if she was spooked. He wasn't too worried, though. He had done it all before. "When did he call it?"

"First thing this morn," Comy said, and they walked together back down the street towards the inn. "Started spreading the word before most men awake."

"He say what it was about?" Bain asked.

"No, but some people saw his daughter come into town last night 'round dinner," Comy said. "Mebbe something to do with her."

"Doubtful," Bain said. He had been glad that woman had left town to get married a couple years ago. She might have been more trouble than her father, when it was all done. That Xander boy was an idiot. Bain had even offered one of his sons, Troyn, to Eliot years ago to try to get control of her and bring the Te'Lyan estate to his family. Eliot laughed him right out of the store. "An emergency Muster is called only in times of crisis, like a war. Breakin' thing shouldn't even be possible any more, not after so many years of the elves keepin' us safe."

Comy knew all this. Bain was speaking his thoughts aloud. "Well, men gettin' ready for the Muster anyway," Comy said. "Some men at the inn now, talkin'."

They were almost at the *Lovely Loaf*. "Let's see if we can stop this lunacy before it starts," Bain said as he entered the common room of his inn. "Let's see if being mayor of this town means anything."

—+—

Aden was still reading when Caleb woke, and the man was furious.

Caleb set his jaw. "You were supposed to …"

"Nothing happened and you needed the rest," Reyan interrupted, giving Caleb a firm stare.

Aden waited while Caleb looked between them. But he sniffed, spat on the ground, and turned to strike camp. When he raised his brows at Reyan, the Prophet smirked. "You're probably not going to get a lesson this morning."

Tamya glowered at him then as Reyan walked off.

"Oh, great," Aden muttered.

They rode back to the northwest. Caleb explained that they would try to catch the road just before the forest of Saten. He stated his confidence the elves would place a guard there. The road through Saten would be hard to find if they didn't catch it before the thick forest began. People could get lost there, and many had.

Other than that first exchange in the morning, Caleb stayed silent and brooding throughout the day. And Aden could feel the anger radiating from the small half-elf sitting behind him.

Leading the way through the rock and brush, Caleb rode before them. For a time, there was enough room for Reyan and Aden to ride side by side.

"I read last night," Aden said.

"Oh?" Reyan said.

"Yeah," Aden said, and his eyes glanced toward Caleb ahead of them. His voice lowered. "I read that prophecy about him. I find it."

Reyan continued to look ahead, as well, his expression unreadable.

"It say, 'the sword that gives him life will take his life,'" Aden quoted. "That mean that if he get this sword he after, on the mountain, it will kill him?"

Reyan frowned and lowered his head. "I had the hardest time translating that one," he muttered to himself. Reyan lifted his head. "It's not very clear, but the implication is that his service as the *Brendel*, the liberation of mankind, will cost him his life."

Aden scoffed, nodding ahead. "He know that?"

Reyan nodded. "Yes, he does."

Aden swallowed. What kind of man went on a quest he knew would cost his life?

"But the translation is difficult," Reyan continued. "The first tongue is very different from the common; hard to get the order right. It could also say, 'the sword that takes his life will give him life.'"

"What do that mean?" Aden said.

Reyan rolled his shoulders. "Not sure. Doesn't make sense, really. Could be largely symbolic that way, I guess." Reyan nodded forward. "If he is the one the prophecy is talking about – and I believe he is – then we'll know which one it means after he lives it." Reyan grunted, his gaze off into his own thoughts. "Maybe it means both."

"Both?" Aden said, his voice rising in volume. He lowered it again to almost a whisper. "He die and live at the end? How that happen?"

"Some things we can't know."

"That seem stupid," Aden said. "Or harsh. Real harsh."

"The Book of Thorns," Reyan said under his breath.

"What was that?" Aden said.

"Oh, something my father used to call the scriptures, the Fyrwrit," Reyan said. "The Book of Thorns. That book has had other names over the centuries. One was the Book of Thorns."

Aden looked at him, his brows furrowed. "Huh?"

"Like a bush of roseberries. Ever had a roseberry?" Reyan asked.

Aden nodded. Once he had tasted the pleasure and sweetness of that fruit, but fresh roseberries were rare and expensive.

"They are called the sweetest of fruit, but the roseberry bush has the longest and sharpest thorns. You have to brave the thorns to get the fruit."

Aden still stared at the man as if he didn't understand.

"The truths of the Fyrwrit are like the roseberry bush. The revelation is sweet and good, but it also pierces the heart and mind, correcting wrong thoughts and attitudes and beliefs. And truth hurts sometimes. That's why they sometimes call it the Book of Thorns."

"Isn't truth good?" Aden said.

"Oh, truth is always better than lies, but truth also costs you something. Every time. But it gives a treasure greater than anything you lose. Every person has to decide for themselves if truth is worth the cost."

Aden let silence continue between them for a moment. "You pay the cost?" he asked.

"If you love El enough," Reyan said. "You will die for him. Or live for him. They are the same thing. Yes, I've paid the cost, many times. And I will again, perhaps many more times, before it is all over."

Aden watched the old man for a minute, a man who had lost his wife and other members of his family for a cause he might never see come to fruition, for a god he believed in even though that god required so much from him. Reyan's body, while somewhat healed, was still weakened from being imprisoned and beaten. Aden could see the man's aches and pains in the morning and evening. Then he turned his head and watched Caleb's stiff, strong back as they wound northwest. Aden remembered the scars he saw there before they went under the Pyts. He still meant to ask the man about those.

Crazy people, Aden thought. But how crazy was Aden to be riding right along with them? And into the shoggin' forest of Saten, at that.

———+———

Eshlyn knew that Bain would try to derail the meeting, as did her father. Eliot swore his family to secrecy and refused to tell anyone what the emergency Muster was about. It wasn't stated in the law, or even in tradition, that the reason for the Muster be given. It might be implied, but no one could refuse the Muster, even the Mayor.

She heard gossip from her brother on how men gathered, drinking at the inn, for hours before the Muster. Bain had argued and threatened the men there, mocked Eliot and his family, and even challenged the manhood of many in the room, but even the ones loyal to Me'Bako had said there was nothing they could do. The tradition was clear. They had to attend the Muster. Eshlyn counted it as a Tablet in her favor. And the town's.

Eshlyn rode back into town on another of her father's horses, a brown gelding by the name of Skylar, a fine horse. Eliot and Eshlyn both agreed that Blackie should have some rest after the long days of travel, and for the ones the mare would have in the future. Javyn was at her parent's house with her mother. Xander and Eliot rode alongside her as they reached the center of Delaton.

It was almost noon, and a large crowd milled just outside the hall, men and women and children. The three of them dismounted and found a place to tie the horses.

"Eshlyn!" a voice carried across the street.

She turned towards the voice and a short, red haired woman in a purple linen dress ran to her and grabbed Eshlyn's upper arms. "Sirah," Eshlyn said.

Sirah half smiled and twisted her pug nose. "What is going on? I heard your father called the Muster. You know anything?"

Sirah and Eshlyn had been best friends growing up. They were not only the same age, but her father had worked for Eliot Te'Lyan helping to herd and breed the cattle. Eliot had also allowed Sirah to attend tutoring sessions with Eshlyn, learning to read and do numbers. Always a happy child, Sirah was full of energy and a little precocious. They got in trouble a few times, but she was a good heart and dear to Eshlyn. She married the son of a farmer to the northwest of town last season.

"Yes, I know ... but I can't say," Eshlyn murmured.

Sirah looked around, scanning the crowd. "Hey, where ... where is Kenric?" she asked.

Eshlyn forced a smile. "We'll talk after. I have to go in with Da."

Sirah's mouth hung open as Eshlyn grabbed her hand, squeezed, turned and walked into the hall. "You – you goin' in?" Sirah asked. Eshlyn heard the amazement as she entered the hall.

The hall in Delaton was arranged in a different way than in Pontus. In Pontus, while there were elders of the town with some influence, the men stood as equals in the Muster. Here in Delaton, though, the men sat on benches facing the far end, where they placed a seat behind a table for the Mayor. Bain already sat there, glowering at any who moved, which was everyone. Eshlyn moved forward to a bench at the front with her father and brother. The men in the room mumbled comments as they passed, as a woman entered the hall.

Bain leaned forward in the chair and pointed. "She can't be in here, Eliot," Bain said. "Get her out of here."

Eliot stood before Bain. "She can be here," Eliot stated. He looked around the room. Then back at Bain. "She's the reason we're all here." Part of the tradition of the Muster included allowing the attendance of people in the Muster that had pertinent information on the crisis. This was to allow non-citizens of the town and other outsiders to be included, if needed. It never mentioned that it couldn't be a woman. So Bain had to allow it, as much as it might seem a technicality.

Bain's glare hardened, but he sat back.

Eshlyn knew this would be difficult, but watching the most powerful man in town dead set against her father caused her to waver even more than she already did. But she made a promise to her husband, and even though she had no physical proof, she would do her best.

It took another few minutes, but the rest of the men settled in their seats, low conversation filling the large room. Bain rapped a wooden mallet against the table in front of him. "Let's get this thing underway," he said, his voice quick and annoyed. "Eliot, you called the Muster. You get first say."

Eliot stood from the bench, walked to the table, turned and faced the men of Delaton. "I appreciate you all being here today. I called this Muster because of my daughter, who you all know. Eshlyn," he called her forward. She rose and joined him, wearing a fine green woolen dress embroidered around the hem and end of the sleeves, her black hair in ringlets and set with silver combs. The men moved uneasy in their seats. "She has something she needs to say to everyone."

Eshlyn stood before the men of her town, men she knew well, men had she dealt with for years as they came through the general store and did business with her father. For all practical purposes, they had done business with her. She was almost as connected to these men as was her father.

Standing straight, her shoulders squaring and her head lifting, emboldened, she began her testimony. She had recited it a few times before this, and the words came easier, flowed better. The men of the town were still and quiet as she described that night. She was nervous, but she took her time. She left out Kenric's claim that he was a descendent of a king. No need to make them think he was more maddy than it already seemed. Eshlyn concluded with a plea.

"So I beg of you, pack your things today, take what you need, and come with us tomorrow to Ketan."

As Eshlyn could have predicted, Bain was the first one to speak. "Have you gone the mad?" he asked, raising an eyebrow with a smirk. "You want the men of this town to pack up their things, leave their farms and ranches and businesses, and all go to Ketan?"

Eshlyn turned to Bain, and said in a calm tone, "Yes."

Tad stood, to the right, halfway back, one of the men more loyal to Bain. "But you didn't see nothin'," he said. "We don't even know what we runnin' from."

"Could be anything," she heard another voice, now to her left, closer to the front. Old man Stav. He worked for Bain. "You don't know for sure what happened in the town. You just ran." Did he mean to accuse her? She felt the guilt of it still.

Eshlyn lowered her head; her heart sank. Not again. What could she say? What could she do? Her mouth felt dry, and she swallowed hard.

Byr took his time standing. Sirah's husband. "No offense, but harvest time coming soon. Can't just all leave and go to the city."

Her father took a step forward. "Listen. I grew up here. I know you all. I wouldn't do anything to hurt this town. But we are leaving first thing in the morn, to the real." He pointed through the crowd to his closest friends; some of them were men Eliot had helped in time of need. "Mark me, all of you. I gave Kenric my daughter, one of my most precious possessions. He was – or is – a good man. If he thought it important enough to send his wife and baby son away, then I believe him. If he thought it dangerous enough to tell us to run, then I believe him and I will run. Have any of you ever known Esh to be untrustworthy in any way? You know not." He took a deep breath. "We gather at the north end of town, first thing in the morn. Anyone want to come with us is welcome."

The men in the room were quiet, looking away or down at their feet, rubbing their beards and knuckling mustaches.. Her father was a reasonable man, a man they all trusted. Did he believe there to be danger, for the real, or was he swayed by a daughter everyone knew he loved more than air? Eshlyn could see the questions in their minds. She had them herself.

Bain stood, laughing. "You want to go up to the city, then go right on in the morn. You want to go and leave your ranch, your herds, run chaos over the plains or in the hands of other men, you go on," Bain said. "It'll take almost two ninedays to get up to the city and back, and that's only if we don't stay there for a while. Crops will need harvest by then. If we do not return in time, some could lose a harvest. That would make it a hard winter. You know all this, though." Bain sniffed in derision at Eshlyn's father. "You always been a little maddy, Eliot, but you let this daughter pull you along by her skirts too much for me. You let a woman call an emergency Muster. A woman! You go too far this time, Eliot."

Eshlyn turned around to Bain, her eyes burning at him. "You listen if you want to live, old man," she said, just as much fire coming from her voice. "What do you want? The head of my husband to show you the sacrifice he made for his wife and daughter? You want dead bodies all around you before you believe me? What will it take? They made that watchtower for a reason; to warn us all. You get your children and that wife of yours together and get on the road with us to the city tomorrow morn." Eshlyn turned back to the men of Delaton, most of which stared at her wide-eyed. "And the rest of you need to stop being scared of a cheating, lying old man. He goes after your wives and daughters and you never do anything!" Gasps came from around the room, then yelling all at once. No one ever talked to Bain that way, except maybe her father. Eshlyn counted herself proud to carry on the tradition. But even her father had never openly called out his adultery.

"You know my father only wants the good for this town," she yelled over top of them. "We'll be waiting at the north end of town tomorrow!" Bain was up and yelling at her, calling her names, ordering her out of the room. Xander moved towards Bain, yelling back at him. Eliot held his son back. Small scuffles broke out all over the hall. She shook her head and left down the middle of the hall, her father and brother right behind her.

She left the hall, bursting out into the light of day, her eyes squinting at the bright sun. Eshlyn walked up to Sirah, waiting there just outside of the hall. She took her old friend by the shoulders and looked into her eyes.

"Esh," she began. "What happened in there? Why are they all yelling –"

"Sirah," Eshlyn said, breaking in. Men were leaving the hall, still yelling and wrestling with one another. "Meet us at the north edge of town tomorrow morn and go with us to Ketan. Do whatever you have to do to get Byr to come with you. Or just come alone. But please, please come with us to Ketan in the morn. You won't be safe if you stay here."

Eliot pulled her along with her brother to the horses where they mounted in a hurry. Eshlyn gave Sirah a fierce stare as they turned and galloped back to the ranch.

———

Just after mid-day, Caleb halted everyone and they dismounted. "You stay here," he told them as they gathered around him. "The main road is a kilomitre north of here, where it enters Saten. I'm going to scout and see if they have a guard posted. Then I'll be back."

He moved to the rear of his horse and grabbed the two sharpened wooden poles that had been made for him in Asya, the ones he used to train with Aden and Tamya, placing them through a loop in his belt, one on each hip. He removed his leather boots and vest and put moccasins on his feet. Wearing his leather pants and long sleeved shirt, he pulled back his hair with a leather cord.

"And if guards're posted?" Aden asked.

Caleb shrugged as he hefted the Kingstaff, light as wood but stronger than steel. "Then I'll take care of them before I get back."

Without another word, he turned and ran north into the brush and through a clearing. The foliage was thicker as he neared the forest of Saten. Caleb continued to run full speed, however, for several hundred mitres.

When he judged he closed in on the road, perhaps within two hundred mitres, he slowed to a trot, crouching, his eyes darting back and forth. He heard a rustle, and he froze. He peered to his right, back to the east, and saw the origin of the noise. A deer bounded away from him.

Still in a crouch, he moved from one thicket of bushes to another, across bare patches of high grass, never making a sound. He moved from tree to grove, from one hidden point to another, for a hundred mitres or so, winding northwest. Soon, he caught a glimpse of the road just ahead, thirty mitres away. He walked slow, bending even lower, his gaze moving from side to side.

He noticed the guard on the road at the entrance to the forest of Saten, just as he had expected. If the men who attacked the elves at Anneton journeyed west along the Galyan road, then this would be the perfect spot to intercept those men. The elves wouldn't enter the forest – an elf hadn't returned from that forest for almost a hundred years – but they would guard the entrance to it. Four Citywatch guards stood on the road, two in front and two behind. They wore gray tunics under silver armor and were armed with long spears with curved blades and gladi at their hips. Caleb watched them for a long moment, studying them. It looked like they had been there all day.

Stretching his shoulders, the scars on his back started to itch, sweat crawling down his spine.

The guard appeared bored, forcing themselves to watch the road and the countryside around them. But they were also well trained, better than the ones in Anneton. Biram and Anneton would have every available Cityguard and other elven official working to find the men responsible for Anneton, at least until a legion from Galya, a Bladeguard, or Wraith could get there.

We have to get into the forest before then, Caleb thought.

But Caleb had bested a whole platoon the other day. Did they think four could stop him?

So he worked his way as close as he could without being seen, which he guessed was about ten mitres away. He was to their right, south of the road. He huddled behind a thick tree. It would be a good position to attack from. A clearing separated him from the guards. He held the staff in his left hand and pulled the wooden pole from his right hip with his right hand. Caleb closed his eyes, making sure he had the terrain memorized in his head, took a calming breath, and moved.

Catching a lucky Tablet, he noticed none were looking his way when he bolted from behind the tree. He had sprinted two or three mitres into the clearing before they noticed him or registered what was happening. By the time the guard closest to Caleb's position caught sight of him, a wooden pole hurtled towards his face. The wood connected across the elf's nose with a sharp slap. The elf's arms flailed, and he fell backwards, unconscious.

Caleb was more than halfway across the clearing as the other three guards reacted, turning his way with their spears pointing towards him at the ready. Caleb reached across his body with his right hand and pulled the other wooden gladus from his belt; in one motion, he launched the wooden pole like a missile, the sharpened end striking a second guard between the legs. It doesn't matter if you were man or male elf, Caleb thought, a sharpened wooden pole stabbing into your groin puts you down.

Within three sprinting paces of them now, Caleb slowed, bringing the staff up above his head and reaching up with his right to twist the staff down and in front of him in time to block the spears that stabbed in at him. He knocked them aside, but the guards parted, jogging back on sure feet, keeping Caleb at spear's length.

As Caleb noted before, they were well trained, and this was a good tactic. The two remaining guards now had him in between them, and they could keep out of range of his staff with their longer spears. He parried their thrusts with ease, but their strategy would force Caleb to make an aggressive move, increasing the likelihood he would make a mistake.

One of the guards reached down to a metallic cylinder hanging from a chain around his neck. With one hand he kept stabbing with the spear; the other hand brought the cylinder to his mouth. It was whistle, and he took a deep breath and blew. Not just any whistle. A grider call. The high-pitched sound cut through the air and echoed.

Caleb continued to parry the strikes from the guard, and he cursed himself for acting like an amateur. They had a grider.

In the midst of his distraction, a spear stabbed low and sliced across his calf. He ignored the pain; he was still able to still walk.

Hearing the screech of the creature from overhead as he blocked the guard to his right, he turned into the spear strike, hitting the elf with a simultaneous elbow to the face and kick to the knee. Both strikes connected, and the elf went down, gasping. Caleb stepped over the guard and kicked down onto his neck, crushing it beneath his moccasin. He turned to face the last guard.

Another scream from above reached Caleb's ears, and his eyes flashed to the sky.

A grider's hairy white torso was tubular and a mitre and a half long with two legs on each side. Each leg bent on three joints and ended in a singular brown talon. A lengthy, thin neck protruded forward, and its head was a long oval with a fierce, curved brown beak. Four large white wings spread from the body, and a narrow tail that terminated with a flat, triangular shape trailed the creature.

It had neither eyes nor eye sockets, but it possessed two large flat nostrils over the beak that flared with cilia that could sense both smell and sound. Its screeches helped it to find prey. The grider was a creature of the large, deep, and pitch black caverns in the dwarven regions far across the ocean. Kryus had bred and trained the griders to attack at a certain scent, which it could sense from a hundred mitres away: the smell of human blood.

The remaining guard did as he was trained and rushed Caleb with the blade of the spear pointed at Caleb's midsection, trying to keep him busy until the grider arrived. Caleb growled and backed away, bringing around the Kingstaff to parry the blade. The elf continued to thrust and sweep the spear, varying his strikes and slashes. *He's good*, Caleb thought.

He perceived a presence behind him, and he dove to the right as a gladus swept through the air. The blade glanced across his left shoulder instead of hacking into his neck, and he tucked into a roll away from both guard. He came to his feet, his calf in pain, to face the guard he struck in the groin. The guard lumbered along, one hand between his legs, but he was very much in the fight.

Caleb had to move on instinct, blocking with the Kingstaff as two guard flanked him again. This would be so much easier with a sword, Caleb thought.

The screech of the grider was closer, so as the guard with the spear stepped into a strike, Caleb moved to the right and reached out with his left hand, grabbing the wood of the spear just below the blade. He pulled the spear toward him, swinging the staff behind him, keeping the guard with the gladi at bay. Caleb thrust forward and brought his forehead into direct contact with the face of the guard in front of him, knocking the elf on his back. Caleb allowed his momentum to carry into another roll. The grider was upon him.

He heard the beak snap, and a talon scraped the back of his right leg as he rotated. Caleb turned over, spinning the staff above him. He connected with the two forelegs of the grider, but the rear legs struck at his torso and took a swipe of flesh from his abdomen before it flew up and away to gather itself for another pass. The four wings gave the grider incredible speed and control.

He sprung to his feet and backed away, keeping an eye on the grider while the guard with the gladi stabbed at him. Caleb leapt to the side and propelled the end of the staff at the elf's throat. It connected with a crunch, and the guard was knocked back, grasping at his neck.

Caleb twisted as the grider was on him again, the staff swinging and blocking the eyeless head as it tried to strike, screeching, all four legs darting in to find a perch. Two got through his defenses, one on his left bicep, the other across his upper right thigh, neither deep, however painful.

He managed to get in a powerful kick to the grider's torso, and the animal flew away again to come back for another dive.

The last guard with a spear strove to get to his feet, blood pouring from his nose, and Caleb rushed toward him. He knocked the spear out of the elf's hand with one end of the staff and smacked him across the face with the other. As the guard fell back, unconscious, Caleb tore off his own shirt, bloody from several cuts, and wrapped it around the guard's neck.

The sound of the grider's screech rose in volume, nearing. He used the bloody shirt as a handle and hefted the elf as a shield, crying out in defiance. The grider descended upon them and ripped into the guard's face with its beak; the body with the talons on its legs. As it tasted elven blood, the grider hesitated. In one final desperate move, Caleb brought the Kingstaff around with his right hand and crushed its skull.

The grider collapsed on the ground, convulsing. Caleb let the torn and bloody elf drop from his grasp. He stumbled over to the creature and finished it with another strike to the head.

And then he immediately fell to his knees. He wanted to lie down in the bloody grass next to him, but he knew if he did, he might not rise again.

He was bleeding from several places, three of them deep gashes, and he was losing a lot of blood. He needed to do what he could to fix that, before he passed out.

Dragging the Kingstaff behind him, he crawled over to one of the dead guard. He began ripping the tunic off the elf and tore it into long strips, which took most of the strength that remained in him. He took a few moments to rest, sitting on his knees, and he almost fell over twice, using the Kingstaff to keep him upright.

It took longer than he imagined, tying the strips of cloth over his wounds: his bicep his calf, his abdomen, his thigh. Two scrapes already stopped bleeding; not worth the trouble. After a few minutes in which he said a prayer to El for strength, he stood and used the Kingstaff as a crutch, limping back to Reyan and the others.

—•—

"I hear somethin'," Aden said.

The three of them sat on the ground behind a copse of trees, the horses tied to a thicket further away from the road.

Reyan turned to him. "What is it?"

Aden shook his head. "Rustling. Can't tell how far." He peered between the trees but couldn't see anything.

"Stay quiet, then," Reyan whispered.

Tamya frowned at them.

Aden heard it again, louder.

"That?" she said.

He grabbed a gladi and stood. "I'm gonna check it out."

Reyan grasped his wrist. "Stay here."

Aden pulled his hand away, and grinned. "No worries," he said. "I be careful."

Tamya got to her feet with a sword in her hand, too. "I'm going with you."

Aden shrugged and headed off towards the road, trying to step without a sound, his knees bent as he walked. He held his sword out in front of him. Tamya followed him.

They rounded another grove of trees, and Aden froze. Movement caught his eye just beyond a thicket fifteen mitres away.

"What is it?" Tamya asked under her breath

He hushed her, crouching lower and stepping forward. Then he heard a voice, low and talking. He stopped again and cocked his head.

"Who is that?" Tamya whispered close to him.

Standing straight, he took another two steps in the direction of the voice. "It's Caleb," he said, and he began to jog, Tamya pacing him behind.

Aden cleared the thicket and saw Caleb five mitres away, head down, muttering to himself, clutching the Kingstaff close to him, using it as some sort of crutch as he trudged forward. He was shirtless and covered in blood and sweat, ragged cloths tied around different parts of his body as bandages, a couple of them dripping blood.

Aden turned to Tamya. "Get Reyan and the horses. Quick."

She nodded curtly, spun and ran back.

Dropping his sword, Aden sprinted to Caleb and grabbed his arms. "Come on," he said. "Sit down."

Caleb stopped but didn't lift his head. "… *the rebirth of the Sohan-el. The sword that gives him life will take his life. He will be inflicted with deep wounds, and those scars will follow him all his days. He is not a man, but a sword …*"

Aden pulled on him, attempting to be gentle and firm, and Caleb resisted at first, but then he looked up and recognized Aden. He allowed himself to be led down to the ground, the leaves softening his fall. Aden tried to take the staff from his hand, but Caleb would not release it.

"*And El will use him as a sword, a blade to cut out the heart of those who would enslave and oppress … He will be born in the land of men but travel far away. His return will be a sign …*"

"I am weary of the fighting, my Lord," Mochus said. "There are so many enemies, so much fighting and death. How long must we fight?"

Yosu said, "Draw your strength from El. Love him above all, and his power will sustain you. Surrender is the only defeat."

"But we have been fighting so long. Battle upon battle we push the demics back, and yet they still come. I feel as if I have been fighting all my days. How much longer until we are free?"

"Peace is not the end of conflict. Freedom is not the absence of chains," Yosu said. "Are you not yet free?"

"Yes, Lord," Mochus said. "But when will it end? When will the fighting end?"

"Oh, Mochus," Yosu said. "The fighting never ends."

-From the Ydu, 5th Scroll, translated into common tongue
by the Prophet

CHAPTER 13

INTO THE SATEN

Eshlyn's head was full of doubts as they traveled from her parents' ranch down to the main road just north of Delaton. Eliot had packed a long wagon full of supplies and necessities. Two workhorses pulled the wagon. Morgan and Eshlyn sat in the jockey box, and Javyn lay in a makeshift crib in the back of the wagon. Two horses were tied to the back of the wagon: Blackie and Morgan's white mare, Princess. Eliot rode his horse, Monny, and Xander trotted Yaysay out front. Other ranchers trailed behind them, three men and their families that worked for the Te'Lyan family and lived on the ranch. They rode horses, their supplies on the Te'Lyan's long wagon, and each child rode saddle with an adult. The road wound to the southeast.

What if she was wrong? The Muster yesterday had not gone well, again. No one believed her. She didn't have any real evidence that there was anything to run from. And her status as a woman hindered the men from taking her seriously, even men who knew her, even Bain, who claimed to be as enlightened as the elves. Yesterday, she had made the division in the town worse, resorting to calling out family secrets, even if Bain Me'Bako was a piece of crit.

What did those dreams mean? Was Kenric still alive? She was more certain he was dead, despite her hope for something different, but those dreams meant something.

Was she doing what was best for the people by asking them to run to the city? Stacked against the reality that she had known her whole life, it was a crazy thing to ask. Nothing like this had ever happened to anyone's knowledge. They had lived safe and isolated for several generations.

And how did she know for certain that whatever happened at Campton would happen at Pontus or Delaton ... or their next destination, Roseborough? Maybe it had stopped with Campton. She had no evidence otherwise. Maybe they were laughing at her in Pontus.

But when she thought back to that night in Campton, heard the conviction in Kenric's voice, she knew in her gut the certainty that they must all get to the safety of Ketan. The men of the Julai Plains were good, strong men, and they would be good in a fistfight, but none knew how to hold a weapon, or even owned one to try. If it came down to any real fighting against a real enemy, the towns would be slaughtered.

How did Kenric get a sword? Had he even known how to use it? She had seen a weapon once, at the festival one season in Roseborough. A group of Cityguard came down to watch the proceedings. Two of them had worn their swords; short swords with a funny name.

She wrestled with the extremes of conviction and doubt as they neared the Manahem road. In the distance, Eshlyn squinted and saw what appeared to be a crowd of people waiting there. A large crowd of people that grew larger as they approached.

People had met them for the journey.

And not just a few people, either. Xander twisted in his saddle and glanced backward at Eshlyn in amazement and excitement. Sitting up in the wagon for a better look, she saw a few hundred people there on horses and in wagons, dressed and packed for travel. And waiting for them.

Her father's closest friends from town were all there   , among others. As they joined the group already gathered, she counted over five hundred people. That was half the town! A woman with a linen bag pushed through the crowd, walking on her feet up to the wagon.

"Sirah," Eshlyn said, jumping down from the wagon and embracing her friend. As she pulled away from her old friend, Eshlyn noticed Sirah's right eye blackened and blue and yellow bruise on her left cheek. "Oh, Sirah," Eshlyn whispered.

Sirah began to cry. "I asked him to come," she said. "I tried to get him to come, but he said he wouldn't. And he say I couldn't go, either." Her face hardened. Her jaw set. "I came anyway."

Eshlyn's own eyes watered as she embraced her friend again. "Good girl," she said into her friend's ear. She pulled away, holding Sirah at arm's length. "Get up into the wagon with my mother," Eshlyn said, and Sirah complied, glancing back at her parents. Eshlyn followed her up to the seat of the wagon, but she stood and stared out over the crowd. Maybe she wasn't such a failure after all. The faces in the crowd turned to meet her.

Her eyes misted and her vision blurred as she looked over the crowd of people. They waited for her to speak, and she wanted to say something that would give them hope, courage. She was overwhelmed, however, and she could not formulate words that would be enough.

"Thank you," was all she could say. "Thank you."

———

Aden sat with the injured Caleb until Reyan and Tamya returned, then he assisted Reyan as they cleaned Caleb's wounds and bound them again with clean cloths from their packs. Caleb was running out of shirts. Reyan placed his hands upon the wounded man, one on his forehead and the other on his chest, and the Prophet closed his eyes and muttered low.

Tamya continued to wrap a dressing on Caleb's calf, but Aden paused and tried to make out the words. He looked down at Caleb lying on the ground, pale and breathing shallow.

Caleb opened his eyes and smirked at Aden. "Told you I'd take care of them."

They gave him water and made him eat something, and he nibbled at the flat bread. He was weak and needed rest, but he insisted they make it into the forest of Saten by nightfall. More elves would come, he said, and soon.

It took all three of them to help him up on the saddle of his horse. He winced at the pain and then nodded when he settled. Aden shared his horse with Tamya again, and they rode the remaining distance to the entrance of the Saten. Reyan paused when they passed the dead elves and grider. He gathered any supplies he could find and one of the spears, laying it across his saddle as he mounted again.

Entering the forest, they made camp a couple hours later once it became too dark to see. Caleb was half-asleep in the saddle already, so the three of them lowered him down to his blanket and let him rest while they set up the camp.

Aden noticed Reyan just beyond the firelight, sitting cross-legged with his hands clasped before him. Aden watched him for a few moments before moving to sit nearby. Reyan had his eyes closed and mumbled to himself. A minute later, Aden asked, "What you do?"

Reyan took a deep breath, sighing to collect himself. Without opening his eyes, he said, "I am praying to El."

Aden's brow furrowed at him. "Like a priest? Why you do no funny stuff like the Nican?" Aden asked. "They light fires or throw water or dirt to please the gods. Why you just sit?"

Reyan scoffed. "A real god doesn't need a show," he said. "El is the only real god, and those that follow him talk to him and listen to him."

"He talk to you?" Aden asked.

Reyan grinned. "I wouldn't be much of a prophet it he didn't. He tells me what to say, the messages to give the people who want to follow him. If I don't listen to him and say what he wants me to say, then I might as well throw dirt or water or burn my eyes with the sun like the Nican. Or I'd just be a madman like they believe I am, after all."

Aden nodded. "So ... what d'he say?" Aden asked. "What do El say today?"

Reyan frowned. "Hard to say. His voice isn't as clear." Reyan shook his head. "Something doesn't feel right. I'm seeking guidance about our journey, about what we are to do, and I'm not getting much direction."

"What do that mean?" Aden asked.

Reyan opened his eyes and looked at Aden. "It means we keep doing what we know is right until we get an answer, a direction. And I think what is right is to stay with Caleb." Reyan turned his head and stared back at the camp, at Caleb, who had begun to rise and gather his things with hesitant and shaky movements. "For now."

Aden nodded. "Yeah," Aden said. "Me too." Then he turned to Reyan, raising his hands palm out. "Not that I hear no god or anything."

Reyan chuckled and began to get up. "Don't worry. You'll know when he speaks to you."

＋

They were in their saddles and riding west in the forest within the hour, and Aden listened to Reyan talk about the forest of Saten as they rode through the day.

To speak of the Forest of Saten was to invoke a number of legends, myths, and dangers, the most notorious of which was the Ghosts of Saten. The elves believed they were the souls of dead human soldiers from the War of Liberation that haunted the thick forest, killing any elves that entered there. Towns had existed along the Saten road through the forest long ago, but nothing lived there now. The elves considered it a place of death, and they had learned to avoid it. Men sometimes traveled through the forest on the road and made it through, and Reyan claimed that he was not afraid of the journey through the forest. But even he glanced warily around himself at times.

Like any place of mystery in the world, the Saten inspired tales. The bloodwolves were a pack of wolves covered in red fur that roamed the forest. Some said they hunted on behalf of the ghosts there, and others said there were several packs and not just one. Tales spoke of wolves as big as a horse, ferocious beasts that would attack men at will.

Other stories were told of the forest: living trees that tore men from the saddle and snapped them in half with their branches and roots, fruit that made a man hallucinate and live out his worst fear, and an immortal black bear that stood five mitres tall, called the Org; a large buck, twice as big as a horse, by the name of the Mfeld, fought the Org every winter for dominance of the forest. Reyan ended his recital of the legends of Saten with the story of a lady dressed in white that sang to men and lured them into a hidden hollow where she dined upon him piece by piece.

It was rare for people to travel through the forest at all anymore, and the survivors never saw a thing. But men all swore by the legends of the forest. Almost any story about the place was believable, especially to men full of ale and smoking Sorcos.

Aden did not know if any of those legends were true. What he experienced of the forest, however, was the darkness. Even in the middle of the day, the thick vegetation of the forest stood like a barrier at either side and hung over them like a dark sky, the canopy blocking out the sunlight.

He could well imagine eyes within the forest looking at him, little orbs from all kinds of unfriendly animals at any time. It made him hunch over in his saddle, and Tamya hunched with him as she rode behind him in the saddle.

As thick as the trees were, strong winds found a way through them, whistling as they rustled leaves and made branches wave overhead. It was difficult to discern the time of day under the thick canopy. The night had been pitch black, but even now a single dim light showed the way. The sun would peek through the canopy at a rare moment and cause them to squint or cover their eyes.

The day dragged on, and Reyan began to tell Aden of the people of the forest. "They were called the Drytweld in the First Tongue," he said. "And they were not a part of any nation of men but were friends with all of them. They were not a nation of their own, more a loose confederation of towns and settlements along the road through the forest. They knew the forest better than most men knew their wives, and it was said they loved the forest more than a man could love his wife, as well." Reyan chuckled. "It was even said that they had a city built in the trees deep in the forest, but it was a secret place, a place where only the leaders of the Drytweld could go, and a deep underground lake watered the city, a lake of power and life."

"Those're the Ghosts in Saten?" Aden asked.

Reyan frowned. "If there are any spirits in these woods, they are not the spirits of men. The spirits of men do not haunt this world when they die; they go to another place. No, the Drytweld did not become the Ghosts of Saten."

Aden thought about ghosts and the men of old, of prayer and madness, what a city among the trees would even be like, and remarking to himself how dismal the forest was ... when through the middle of the day and into the afternoon, the sky began to darken with black clouds, blocking even the rare glimpses at the sun. Then it began to rain. They heard the sound of it first, pattering on the canopy above, periodic drops of water falling upon them. Then the rain thickened and the canopy was soaked through. Within minutes the travelers were wet to the skin.

And Aden realized how much more dismal the forest could be.

———

Eshlyn had traveled alone with her son until the people from Delaton joined her. The feeling of loneliness and isolation had been overwhelming at times. She didn't realize how alone she felt during those times until she saw the crowd of people camped out upon the plains for the night along the Manahem road that evening.

She nursed Javyn once more before settling him in, the stars and the three moons of Eres – the green of Cynadi full now – shining upon the residents of Delaton that had come with her that morning. She heard the sound of a drum, a mandolin, and a fiddle off on the other side of the road through the low din of the camp, and she smiled. Shew and his family must have brought their instruments. After checking the bundle on Javyn again, Eshlyn stood up and began to walk away from the fire her father had started.

"Where are you going?" Xander asked as she brushed off the front of her woolen dress.

"I'm going to walk around a mite," she said and left at his grunt.

She walked towards the sound of the music, the hollow and deep sound of the drum a hypnotic rhythm that seemed to draw her. She passed people as she wound her way in that direction, men and women and children looking up at her with a smile and saying hello. She paused at one family from a farm that reached almost to the western edge of the Saten, and checked on them. Their baby had a slight cold, and they were concerned about the night air. Fires were rare in the camp since bush and tree simply dotted the landscape and dead wood was scarce, so Eshlyn asked her father's friend, Grolm, if the sick baby and family could share their fire. Of course they could, Grolm had replied, and with that taken care of, she continued her walk to the music.

Hearing the melody now, it was an up-tempo jig that she had heard many times at market. Stew liked to play and entertain people at market, and his wife was a gem on the fiddle. Stew's son could play that drum for a week straight with that little mallet. Several families shared the fire and clapped along with the tune, a song about a fat and beautiful woman who had to choose between a farmer and a rancher, both vying for her attention. The woman had them go through a series of comedic contests before she would choose, each contest more outrageous than the last. She chose the blacksmith in the last verse. Stew himself played the mandolin and sang the tune, several joining in as their favorite lines came along. The song could go on forever if someone could make up a verse on the spot, and a few of the men and women at hand did just that. The laughter warmed Eshlyn's heart in a way that also wounded it. She wished Kenric could be there. She could just picture him with his pipe clapping along with the jig.

A few people danced on the outskirts of the group, and Eshlyn had to dodge those merrymakers as she rounded Stew's crew, smiling to people who greeted her as she passed. The people of Delaton were good, strong stock, and everyone else claimed to be fine and in no need.

Eshlyn thought of Kenric then, of how she had followed him to his home in the small town of Campton, and their dreams of growing the farm and business together, of seeing Campton come together and becoming more of a community. It was difficult at first, but two stubborn and independent souls learned how to work together and lean on the other's strength. They did everything together. Even after the happiness of the pregnancy, and the birth, they were more a team than ever. She wished she had him now, wished she could talk to him, see him smile reassuringly at her self-doubt. But she would have to do this without him.

She made it back to her family's camp, the fire burning low. By the time she lay down on her blankets, the noise of the camp had died down and quiet reigned over the grasslands. She slept, a breeze caressing her face.

She dreamt again that night, a furtive dream where she struggled with a dark figure, too big and monstrous to be a man, who tried to reach past her and kill her son. She couldn't see any of his features, but she wrestled with him, Javyn beginning to cry behind her. She felt so hopeless in the dream.

Then she heard Kenric's voice. Hurry, Eshlyn. Don't give up. Keep fighting. His voice was so clear, desperate and pleading.

She woke with a cry, breathless. She felt for Javyn next to her in the dark, pulling him close to her.

Perhaps she wasn't doing this without him after all.

CฎAPᴄᴇR 14

GฎOSᴄS

Aden had slept in the cold and wet before, many times even in the snow under a back door in an alley in Asya. Tamya tried to brave the rain, and she was almost successful; her shivers belied her true struggles. Reyan also shivered and snored even louder that night, when he slept. Most of them didn't sleep very much at all. The lightning and thunder alone would have kept most of them awake, but the wet and the added chill made it a fitful night.

Caleb moved much better than the day before. They were running low on supplies, and Caleb expressed his concern for the horses. The rain replenished their canteen and water bags, but the horses would need real feed before long.

Aden and Tamya practiced the sword while Caleb sat nearby, eating his breakfast. They slipped on the wet leaves, wiping the falling rain from their face, and Caleb even chuckled once when Aden found himself on his back trying to shuffle forward on his feet too quick.

They rode through the day, bodies aching, quiet due to their lack of sleep and large drops of rain keeping them soaked. As safe as they might be from elves, the Saten could be a dangerous place, so Caleb had them ride with weapons at hand.

Aden's mind wandered often as they traveled. There had been some frightening and exciting times, to be sure, but there had also been long hours and days of passing trees and fields and now a thick forest. Everything began to look the same, and Aden often lost time as the monotony drowned him. He thought about times in Asya, about people that he had known, people on the street and people like Freyd. He even wondered about Chronch and what had happened to him.

Riding with Tamya made him uncomfortable. He could bear most anything with a shrug, but long hours of the beautiful woman pressed up against him affected and embarrassed him. He wished to ride with Reyan again but dared not begin to explain why. He tried thinking about something else, but that was difficult. The readings from the Fyrwrit confused him, and reviewing the sword forms only brought her to mind again.

By second hour of the afternoon, the rain stopped, and the sun shone again through the trees. The heat of the day began to bake the wet forest, and a mist rose on the ground, as if the dark forest needed any help looking ominous. After a few hours, their clothes dried in the afternoon heat. And Aden began to sit up straighter. He felt just a little lighter.

Maybe the forest wouldn't be so bad. He could understand how the dark trees around him could conjure any number of wild fancies, but he was more reasonable than that. Riding into the late afternoon, Aden even thought about asking Caleb about those scars on his back.

The faint sound reached Aden's ears in the evening, distant and mixed with the stirring of the trees, leaves cracking, steps on the road. Aden cocked his head and turned back behind them. The sound grew louder, and Caleb stopped his horse. His face soured, and he turned to look as well.

Reyan and Aden both drew rein, and when the soft noise of hooves quieted, a rising pattering upon the road became clear. Aden turned his horse perpendicular to the road to peer back along the path. He saw only shadows and mist, but his hair stood on end at that sound.

Then a howl carried through the night, a long, chilling and threatening wolfish wail. He saw Reyan stare at Caleb. "You know what that is," Reyan said.

Caleb shook his head. "Break me," he said in a strained whisper. Then he yelled, "Ride! Everybody ride!"

———

Waiting until the other mounds were beyond him, Caleb kicked his stallion. They galloped at a good pace, but he knew they couldn't keep this up. The horses didn't have the stamina. This was a sprint to see if they could find a safe place, a hiding place. Maybe they could climb trees and leave the horses for the pack, but the trees were slick with rain and moss. Any scenario Caleb could think of ended in death.

He held the staff out at his side and saw Reyan at the front of the group with the spear across his saddle. He knew the man had some ability with a weapon or two, but he was no warrior. Reyan was quite the hunter back in his prime, with a bow, but he wouldn't last long in a fight now. He was in no condition to fight, and Caleb hoped it didn't come down to that.

But it probably would.

They raced through the mist and the stillness of the forest. It was warm, but evening was arriving. Caleb's eyes darted forward and around them, looking for anything that could provide them cover. He prayed to El, begging the Creator for anything that would save their lives.

The pack of bloodwolves closed the gap. He managed a peek behind him, under his arm as he rode, and he could see shapes and shadows moving behind him. Spurring his stallion, he urged the others in front of them to ride faster, but he knew he they were going as fast as they could. He hung back five mitres or so behind the others. Maybe he could keep the bloodwolves at bay. But he wouldn't last long, either, wounded as he was.

Caleb heard the breathing now, an eerie sound since snarls and growls didn't yet accompany their attack. He turned and looked again.

They were large animals, not as big as horses, but perhaps half the size. The bloodwolves did indeed have long dark red fur. Their mouths were open as they ran, their paws beating the road, jostling one another for position, and baring yellowed fangs at him. He could see six of them. No, he did not want this to come to a fight of any kind.

The stallion was a good horse, but it wasn't a trained warhorse. Caleb did his best to keep it from bolting ahead of the others. His left arm struggled with the reins as his right held the staff.

Snapping, snapping of jaws behind him among the pounding of hooves and paws upon the packed dirt of the road. Now the bloodwolves were snarling, nipping even at one another, growling as they were mere paces behind Caleb's horse. Caleb pulled his horse back a couple mitres further behind the other riders before releasing the reins with his left hand and guiding the horse with his thighs. His jaw clenched as the wounds on his thigh and calf stung with pain.

Twisting in his saddle, he began to spin the staff from one side of the horse to the other. One bloodwolf got close to the back legs of the stallion. Caleb moved the horse to the left with his thighs and spun the staff back to the right, connecting with the eye of the bloodwolf with a wet sound, and he heard the large red animal yelp.

Emboldened, he began to move the horse back and forth, striking out as he could behind them with the staff. The lacerations on his body – bicep, shoulders, abdomen – protested with constant pain. He ignored them. He connected with another wolf, but this enraged it further.

Caleb rode ten mitres behind the others, and he could hear the panting of their horses – they were already tiring. Soon they'd be running blind through the Saten as darkness fell. Out of his periphery, Caleb saw a clearing with the ruins of an old structure on the right.

All six wolves were still in pursuit, and the one with a wounded eye came up on his right again. Yelling as he embraced the agony of his body, Caleb brought the Kingstaff up and around then down upon the wolf's skull. The beast exhaled with a snort and then dropped to the road, causing three others behind it to stumble.

He heard a horse neigh in distress, a high pitched and disturbing sound. Caleb turned forward just in time to see Reyan's horse pitch forward, the horse's front legs buckling – had it stumbled on something or just collapse? – and then it went down, throwing Reyan forward and landing on its side, skidding on the road. The old man tumbled to his back.

It would be a fight after all.

Caleb was filled with pride to see that Aden did not hesitate to pull up hard on the reins of his horse, slowing to the spot where Reyan had landed.

"Get him and your horse to that clearing!" Caleb shouted. His only hope – their only hope – was to put the ruins at their back and keep the wolves from flanking them. In a defensible position … maybe. They had a chance then.

He kicked his horse with his heels and watched as Aden and Tamya both leapt from their horse to where Reyan had begun to rise, favoring his left arm but still holding onto the spear with his right.

Grabbing the Prophet with surprising speed and strength, Aden moved the man to the clearing while Tamya grabbed the reins of their horse and ran towards the clearing, as well. Reyan's horse was down. They didn't even bother with the animal.

Caleb was now at the clearing, and his stallion still ran, slowing, as he jumped off the horse to the right of the animal. He hit the ground running but stumbled in pain, pitching forward to his knees, hopping up to a fast limp. Tamya reached out and grabbed the reins of his horse as it neared her.

The clearing had once been a structure, and two stone walls met at the far end. Caleb turned and faced the oncoming wolves and shouted, "Tamya! Keep the horses in the corner!"

The bloodwolves stopped just outside the clearing as Caleb turned to meet them. His staff was extended, and he crouched low. One animal attacked the flailing horse on the road, and four more surrounded the group and bared their teeth at them, growling, their hackles rising, panting and out of breath. The wolves snapped their jaws at the air and crept forward.

Time slowed, and Caleb felt blood running down his calf. He saw a spear extend next to him. From his periphery, he noticed Reyan, his left arm tucked at his side, his face a grimace of pain, but the elven spear raised toward the wolves. "You all right?" Caleb asked.

"Doesn't matter," Reyan said. "Are you?"

To his right, both Aden and Tamya stepped forward, their gladi in their hands, doing their best to stand in the forms he had taught them. *Tamya must have tied the horses to something behind us.* He could still hear them neighing and stirring in the dead leaves. He was so tired, leaning against the staff, but he snarled back at the wolves.

"Keep a tight formation," Caleb said to the group. "Tamya, beside me. Aden, take the flank … the end. They will try to get between and around behind us. Let me out in front."

The bloodwolves arrayed themselves in a half circle around the humans. They attacked.

A singular wolf, perhaps the leader of the pack, leapt at Caleb first, and Caleb met the wolf with a strike across his snout that crushed bone and split skin, leaving blood on the staff. A split moment after three more pounced, and Caleb struck one down, which scrambled to its feet and retreated shaking its head.

Caleb heard the sound of wolves crying out in pain to his right and to his left, and quick half glances showed him Reyan slicing across the leg of one wolf and Aden stabbing deep into the shoulder of another as it knocked Tamya back with its paw. The wolf in front of him was still dazed, but it shook its head and charged him. Caleb struck the right side of its head, twisted the staff and brought it up on the animal's windpipe. The wolf went down, but another approached him from the road, the blood of the horse in its teeth, growling at him.

He stepped back to gather his strength and saw a wolf with a gladi sticking from its shoulder bearing down upon Tamya. Aden leapt upon the wolf's back, throwing his arms around its neck as it swept at Tamya with large paws. She no longer held her sword and Caleb noticed another wolf dead on the ground nearby with a gladi through its skull.

The wolf before him charged, and as Caleb shifted his weight, his leg buckled in pain, and he dropped to his knees. He barely had time to raise the Kingstaff across his body in defense as jaws snapped at him. He fell on his back, the large wolf pressing. Caleb shoved the staff into the mouth bearing down upon him, claws raking his chest.

To his side, a bloodwolf tore the spear from Reyan's grip, spitting it away and pouncing upon the old man. He put out his wounded left arm, and the wolf grasped the limb in its teeth. Reyan cried out as he was tossed aside against the stone wall. He kicked out at the wolf, holding his bloody arm, but the wolf shrugged it off, taking a slow step nearer.

Caleb roared in frustration and anger, pinned as he was beneath the bloodwolf, his arms burning, his strength failing.

Then the wolf upon Caleb shuddered and became dead weight. Caleb looked up to behold an arrow protruding from its eye.

More arrows entered the clearing from the forest across the road, precision shots that took down the other two bloodwolves, one arrow that sunk deep into the animal's head, missing Aden's jaw by a centimitre.

The halt in the action was abrupt. Shocked, Caleb pushed the dead bloodwolf off of himself. He saw Reyan sitting against a wall, holding his arm with a grimace, a wolf dead and riddled with arrows at his feet, and Caleb turned to see Aden rolling a dead bloodwolf off of Tamya.

Caleb managed to get to his knees, holding the Kingstaff before him and looking into the forest. He wasn't sure if he could stand if he wanted to.

Men began to come out of the forest from across the road, led by a tall thick man with long hair in matted black coils and a thick black beard. He wore a short green tunic and deerskin pants and moccasins, as did the men with him. The tall man had black Liorian skin and wore a long sword at his back. He held a bow with an arrow nocked, as did all of the men behind him.

They approached the clearing, seven of them, and they all wore swords, gladi. Caleb faced the tall man.

"Thank you, Athelwulf," Reyan said.

Athelwulf's dark eyes widened as he saw Reyan, and he bowed. "It is our honor, *Arendel*," he said to the Prophet, his voice low and deep. "Welcome back to the Saten."

Aden and Tamya looked at each other and then back at Athelwulf. They lay still, panting and bleeding.

A small figure from the back of the small group stepped forward. Then it spoke, the voice of a woman. "Uncle Reyan?" she said.

She moved closer. Caleb could see the blond hair tied back in a leather cord. She was small and lean. She had a round face with a button nose and full lips. Her cheeks were flushed. She moved towards Reyan, then hesitated. Caleb said her name in a choking whisper. "Carys?"

His sister turned her head in his direction. Her eyes narrowed in the waning twilight. Then they bulged. "Caleb?" she said. "Cubby?"

He nodded at her. "Yes!" he said, and he dropped the Kingstaff as she ran at him and launched herself into his arms.

"Cubby!" she shouted in glee. "You're alive!" She wept against his shoulder. Her arms were wrapped around his neck, squeezing so it hurt, but he didn't care. He couldn't help but smile and chuckle in joy. He caressed her head and closed his eyes. The smell of her, even after all these years, brought back memories of immense tragedy mixed with a sense of home he hadn't felt in almost twenty years.

"I found you," he whispered. "Thank El, I found you."

"I never gave up hope," she said. "Never. I always knew you were out there somewhere."

When he opened his eyes, the other men with Athelwulf surrounded them, looking at both of them as they knelt in the midst of the clearing, dead bloodwolves all around them. Even Athelwulf frowned. Carys pulled away enough to turn to them. "This is my brother," she said. "Caleb."

Athelwulf smirked at them. "Then El has shown his goodness this day. Your brother back from the dead. Well met, Caleb," Athelwulf said. He glanced around the clearing then up at the canopy. "Night comes and we should get you to camp. You are wounded. I will have my surgeon look at you." Athelwulf turned to one of the men behind him, a young man that appeared to be Aden's age but taller. "Run back to camp and set up a site for them." The young man turned without hesitation and sprinted into the forest.

Caleb used the staff to stand to his feet. Carys stood with him, her arm around his waist. He could stand, after all. "Thank you," Caleb said to Athelwulf and his men. "I thought we were finished."

Athelwulf nodded once. "The bloodwolves are a danger here in the Saten," he said. "We had been tracking them, just to know their location. We heard them attacking and ran as soon as we realized they were hunting humans."

"Well, we're in your debt," Caleb said.

"It is nothing. Come with us back to the camp. We are losing light."

Aden stood now, and he chuckled. "Yeah, Cubby. Let's go."

Aden felt blind as they rode through the dark. He and Tamya shared his horse, and Reyan rode behind Caleb. The horse on the road was dead, torn to bloody pieces, but they managed to salvage the saddlebags. Athelwulf led the way back into the trees and through the forest. How Athelwulf found his way through the forest in that situation was beyond Aden, but he trusted the man. He had saved their lives.

They rode in the dark a few hours in silence but for the crunching of dead leaves with the footfalls of the horses. Aden didn't hear Athelwulf or his men walk at all. Swaying several times in the saddle, Aden could have slept if not in so much pain. Once, one of Athelwulf's men had to steady him. How did the man see him when it was so dark?

He began to see a hazy yellow light in the distance through the trees. He thought the horse passed through water, something wet – a stream maybe? – and within a few minutes he could see several smaller lights. He smelled the aroma of cooking food, and soon they wound their way through several campfires shaded by canvas or deerskin blankets to disperse the smoke and contain the light. The men brought them to a campfire where a man with long white curly hair and a long white beard awaited them. He smiled a toothless smile, and he waved them forward with long bony arms.

Athelwulf's men laid the three wounded around the campfire. Caleb and Carys sat nearby. Athelwulf's men left after getting their charges situated, but Athelwulf stayed, sitting on a nearby log. "I will care for the Prophet," Athelwulf said. "Dackwell, you begin with the young ones. Carys, can you tend your brother?"

Aden saw Carys nod, and Dackwell handed her a small leather bag full of ointments and other things. Dackwell came back to Aden and Tamya. "Oh, yes," he said, looking at their injuries. He frowned as he tore off what remained of Aden's shirt. He tore off the legs of Tamya's breeches and the sleeve of her tunic to expose her wounds. He looked at them both and spoke with a toothless lisp.

"My name is Dackwell. Oh, yes, well, Ath just said that," Dackwell giggled at himself as he poured an ointment from his own bag into his hand. "This will cut down on the pain and keep you from infection." When he placed it on Aden's chest and abdomen, Aden squealed. "Oh, yes, well, it will hurt at first, but it will make it feel better soon. Promise to you."

Dackwell was correct. Within moments, the pain had subsided, and Aden laid back, his eyelids heavy. When Dackwell put the same ointment on Tamya, she grunted but set her teeth. Well, she'd been warned, after all. Dackwell got out thread and needle and began working on the deepest cuts.

Aden turned to see Reyan moan in pain on the other side of the fire, and Athelwulf spoke to the Prophet. "The arm is not broken, but the bloodwolf severely damaged it. I will mend it best I can." He frowned at Reyan. "I wish we could have arrived earlier. Your arm may never be the same."

Reyan glanced over at Aden and Tamya, then over at Caleb and Carys. "We are alive, my friend. And that is enough."

Aden faced Athelwulf. "So … who are you people? The people of the forest?"

Athelwulf ran his hand through his thick black beard. "The Drytweld?" he said. "Few of those remain in the forest. Many are like Carys and me. They have come from near and far – from every nation of men – to find refuge, and we teach them. And they join this army."

Aden's brow furrowed. "Army?"

"Yes," Reyan said. "These are the Ghosts of Saten."

Caleb sat there with nothing on except for his leather pants, exhausted, and leaning against a tree. He sat with his sister, close enough to have the light of the fire but far enough to give them privacy.

"You're a breakin' mess," Carys said, looking him over, a water bag and wet cloth in her hand. The scratches from the bloodwolf added to the cuts and gashes over the rest of him.

"You have no idea."

"I almost don't know where to begin," she said.

She smiled through a tear. He reached up and touched her face.

"How about you tell me where the shog you been the last fifteen years?" she said.

"Sixteen years."

"Whatever."

He told her. He began with the abduction by Galen, the opportunity to become a Bladeguard, and then his ultimate return. He told her how he and Aden broke Reyan from the Pyts and what happened in Anneton. She made comments here and there, but then she fell quiet.

She wouldn't meet his eyes. "You never said goodbye."

"I wanted to, Car. But there was no way."

"You could've told him to shove it up his arse," she said.

"Yeah, I could've."

He watched her as she stitched up his calf. Even though he remembered her as that little girl—the one he held in his arms and protected as their mother had screamed—she had grown into a woman. A woman who could use a bow and stitch a wound as well as he had ever seen. He shook his head in disbelief.

"What brings you to the forest?" she asked.

"I think you know," he said. She may not have remembered their father reading the prophecy of the *Brendel*, repeating it like a mantra, but she heard the Prophet enough over the years to know it. And she would know how important it was in Reyan's mind. "I'm headed west."

Her hands dropped to her lap, and she groaned. "You're going to try to find the Living Stone."

"Yes." She rubbed ointment on the rest of the cuts not deep enough to stitch. "I know what happened to Aunt Kendra. I heard at the Citadel."

She nodded, her eyes watery.

"Have you seen Earon? Do you know where he is?"

"No. He was … angry. So angry." Caleb kept himself from looking over at Reyan.

"We left a message for him in Galya, so he could meet us in Biram. Maybe he'll be there."

She sniffed and sighed. "It would be nice to see him again."

"How did you get here? With these people?" Caleb said.

"We met Athelwulf once after … after you were gone. So after Aunt Kendra, I just ran. I had to get away from him, and I thought to come and find Athelwulf. I remembered how he made me feel safe." She paused.

Like I used to, he thought.

"Well, I didn't know exactly what I would do, but I came. I learned how to fight, how to hunt, how to shoot, how to be a woman of the forest. I found a home for the first time."

Caleb reached out and touched her arm, smiling at her. "I'm glad. And glad to be together again."

"But you'll be leaving soon, right?"

He shrugged. "Soon."

"You could stay," she said.

He shook his head. "I need to go, try to find the Stone before the autumn."

She scoffed and glanced at Reyan. "Now you sound like *him*."

CHAPTER 15

THE TOMB

Aden woke late, the sun full into mid-morning before rolling out from under the small shelter built between two trees in the forest. His chest was wrapped in cotton cloths under a new tunic, and his wounds still pained him. He didn't know how long he slept. He barely remembered being placed under the shelter at some point in the night by Dackwell and Athelwulf, and as he awoke and stretched, groaning with soreness and pain, he could see the camp close around him.

Several firepits surrounded by small shelters or low tents were scattered through the forest. Men and women were up and about at various activities, stringing bows, mending clothes, even laughing and conversing. Reyan was up, as well, his left arm in a sling, and he read the bigger book, the Ydu, nibbling at food in his lap as he sat next to the firepit. Caleb and Tamya were nowhere to be seen.

A nice breakfast was laid out for Aden on the ground: berries, venison, a small cracker, and his water bag filled. Starved, he sat to eat a pace away from Reyan.

Reyan stirred and looked up from the book as Aden sat next to him. "How are you?" Reyan asked.

"Still hurts, but I'll live," Aden answered in a muffled voice through the food in his mouth. Reyan grunted his satisfaction. "Where's Caleb?" Aden asked. "Tamya?"

"Caleb was gone before I woke," Reyan said. "He is probably with Carys. They have much to talk about. Tamya went to talk to some of the others in the camp."

Aden nodded and then pointed towards the book. "What you reading?"

Reyan's brows lifted a little before answering. "Oh. Well, just about Yosu, from the sixth scroll." Reyan nibbled on a small blackberry. "How have your readings been going? What do you think of the Fyrwrit?"

Aden shook his head. "Not much I get. The reading is hard. Big words." He took a sip from his water bag, wiping his chin with the back of his hand, grimacing at the slight pain it caused. "Why do elves want t'keep people from readin' it? Seems harmless. Nothing about them that I read, nothing against them. Only words about El and Yosu and people living a way or no. Don't they have their own gods? Why against th'god of men?"

"That is part of it," Reyan said, closing the book and turning more towards Aden. "But truth has power, more power than swords or armies. The words in these books, the testimony, the teachings, they speak of where humans – and elves and dwarves – came from, who created us and that there is only one god, not many. That is not 'harmless' to them."

Aden shrugged. "So? What so bad 'bout people believe diff'rent?"

"Because different beliefs cause people to act differently," Reyan said. "These books speak of a creation, and a single Creator, a designer that gives men, all races, purpose and direction. The light exposes darkness, and man will long to be free from within, from faith, hope and love. This is what Yosu came to show us, but it cannot be forced upon anyone. And it often takes great sacrifice, just as it cost Yosu. Many will balk at such a sacrifice and reject the truth to seek their own ways.

"The elves believe that these ideas are fables and therefore dangerous to safety and peace, their control and colonization of Ereland. They assert it is … delusional to believe such things, that it is real. At first, Tanicus tried to discredit and discount the Fyrwrit and the Ydu, but some men still believed and would not bow. So he did what he thought he had to do: violently wipe out the roots of any rebellion and insurrection." Reyan took a deep breath. "But truth survives. Truth is not a thing you can kill."

"You keep speakin' 'bout Yosu," Aden said. "Who was he really?"

"El came as a man, as one of us, to show us how to live as El in this world and so we can then be with El in the next world."

Aden looked at Reyan in confusion.

Reyan sighed. "You ever hear the story of the wolfchild?"

"I think there's a theater about it," Aden said. "The boy raised by wolves?"

Reyan nodded. "Wolves found an abandoned baby and raised him. All the boy knew was the life of a wolf. He ran like a wolf on all fours, he snarled and growled and howled like a wolf. He hunted and tore into his food like an animal. Once he was found by humans, he was an adult, physically, but he knew no language and was nothing like a human being. He thought and behaved like a wolf. It wasn't until he was able to spend time around humans that the wolfchild began to stand upright and behave like a human."

Reyan paused, looking up into the forest canopy. "Humanity was lost and immersed within a world of violence, corruption, lust, greed," he continued. "I have seen much of this beautiful world, but humans are capable of great darkness, great ugliness. And if this is all that humanity knows, its only example, then that is all it will be. So El came as a man, Yosu, to show what we were created to be, how all three races were created to live and be.

"We were like the wolfchild, living as less than human until shown a different way. But just as the wolfchild had to make a choice, to stop living like an animal and live like a human, we have to make a similar choice to stop being the people we thought we were and become something greater, to live as Yosu, to live as El."

"You mean live like a god?" Aden asked.

"Not to be a god, but to live in El's ways, yes," Reyan corrected, turning back to Aden. "The greatest love El has shown us, to be like him. And that reward is worth any cost, any sacrifice, and worth any cost to speak to others about it." Reyan smiled. "And so I do. Willingly, as my choice. Because I love El."

Aden glowered at the Prophet. "I see so much of that ugly, too."

Reyan looked down at the Ydu in his hand, running his hand over the leather cover. "We all have," Reyan said. "Sometimes it is hard to have faith, hope, love."

"But you still do?" Aden asked. "After all of it? You still do?"

"Yes," Reyan said. "One day I will shed this skin, this old skin, and I will be given a new skin in a new land, the Everworld, to be with El, to see him face to face. Perhaps I will see the redemption of man while I live here." Reyan's eyes became wistful. "But even if I don't, being with El forever is reward enough."

A long silence passed between them. Leaves rustled nearby, and Aden twisted on his arse to see two people approach their site, Athelwulf and Carys. As they stood a few paces away, Reyan's eyes dropped.

"Aden," Athelwulf said. "Come. Walk with me."

Aden rose, grabbing the last slice of venison, trying to gauge the sudden and palpable tension between Reyan and Carys, looking back and forth between them as he came close to Athelwulf. Carys ignored him as he passed her, and Athelwulf turned on his heel and began to walk without a word. Aden gazed behind him once as they walked into the trees to leave Carys and Reyan behind them.

Carys stood two mitres away. She took measure of the man who sat next to the firepit. He seemed so much older, even smaller than she remembered him, hunched as he was over one those books that consumed his time, time he never had for anyone else. He had less hair, and what he had was whiter than before, his beard even thinner, his left arm in a sling. He was a shell of the man she had known, had sometimes feared, had loved, had oftentimes admired, but who had also caused her so much bitterness.

Her breath was shallow, her heart beating, but she didn't know what to say, how to start. But she had to say something. Opening her mouth, she closed it again, her mind blank. He sat there calm and still, simply staring down at that book. Maybe he didn't know what to say, either.

He turned up towards her at last, and his eyes were filled with water. Reyan grinned at her. "Hello, Carys," he said. "I am so glad to see you well." His face was full of sadness and … is that shame? "I am so sorry about how things last ended between us. I regret the way I acted. I do not blame you or Earon for leaving so angry after your aunt's death. It was my fault, and I take the blame. I have no excuses. But I do ask you to forgive me. Please."

Carys shook her head and took a step closer to him, raising her hands in exasperation. "What are you doing?" she asked. "You trying to make me feel sorry for you or something? If you were so sorry, did you look for me or ever wonder where I was?"

"I did wonder, often, and prayed you were well," Reyan said. "But no, I didn't search for you. Time passed and I … I didn't know where to start, so I just asked El to help us find one another again."

"Well, good to hear he answers someone's prayers," she said before she could stop herself. He winced at that, and she regretted saying it a little. Athelwulf made her come to talk to the man, and she thought she had been ready. But the bitterness and the pain were still close enough to the surface and they boiled over a thin veneer, thinner than she had realized, especially after seeing him last night in the clearing among the dead bloodwolves, the first time in years.

She had heard rumors of him, and once Ath told her that her uncle had been through the forest and with a different camp, but never hers. Reyan had either avoided her or El had kept them from each other until this moment.

Reyan frowned. "Not all of my prayers, but I am glad to see you are well."

She didn't feel so well at that moment. She took another step towards him. "I was eighteen years old," she said. "I don't even remember my parents, and then my brother is just gone, and then Aunt Kendra killed. Earon just disappeared. You were all I had left! But you had your work and not enough time for anything else."

Images flashed in her brain, the small house in Falya where she had begged him to talk to her, to help her have faith in a good El again after Aunt Kendra. Earon had run without even trying to speak to his father. But she couldn't do that. She pleaded with Reyan for something, anything. But he had said nothing, setting his jaw and walking from the room.

"I know," he said. "And I'm sorry. I didn't know how."

Carys shook her head, taking another step towards him. "You bare your soul to anyone who will let you, share truth and messages with the world, but you wouldn't share your grief with me, or with your son. I know you lost her, too, but I needed you to share that with me. But you hid from us."

He nodded. "I threw myself into my work, I know," he said. "I had to make her sacrifice ... mean something. But I was wrong. I realized later that it was not my place to make her life mean something, but I was so lost without her. I didn't know how to share that with you, with Earon. I thought I had to be stronger, harder than ever."

"Running away, pushing us away, that wasn't strength," Carys said, moving a pace forward.

"No," Reyan agreed. "It wasn't."

Carys took a deep breath, squinting at Reyan. This was the most genuine conversation she had ever had with the man, and it made her angry. It didn't make sense, but after all those years of wishing, desiring to have something real with her uncle, and having it here, now, made her furious. Carys didn't know if she could trust it. She wanted to lash out at him, but this time she found the strength to keep her mouth from letting the words loose. She turned away from him, crossing her arms, her head bowed.

"I wish I could have given you all that you needed then, but I can't. That time has passed. All I have is today. And today, I ask for your forgiveness." He said it like he needed it. And that made her even angrier. Was this just some cathartic moment for him? Did he just desire her forgiveness to ease his own conscience? Well, break that! Break him for still being so selfish!

Facing him again, she was ready to yell and scream at him for his selfishness, for the life of running and hiding she had with him, the silence and distance she had always felt from him. But when she saw him now, sitting cross-legged on the ground, his left arm in a sling, she didn't see the hardened, cruel, selfish man she had built in her own mind. She saw a man in pain, more than just the recent injuries, and her heart began to soften. But that softening scared her.

She had lived with the bitterness and anger for so long; they were like old friends and had been such a big part of her. Carys crossed her arms over her chest, breathing in short through her nose, clenching her jaw to keep the words and the caustic nature of her own heart within her. She couldn't look him in the eye, so she bowed her head. "I'm sorry," she said, but she couldn't have said why.

Turning, she walked back into the trees and left the Prophet alone.

———

Aden followed Athelwulf as they walked through the camp, winding through different sites and greeting different men.

"You called Reyan somethin' last night," Aden said to the big man. "You called 'im a different name."

Athelwulf nodded. "Yes. The *Arendel*. Do you know of the prophecies from the scripture?"

"I know of the *Brendel*," he said. "That maybe Caleb is him."

"The Prophet and I spoke of this last night," Athelwulf said. "I am eager to speak with Caleb more. Perhaps El has decided it is time for man to rise again."

"What be the *Arendel*?" Aden asked.

"He is *the dayspring of the dawn, the light, the messenger that announces the coming redemption*," he answered. "It is an obscure passage, but many believe that Reyan is this person."

"What he supposed to do?"

Athelwulf sniffed and grinned through his heavy beard. "Exactly what Reyan is doing. He tells people that El is about to bring a revolution in the hearts of men."

Aden saw men of every nation, many from Manahem and Asya, but several also had the black skin of Lior and the light brown of Veradis. He even saw a woman or two with a sword on her hip and a bow across her shoulder. They were all strong and healthy.

"Where did all these people come from?" Aden asked. "I even see some from Veradis and Lior, like you."

"The people of the Saten, the Drytweld, had dwindled over the years. They managed to keep the elves away, but they suffered heavy losses over the first hundred years." Athelwulf sniffed, and as Aden looked up at the tall man, Athelwulf blocked out the sun as it tried to peek its way through the canopy. "But other men heard of the rebellion of the Drytweld, and they came to join, to live free from the elves here. Over time, more people came, some families."

"There're other camps?" Aden asked. "How many are you?"

Aden began to hear a strange sound, like a man screaming in pain and torture, distant.

"There are several thousand of us," Athelwulf stated. "And several camps like this scattered throughout the forest. Each camp is its own community and makes its own decisions, but we are united and our communication is quick and good."

"I'm seein' women," Aden said. "Do the women fight? There're children?"

"Women are as free to fight as the men, although many choose to stay with children if they have them," Athelwulf said. "Several of the men you see here have families, as well."

"Where're the children?"

Athelwulf took a moment before answering. "The children are somewhere safe."

Aden again heard the sound of a man screaming, muffled and distant, but it grew louder as they walked. He looked up at Athelwulf, his brows raised in a silent question, but the large man did not respond.

Athelwulf led Aden by a small hill in the forest, a thick trunk of a large tree planted atop it. The roots of the tree extended down the small hill, and in between two thick and gnarled roots hung a thick piece of canvas in the shape of a curved door. The sounds of a man yelling and in pain came from a place dug out underneath that tree.

Aden stopped in front of the canvas door, standing still and staring at it. Athelwulf paused as well, taking a few steps back to stand with Aden. "What is that?" Aden whispered.

"That is a place we call the Tomb," Athelwulf explained. "Every camp has one. Well, most of them."

"Who ... what is it?"

"Many men come from the world of elves, and they are addicted to Sorcos," Athelwulf said. "Sorcos is an evil thing. It is addictive and destructive. To be a member of the Ghosts, to live and fight with us, you must be free of bondage, of all addictions. So we have a place where a man or woman must go to be free of the addiction. It is a painful process that takes time. Sometimes a long time."

Aden had heard of the addictive properties of Sorcos. His Jo had been addicted to the crit. "He's in there alone?"

Athelwulf nodded. "It must be alone. His freedom must be his own and not based on the dependence of others, else we are no better than the elves believe us to be."

"I hear some die if they no have it," Aden murmured. The man's screams were unnerving, like someone was cutting his skin from his body.

Athelwulf grunted. "Most do survive it. Some do not. But death is better than slavery," Athelwulf said with conviction. "That is why we call it the Tomb. One way or another, you die in that place. Those who emerge are reborn as free."

Aden wasn't so sure. The way that man cried, it sounded as if anything were better than the withdrawal.

"Come," Athelwulf said, turning to go further into the camp again. "We must leave him be."

Aden hesitated, but he followed, leaving behind the Tomb but carrying the memory of it with him.

—+—

That night, many of the men gathered in one of the larger clearings in the camp around the firepit there. The firelight illuminated the area, and Reyan sat in the middle next to the raging flame. The men and women of the camp were packed around him, the group extending even into the trees. Reyan spoke, loud and firm, encouraging them and telling them of how the world could be and the hope of the Everworld.

"Remember to pass truth on to others, to your children. Truth never dies, but the strength of men fade as we fail to pass these truths on to the next generation. We live short lives, and we must be diligent. As we do this, man will grow strong again, and tales of old will become reality to us all again." The men and women of the camp nodded.

"As an example," Reyan continued as if it just came to him. "The Ydu speaks of the demics that come out of the mountains to the south every few hundred years ready to kill and slaughter men, women, children, animals, anything that lives and bleeds, and they threaten with an even greater horde if they can find the Key that permanently opens the gate to the Underland. All of the nations of men, the whole of Eres even, are at risk of death in those times. Men don't live more than eighty or a hundred years at most. How are they to guard against such destruction, from keeping such devastation from finding them unawares? They warn their children and grandchildren. They teach them to keep watch and wait. Be diligent, they tell them. Be strong and fight together, as one, for the life of men and all races."

Caleb sat with Aden at the back of the group and noticed Reyan looked more energetic and full of life than ever. Caleb had been worried just after rescuing the man from the Pyts, but he had worried in vain. The man would probably outlive Caleb. Almost definitely. Carys sat just in front of him, and he laid a hand on her shoulder. She looked back and smiled at him. It had been so long since he had family around him. Too long.

Aden stood, rolled his shoulders, and walked further into the forest to an empty fire nearby. Caleb frowned, watching him for a moment. He stood as well and followed Aden. Striding into the empty site, Caleb sat on a nearby stump. "You all right?"

Aden had his head down, his face dark and brooding. "Fine."

After a minute, Caleb said, "Okay," and began to get up to walk back to sit with Carys.

"I see him before," Aden said, just loud enough for Caleb to hear.

Caleb froze a moment, then sat back down on the stump. "Who?"

Aden heaved in a deep breath. "Reyan. In Asya, long before he in the Pyts, I see him, hear him before." Aden looked up and past Caleb to the group listening to Reyan speak. "Like this."

Caleb didn't say a word. He just sat still and quiet.

"You probably hear 'im say stuff a lot, you were a kid," Aden said. "You hear same stuff all th'time."

"Well," Caleb said. "Not exactly the same. He says it different every time. I don't remember him ever saying it the same way twice. He seems to say what is needed for that group, what they need to hear." Caleb glanced over to Reyan, as well before turning back to Aden. "He really does have a gift." Caleb watched Aden for another minute before saying, "How did you see him? In Asya."

"My – the man who used t'watch out for me, Jo, he want to go see him," Aden said.

"Was Jo your father?"

"No," Aden said. "Maybe. I don't know. But he want to go see this Prophet. He don't say much 'bout it, but he kinda clean up, you know. He was addicted to Sorcos. Many are, but he was bad, sometimes mixed it with ale." Aden looked up at Caleb. "He never let me have any, though. He say not for nothin's, not for nobody's. But he have some a lot. Sometimes he fake a sick to get some from the Ministry. But he keep away from it for a day or two, close to three. And he find a way to clean his clothes, the rags they were, and he clean up. Just t'see this man, this Prophet."

Aden rubbed the sleeve of his tunic across his nose, sniffing. "Anyway, he say I no go, but I follow him anyway. Not much he do 'bout it. He go to this back room in a store, and there be maybe fifty people sittin' in there, and this man walk in. Reyan." Aden pointed over to the Prophet. "He start speakin', and I never heard this stuff before. His eyes ... they like fire ... like now, like he can see right through you, like you not there but you are. Like he somewhere else and here all at once. Jo, he stay the whole time, but he run off right at the end."

Aden shook his head. "He stay clean another day before the pains hit him. It was bad. He try to not take any more, say he kick it, but he couldn't take the pain. I give it to him, 'cause he in so much pain. Maybe I shouldn't give it to him. Maybe I should let him die instead of be slave to that crit."

"You were doing what you thought was right," Caleb said. "It's not your fault. You thought you were helping him. You were just a boy. No shame in what you did."

"You believe that?" Aden asked. "Even though I think it right, but it not, that still okay?"

"I think you wanted to help, and you didn't know better," Caleb said, "and yes, that makes it okay. But you know better now. Be different now. Don't judge the child you were based on the good you learn as you become a man. There's no good way from there." Aden just sat quiet, looking down. "So when you met me, and I said I needed your help breaking him out of the Pyts, you didn't take money ... you made the deal you did because ..."

"Because I wanna know is it real," Aden said, his voice choking. "I wanna know is this man I saw the real. It been years before, but I remember. So I want to go with you. I don't even know what it all mean, but I know I need to go. For me. For Jo. For him." He pointed again at

Reyan. "I don't know, but I'm scared. Where do I go from here? How do I stop? I seen too much and know too much. I can't go back."

"Well, the offer still stands," Caleb said. "You're a good fighter, fast and strong. They could use you here. Or you could go somewhere else, take a good portion of coin with you for a fresh start. I have enough."

Aden scoffed. "No," he said. "I can't do that, not now. I see too much, read too much."

"Or you can come with me," Caleb said. "I told you that you could. But I understand that you're scared. It is dangerous. And it only gets worse from here."

Aden shrugged. "I don't know," he said. "I just don't know."

Caleb nodded. "Well, I'm leaving tomorrow," he said, standing. "Decide by then." And he walked away and back to sit with Carys. Aden needed to make this decision alone.

✦

Tamya also sat apart from the crowd, sharpening her gladus with a stone. One of the Ghosts had shown her earlier that day how to do it. Her injured shoulder hurt, but she pushed that pain aside as she had other wounds, deeper wounds, for days. The rhythm of the stone against the elven steel comforted her. She sat far enough away from the crowd to hear Reyan's voice as a droning, low sound. Every now and then, the crowd would react, but she heard those sounds in the distance.

Distracted as she was by her own thoughts in the dark, she didn't hear the man walk up beside her until he was almost on top of her. She turned to see Athelwulf, the large man who was some type of leader here, sit next to her. His dark hair and beard and black skin made him seem like a shadow even near the fire that provided the light she used for sharpening the blade.

"You are doing a fine job," Athelwulf said, and he held out his hand to see the blade. She hesitated and then handed it to him. He turned the short sword over in his hand close to the fire. "The elves make fine weapons, fine blades, I'll admit. They are skilled in many things."

Tamya sat in silence, staring at him.

Athelwulf reached out his hand for the sharpening stone, a round, fist-sized stone. She waited a moment and then handed it to him.

"Swords are dangerous," Athelwulf said. "The finer the blade, the more dangerous they are. The elves know this, so they keep men from having weapons. But the sword isn't the problem." Athelwulf held it out to his right side, away from Tamya, and spun it with a flourish. "The sword only responds to the evil or good within the heart. Some use the sword to protect, for something good. Others for selfish reasons, to destroy. No being is above this reality. The elves are proof of this." He began to sharpen the sword himself, the stone ringing against the steel. "Take the sword from the being, and he can still find a way to kill," he continued, glancing down at her. "Or she." Athelwulf handed the sword back to Tamya along with the stone. "This sword is sharp enough. Won't get any sharper or finer. It is the hand and the heart of the one that uses it that needs sharpening."

Tamya eyed him, trying not to be intimidated by the man's sheer size. "Caleb has been teaching me," she said.

Athelwulf nodded. "He seems a fine man," he said. "And he's done well. You survived against the bloodwolves longer than most. You learn quickly."

"I want to learn more," she said. "I've learned lots today."

Athelwulf inclined his head towards her. "Of course," he said. "We have a good camp here. Some say the best. You could learn much here."

Tamya scoffed at him. "I could stay here?"

Shrugging his shoulders, he said. "And why not? As long as you agreed to abide by the rules, you are more than welcome. Anyone is."

"Even a half-elf?" she asked.

"Rare, to be sure, but does not matter," he said. "El created all peoples. There is much to learn, but as I said, you seem to learn quickly. And the people here are hard but kind. They will accept you if you take it seriously. You would be responsible to help take care of others, pull your weight, and fight with us to protect the forest and weaken the Empire, if the opportunity arises."

Tamya looked over the sword. "You could teach me to fight?"

"To fight, to hunt, to shoot, to make your own clothes, to bind wounds, yes," Athelwulf said. "We must all learn it all, to some degree. It makes us stronger."

"You fight elves?" she asked.

"From time to time," Athelwulf said. "The Empire sends soldiers and … others … into the forest more than they tell. We can take care of them and see they never return."

Tamya frowned in thought, still staring at the sword and the fire behind it.

"But you will also learn why we fight," Athelwulf said. "We do not fight for revenge or hate. I think you know this."

Athelwulf stood, brushing his hands together. "You speak to Caleb," he said. "You are one of his companions. I would hate to steal such a fine pupil." He smiled at her. "I must get back." He walked back towards the crowd, beginning now to disperse, talking with one another.

Tamya turned the blade in her hand as he walked away.

Just after dark that night, over five hundred citizens of the town of Delaton arrived in Roseborough.

Roseborough was a larger town, almost five thousand citizens itself. The Manahem road split into four other roads as it entered the town. The townspeople of Delaton camped just south of town. Roseborough had three inns, one large and two smaller like the boardinghouse in Pontus, but that wouldn't hold a fourth of their crowd. And since they were all one town, and Eliot himself as the example, no one went for an inn, despite the fact some had the money and could pay for the luxury. They arrayed themselves on both sides of the Manahem road, just like they had the two nights before.

The Te'Lyan family and others sat around the Te'Lyan fire that night. "We'll go into town tomorrow," Eshlyn said, looking at her father, who nodded. "And we'll speak to Mayor De'Sy. We'll try to call an emergency Muster here, but as we all know, things work differently in Roseborough." Several rolled their eyes, and Sirah's father chuckled. "But we will stand firm and stand together. We will speak with the Mayor tomorrow. But either way, the day after, we ride further to Ketan." Eshlyn looked into the eyes of the men and women around her, at least fifty of them. "Spread the word to your neighbors. Get more supplies here in town if you need them. Be packed and ready to go morning after morrow."

CHAPTER 16

ROSEBOROUGH

Mayor Crystof De'Sy had been dreading this meeting ever since he got the pigeon from old Bain.

Roseborough boasted five thousand citizens, and apart from Ketan, only Biram was larger in Manahem. Mayor De'Sy did his best to keep friendly with the elves but keep their control at bay. Kryus barely ruled Ketan, so it didn't have the resources to be responsible for Roseborough. It had worked for hundreds of years, and all to their advantage.

The Mayor lived in a sprawling estate across the street from the gathering hall, which had been expanded in recent years to take up the whole block, and the Mayor swelled with pride at the thought of the six-year construction project he had spearheaded. Now it was named the De'Sy hall. There was a sign and everything.

His father before him had been Mayor, and Crystof knew that Roseborough could be so much more through progress and growth. He and Bain had that in common; the difference being that here in Roseborough Crystof didn't need the approval of the council to make decisions. Crystof delegated what he felt too busy to handle.

Mayor De'Sy was forty-seven years old. He and his wife were both from the upper class of the city. A man of average height and impeccable taste, Crystof De'Sy always wore his best silk shirt and cotton pants with low cut leather shoes that shone in the sun. Over his shirt, he would don a cotton jacket, a leather and fur lined one for the winter. Crystof had dark blond hair, cut short in the elven style, a clean-shaven face, piercing blue eyes and the body of a man ten or twenty years younger. He lived in moderation; his father had been a man of greed, and it had almost ruined him and the family.

Roseborough also employed a handful of men as a type of Cityguard. They didn't carry swords, but they had clubs and thick arms that would intimidate even the most belligerent. He kept them around for the rare times they were needed. Next door was the Mayor's office that also housed a small meeting room for the council and a three-cell jail.

Crystof's assistant, Diles, came to him back in his study at the house—Crystof reserved the office for official meetings. "Sir, Eliot Te'Lyan here to see you," Diles said. "With his daughter, Eshlyn Se'Matan."

Leaning back in his chair, Crystof rubbed his temples with his right hand. The message from Bain, sent by pigeon two days ago, still sat on his small writing desk, on the front corner. Crystof took the message in his left palm. Lowering his right hand, he Diles. "Thank you, my friend," he said. "Please seat them in the front parlor. Let them know I'll be right with them."

He had gotten word first thing this morning that half the town of Delaton camped just south of Roseborough, so it did not surprise him. Also, Eliot was a good man. Crystof had met Eliot a handful of times, but the man never annoyed him half as much as most of his own constituents. He should be able to have a simple conversation with Eliot, but Bain had warned him of the daughter. A wild Tablet if there ever was one, Crystof had heard.

The Mayor of Roseborough couldn't help but think of all the suitors Eshlyn had spurned. His own son Brus had been one of them. She laughed at the boy as if he had been a cow wearing an apron, and in the end, he heard she married some grain farmer in Campton, that dark hole in the world. But Crystof dealt with difficult people, even pushy women, all the time.

The camp of citizens from Delaton made him nervous. He had no reason to be. They were good people. But knowing they squatted just south of him, and why they were there, tickled the back of his brain, as if he should know something that he didn't.

After making them wait a sufficient amount of time – people should not believe a Mayor was at their beck and call – Crystof walked from his study down the long hall to the front parlor, well lit this morning with large bay windows that let the eastern sun shine well into the room. He fixed a smile on his square face and poured a trusting and caring look into his blue eyes as he opened the door and greeted Eliot and Eshlyn.

Eliot stood, looking tired, although Crystof guessed that was due to the days on the road, and extended his hand. Crystof grasped the hand with a firm shake as Eliot returned the smile. Hanging back, Eshlyn stood her hands clasped in front of her. Bain warned she would tell some crazy story. Crystof would make her wait. It was good to let people think about what they asked of those that ruled over them before having a free audience.

Crystof introduced himself to Eshlyn, who smiled for an instant before returning to the scowl. She was from Campton, after all. "Please, sit," he invited, the smile never leaving his mouth. He sat across from Eliot, making a point to keep Eshlyn off to the side. She glanced at her father with a look that spoke volumes. She was the reason they were here and would try to push and control her father.

"Why don't you tell me why you've come to see me today," Crystof suggested in a casual tone. "What can I do for you?" He leaned back on the feather couch.

Eliot turned from Crystof to Eshlyn before turning back and saying, "Well, I know this is sudden and difficult to understand," Eliot said. "But we need you to call an emergency Muster."

Mayor De'Sy squinted at the both of them and rubbed his chin. An awkward silence passed. "That is next to impossible," Crystof said. "We have thousands of people to consider, and getting word to them could never happen by the end of the day. We haven't had a Muster at all in a long time, not that I ever remember. Too many people."

Finally, Eshlyn broke in. "But every man – and woman, too – needs to hear what we have to say," she said, the words rushing out of her.

Eliot's eyes narrowed at his daughter.

She pushed on anyway. "There is a real danger to everyone in this town, and we need to get them all to Ketan."

Crystof chuckled behind his hand. "Don't be ridiculous. That will never happen, not a Muster. Not in this town."

Eliot forced another smile, and he leaned in closer to Crystof. "I am an elder of Delaton, neighbors just to the south," Eliot said. "We are … acquaintances, if not friends, Crystof, and I believe, as my daughter claims, that we have something very serious to discuss with the men of this town. We come to you and ask for audience. You can't just forget the ways of the old men so easily, to the sure. You may not have Musters here anymore, and I understand that, but you cannot refuse to hear us on behalf of the town. Then we would be men no more. We would be elves." Eliot said it as if that would be a horrible thing.

Taking his time to respond, Crystof thought through Eliot's plea. Crystof didn't appreciate getting in the middle of the power struggle between Eliot and Bain. If Bain wanted to be a real mayor, then he should handle this breakin' crit and not let it spread out of the borders of his town onto De'Sy's doorstep. Bain would never be a man of power that way. As understanding as the elves there could be, they would see to that. But he didn't want to just reject Te'Lyan. Eliot was a good man and deserved better than that, even though he tied himself to his daughter's apron.

He took another minute to give an answer, finding the torture in Eliot's daughter satisfying. This was easier than he thought it would be. "I'll tell you what I will do," Crystof said, sitting straight. "I can call the council together for a meeting later this afternoon. Most of them are here in town; that should be easy enough. You can make your case then, and we will make a decision."

Eliot took a deep, sad breath. He knew. Te'Lyan wasn't stupid. He could tell that their meeting would be fruitless. He might even know that Crystof had gotten a communiqué from Bain since Eliot decided on this fool errand. Give the man credit, but what could he do? He would take what Mayor De'Sy would give him.

"No," Eshlyn said, standing to her feet. "That's not good enough. Don't be manipulated by that Mayor Bain, sir." Eliot stood now with her, putting a hand on her arm to calm her. "No, Da, he needs to realize that he holds the fate of this town in his hands and needs to call an emergency Muster so everyone can hear what's going on and make a decision."

Crystof rose to his feet and lifted his hands to the sky as in surrender. "I told you, that is impossible," he said.

Eshlyn glowered at him. "I bet you would call a Muster if you needed it to take more taxes for another building with your name on it," she said, a dangerous tone to her voice.

For the first time, the smile almost left Crystof's face. He ignored Eshlyn and faced Eliot. "I shall see you this afternoon, Mr. Te'Lyan," he said. "In my office. Think carefully whether it be wisdom to bring your daughter. Good day." And Crystof left the parlor to go back to his study, gesturing for Diles to show them out.

Now he really had a headache.

┼

The cool air blew through the trees as Caleb finished saddling his stallion in the clearing on the northern side of the camp. Several new linen tunics and deerskin breeches were packed in his bag, along with other fresh supplies for the journey. Caleb's wounds were healing, and despite the soreness all over his body, he felt good.

Aden walked up first, carrying his saddlebags and leading his horse into the clearing, the gladus at his hip. One of the Ghosts had helped him fashion a better scabbard for the sword out of deer leather, and he wore it awkwardly.

"Good morning," he said to the young man.

Aden wore a constant frown, his face conflicted, but he answered, "Morning."

Reyan then walked out of the trees with Athelwulf at his shoulder, leaning down to listen to the Prophet talk as they moved. Reyan carried his things, as well, and Tamya and Carys trailed them. Carys moved into the clearing last, her bow on one shoulder and a pack in her hand. They all stood around Caleb's horse, gathered there and greeting one another.

Athelwulf reached out and pressed Tamya forward. "I believe this young woman has something to say," Athelwulf said.

Tamya grimaced and looked up at Caleb. "I want to stay here," she said. "I think I want to stay here with the Ghosts of the forest."

Caleb turned to her, his eyebrows rising. This was more than he had heard from her the whole trip. She spoke it like a request. "You are free to stay anywhere you choose." He looked over at Athelwulf. "As long as it's okay with him."

"She is free to stay," he said. "We have already spoken."

His feet shifting, Aden gulped at Tamya. "Are you sure?" he asked her. "We could both double up. There's plenty o'room."

Tamya's head tilted to one side. "I am staying," she said. Aden's head bowed low.

Athelwulf looked at them all, then, taking them in with a turn of his head. "I understand Caleb must go on to the *Ebenelif*, to fulfill the prophecy of the *Brendel*, but the rest are welcome to stay," he said.

The group was silent a moment at the mention of the prophecy, and Caleb's eyes tightened. A part of him wanted to resist identifying himself by that term – it felt arrogant to claim a prophecy – but what could he say? Athelwulf spoke true. Caleb would try to find the Living Stone, and they would know the reality of the oracle one way or another.

He turned to Reyan. "Please feel free to stay," Caleb said to the Prophet. "This could be a good place for you. You're injured and need to rest. You could help encourage the people here, and they would protect you. I can do this alone."

"It would be an honor to have the *Arendel* among us," Athelwulf said, and Carys' eyes averted, her arms crossing over her chest.

Reyan squinted at Caleb. He also looked around the group, first Carys, then Athelwulf, pausing just a moment on Tamya as if considering something important, but he ended staring at Aden. "What about you, then?" Reyan asked the young man. "What have you decided?"

Aden took a deep breath, his eyes dancing back and forth between Reyan and Caleb. "I said I'll see it to th'end," Aden said. "And I mean to." He set his jaw and met Caleb's gaze. "I'm going with you."

Reyan waited a few breaths, still facing Aden, before saying, "My father was a gifted man, as well, but he never felt the drive to travel, to speak and spread the truth. My journey is not yet done. I am going with Caleb as well."

Caleb breathed heavy, disappointed. He had hoped they all would stay, and he could go on his own. He would travel faster and safer by himself. But it wasn't meant to be. At least Tamya would stay.

"I'm going with you, too," Carys said, glowering at Caleb. "Since you didn't ask."

"What?" Caleb said. "I – I thought you had a home here. Athelwulf said – "

"Doesn't matter what Athelwulf says," Carys interrupted. "I'm going with you, at least as far as Biram. It would be good to see Earon." She patted the bow on her shoulder and lifted the bag. "Packed and ready to go.

Looking over at Athelwulf, Caleb saw the tall man smirk back at him. "She has always been free to come and go as she wishes." Athelwulf turned to Carys, his dark eyes full of kindness. "I will be sad to see her go.

She is a leader and a sister among us, but we will survive. El will always show his goodness."

Caleb took another deep breath, rubbing his face and his beard. "Okay," he said.

Just as Caleb began to realize they would have to ride double on both horses, another young man walked into the clearing from behind Caleb, leading an old mare behind him. The young man handed the reins to Athelwulf, who stroked the horse's neck with a gentle touch. "This is Ingrid," Athelwulf said. "An old friend. She is not fast, but she will be loyal and do what you need."

"You're giving us a horse?" Caleb asked. "Don't you need her yourself?"

"El teaches us to give freely to those in need—even our greatest possessions—so we give to you," Athelwulf said. "She has worked hard and well for us, and she is old. But I would give whatever the Prophet needs."

Speechless, Caleb began to reach into his saddlebags. "I have money," Caleb said. "More than I need. Please take as much as you like …"

Athelwulf scowled at Caleb. "Coin? Have you become an elf to think that coin solves any problems?" Athelwulf snorted at him. "Coin solves no problem. Coin only creates them. And what would we do with money? We go to no cities or towns; we make what we need and take care of one another. No one has lack here. Coin has no place among us." Athelwulf shook his head. "Save your coin. You take a sister from us and now an old friend in Ingrid. We give them freely. Do not sully our gifts with talk of coin."

Caleb froze in place, and Reyan stood with his lips pursed. Aden's eyes bulged back and forth between the men like he expected a fight. "I'm sorry, Athelwulf," Caleb said. "Forgive me."

"Of course," Athelwulf said. "All is forgiven and forgotten." He began to help place Reyan's saddlebags on Ingrid.

"I don't understand," Reyan muttered to Caleb as they stood close. The Prophet glanced back at Caleb's sister. "I thought Carys hated me."

Caleb chuckled. "She doesn't hate you, old man," he told him. "She never could. Her coming with us doesn't have much to do with you, though."

Reyan's left eyebrow rose.

Caleb grinned. "I told her yesterday that we might see Earon in Biram," Caleb said. "That I left him a message in Galya."

"Oh," Reyan said. "That foolishness about how they fulfill the prophecy, too."

"Maybe that," Caleb said. "But also … well, I think she developed a little crush on Earon over the years."

Reyan's head whipped around. "What?"

Caleb chuckled again. "What do you expect?" Caleb said. "I was gone, and you were busy. And Earon was always a pretty good-looking guy, you know, despite being your son. And smart. Smarter than I was. What did you expect a teenage girl to do?"

Reyan scoffed. "But they're cousins!" he said in a whisper.

"So? Cousins have married before, you know as well as I," Caleb answered. "No real rule against that." Caleb scoffed. "You know, for a Prophet, you sure miss a lot."

Athelwulf and Aden remained quiet and busy, Aden biting his lip. Tamya rolled her eyes and checked the saddle on Aden's horse.

Carys stood in front of Athelwulf, who turned to her with a sad smile. Her countenance fell. She looked up at him with tear-filled eyes. He laid his hands upon her shoulders. "You came as a scared young girl and leave as a strong sister-warrior," Athelwulf said. "I am very proud of you, and I hope El shows his goodness to us by allowing us to see one another again. Someday."

Dropping her bow and quiver to the ground, she threw her arms around his neck, and he bowed low to lift her, embracing her. "Thank you, Ath," she said. "You are my brother forever."

Caleb frowned at them. He felt uncomfortable with the display, but what could he say? He should be glad she had a man who had protected her and acted as a big brother while he was away. He should be. But he wasn't.

"Come on, then," Caleb said, getting up into the saddle of the stallion. Aden mounted his horse, and Reyan was soon atop Ingrid. "We need to get back on the road."

Carys pulled away from Athelwulf with a final smile and gathered her bow and quiver from the ground. She walked towards the horses, between Aden and Caleb, and Aden reached down with his right hand to help her up in the saddle with him.

"No," Caleb said, and Aden hastened to pull his hand back. "She rides with me." Carys grinned at Aden, rolled her eyes, and stepped over to Caleb's arm.

"I ride in front," she stated. "I'm leading this one." Caleb hesitated but further extended his arm to pull her up in the saddle in front of him, scooting back. The stallion shifted with the extra weight.

Athelwulf waved at the group as they formed up to ride into the forest, Caleb at the lead. "Goodbye friends," Athelwulf said. "May El's goodness shine upon you always."

They waved in return, Aden taking one last look at Tamya as they left.

A few mitres into the trees, Carys spoke up. "And we're not going to the road," she said.

"The road will be faster," Caleb said.

"We're going to another camp, through the forest. I've lived in this forest long enough to know this is both the safest and the fastest way. Don't worry, Cubby," she said. And she led the way while Caleb heard Aden's muffled chuckle behind him.

—

"We don't have all afternoon," Mayor De'Sy said, still looking impeccably dressed and confident. "So please tell us what all this is about."

The small office was filled with six men besides the Mayor. They didn't introduce themselves and sat around on wooden chairs with the Mayor in the middle. The men were older, all frowning. They seemed bored. Eshlyn sighed at the prospect of another audience against her from the start.

Eliot nodded. "Thank you," he said. "I believe I'll let my daughter begin." Eliot and Eshlyn sat facing the representatives of Roseborough, Xander standing behind them.

Mayor De'Sy waved his hand at them to continue. "I apologize. I have much to do today."

Eshlyn told the story of that first night in Campton, so long ago, twelve or thirteen days ago now. It was all a blur to her in that moment, but she had told the story several times. Many on the road to Roseborough from Delaton had asked her for more detail, and she was able now to tell the story without leaving out anything important.

Even as she went into the screams, the horrible sounds of the town under attack, the men before her never changed expression. It was as if she told them about simple figures in a databook from a harvest thirty years ago instead of the death of real human beings. The harvest might have affected them more.

"So just as my husband asked of me, I'm taking my son to Ketan for safety," Eshlyn concluded. "And I'm telling everyone I can to do the same. Here we are, now, asking you to mobilize your town and move them into the city walls of Ketan."

Mayor De'Sy looked at her with a familiar countenance, like she was breakin' maddy. He shook his head. "You can't be serious," he said.

Eliot leaned forward now. "To the real, we are," Eliot said. "I can vouch for Kenric's character, and if he thought it be that serious, it be that serious. So we go and we ask you to move your people into the city."

The Mayor's eyes tightened in a rare response. "Let me ask you," De'Sy said to Eshlyn. "Did you speak with the people of Pontus?"

"Yes," she said. Still no reaction from the other six men. Were they even awake?

"And how many from Pontus are here with you?" De'Sy asked.

"Well ... none came from Pontus," she said.

"And from Delaton?" he asked.

Eliot spoke up. "More than half the town," he said.

"There are over five thousand people in this city," he said, emphasizing the last word. "It would take weeks to get them ready to go for a prolonged stay in Ketan. It's just not practical."

"I'm not talking about practical," Eshlyn said. "This is a crisis. I don't know what happened to Campton and to my husband, but there is no time to waste, I promise you."

"You promise me?" De'Sy said. "Even if I believed something happened at Campton, do you have any evidence that it is coming this way?" Eshlyn pursed her lips. "Of course you don't." The Mayor turned to Eliot. "I know you and Bain have divided the town down there, but you can't expect me to take sides in one of your little tiffs."

The Mayor spoke in a low, compassionate tone to Eliot. "And let me ask you to do something, beg you, for your own good. Go back to Delaton. Go back home, Eliot. Please. You are throwing away your business and your place in that town. You will look like a fool when this is all over and Bain will take full advantage of that. And I can't say that I blame him. Who would want such a fool to have any influence in their town?"

Eliot clenched his teeth and his brow furrowed. "You can believe what you will 'bout me or mine," he said. "But I will stand by true and good and right. And you will end up the fool. More than fool in the end with a town dead around you."

Mayor De'Sy sighed and shook his head. "Well, this meeting is over," he said. "You may see yourself out."

Eshlyn stood to her feet in a bound. "You can't!" she said. Not after the partial victory in Delaton. She couldn't fail here. Thousands of lives were at stake. "Call a Muster of the whole town." She turned to the men. They weren't even uncomfortable. Bored. "Call all the men. Please. Let me speak to them."

"No," De'Sy said. "You won't create a panic or push your way in our city. You may go where you like, but you leave our city alone. Or there will be … trouble you don't want."

Eshlyn's jaw dropped. She was trying to save this piece of crit's life and he was threatening her? She took a step towards the Mayor, and she heard her father say, "Esh," in a firm tone that she knew well. She stopped. Eliot grabbed her arm. Xander was also close to her, a scowl on his face.

"Come. Let's go," her father said.

———

Nafys Che'Wyl was a tall hulk of a man and strong. If he hadn't been one of the guardians of the city of Roseborough, he would have no end of backbreaking work hauling or plowing something. That's what people thought what big men were for, until he was made one of the guardians.

The Mayor had recruited him six years ago, and Nafys accepted a life of roaming the streets of Roseborough to keep them safe. It was a boring job. And it was good to be bored. Most of time his job was to break up fights at the inn or the tavern across town, using his club on actual criminals a handful of times. And the town paid him for this.

He saw Eshlyn and her father Eliot earlier that day. He didn't know Eshlyn, but he heard of her marriage to Kenric, a man he called his friend. Eliot he did know, a wealthy man from Delaton with a reputation for being generous. Her features were so similar to Eliot's that their relation was unmistakable. Eshlyn was a little more notorious, and he could see why many had desired her betrothal. Not only was her father wealthy, but she was one of the most beautiful women he had ever seen. Kenric landed a goddess, but that didn't surprise him. Kenric had a quiet, mysterious strength about him. Women tended to love that sort of thing.

Nafys himself was more of a clumsy oaf most of the time, except when it came to a fight. He always did a good job finding a way into a scuffle when it happened. But he didn't like to fight. He preferred to sit next to his hearth and smoke his pipe with a mug of ale in his hand, his wife sitting next to him.

He had found a wife who also loved a quiet life, a good woman, good and round and warm with pretty eyes and an easy smile. He didn't need pretty, though. He knew from his own parents that a good long life with a woman meant friendship and companionship more than sex and passion. Although his wife gave him plenty of that, too. Good woman.

Kenric came almost every season to Roseborough, for the trade after the harvest or the festival in the spring. They met one year at the festival, the first year that Nafys had begun to serve as a guardian of the city, and Nafys had liked the man from the beginning. They had ale after ale at the tavern on the other side of the city, smoking their pipes and swapping stories. He was the only guardian in Campton, but it sounded as if even that position was somewhat superfluous. At one point, Kenric had smiled and eyed the club at Nafys' belt. "Do you know how to use that?" Kenric asked.

Nafys shrugged. "What is there to know?" he asked. "Just a club."

Kenric smirked. "I can show you," he said. And so the next day, both with quite a hangover, Kenric showed Nafys some moves that were simple but helpful. And they had been friends ever since.

Seeing Eshlyn that morning, he kept his eye out for her again. She and her father did not seem happy. He saw her and Eliot and another young man coming out of the Mayor's office in a huff, and he intercepted the three of them before they got on their horses. Eliot took a step back upon seeing the hulk of a man before him carrying a club, and the young man took a step forward to protect his sister. Eshlyn stood still and faced him.

Nafys raised his hands palm outward. "It's okay," he said. "I'm a friend of Kenric's." They eased, looking at each other. "Where is he?" he asked.

Then Eshlyn told him her story, and he knew he would be leaving Roseborough the next day. He wondered how many he could get to go with him.

CHAPTER 17

MERCY

Eshlyn rose before first light to organize everyone, and while the citizens of Delaton were efficient and quick, it still took an hour and a half to get everyone up and on the road heading north through Roseborough. On Lyndae, the middle of the week, the people of Roseborough bustled about their business, getting ready for the day. But they had never seen five hundred people packed and riding through the city on a journey, so the bustling halted. People stared. The citizens of Delaton walked on, ignoring others for the most part.

Xander's friend, Joob, waved at shopkeepers, a blacksmith, and others as they rode by. He took time to greet the lovely ladies he saw, whether they were married or not, tipping his wide-brimmed hat at them as if he just won the Festival horserace and would receive lurid attention as part of his reward. Eshlyn would have been more embarrassed if she thought more of Joob.

Eliot led the caravan to the left of the De'Sy hall, past the open windows of the Mayor's house, and Eshlyn could see the Mayor and his wife peering at them with expressions of odd disappointment. Towards the northern end of town, the caravan slowed as a small group, packed and ready for travel, waited to meet them.

Nafys nodded to Eshlyn, riding in the wagon with her mother, Javyn lying across her lap. She smiled at him and handed her son over to her mother. She stood to greet the newcomers to their caravan from Roseborough. She did a quick count in her head. Fifty? Just about fifty. Looked to be Nafys' family along with six or seven other families and a few stragglers. Fifty out of five thousand. She fought the discouragement and feelings of failure while she took them in with a glance. It was something.

"Welcome to our caravan," she said, trying to project her voice without yelling. "I do not know what good Nafys here has told you, but my husband saved my life while fighting a great threat in the very small town of Campton. He begged me to get our son – and as many people as we can – to safety behind the walls of Ketan.

"It is said that the old men believed the greatest love was to give your life for neighbors and friends. I know many of you and your generosity. We must care for one another. If you have need on the journey, let others know. If you see a need on the way, try to meet it. Be neighbors to one another, and we will be in Ketan before you know it. Thank you," she concluded with a wave, and she saw several of them calm at her words.

She sat down and nodded to her father, who waited for her signal, and as they began riding northward along the Manahem road, the small group from Roseborough melted into the caravan.

Eliot moved his horse next to the wagon and leaned close to Eshlyn. After a few moments of silence, he said, "You think the old stories of kings and queens are only that, stories, but the way you spoke, Esh, I could believe you were a queen." He shook his head and rode to the head of the column. Xander smirked at her and followed him.

Eshlyn wiped at her eyes. That wasn't the first time someone had called her a queen.

———

Carys led them through the forest like a master. Aden saw a wall thick with trees and brush, but somehow Carys would find the perfect space between two trees or a tree and a large bush and have them through and on a discernible path again northward. They crossed a stream, refilling their water bags and canteens, watering the horses. While Aden's first impression of the forest of Saten was one of foreboding, he began to enjoy the scent of the trees and the stirring of the leaves as the wind blew the forest.

The tension between Carys and Reyan was obvious, but it didn't suffocate the group while they traveled. Caleb and Carys were able to talk freely, and Reyan even laughed a time or two as brother and sister reminisced about their times together, some with Earon. Reyan was quiet, though. Aden knew what it meant to remember some good times and wince at the pain. Reyan seemed to experience that in spades.

He saw why Carys found such a home here. At first it seemed so dangerous, but the forest was a perfect place to hide, and Aden felt he was hidden from the world. And he knew the value of having a place to hide.

The next camp was just beyond a river they had to ford. The Ghosts there met them warmly, as if they had known of their arrival, and again Ingrid got almost as much attention from them as the Prophet. What had that horse done?

After unsaddling the horse and feeding it, Aden worked with Caleb for his hour lesson. Caleb thought Aden healed enough for more strenuous physical activity, and he made good on his promise. Carys watched and seemed impressed. Why that swelled him with pride, he wasn't sure, but he didn't want Caleb to see it. He could imagine that staff smacked against his head.

Reyan spoke to the Ghosts of the camp that night, although tonight he excused himself earlier and the people of this camp were gracious and allowed him space. Reyan walked back with Aden to the fire they shared. Caleb and Carys hung back with some of the Ghosts to talk.

As Aden began to settle in for the night, Reyan sat next to him with the leather bag full of the four books, the Ydu and Fyrwrit in two languages. After a moment of silence, Reyan sighed and put the leather sack of books in Aden's lap.

"Here," Reyan said. "I want you to have these."

Aden froze, and his mind was empty of thought. "But – but –" he stammered.

"I've been thinking," Reyan said. "You should take care of them for me."

Aden's hands were in the air just above the leather sack, and he turned back and forth from the books to Reyan. The man had just come and plopped down his prized possession in Aden's lap.

For some reason, Aden thought of how Jo always protected every scrap of his food like it were gold. Or Sorcos.

Aden found some words bouncing around in his head to say, "But I don't even know what I believe," Aden said. "Aren't these for people who believe?"

Reyan smiled. "Yes," he said. "Good. You've been listening." Reyan turned from Aden for a moment, then back again. "You see, I think you do know what you believe. But you're scared. And you sure have a right to be. We all do. But I'm an old man. Being thrown from that horse and having to fight off those bloodwolves got me thinking. I need to pass these on to someone who will take care of them. Read them, copy them maybe." Reyan grunted. "Although I don't know much about your handwriting," he muttered. "Might want to see that first."

"But why me?" Aden said. "Why not Caleb? Or – or Carys?" Aden moved his hands, gesturing to the north. "And Earon? Your son. What about him?"

"We'll see," Reyan said. "Caleb has a different role, and even with a prophecy, no one knows where or how that will happen. Carys … she believes but I don't know if she would take them from me right now. And Earon," Reyan paused. "He did love these books when he was a boy, and he loves them still. Always will. I think he has his own path, though."

"What's his path?" Aden asked. A Prophet would know, right?

"Don't know," Reyan said. "Just his own path. I pray he finds it."

"That still no answer my question," Aden said, laying his hands on the books. He could feel them under his palms, the hard covers, the corners. He tried not to savor it. He spoke in slow firm words. "Why. Me."

"I think you're more a part of this than you realize," Reyan said. "Or maybe you do realize it. You haven't said much more than you're along for the ride, but people like you don't just … exist. They are put on Eres for a reason." Reyan squinted at Aden. "You grew up on the streets, right? But you taught yourself how to read. Do you know how rare that is? I think you do but won't say. Well, I will. And you aren't hopped up on Sorcos.

Again, rare. And when a man you don't know asked you to help him free an old man, you turned down a fortune and asked to be on this dangerous journey."

Reyan chuckled. "People like you don't simply exist. You are one in a million, boy, maybe one in a billion. And I think you might be one of the few that has the courage to read those books like you believe. It will scare the crit out of you, to be sure. But I think you do. So until you give them back and say you just don't want them, I want you to hold on to them for me."

"I don't know what to say."

Reyan grinned. "That's okay, boy. Keep reading those books and listen for the Voice, and you will. One day, you will."

———

Ko was a small demic, which meant that Ko was a hungry demic.

Being small meant that when a group of his fellow demics came upon a human or other animal, he always found himself pushed away under threat of his life. And if the others, bigger ones, ever experienced real hunger, he would be the first to feel their tusks in his flesh.

There was one advantage to his size. He was faster than the others. But the rule and instruction that sounded in his head told him to stay with a group. Demics weren't capable of much more organization than that. Stay in a group. Run down living things and destroy them. It was simple. It needed to be. But staying in a group never fed him, and his size kept him from eating one of his brothers if he starved. So he did a desperate thing.

He ran ahead of his group, used his speed to run faster than he ever had in his long, miserable life. The others screeched and cried out at him in wordless displeasure and anger, but he was hungry. He also knew, from the past two human places they had feasted upon, that if he took the first available meal, the others were fast enough to catch up with him, and his victory would be short. So he ran through the large buildings in the middle of the human place and ran with all his speed outside of the center of the place and followed a road where he could smell a human.

Ko's demic eyes gave him clear vision in the night, and he soon saw a human, a male, walking alone on the road with something in his hand, some sort of small tree. The human smelled sour, but that didn't matter. The flesh would taste good either way. The hunger within Ko rose up and overwhelmed him, and as his breath quickened, Ko snarled and frantically rushed the human.

Byr shouldn't have hit his wife. He knew that. Few in town would have ever addressed it with him. Men who laid hands on their wives weren't exposed, much as Bain's adultery was buried in the field, but the town would know. And they did. Some men treated him the same. Others were civil but curt with him. The women, however, were a different story. Their anger simmered beneath the surface, well hidden, but he wasn't a complete idiot, despite what people said about him. He caught the stares and the hard looks.

How they had seen or known, he couldn't say. He thought Sirah had left with Eshlyn and more than half the town that day. But all it took in a small town was one glimpse of her face, her eye, by anyone who had remained and the whole town knew within hours.

Byr had stayed late that night at the inn and gotten roaring drunk. The innkeeper kicked Byr out a little past midnight. Byr didn't want to go home; the house smelled like her, the furniture and farm reminded him of her, which made him both angry and depressed. They felt the same most of the time. So he spent what time he could, and what little coin he had left, sitting and drinking ale at the common room of the inn most days and nights. There was work at the farm, but he couldn't make himself do it.

But Sirah had made him so angry. She first asked and pleaded with him to leave with her. She had known, like everyone else in town, that Byr was one of Bain's men, one of the men that owed his livelihood to the Mayor. It had been like that with Byr's father, too. What did the woman expect him to do? Bain had been clear. Anyone leaving with Eliot Te'Lyn would face consequences and lose out in the end, if Bain had anything to do with it. And Byr knew what Bain could do in the town, for or against him. So how could Sirah expect him to make a choice like that? He couldn't. And when he told her that, she said things that questioned his manhood. Wasn't he his own man? she had asked him. Was he one of Bain's crinkles? The anger had taken him by surprise, and he lashed out. More than once. He wasn't an idiot. The irony that he hit a woman in a reaction to questioning his manhood wasn't lost on him.

For the first time in his life, he regretted that they didn't have Sorcos in the town. He knew Bain would be for it. Either way, Byr would have to go all the way to Ketan or Biram to get some of the drug. He heard it made people forget. And he wanted to forget.

While Byr didn't want to go home, where else could he go? He was really drunk, so he might pass out at any moment. Thankful for the sturdy walking stick he managed to remember to bring with him today—he had stumbled home and scraped his knees and elbows on the way home last night—Byr trudged down the road to his farm.

It was a clear, cool night, and the wind blew past his ear. He heard the tall grasses on both sides of the road rustle. Then he heard another sound, a snarl, and distant heavy breathing. As drunk as he was, it took him a moment to react. He stopped walking, leaning on the walking stick, cocking his head, his eyes drooping as he concentrated. Footfalls, more like a gallop but something light. The snarling neared him in a rush. Thinking it odd, Byr wasn't too concerned – too drunk to be too concerned – as he turned around.

When he saw the creature leaping at him, all he could do was fall to the ground, crying out as he dropped back and to his left. Since he pulled the move at the end of his initial turn, he landed more on his back as his momentum continued to carry him around. The air left his lungs, but he saw the creature fly past him with an angry screech.

The monstrous little imp landed on the road a pace past where Byr had just stood, and all Byr could do was react again, lifting his walking stick up to protect himself as the creature jumped at him again, colliding with the stick. Byr used the stick to flip the monster over his head, the monster clawing at him and scraping his right shoulder as it was flung into the grasses to the side of the road.

Byr scrambled to his knees, twisting to face the thing – he could see black eyes, black teeth, red skin – as it flailed in the grass for a second or two before recovering and running back at Byr. He had played Qadi-bol with the other boys in town, little town games when they were bored as kids. He hadn't been terribly good, not as quick on his feet as some of the others, but they always praised his striking ability. He had been the marksman, so when he swung the walking stick at the creature, he connected with enough force and precision at the side of the creature's head – were those horns? – that the little monster was knocked unconscious and fell about a mitre to Byr's left.

His breath came short, hyperventilating, and he stayed there on his knees, the walking stick held in front of him for defense, his eyes bulging, his mouth wide. He gulped down the night air.

"What the breakin' shog!" he exclaimed when he had enough breath to speak.

Getting a good enough look at the monster now, he leaned forward in complete shock and fear to see the little human-like figure with dark red skin, black claws and horns and teeth, wearing only a loin cloth.

Fear overcame him, and as usual, he reacted violently. He brought down the walking stick on the creature's head over and over, black blood and gore covering the walking stick and the ground, until the head of the thing was nothing but a flat, black and red mess on the road.

He sat back – was he crying? – on his rear end, the walking stick falling to his side. Then he heard the screams from town. Two kinds of screams. Several of them just like the one that came from this little creature. And several of them were human. And he remembered what Eshlyn had said in that meeting in the town gathering hall that day, and he thought of Sirah.

Crit. He was a complete breakin' idiot after all.

He tried to think, lifting a hand to his foggy head, of what Eshlyn had said that night, of what Sirah said. North. Ketan. Right?

As inebriated as he was, fear drove him to his feet. He grabbed his walking stick on the way and ran northward through the grasses to meet the Manahem road, leaving the sounds of Delaton dying behind him.

He had never been fast on his feet, and he fell several times trying to sprint through the grasses. Byr never even took time to notice any injuries or wounds. He didn't feel them. He stumbled to his feet and ran on. He made it to the Manahem road out of breath, but he didn't stop. The road gave less resistance, so he continued to rush north.

The noise of his own labored breathing – and weeping? – filled his ears, but he heard the noise of a wagon coming up the road behind him. He managed to twist to look behind him, but he lost his balance and fell to the road as the wagon approached. He was sure that it would run straight over him, but thankfully they saw him, and the wagon slowed.

"Kyv?" Byr said as his eyes were able to focus enough to see the man driving the wagon pulled by two horses. Kyv was a strong man, a good farmer also to the north of town, and he stood enough to look down to see Byr sprawled on the road. Kyv's wife and son were also in the wagon.

"Well, get in, man!" Kyv said. "We're getting out of here!"

Byr didn't need another invitation. He scrambled to his feet, stumbling but jumping on the back of the wagon. Kyv was already urging the horses forward at a full run, and Byr had to grab the side of the wagon amidst loose bags and supplies as the wagon lurched onward.

The boy – Byr couldn't remember his name now – sat huddled in the back of the wagon, and their eyes met, Byr wondering if his were as filled with fear as the boy. The boy was crying, too. Kyv's wife sat in the jockey box with her husband – Dyra was her name, he could remember that one – and she looked back at him, her blond hair whipping around her face.

"I saw one!" Byr shouted. "I – it was … horrible!" He had lost his walking stick somewhere.

"Saw one!" Kyv shouted back at him, the wagon racing at top speed along the road. "I've got one!"

"What?" Byr yelled. The boy caught his gaze again and glanced down at a canvas bag in between them. The boy was huddled away from that bag.

Sitting up in the back of the wagon, Byr dragged the bag towards him. He pulled it open and drew out the round, wet object. It was a small head, childish in size, with red skin, small black horns, dead but open black eyes, and black teeth in a slack jaw. He dropped it back in the bag and wiped his hands on the torso of his tunic with a grimace. Then he turned, leaned over the side of the wagon, and vomited.

Chapter 18

Scars

Caleb rode with Carys as she led them out of the forest of Saten that morning. She and Caleb had talked, and he suggested that they stay clear of the road at the entrance of the forest. The elves had likely sent more pigeons to Taggart, and just as they set guard on the other side from Botan, they would have a presence along the road on the northern entrance to the forest along the main road. They might also have patrols, he explained, so they would have to move careful and be watchful, even away from the road. The four of them exited the forest without incident.

Taggart was once a city-state that flourished in trade but had been caught trying to keep the peace between other nations of men. After centuries of peace, Erelon and Manahem went to war, and Taggart became a strategic position both wanted to control. The fighting stopped with an armistice, but the two nations were ever at odds. The Drytweld and the People of the North withdrew into their tribal lands as Taggart, once a neutral place of peace and prosperity, became a military outpost for Erelon.

Once Tanicus decided to liberate man from their own aggression, corruption, and violence, he brought his War of Liberation upon the world of men. Erelon made their final stand at Taggart. King Judai of Mahanem offered his aid but was rejected by the warlord generals of Asya and Galya. Taggart held out for a whole month before succumbing to the superior military might of Kryus.

The elves turned the city into their own military base to the west. They waged their campaigns against King Judai and Manahem until the final surrender of Ketan. Taggart was now the primary Kryan military outpost to the west.

Therefore, Caleb had them camp several kilomitres to the west of Taggart, bypassing the city altogether, keeping as far away as possible just to be safe. Carys suggested she could go into Taggart and buy more supplies, maybe a horse, but Caleb saw it as too much of a risk. He insisted against it, arguing that they could make it to Biram, where Reyan had old friends and connections that would help them without the danger of walking into an elven military complex and flashing gold. She finally agreed. He was grateful.

Caleb went through two new forms with Aden that night in their lessons. The young man learned well and had all but mastered the few Caleb had taught him so far. Aden was fast and strong for someone so small, and he proved to be intelligent, too. Caleb could see the injuries still pained Aden at times, so he eased up as the sun ducked down the western horizon.

As Caleb and Aden sat at the fire, Caleb noticed Carys examining Reyan's arm, both of them tense. Reyan could barely move it. "Does it hurt?"

He shrugged.

Frowning, she nodded. She bandaged the arm and replaced in in the sling. Upon seeing Caleb and Aden, she pointed a finger at them. "Get those shirts off, gents," she said. "I need to look at those stitchings."

Caleb heard Aden gulp, but they both complied. She examined Aden first, and Caleb tried not to grin at how uncomfortable Aden seemed. "Not infected. Dack did a good job, and you heal well," she said.

Aden smiled as he shouldered his shirt back on. Carys then investigated the wounds along Caleb's chest and abdomen. She took off his boot and rolled up his pant leg to scrutinize his calf. "Pretty good, too," she said. But she hesitated while moving to Caleb's side.

She touched the scars on his back. "How did you get these?" she ventured.

The whole group paused, silent. Scars covered his back from waist to shoulders. Even Reyan looked at him with sadness in his eyes. While he thought of Danelle every day, he hadn't told the story since it happened. It wouldn't bring her back, but maybe people he cared about would understand how important she had been to him. So he told her story.

"Her name was Danelle," he began, and Aden and Carys looked up at him, startled. Reyan continued to gaze downward. "She was a slave at the Citadel where I trained with the Bladeguard. They liked to have young women as slaves. They used them for sex, a convenient indiscretion and pastime for many of the teachers and students. Except for me.

"I noticed Danelle as soon as she arrived from Landen. I mean, I was twenty-five years old; I noticed all the servant girls, but I was drawn to her right away. She did the laundry, so she would deliver clean clothes and sheets to my room. She was beautiful. Long dark hair, green eyes. I couldn't bring myself to speak when she was around, even though I saw her every day.

"Soon I heard a couple of the elves talk about her. She developed a reputation for rejecting the advances of the elves in the Citadel, which was dangerous. She couldn't officially get in trouble for it, since talking about such things in the open would taint the official position that the Bladeguard were honorable elves. Elves like to keep up appearances. The fact that she spurned the elves in the citadel, willing to embrace that danger, only made her more appealing to me.

"One day I was walking through the Citadel, and I heard noises from one of the students' rooms. I had my own place near Galen's quarters, apart and away from the others, but I was free to roam the complex. I heard low male elf voices, and Danelle's voice, too, angry and desperate in her tone. I broke into the room, which was stupid, and found two elves cornering her in the room. It was Saben's room, an elf who had been a student just two years longer than me, and one of the visiting Bladeguard, Cyprian, was there in the room with him.

"It was obvious what was going on, and Cyprian told me to get out. None of us had weapons – it wasn't against the rules to have them, but tradition held that Bladeguard didn't wear their swords or carry weapons outside of training rooms. I wouldn't leave the room, even as they tried to force me out of the room, and in the ensuing scuffle, Danelle ran past us and got away. We all came away with some scrapes and bruises, but no one the worse for wear.

"The rumors spread through the Citadel. The next day Saben challenged me to a duel with practice swords. Since Cyprian was a full Bladeguard, it was against the rules for him to fight me, but Saben was a fellow student. He could issue the challenge.

"The Master of the Citadel, Galen, had been … well, upset would be a kind word. He yelled at me – about how reckless I was, how stupid I was. Cyprian could have me killed and few would care. I didn't have the same rights as an elf and would find the whole system arrayed against me. I knew that, but I couldn't just stand by and do nothing.

"Galen begged me to deny the challenge, accept a punishment. But I chose the duel anyway.

"The whole Citadel showed for the duel. As we faced each other with practice swords, swords of unsharpened steel that could still break bones, I told him that I would fight him on one condition: that if I won, Danelle would be mine and no other elf could touch her in any way. Galen's jaw dropped in shock. But I made them all agree before I would fight. This didn't win me any friends, but I didn't have many to begin with. They agreed, wanting to see me beaten by Saben.

"Saben was a good student. He was older and had more training. I had more one-on-one training with Galen, but everyone believed Saben would be one of the best Bladeguard within a decade or so. And what was I going to do if they went back on their word, on the off chance I won? Fight them all? No one is that good. I was placing confidence in the word of elves that I could not trust. Win or lose, I would make Danelle a target anyway." Caleb laughed. "No, pretty stupid, looking back, but I did it."

"So after they agreed, we fought. We wore thick leather tunics to keep the dull swords from penetrating and delivering a killing blow, but the head was fair game, and once or twice over the last few hundred years, elves did die in a duel in the Citadel. Most fights are over within a handful of moves. They just don't last long. This one wasn't over quickly, however. We fought for almost a half hour. In the end, I won. I broke Saben's right arm and left leg with the practice sword.

"Galen was still upset with me, but I was pretty proud of myself. At least, I was until the next morning when Danelle came storming into my room, yelling at me that she didn't need my help or protection or anything. I was speechless, and she just ran out. The elves did leave her alone, though.

"Over time, Danelle began to soften towards me. Cold greetings became warmer, and then we started having conversations. I won't bore you with all the details, but we fell in love. I was probably in love with her from the first day I saw her, but that grew as I got to know her. And even against Galen's wishes, we got married."

Caleb grinned as he glanced at Carys. She gasped, her eyes wide and bulging. "You're married?" she squeaked.

"Yeah," Caleb said. "But no one in the Citadel knew. She and I were alone and spoke our promises to one another in private. We kept it as secret as we could. Only Galen knew. Others felt that I had claimed this servant as my own, and as long as I didn't go outside my race or keep the other elves from the rest of the servant girls, they ignored me.

"I told her everything. I told her about my life and the Prophet and what I believed. I held nothing back. I needed to confide in someone, a human. If she had been a spy, she could have turned me in and I would have been finished.

"But she wasn't a spy. She believed with me, and I think that I might've gone insane without her there, carrying the burden with me, especially after hearing how Aunt Kendra was captured and executed by the Kryans.

"But as I said before, this was a place where people had been trained in espionage and strategy. You could keep few secrets, and after five years into my relationship with Danelle, Saben figured out that it was more than a student-slave girl thing. Whether he knew we were married or not, I don't know, but that didn't matter. He knew that hurting her would do more than inconvenience me. It would wound me beyond measure.

"It didn't take much. All he had to do was report a very expensive item missing – a ruby ring from his mother – and accuse Danelle. They didn't even need proof. She had no right to defend herself, so they prepared her punishment.

"My first instinct was to kill him, challenge them all to a duel, whatever. Galen stopped me, calmed me down. But he knew me well enough. He knew that I couldn't watch her being whipped, not when her only crime was her association with me. So he suggested another solution.

"The Citadel had an old tradition, rarely if ever used, that a student could take the punishment of another in the Citadel, on their behalf. It was something passed down from the ancient *Sohan-el*, but the elder elves knew the tradition and would uphold it. It was designed to create camaraderie within the Bladeguard if another student were caught in some minor infraction and were to be punished. Extending it to a servant within the Citadel was something of a loophole, but Galen thought the tradition would hold.

"And it did. There was arguing after Galen and I suggested it to the other masters of the Citadel, but in the end they conceded. There was no hiding that Danelle and I were in love. The whole Citadel showed up again, this time to see me receive fifty-one lashes with a whip. An elf named Zarek, the Master of intelligence and espionage, happened to be at the Citadel and volunteered to administer the beating. They strung me up in the courtyard and even brought out the servants—Danelle most importantly—to watch.

"Danelle was stronger than I was. I think that's why I needed her, loved her so much. I could never have stood there and watched her endure the beating as an innocent woman, and she was innocent. It was a weaker thing to take that beating. I could take physical pain, had been trained to welcome it, but I knew that it would break me to see her flogged.

"Zarek beat me until I fell unconscious. And he finished the fifty-one lashes even after I passed out. When I awoke, I was lying on my stomach with bandages and cloth covering my back. Galen had tended me himself with medicine to stop the infection and other herbs to hasten the healing.

"I asked for Danelle, but they wouldn't answer me. And after two ninedays, I was able to get up and walk. In the end, they told me that Danelle had disappeared the night after I had been beaten. She was just gone."

Carys groaned. "What did you do?"

"What did I do?" Caleb repeated. "I searched for her for days, but there was no sign of her. No tracks. No witnesses. She had disappeared. And I didn't know, couldn't know what happened, and that hurt more than the beating. If one of the Bladeguard had decided to kill her, I would never find her and they would never admit it. Not to me."

He sighed. "I finished my training, that's what I did. I channeled all my anger and pain into becoming a Bladeguard, and six months later I got the tattoo on my arm. Galen gave me a letter of Regency with the Emperor's seal and a bag of gold, and I was headed to Asya."

Carys reached out with her left hand and touched his arm. He was still and quiet. "I'm so sorry, Caleb," Carys said. Aden watched him with a pained look.

Reyan sniffed, shook his head, and lay upon his bedding, pulling his blanket over himself and turning away from the group.

＋

Thoros sat on a wooden table in the large room he assumed men used for dining, the unforged sword in his hand. Around him, nine demics crouched over human bodies, humans that once inhabited this house, feeding upon flesh, picking the bones clean of meat, drinking the blood with satisfied growls and grunts. The room was lit by a single lantern on the table.

He stared at the man sitting in a chair in the corner, an older man with gray hair and big blue eyes. The man was unbound but caught, his face gaunt with terror, glancing from the demics that fed upon his family to Thoros and back again. The man wore a short pair of pants and nothing else. He was covered with his own vomit and waste.

Thoros spoke to the man. "What is your name?"

The man's brow furrowed. "Huh?"

"Your name."

"Bain."

"Bain." Thoros repeated. "Have you ever been hungry? Truly hungry. Starving, feeling like you would die from it at any moment?"

The man shook his head.

"These demics have been starving for hundreds of years, but they did have one advantage. They could eat one another, and they did. But that was not an option for me. I eat something that does not exist in the Underland. So I starved for a thousand years, but there was no sun, no changing of the season to mark the passage of time, only a constant, desperate hunger. And now we are here above."

"I don't understand," Bain said.

Thoros took the unforged sword and stuck it in the table next to him. The demics became agitated, turning to regard him. They did not like the presence of the sword.

"Do you know what this is?" Thoros pointed at the sword with a talon.

"A – a sword?"

"Yes, but a special sword, a sword from El. A sword wielded by his warriors, the *Sohan-el*. It is the one thing in this world with the power to defeat me. And yet I continue to carry it." Thoros pulled the sword from the table. It was heavy, even for him, and he wondered how a human could lift it. He held it out before him. The demics cowered.

"I possess memories that are not my own. Fourteen Demilords have gone before me, each with thousands of demics, searching for the Key to free us all from our exile. Each of their memories in my head, and they each tell a different story but with the same end: defeat at the hands of a *Sohan-el* and an unforged sword, like this one. But no Demilord has ever wielded one himself. Perhaps that will be the difference."

Thoros lowered the sword and considered Bain. "My memories tell me of a great city to the north of here."

"Ketan."

"Yes. Do they have a *Sohan-el*?"

"I don't know what that is."

"You have never heard of the warriors of El?"

The man shook his head.

No *Sohan-el*? What if one did not exist in this age? The Key called to him from the city, a pulse within his mind, stronger the further north he traveled. He would need to feed upon the soul of a Sohan-el for it to work.

"Does Ketan have an army?"

"Army? No. Just a few hundred elves."

Only a few hundred elves to protect a human city? No *Sohan-el* to protect the Key? Had man become that weak? He smiled, and Bain tried to retreat further into the corner.

He would get the Key first and find the *Sohan-el* later, if he could.

But for now, he was hungry. He stuck the sword back into the table, rose and walked toward the man. He laughed at Bain's screams before he drank his soul.

CHAPTER 19

HEALING

The next morning, after Caleb gave Aden his hour lesson, Reyan and Aden worked together to put out the fire and gather up the camp. Caleb did a walk around the camp to cool down from the workout and asked Carys to walk with him.

Clumps of trees and bushes were plentiful and the long, green grass brushed their legs as they walked. The sun still sat just above the eastern horizon, and Caleb heard a bird call off to his right.

"He loves you, you know," Caleb said.

Carys flinched and looked up at Caleb with a frown. "Who?" she asked with accusation.

"You know who," Caleb said. "He was grieving, too."

She scoffed at him. "That doesn't excuse what he did."

"No," Caleb said. "Not trying to make excuses. I'm just saying that even though you may not believe it, he loves you."

"He barely ever took time for me, or you, for that matter," Carys said. "He left everything for Aunt Kendra to do! He just went about his life as if we weren't even there."

"He wasn't around a lot, that is true," Caleb said. "But he was around, though. And there were good times with him."

"Why are you defending him?" Carys asked. "You hated him when we were kids."

Caleb shook his head. "I never hated him," he said. "I might have said that, but that was just anger and my own grief talking. And I was young. We say things we don't really mean when we're young."

"We lost our parents," Carys said. "We needed more than he gave. You needed a man in your life. His own son needed him more than he got."

"Probably true," Caleb said.

"Probably?" Carys lifted her arms in frustration at him. "What is your problem?"

"Well," Caleb said. "Maybe I know what it is like to lose a sister. Not like he lost his, mind you, but enough to relate. If he loved his sister half as much as I love you ... And I know what it is like to lose the love of your life, the woman that you relied on, the one that made you strong. Having to go on alone again is ... well, it feels impossible, but you find a way." Caleb shrugged. "Maybe not the best way, but you find a way. And maybe he wasn't what he should have been ... or could have been. But maybe he wasn't so bad, either. Maybe he did the best he could. Maybe he is human after all. Maybe I have to let him be." Caleb frowned. "That's all I'm saying."

Carys crossed her arms as they made a final turn in their circle back to the camp. Caleb ducked under a low branch.

"I do know, though, how blessed I am to have found my sister again," he said and put his arm around her. She groaned in sadness, not able to look at him, but she melted into his chest. They stopped walking so he could let her fall into his embrace. "El has shown his goodness, to the sure."

———

The First Men built Ketan. The walls of the city had never been breached.

The river Rumer flowed from the northeast down to the valley just before Lake Avahu. Ketan was erected in that valley against the south side of the river. The Manahem road ran straight north into the city, the one entrance through the stone walls, eight mitres thick.

As Eshlyn and her father led the caravan through the plains, they could see the imposing city from far in the distance, the dark gray stone rising above the horizon, and the four battle towers rising even higher. As they neared the city, Eshlyn craned her neck to see the walls reaching a hundred mitres into the sky, and she marveled at the city that even the mighty Tanicus had not been able to conquer.

The flat, smooth wall grew closer as the Manahem road widened toward the city gates: large rectangular doors made of iron. The gates had a battle tower on either side, smaller than the main towers but still thick and strong. The city walls extended from the river, continuing around the city and protecting any that dare attack from the south. Shorter walls protected the city from the north along the river. The Kulbrim dam to the west of the city regulated the rushing waters of the river. Two main towers at either side of the gates gave perfect firing angles back at the entryway and would surround any force that tried to fight their way in on that field.

The caravan of travelers hunched a bit, looking up as they neared the gates of the city, feeling vulnerable and surrounded, though no army stood in those towers ready to rain arrows down upon them. It was too easy to imagine.

Eshlyn and her family stopped at the open gates to the city of the Ketan, the caravan extending far behind them. At the gates, thirty elves stood in Cityguard armor, twenty of them with spears and shields along with the gladi at their hips, the other ten with a good gladus at the ready. One elf walked to intercept them, his armor accentuated by a silver helmet with a blue plume.

He eyed the caravan, peering as much as he could around Eshlyn and her father as they walked on their feet towards him, and as Eliot,

Eshlyn, and Xander halted in front of him, he eyed Eliot and said, "What is this?" He pointed at the caravan.

The other guard paid more attention at his tone, also nervous at the large group of humans headed into the city. Spears leveled out, and shields were raised.

"We are citizens from Delaton," Eshlyn said, standing by her father. Like most of the people in the caravan, she had never been to Ketan, but she steeled herself and met the elf's eye. "My name is Eshlyn Se'Matan, and this is my father, Eliot Te'Lyan. And this," she pointed behind her, "is my brother, Xander." As he looked at her in confusion, Eshlyn asked him, "What is your name?"

"My name?" he said. "I am Lieutenant Ryus, but you haven't answered my question. What is this?"

"As I said, we are citizens of Delaton, a town to the south," Eshlyn said. "And we have come here for refuge."

"Refuge?" Ryus asked. "Refuge from what?"

"We will need to talk to the Steward tomorrow," Eshlyn said. "But there is a crisis here in Manahem. The town of Campton was attacked days ago, and we have come to the walls of Ketan for safety."

Lieutenant Ryus looked again at the caravan. "I'll have to talk to my superior about this," Ryus said. "I cannot allow you into the city until I do."

"We are only a few hundred people," Eliot said. "Surely there is enough room for us in the great city of Ketan."

"Not the point," Ryus said, turning now to the guard behind him. "Hold them here," he told them. "Don't let them enter until I get back with the Second Captain." The guard behind him formed up to block the way as Ryus gave them one last glare before stepping through the gates, getting on his horse, and riding off to the right.

Eshlyn rolled her eyes at Xander, and Eliot gave them a firm look. "Be patient," he said. "We won't get anywhere by trying to force our way. People will only get hurt."

"I know," Eshlyn said, but that didn't make the wait any better.

Over the next ten minutes, some of the men of Delaton strode up and asked about the hold up, and Nafys joined them, as well. Fifteen men stood with Eshlyn and her father as Lieutenant Ryus returned on his horse with another elf riding next to him, this one with a silver helmet and a red plume.

The Second Captain surveyed the caravan from his horse, standing in the stirrups for a better view. "What is this?" he asked the group standing at the gate. "Who are you?"

Eshlyn sighed before speaking. "I told Lieutenant Ryus here," she said. "We are citizens from Delaton to the south and we've come to stay here in Ketan for safety."

The Second Captain frowned at them. "Ryus said something about refuge. You're seeking refuge?"

"Yes," Eliot said. "Towns have been attacked, at least one, to the south, and we have come to the city for protection until it is safe."

"Attacked?" the Second Captain asked. "By whom?"

Eliot shrugged. "We don't know," he said. "But a town has been lost and we decided to travel here."

"What is the problem?" Eshlyn asked. "You have a large city in there, and all we want to do is get inside the walls before dark tonight and find places to stay."

"I don't know how we could take all these people," the Second Captain said. "I don't know if the inns have the room ..."

"Then let us find out," Eshlyn said. "There are families here that would share rooms, and most are willing to pay. The others would be willing to work for room and board ..."

"You don't all have the coin to pay for an inn?" the Second Captain said. "I can't just let you in to sleep on the street."

"Then where would we go?" Eliot said.

The Second Captain pursed his lips and shook his head, thinking. "I don't know, but you can't all come in the city yet," he said. "The Steward doesn't like surprises like this. I'll need my superior's approval to let you in the gate."

"Oh, by the nine gods ..." Xander said. "Are we to just camp out here tonight? We won't go back." Any human who heard that nodded or voiced their approval.

"You've been camping to get here," the Second Captain said. "One more night won't hurt you. I'll get the First Captain down here first thing in the morning."

Many cursed, and others complained, but as Eshlyn looked into the eyes of the Second Captain and the guard behind him, she knew they were not getting in tonight. "Come," she turned and said to the men and women that traveled with her. "We will camp outside the walls." The thought of sleeping surrounded by battlements bearing down upon her gave a chill, but she put on a brave face. "We will survive one more night."

The residents of Delaton and Roseborough knew she was right, and they possessed confidence in their own ability to brave the elements, but many had looked forward to a warm, dry bed and a roof over their head. Angry and disappointed, they turned back to their wagons and horses to spread out and camp just outside the walls of Ketan. Eshlyn saw the Second Captain relax.

She caught his eye and held it. "First thing in the morning," she said. "The First Captain."

He nodded to her and turned his horse back into the gate.

She walked back to the wagon with her father. "We'll set up some men to watch overnight, just in case," Eliot said to her while she stewed. "Just in case."

———

Carys watched Reyan. He still limped a little when he walked; his left arm was still in the sling. It would never be the same, but he clenched his fist and then extended the fingers. The exercise hurt him. He would wince every now and then, gritting his teeth. Despite being wounded, he kept going, moving, pushing forward.

They had settled in for the evening, and Caleb and Aden were in a nearby clearing to continue training in the sword.

Her heart began to soften towards her uncle yet again, and she resisted it. She wanted to yell and scream at him for his selfishness, for the life of running and hiding she had with him, the silence and distance she had always felt from him. But when she saw him now, she didn't see a hardened, cruel, selfish man.

She saw a broken man; a man so wounded he didn't even know how to speak it, despite his eloquence when it came to other matters. She saw weakness in him, but also the strength to keep moving forward, all but ignoring the pain as he continued on his path. He kept taking hits and wounds and never stopped. Had he carried this brokenness all this time? All this pain? Why had she never seen it?

And she knew she couldn't add to it. A part of her broke on his behalf, and the bitterness and anger melted. All she had left was compassion. It was hard to let the old friends go—the bitterness and ugliness within her—but let it go she did.

He had done the best he could. She saw it in a moment of such clarity that she could never have lived with herself if she didn't forgive him. She didn't even know if she needed to forgive him anymore. He was both the weakest and strongest man she would ever know. And she hated that this was the first time in her life she had seen it.

Reyan sat now, cross-legged in front of the fire, and Carys rushed and knelt next to him in the leaves of the forest, Reyan's head flinching, his eyes wide. "I'm sorry," she said. Tears blurred her vision. "Forgive me. I shouldn't have said those things to you before."

Reyan's face was pained. "No, Carys," he said, leaning closer to her. "It wasn't your fault. You had been through so much, and I pushed you away. It was me." He reached out to her, touching her arm. "It was me."

"No," she said. "It was both of us, then." She felt tears running down her cheeks. "I just missed her so much."

He hunched over, grimacing, a tear running down his face and into his beard. Bowing his head, he reached out with his right arm and grabbed the back of her head, pulling her towards him. She didn't resist; she pressed herself against him, buried her head into his shoulder, the smell of him so familiar. In that moment, as she heard him sniff in her ear, he said the words that she had always longed to hear from him. "I love you," he said in a whisper – not meant for the crowds or anyone else, just for her. "I love you, Carys. I always have and I always will."

CDAPTER 20

THE ACAR

Macarus, the First Captain of the Cityguard in Ketan, rode his horse, a red stallion with white mane and tail, ahead of the small contingent towards the gates of the city. Behind him rode Lieutenant Ryus and Second Captain Aetos on their horses. The three elves were all silent. Macarus was not happy this morning, for several reasons, and his subordinates practiced wisdom by keeping their mouths shut.

The First Captain was tall for an elf, as tall or taller than most human men. His long black hair hung straight from his head, and his teardrop face was accentuated by his long beak nose, dark blue eyes, and a frowning mouth. He was also thicker and stronger than most elves. Some elves mocked him and wondered aloud if he were part human. He wasn't. Macarus hailed from a powerful house in Kryus, his parents both elves, his mother a leader in the Lord's Senate. He was simply taller and stronger than other elves.

Macarus fingered the sword resting in the hilt at his left hip. It was as fine a blade as one could have in the Empire, as fine as any Bladeguard. He had trained in the sword and could be considered a master, but the opportunity to be a Bladeguard had passed him by centuries ago. His size worked against him, despite his incredible athletic ability. Elves assumed a big elf unintelligent and treated him as such. Macarus was a warrior at heart, but a noble one, so he had joined the army. Not the most prestigious of careers for a son of a great politician like his mother, but he proved himself a fine militan and rose within the ranks.

During the siege of Ketan those centuries ago, he had been an officer in a legion as they broke time and again against the great walls. How he had survived the campaign for so long on the front lines he would never understand, all by the power of the nine gods he supposed, but his superiors had asked him to name any post he liked in the new colonies in honor of his service. He chose the First Captain of the Cityguard for Ketan.

He could have chosen a position back in the Kryan homeland. Macarus was a hero of the Empire and the son of a powerful politician. But the War of Liberation had changed him. He had once believed that what Kryus did was for the best of humanity and Eres itself, but his misplaced idealism had been exposed in the reality of numerous abuses during the War. So he thought, as First Captain, he could keep the abuses in check. And he did. Ketan, and Manahem in general, already had special considerations from the Emperor from the negotiated peace with King Judai, so he felt it his duty to make sure those special considerations were honored. And while his conscience remained clear when it came to how the humans were treated in Ketan, his actions did not bode well for any future promotions. He had been First Captain since that day to this.

But this wasn't why he was unhappy today. He had accepted the sacrifice of his career for his morality long ago. His unhappiness could be attributed to two things. First, the Second Captain had waited until the morning to tell him a large group of humans camped outside of the city walls seeking refuge. Second, those humans had to spend the night outside when they should have been allowed in the city.

Macarus and the other two elves exited the gates, riding past the guard, and a small group of humans waited for them there.

A middle-aged man and a young woman stood holding the reins of their horses. The older man was above average in height and still in good shape for his age. The woman, his daughter it seemed, froze him for a moment with her beauty. Macarus halted his horse in front of them and scanned the field beyond the gates, the camp of humanity spread out and around him. Not that many people. They could have found a place for them last night.

"Greetings," he told the two humans before him. "I am the First Captain of the Cityguard of Ketan. My name is Macarus." He pointed to the two elves behind him. "I believe you met Lieutenant Ryus and Second Captain Aetos last night."

The older man glanced at his daughter and then back at Macarus. "My name is Eliot Te'Lyan," the older man said. "I am an elder from the town of Delaton. Most of these people are citizens of Delaton. This is my daughter, Eshlyn Se'Matan."

Macarus nodded at them. "Well met," he said. "Please explain your petition."

The woman, Eshlyn, stepped forward. "We have come because a town was attacked several days ago. By what we do not know, but we have come to the safety of the great city of Ketan until we can know our homes are safe." She peered deeper into his eyes, looking for something. "We come for refuge."

Macarus leaned over in his saddle. "Do you know how long you will be staying?" he asked.

Eliot shook his head. "No," he said. "We don't. Until we know our homes are safe. We don't know how long that will be."

"The Second Captain said you don't have the coin to all stay in an inn or boardinghouse," Macarus said.

"That is true," Eliot said. "But we may have enough for a time. And we are willing to work and earn what we need."

"And we require an audience with the Steward," Eshlyn stated. "We must discuss with him the crisis here in Manahem. It is his responsibility."

Macarus sighed. "Yes. Indeed it is." He sat up in his saddle. "Come," he said. "I will take you to him."

He could see the surprise in the eyes of the other two elves as he turned his horse and waited for the humans to get in their saddles. Once they were set, he nodded to them and led them into the city of Ketan.

The Manahem road continued straight through the gates and became the main street of the city. First they passed the main military complex on their right. With over five hundred Cityguard to use in the city, Macarus held the city more than secure. Most of the elves in the Cityguard were bored with the lack of activity and crime. Macarus considered that an achievement.

After passing the military complex, they rode past apartment buildings and homes on both sides of the road. Soon the main road through the city led them straight to the Inner City, the complex of administrative buildings and the palace behind a second wall of dark gray stone. They passed through iron gates under an arch in that inner wall, and the guards there watched them with threatening eyes. But with Macarus at the head, they did not move.

The small procession rode through a green grassy courtyard with benches and trees uniformly spaced around an oval field. Administrative buildings rose at either side as the road continued toward the palace of Ketan, a massive structure with wide stairs leading up to iron doors gilded in a design reminiscent of the Bladeguard tattoo: a tree growing out of a stone.

Macarus stopped at the palace stairs and dismounted while servants came to gather his horse and hitch it to a nearby post. The others followed suit. He waited while Eliot and Eshlyn allowed their horses to be taken, too. They appeared nervous.

"Do not worry," Macarus said. "The horses will be fine." He turned to the Lieutenant and the Second Captain. "Both of you wait here," he told them.

His officers frowned at that, but they obeyed orders well enough. Laying his left hand on his sword, he led the humans up the stairs to the doors of the palace.

Since surrender had been negotiated, the city of Ketan had not needed much rebuilding. The palace was just as it had been the first time he laid eyes upon it centuries ago rising fifteen stories tall and stretching almost half a kilometre to the back wall of the city, against the river Rumer. A beautiful rectangular building, it was surrounded by four other stately buildings used to serve the palace: stables, servant's quarters and the like. A tall blocky tower extended out at every corner of the palace, each crowned in a perfect spire.

They entered the palace, walking down a long hall with opulent decorations along the walls – golden candelabrae, red velvet couches, and long tapestries that hung from the ten mitre ceiling. The tapestries were the main changeover from the previous reign. Once, they had depicted ancient heroes and stories from the human history, the Ydu. They had been beautiful and exquisite, but Tanicus burned them upon surrender. He replaced them with pictures of himself conquering King Judai, standing over him with a long sword and the king frightened and begging for mercy. Another tapestry showed men and women and children worshipping Tanicus as he handed them food and medicine.

Macarus guided them through the palace in silence; the humans walked in a hushed and awed silence. Few ever came this far, and fewer humans nowadays.

They took a right at a crossway and stopped at a large office on the right. Gold letters were written on the door: *Second Assistant to the Steward, Chamren Ke'Ladi*. Macarus did not knock before entering.

Chamren hastened to stand to his tall height, acting nervous. But the man was always nervous. He was tall for a human with wide hips and narrow shoulders, slightly overweight with a long head and a very weak chin. His thin narrow mouth always hinted at a smile but never quite achieved it. His curly red hair framed his face – a long nose, green eyes, and low cheekbones. It always amused Macarus that Chamren treated him with such deference even though his position outranked the First Captain.

The only official human administrator in the Empire, Chamren was a genius at taking care of the day-to-day details. In any practical terms, he had more influence over the city than the Steward. And he possessed more knowledge of the city than any other being, elf or human, in Ketan.

"Yes, First Captain," Chamren said. After two years of trying to correct the man, he would only use the proper title, no names, so Macarus gave up. "How may I be of service to you?"

Macarus pointed to the humans behind him. "We need to see Desiderus," Macarus said. "Take us to him, please."

Chamren bowed and stammered his way around the piles of papers on his large desk. "Yes, well, yes, okay … um, well … you see, we will have to see if he's in today," Chamren said.

Interrupting the man, Macarus said, "Just take us, please."

Chamren waited until they parted to exit into the hall and led them further down into the palace. They came upon another crossway, and Chamren shuffled to his left, Macarus and the humans following. Coming to another door, this time they knocked. Written here: *First Assistant to the Steward, Unitian*. Chamren shifted his feet and wrung his hands. The man could never stand still.

The door opened, and a male elf with brown hair cut short scowled at the four beings in the hallway. He looked up at Chamren. "What?" he demanded.

"Yes, well … uh … excuse us, if you please, First Assistant. You see, the First Captain here … he would like to take these … uh, humans … to see the Steward," Chamren said.

"The Steward is very busy today," Unitian said in a casual tone after eyeing Eshlyn and Eliot. "You know that."

"Yes, well, the First Captain here …" Chamren began.

Macarus stepped forward. "These people would like to see the Steward," he said. "They believe it to be of great importance to Manahem."

Unitian rolled his eyes. "Of course they do," he said. "We all believe that what we want is imperative, but the Steward is an important elf and cannot be bothered all the time with these trivialities."

Macarus breathed deeply. "All the time?" he said. "When was the last time that we had a group of humans claim that their town had been attacked, who came to ask for refuge? I cannot remember a time."

The First Assistant peered at Macarus. He knew well that Macarus had been here even longer than Steward Desiderus. "Well, it must wait until tomorrow," Unitian said. "He is too busy today."

Macarus knew that tone and those words. He knew the kind of things Desiderus busied himself with. Macarus would get nowhere today. "What time should we come tomorrow?" he asked.

"I shall have to get back to you," Unitian said. "I shall check his schedule and see."

Eshlyn burst forward herself. "Please, sir," she said. "This is very important. The whole colony of Manahem might be in danger."

Unitian's eyes popped, and he looked from Eshlyn to Macarus then back again. "I said … I shall have to see," he said in a terse voice.

Chamren's shifting feet sped up a little, but he spoke. "Well, First Assistant, if I may say, um … uh, I believe the Steward's schedule is quite free in the morning. The humans could come back then." Chamren cleared his throat, becoming a half cough. "I could write them in for you?"

Macarus fought a grin and turned to Unitian. Chamren was braver than people realized. He just found his own way to be so. "We'll be back in the morning," he said to the First Assistant. "Have Desiderus ready. Tell him he has an audience with his First Captain." Macarus spun on a heel and walked back down the hall, the three humans having no choice but to follow him. The door to the First Assistant's office closed behind him.

"But … where will we go?" Eshlyn asked. "Are we to stay outside the city walls again?"

"No," Macarus said, walking quickly more out of frustration and annoyance than any real haste. "Chamren, there are a few hundred humans camped outside the gates as we speak, since last night, and they need a place to stay for an indefinite amount of time. What do you think?"

Chamren's shuffling feet stumbled but then resumed. "Oh, my," he said. "I'm not sure." Chamren was quiet for a few moments. Macarus let the man's mind work. He would come up with a solution if anyone could. Chamren gasped. "Ah! Yes, well, um, you could maybe put them into the old abandoned tenement on the southeast side of town. It is still structurally sound. Empty, but sound. A roof over their heads, at least."

Good man, Macarus thought. "How does that sound?" he turned his head to Eshlyn as they walked.

He could read the satisfied look on her face. "That will be to the fine," she said. "Much to the fine."

———

Aden rode third in the line of horses on the road towards Biram and Ketan. Last night, as he and Caleb returned to the camp, the tension between Reyan and Carys had vanished, and they sat together, close together, talking in hushed tones with one another. Aden saw Caleb only smile and join them at the campfire. Soon they had all eaten and relaxed, and Aden felt a shared peace and affection between them that he had never experienced.

They began to share stories of their life from long ago, laughing at their own mistakes and quirks and passions. Carys even requested they sing a song together, and they made sure to include Aden in the revelry, teaching him the lyrics and the melody. Soon his voice rose with theirs, and even Reyan's tonal disaster of a voice sounded joyful.

For the first time in his life, Aden forgot pain and loss and struggle. For a moment, just a moment, he felt as if he belonged.

The group laughed together later into the night, and Reyan was the first to admit he needed some rest. Everyone soon followed his lead, Caleb kissing his sister on the forehead before they curled under their blankets, as well. Glad of the evening, Aden also turned in.

The next day they rode early, and Aden's lesson with Caleb was short. They had a lot of ground to cover, according to Caleb. The group rode in silent contentment that caused Aden a certain satisfaction that he couldn't explain, but he enjoyed it.

Just after mid-day, however, that mood changed. No one in the group said a word. Nothing had happened. But the vegetation became sparse, turning brownish and desolate as they traveled. Soon, Aden all that remained was flat, black, parched, and cracked earth. No trees. No grass. Nothing lived. Aden could smell something putrid, like dead bodies mixed with crit. Similar to what the experienced under the Pyts, the scent was faint and more ominous. Over the next hour, the scent got worse, more acidic. And Aden could see a body of water up on his right, to the north of the road.

"What is this place?" Aden asked in a whisper. Even that sounded too loud.

Caleb looked around from his saddle with Carys to share a glance with Reyan. Reyan sighed and coughed. "This is the Acar," Reyan said. "Have you heard of it?"

"I hear the name, but … didn't know …" Aden said. He had heard it as a curse in Asya.

Reyan didn't turn around, but he glanced at the body of water they neared. It looked black, even darker than the blackened gray of the land around them. "It is short for *Acarleasharam*," Reyan said. "In the First Tongue, that meant the place of destruction, or death." Aden scanned the landscape, his shoulders hunching forward in the saddle. An appropriate name, he thought. "The place here, it used to be a thriving town," Reyan continued. "But it is now called *Mewatamel*, the dead water."

"What happened here?" Aden asked.

"You know of *Tebelrivyn*, the elven magic of Worldbreaking," Reyan said.

"I know of it. Illegal," Aden said.

"This place is one reason why," Reyan said. "The workers of magic began long ago, not long after the time of the first *Sohan-el*. They found they had the ability to manipulate nature, to control the different aspects of nature – light, heat, water, earth, and the like. Only elves, or those with elven blood, were capable of this magic. The men and dwarves were unable to do it. But over time, the elves also learned that the working of that magic had a cost. These sorcerers had to take from the resources of life around them to work their magic. To make a stone more powerful or to manipulate it, rocks and earth around them would become brittle and empty or lose coherence. To give more water in one place made the region around them more dry and dehydrated. Some could even give themselves more life and strength, even longer lives than they already had, but they took the life from others when they performed the rituals.

"Another effect of the magic was that as the sorcerer grew in power and proficiency, the elf would go mad. Whether some form of dementia or violence or paranoia, the practitioner went more insane the more power he or she drew. As the magical discipline grew, the sorcerers became tyrants over the nations of elves, and they terrorized the land of men.

"The two most powerful Worldbreakers, as they began to be called, were lovers and traveled the world, performing their magical miracles. Their names were Heru, a female elf, and Saemys, her husband. Heru and Saemys traveled through the land of men and became more violent as they began to require people to worship them and do their bidding. As they became more dangerous, killing any human who dared oppose them, two *Sohan-el* came to stop them.

"The two *Sohan-el* were great warrior leaders of the old world. They confronted Heru and Saemys here, where the town used to stand, here near the River. The town had been evacuated for a day or so by their elders by the time Gibryl and Jato battled the Worldbreakers."

"Did magic not affect them?" Aden asked.

Reyan paused before answering. "Yes and no. An unforged sword protects the bearer from being directly affected by the magic. But things around the *Sohan-el* can be manipulated, so the battle was still fierce. But ultimately, after a day of battle with the two Worldbreakers in an empty town, the *Sohan-el* killed Heru and Saemys."

"If they kill 'em," Aden said. "How did this happen?"

"The Worldbreakers had drawn so much power into themselves, that once the unforged swords killed them, the resulting release of that power leveled the town, poisoned the land within a three kilomitre radius, and produced a crater. That crater has filled with water, poisoned water, over the centuries.

"And so after that battle, the world of men made the magic of *Tebelrivyn* illegal, and the empires of elves in Eviland followed suit over time and other events like this happened there." Reyan looked at the lake, just at the right of them, the water eerily still and black. "But none of those events were as destructive as this one," Reyan said. "This was the worst of them, since it was two of them at once."

"What happened to the two *Sohan-el*?" Aden said. "Did they die?"

"Just as there are legends and myths after such events, like the forest of Saten," Reyan said, "legends of what happened after the battle here at the Acar are difficult to sort through. Some say they survived, protected by the unforged swords. Some say they also were poisoned and died weeks later. Others say they disappeared at the moment of the release of dark energy, and the unforged blades were all that remained. Those swords were exhibits in the throne room of Ketan for hundreds of years. Until Tanicus."

"What you think happened to them?" Aden asked, trying not to look at the dead water moving behind them as they traveled.

Reyan glanced at Caleb's back, then his head bowed low again. "I don't know," he said. "I just don't know."

—+—

It took several hours to get the residents from Delaton and Roseborough into the abandoned building on the southeast side of the city, and it took another two or three hours to get people settled in where they felt comfortable. Who would share rooms? Who needed their own rooms? Chamren and Macarus oversaw the operation, and they helped a great deal. The city held about fifty thousand humans but it had been built for many more, so there were other empty buildings around the city. But knowledge of which ones were safe or not was invaluable. Chamren had that information, and Macarus kept them from being unduly molested by the rest of the Cityguard.

Eshlyn sat cross-legged on the floor of her room next to her mother and nursed Javyn after the long day. Even still, a young married couple came to see her about getting their own room. The husband had two children from a previous marriage. She suggested some options while she nursed Javyn, and they ended up putting the two children in the same room with some older children from families they trusted and who might be willing to help watch them.

As they left and her mother went to see if Eliot needed any assistance, Eshlyn took the chance to enjoy a quiet moment with her son, a moment that had been rare over the last ninedays and a half. She stroked his fine hair, and he cooed at her when her dirty fingernails brushed his pure and soft cheek.

She remembered how happy Kenric had been when he had found out she was pregnant. To be honest, Eshlyn had been nervous to tell the man she loved she carried his child, nervous about how he would react. She had no evidence that he would react in a negative way – on the contrary, he was sensitive and content about most things – but she had images of his anger or resentment or disappointment, as uncharacteristic as they might be. She realized how silly those thoughts had been when he reacted with such joy and happiness, that all her fears dissipated. He pulled her into a tight embrace, and they entered a new phase of their life together, waiting and planning to be parents.

Over the next eight or nine months, his joy and happiness never wavered. He was as caring and attentive as a man could be. His dark silent times were gone, and she could see a life with Kenric full of light and hope.

When the baby was born, Kenric saw it was a son, and he wept. They named him together, and Kenric was ecstatic at the name Javyn. The first time he held the boy, he sang him a lullaby his father had sung to him, and the depth of nostalgia and love in Kenric's eyes drew her like never before. If she hadn't been in love with him before that moment, that second would have sealed her heart to him forever.

So in the abandoned tenement in the great city of Ketan, behind the thick walls Kenric told her to reach, she remembered that last night with him—that night where she had failed in so many ways, to kiss him, to tell him she loved him more than life itself, to tell him he was the greatest man she had ever known. And then Eshlyn recalled his last words, part of which was to sing his lullaby to his son.

The tears flowed from her cheeks in a constant stream. She could taste them in the corners of her mouth. Feeling the golden marriage

bracelet upon her cheek as she wiped the tears, she sang the lullaby she
had heard so many times to Javyn, born without her knowledge with the
blood of kings, choking on the melody through her weeping.

> *In another age, the children lead*
> *The sons are kings, and daughters queens*
> *The crowns will bow at dragon's feet*
> *And thrones will fall to find the Key*

CHAPTER 21

HARD EVIDENCE

Desiderus' childish, cherubic face frowned as he waited with his assistant, Unitian, for his meeting with Macarus, ready to give that pompous elf quite a piece of his mind.

He sat in the throne room of the palace of Ketan, lounging on the large iron, silver, and gold throne that sat upon the dais at the end of the enormous room with a dome ceiling. It was once King Judai's seat, as fine a throne as ever constructed, so Tanicus left it as a sign of the Kryan conquest, seating an elf in the seat of power. Even though Desiderus was a fat elf, his girth still did not fill the seat of the throne, the armrests the golden heads of dragons and the back of the throne a large iron tree with gold leaves. The base of the throne was iron in the shape of a rock with silver veins decorating it. Unitian stood at his left. Two Cityguard held their position two stairs down from the throne. Another six stairs led down to the vast marble floor.

Desiderus was dressed in a long golden silk robe with a white satin sash as a belt around his round belly. The robe almost hid his short, chubby arms and legs. His curly black hair fell to his shoulders. As he narrowed his blue eyes at the double doors that led into the throne room, he touched his face with chubby fingers covered in jeweled rings.

He remembered the first time he entered this room, hundreds of years ago, just after Tanicus had won the long siege of this city. Desiderus was from a large and powerful family in Kaltiel, the capital of Kryus, a wealthy family that had fallen from power just before the War of Liberation, all due to Desiderus himself. He had been a young elf and full of his own thoughts of reigning the Empire. He made a play for the High Evilord himself, a power play to unseat Tanicus that was a complete disaster. After making Desiderus wait in a luxury dungeon for two decades, Tanicus offered Desiderus this post as Steward of Ketan. Desiderus had been forced to choose between staying locked up in Kaltiel or leaving his homeland forever for an insulting position in the new colonies in the land of men.

Because of the peace made with King Judai, Ketan and Manahem allowed the most freedom for its human inhabitants, which meant Desiderus had the least amount of power of any of the Stewards in the new colonies. Even the Stewards in the smaller towns like Anneton and Vicksburg had more power. And Ketan was the farthest city away from the Empire, all further evidence Tanicus was a deft politician, keeping

Desiderus in a weak position far from the center of power and in debt to the Emperor's compassion.

A luxury prison was still a prison, however, and so Desiderus took the deal. He thought, over time, that he might be able to turn his Stewardship into another play for power, but between the independence of the citizens of Manahem and Macarus holding him accountable to the peace, Desiderus was trapped in this human hell for the rest of his life.

So he took his pleasures where he could find them. He ate and drank to his heart's content, and often beyond it. He consumed the prostitutes of the city, young and old, male and female, it didn't matter. His wife had long left him to return to the capital. She married a middle class elven merchant, but she believed it a better position in life than the wife of the Steward of Ketan. She was probably right. He also acquired jewelry and gold trinkets, his apartments full of them. Possessing them did not satisfy or excite him, but the hunt for them did.

Unitian coughed, rousing Desiderus from his deep thoughts as he heard footfalls just outside the door. Unitian was a fine assistant, knowing his place as the one responsible for allowing Desiderus his time to entertain his pursuits, waiting to get him involved when necessary. Most days even Macarus would not have been important enough to get Desiderus out of his vast apartments upstairs, but Unitian said that Macarus had brought humans, not even citizens of Ketan, into the palace. And that Macarus possessed that look, that look on his too handsome face that communicated he would be stubborn about this until he got an answer.

Macarus entered the room first as the wide, golden double doors parted. Desiderus and Macarus had developed an understanding over the years. Macarus left Desiderus alone, unless Macarus decided that it was important enough to involve the Steward. Desiderus went along with the understanding because days like today were rare, and he didn't want conflict with the First Captain of the Cityguard, an elf who had also been installed by Tanicus himself. He didn't know what would happen if it came down to a real play for power between them, but Macarus had the advantage in pure combat. He had learned how to use that sword through endless battles with men, and he carried it with the kind of quiet confidence that didn't need the threat of words to confirm them. The First Captain carried the loyalty of the Cityguard; they worshipped him. And Desiderus suspected that Macarus secretly believed that humans and elves were somehow equal. He couldn't prove it, but if he did …

Desiderus had his own advantage, however. Macarus was an elf of morality and principle – those kind were often weak and most vulnerable since they played by rules. Desiderus played by no standard save what was best for himself, and there lay his advantage over the First Captain: in politics.

Chamren followed Macarus into the room, his shuffling feet annoying the Steward from the first second. The man was a fool and an idiot, but he somehow kept the city afloat. Unitian relied on him too much. Ketan was the only city that had a human so involved in the running of the city. It grated on Desiderus to no end.

Entering the throne room after the First Captain and Second Assistant were two humans. A woman walked in behind Chamren, one of the most beautiful women Desiderus had ever seen. His small blue eyes took a long moment to drink her in. She noticed his eyes and scowled at him, but that didn't keep him from continuing to admire her. Behind her was a man, middle aged but strong and above average in height. At first, being around humans, he had thought they all looked the same. He couldn't tell one apart from another, besides males and females, but after a few centuries of being forced to deal with humans, he could tell these were related somehow.

Macarus led them before the dais, and he did a polite little bow with his hand on the hilt of his sword. "Steward Desiderus," he said with that melodious voice of his. "Thank you for meeting with us this morning. We come to bring before you a matter of possible crisis in Manahem. I believe it is urgent."

Manahem, and Ketan for that matter, could burn to the ground and all the humans with it for all Desiderus cared. He waved dismissively at the unknown humans standing just behind Macarus. That woman still scowled at him. "Who are these humans?"

The woman stepped forward. Bold and confident. He thought about putting her in the dungeon. For later. He had friends down there, elves that would keep certain things quiet. "My name is Eshlyn Se'Matan," she said. "This is my father, Eliot Te'Lyan. My husband was Kenric Se'Matan, the guardian of the town of Campton."

He sneered at her. Humans and all their names. "Never heard of him."

She took a calming breath. He could read humans well enough by now, and he perceived the violence in her eyes. She thought about striking him, the Steward! Astounding. A week in the dungeon before being brought to his apartments might do her some good. "Nevertheless, our town was attacked by an unknown force fifteen days ago, and we have come to seek refuge in the mighty city of Ketan until this crisis is known and passed." She took yet another step, her foot on one of the stairs up to the throne. "And to ask you for your help."

"What help could the Steward give the towns to the south?" Unitian asked in a derisive tone.

"Indeed," Desiderus agreed.

This time the father spoke. "We ask that you send a small force to scout and report back the nature of the threat," the father said. "And possibly send a pigeon to Biram or Taggart for reinforcements."

Desiderus smirked at them. "The towns to the south have made it clear they enjoy their independence from the powers here in Ketan," he said. "Which includes me. And Macarus, and even Chamren there. Now you ask for our help? You have quite the gruts to you, little girl." He shook his head. "No. You may stay in the city for a few days. But you will receive no help from this Steward."

The father sighed, dejected, but Eshlyn took another step up towards the throne. Unitian flinched back and the two Cityguards moved forward, their hands on their gladi. "Aren't you the liberators we've heard so much about?" she said. "Haven't you come to save humanity?" Was she mocking him? She didn't even acknowledge the threatening stances of the Cityguard that stood before her. "Well, humanity might actually need saving. There are other towns, other citizens of Manahem, under your care, that may be in great danger. And your own life might be at stake."

Desiderus laughed. Then he glowered at them. "Do you have any idea what type of force or threat this is?" They didn't answer, but Eshlyn's face tightened. "Do you? No, I see you do not. If I send a pigeon to Taggart, asking for reinforcements, I look the fool. If I send for reinforcements, and they come, and nothing happens, then I've caused a panic in the Empire and will be held responsible. We are safe here, little girl. These walls have never been breached. Even Tanicus himself couldn't break into this city! You think some unknown threat could?" He chuckled again. "The independent towns to the south can take care of themselves. We will wait here for further word. And we will not send a pigeon." Desiderus met Macarus' gaze. "And by my orders, we will not send a scouting party."

He could see Macarus' mind working, wanting to answer and argue, but Macarus knew that once orders were official, in front of witnesses, he was under threat of punishment if he disobeyed. Again with the following of rules. Desiderus didn't even try to hide his grin. The First Captain forced himself to bow and turned to walk back out the door.

Chamren followed without comment, and so did the father. But Eshlyn stood still, with one foot on the second stair from the lower floor, her green eyes full of fire and locked on Desiderus.

"Eshlyn," the father said from the doors to the throne room. "Come. Let's go."

She waited a moment, her face angry, then she turned and walked out of the room. That one was trouble.

Eshlyn and Eliot walked with Chamren, the three of them right behind Macarus. She thought she heard the elf Captain mutter under his breath, "That fool." But she wasn't sure, and the elf wouldn't repeat it if he had said it. They wound through the halls of the palace back out to the main entrance. Xander stood there with Lieutenant Ryus and two other Cityguard with the horses just outside the main entrance of the palace.

Xander looked at Eshlyn with expectation. "Well?" he said.

Eshlyn couldn't speak, she was so angry. She mounted Blackie. Eliot breathed deeply as he pulled up into his own saddle. "The Steward offers no help and will not send a pigeon for reinforcements or a scouting party down the Manahem road to check on the other towns," Eliot said.

Xander cursed as he also got up on Yaysay. He looked at Macarus. "Can't you do anything? Send anyone?"

Macarus, now on his horse, shook his head. "We need his permission to send a pigeon that asks for reinforcements, or at least the First Assistant. But Desiderus himself made it clear his orders were that we couldn't help at all. If I send any elf, either south or east, he'll have my neck in a vise and could remove me of my position."

Chamren also sat on a horse, appearing uncomfortable on the animal. Eshlyn and the rest of them followed as Macarus led them out of the palace complex. The Lieutenant and the other Cityguard stayed while Macarus and Chamren took Eshlyn, Eliot, and Xander back into the streets of the city.

"We tried," Eliot said. "We'll wait here for a time to see if anyone from the south sends word. We can be comfortable here for a few days, at least, and he did say we could stay in the city."

Silence hung over them for a time while they rode beneath the arch and back to the southeast part of the city where the humans from Delaton and Roseborough waited for news.

"What if you didn't send an elf?" Xander asked.

Chamren squeaked a little gasp. Macarus turned around in his saddle as they rode to look at Eshlyn's brother. "What?"

Xander cleared his throat. "What if you sent a human?" he clarified. "What if … what if I went to Biram, or Taggart, and tried to speak to the authorities there? Do you think they might listen?"

"That's crazy," Eshlyn said. "You're going to ride all the way to Taggart? That's almost a ninedays there. And alone? They're not listening here to us now. Why would they listen to you there?"

"They might if the First Captain sent a letter with him," Eliot said.

Macarus scoffed. "That is essentially taking my life in my own hands," Macarus said. "You heard his orders in the throne room."

"Yes, true … yes," Chamren began. "And you are bound by oaths and law to obey. But … just perhaps, what if you didn't send for reinforcements like we asked and were denied? What if you asked for, say, a change of the guard?"

"That isn't due for another year," Macarus said.

"But it is not illegal … and not disobedient," Chamren said. "If you sent a letter with young Xander here to the First General at Taggart, a missive explaining why you need the change to happen sooner, they may send at least another two hundred guard. If not the full five hundred, if you request it."

Macarus grinned at Chamren as he slowed to ride closer to him. "And what would my reasoning be?"

Chamren stammered for a moment before speaking, his hands fidgeting at his short red beard. "W-well, I mean to say," Chamren began. "You could say discontent among the Cityguard, or perhaps they need further training, or the need for fresh faces to root out some sort of crime." Chamren shrugged. "Just ideas."

"And good ones," Macarus said. "But would they do it?"

"It has been my experience in the Kryan Empire," Chamren explained. "That anything communicated – with the right seal and authority – will be done. If it looks official enough."

Macarus nodded. "And you can make it look official enough," he said with confidence.

Eshlyn looked at them both with bulging eyes. "Are you seriously considering this?" she asked. "You can't send my brother off to an army and hope something works."

Xander turned to his sister with a frown. "I want to do this, Esh," he said. "I've got a good horse and with enough supplies, and the letter like they're talking about, we could get some more help if something happens here."

She groaned at her brother. "What do you think this is, Xan?" she said. "This isn't just playing with your friends or getting excited pulling some sort of prank. This could be really dangerous. I hear there are bandits on the road out to Taggart."

Xander's face turned dark. "Break it all, Esh, I know this is serious, okay?" his voice rose in volume. "Kenric was a friend and a brother to me. He was one of the only people that saw something more in me than just a playful kid around town. I want to do everything I can to protect you and Ma and Pa … and Javyn. This is important. And this is something I can do. I'm going to do this."

She shook her head. "I just lost Kenric," she said. "I don't want to lose you, too."

"You won't, Esh," he said. "I can take care of myself. And I'll travel fast and light. I'll be fine. You'll see."

"You can't go alone," Eshlyn said.

"He might be safer alone," Macarus said. "A group is a larger target for bandits, and a lone rider can travel faster. Hide better."

"You don't know how to fight with weapons or anything," Eshlyn said to Xander, ignoring the First Captain.

"What human does?" Xander said. "It is a risk I'm going to take." Then Xander shrugged. "Joob could always go with me …"

"Ha!" she exclaimed. "He's the one that gets you into trouble!"

Xander's eyes darted about. "Yeah, true," he said. "But … uh, there were also other things that we did that no one ever knew about. He can be pretty … sneaky."

Eliot raised a brow at that, and Chamren hid a grin. "No more than two," Macarus said. "If you trust this man … Joob? If you trust your life in his hands, then he may be a good man to go with you. If he can be discreet."

"Discreet?" Eshlyn cried. She remembered his name around Delaton: Joob the Boob. "Not a chance."

"I do trust him," Xander told Macarus, and he faced Eshlyn. "And he can be discreet. Trust me."

Eshlyn bowed her head, realizing she wouldn't be able to change this. Eliot rode close to her and put his hand on her arm. "It will be okay," he said to her. "Those boys will look out for each other, and the real danger is south." Eliot then turned to Xander. "One condition, though. Joob agrees that you do all the talking and dealing with the elves in Taggart. Or you don't go. Understand?" Eliot used that fatherly tone that she and Xander knew allowed no negotiation.

Xander nodded. "Yes sir," he said.

"I'll give him enough supplies for the journey and coin to stay in safe places in Biram and Taggart," Macarus said.

"I have some extra coin, too," Chamren said. "If you need it."

"I'll be okay, Esh," Xander told her. "You'll see."

She didn't know if she trusted statements like that anymore.

—+—

Mayor De'Sy sat in the parlor of his house, sipping hot tea and reading an old elven epic novel about three elves in love with one another and how they had to fight the dwarves to consummate their love.

His wife, Kayan, was out having tea, as well, at the inn this afternoon with the wives of the elder's council. She entertained them there at the common room of the inn once a week. De'Sy knew the influence a woman could have on her husband, and the town would go along with any plan if the women believed it were their idea. They would nag their husbands accordingly. His wife called it her weekly "tea social," but he and his wife knew the real agenda.

The knock came to the door, and he started at the pounding. He spilled a drop of hot tea on his leg, and it stung. He wiped it as dry as he could with a curse while he set down the tea and book on the small table next to him and rose in a huff to answer the door.

Crystof De'Sy opened the door to two men he did not recognize. Behind them, out in the street, was a wagon with a woman and a little boy. The two men and the people in the wagon all looked sleepless and haggard, dirty. The two men had circles under their eyes, and they appeared desperate. He wasn't comfortable around desperate men.

"You the mayor?" one man asked.

"I told you," the other said. "He the mayor and he live here!" The second man had a canvas bag in his hand.

"I know, I know," the first man said. "Just trying to be polite."

"Just tell him already!" the second man said.

"I am the Mayor," he said. "Perhaps you gentlemen would like to come back later." He wanted some of his town guardians there to help him, maybe run these fools out of town.

"Can't come back later," the first man said. "We'll be heading on our way as soon as we do the right thing and tell you what's coming."

"I'm sorry …" Crystof said, ready to slam the door on these maddys just in case.

"Tell him, Byr," the second man said.

Byr took a deep breath. "A woman come through town here just a few days ago, I bet," Byr said. "With her Da, Eliot. Her name Eshlyn."

The Mayor's brow furrowed. "Yes," he said.

"Well, we didn't listen to her and we barely got out alive," Byr said. "The whole rest of the town is dead, eaten by little monsters!"

He didn't smell ale on the men, but they acted drunk, to the real. "You can't be serious," he said. "She never saw anything. How do you …"

"We know 'cause we saw them," Byr said. "We gotta show him, Kyv."

"Okay," Kyv said, bringing the canvas bag up to his chest and reaching inside it.

"Look, gentlemen, if you'll come back tomorrow, I'm sure we could …"

Kyv took a small head out of the bag, holding it by one of the small black horns, a head with red skin, beady black eyes, black teeth and tusks frozen in a snarl, and black blood smeared all over it. And it smelled. Badly.

The Mayor of Roseborough puked up his lunch all over his black leather shoes.

"I happen to be out at my barn late that night," Kyv said as the Mayor tried to recover, as if seeing a man empty his stomach the most natural thing in the world. "The horses were to makin' noise. And I keep my ax I use for cutting wood, I keep it right there at the barn." He lifted the head in front of the Mayor's face again. "And this little critter come jumpin' up at me with about three of his friends. All those shoggers try to eat me! All I know to do is pick up that ax and start swingin'. I kill 'em all 'fore you know it. Just a couple scratches on me. Then I cut this shoggin' one's head off to show people 'fore I wake up the wife and boy and get in the wagon. Just in case no one believe me. Seem like a breakin' nightmare to me anyway."

Byr nodded the whole time. De'Sy really wished that Kyv would stop waving that hideous head around. But he was pretty sure that if he tried to speak, whatever was left in his belly would come up.

Mayor De'Sy realized how wrong he had been. He thought of Eliot and Eshlyn. He thought of half the town of Delaton that passed through a few days ago, people he thought were insane. And the fifty or so that left with them that day, Nafys his best guard one of them, how he had cursed them that day. Looking at that severed head, he could believe the rest of the town of Delaton was dead.

Then he thought of his own city, Roseborough, and the thousands he had here.

Then the Mayor tried to speak. "How many ... of these things ... are there?" he asked, wiping his chin again.

The two men exchanged a glance and shrugged. "Not sure," Byr said. "Could be thousands, I think."

Kyv nodded. "Yeah," he said. "At least thousands."

"And how close are they to Roseborough?" the Mayor tried to ask while keeping his voice from squeaking.

"They maybe a half day or more behind us," Byr said. "We hear them sometimes at night, far behind us, but hard to tell on the plains. They seem like to travel at night. We travel during the day, rest the horses only when we need to."

"We stopping to warn you," Kyv said. "Then we moving on while there still daylight and they stopped." Kyv put the head back in the bag. Thankfully.

The Mayor blinked and rubbed his face with his hands. He was suddenly very tired. "So you're telling me they could be here tonight?"

"Or 'morrow night," Kyv said, shrugging at Byr, who appeared to agree. "We not stayin' to find out." Kyv turned and walked back to the wagon. "We leavin' now." Byr spun and followed him with a quick apologetic glance at the Mayor. Kyv was up in the wagon, the boy, apparently his son, tugging at his sleeve. Byr got in the back of the wagon.

Kyv tossed the canvas bag with the monster head in it back at Byr, who caught it and set it aside.

Kyv gave the Mayor a sober look. "Get your people out if you can, Mayor," he said. "Get them all out." He snapped the reins of the horses, and they rode off.

The Mayor would listen this time.

Chapter 22

A Call for Help

Tightening the saddle on Yaysay once more, Xander stood a half kilomitre south of Ketan, the walls and towers still imposing upon him from that distance. After living in a small town his whole life – and he hadn't known how small until coming to Ketan – the existence of something so large unnerved him. He checked on the clamps to the saddlebags for the fifth time. Joob borrowed Monny, Eliot's horse, finer than Joob's own and better for a fast and long journey, and he waited to get going. Joob had said goodbye to his own parents in the city.

Xander had spoken sharply with Joob when offering to take his friend with him. Joob grew excited at the chance, and Xander had to punch the man in the arm to get him to settle down and focus and agree to his father's terms. Joob came along as backup on the road, but he would not be talking to any elves or anyone in authority.

Once he felt Joob understood that – it was difficult to tell sometimes with Joob – then they began making plans. Joob began talking about all the fun they would have on the road together, the two boys like old times. Xander told Eshlyn yesterday he knew the seriousness of what was happening. He couldn't say the same about Joob.

Surrounding him and Joob were Xander's parents, his sister holding Javyn, Chamren and the First Captain, Macarus. Morgan Te'Lyan whimpered next to her husband. He thought Eshlyn had been against his going, but Morgan threatened to tie him up in the abandoned building they all inhabited. And he believed her to be serious. Eliot talked her away from that action, and she now just stood there with tears in her eyes. Xander thought the sight of her crying there in the dawning light before he left more effective than if she had tried to tie him up.

It had taken most of the day yesterday for Chamren and Macarus to draft the letter to the First General at Taggart. The Steward in Biram would not give up any of his own Cityguard for Ketan, so it would have to be Taggart, although that were six or seven good days of riding away. Chamren and Macarus also had to make very calculated decisions about what seal to use and how to word the letter. Could they use the seal of the Steward? No, that was too much of a risk. But was the seal of the First Captain enough authority? Better that than nothing, and Desiderus' reputation preceded him. They should consider the request from the First Captain alone.

Xander and Joob could make Biram in two days and Taggart in another four if lucky. And Xander had always been lucky. Truth be told, Xander was terrified. He acted nervous and playful to hide the terror he felt. Not too playful, though. He didn't want to give Joob any ideas.

Eshlyn shook her head. "Maybe I should go," she said.

Xander turned to her, stealing a glance at the baby in her arms. "What?"

"Maybe I should go," she said. "I'm the one everyone is trusting to believe this 'crisis' we are in … I should take the risk."

Eliot and Morgan both spoke over one another against the idea. Xander took his sister by the shoulders. "You know that is maddy," he said. "Our people look to you as a leader here in the city. They take comfort from you somehow, along with Da. And who is going to take care of Javyn when you go? Or you gonna take him with you? After telling me how dangerous it is? You, more than anyone, need to stay." Xander grinned at her. "And don't worry. I can take care of myself. Remember that time Joob and I got in a fight with four of Bain's sons?" He chuckled and raised clenched hands. "I took out two men with these fists."

"And you had help, remember?" Joob said with a smirk "We breakin' showed those Me'Bako boys, to the real!"

The group ignored Joob while Xander embraced Eshlyn, and she fell against him. "I don't like this," she said.

"I need to do this," he told her. "I'll be okay."

Xander pushed her away from him as his Da and Ma both pulled him close to tell him goodbye. Chamren shook his hand, putting on a brave and comforting face. Joob was already up in the saddle on Monny, grinning.

Stepping forward, Macarus handed Xander an envelope. "Whatever you do," Macarus said. "Do not lose this." Macarus then handed him a small purse. "This should get you lodging in Biram and Taggart, along with a little extra for food if you need it. I also put in the letter a request to bring you back with them if they should come. So you should be safe once you reach Taggart." Macarus gave him a stern look. "Your sister is right. The road can be dangerous. Try to avoid people on the road as much as you can, and sleep far from the road. You understand?"

Xander nodded. "Yes. Thank you, First Captain," Xander said. He turned, took a deep breath and mounted his horse, trying not to shake in fright.

Xander Te'Lyan waved at his family as he and Joob rode off at a trot, leaving the city of Ketan and their loved ones behind as they rode east to Biram. Xander's family did not wave back. But Chamren did.

The fire burned down to orange embers that gave off plenty of heat. Aden turned, grunting and sighing as he found it difficult to sleep. Caleb and Carys slept on the far side of the camp. Reyan was close to him but facing away. Aden whispered across the mitre over to him.

"Reyan." No answer. Aden attempted again. "Reyan."

The Prophet sniffed. "Yes?"

"Why do he have to die?"

"Who?"

"Caleb," Aden murmured. "Why do he have to die?"

Reyan was still for long enough that Aden thought he might have gone back to sleep. But the old man rolled to his back. Aden could see yellow and red reflections in his eyes.

"A sword is a tool of violence. In the right hands, it can win battles, protect the innocent, punish the oppressor, and even win freedom." Reyan swallowed hard. "But it cannot maintain it. You cannot rule by the sword. That way leads to more bondage and tyranny. The sword must be set aside for peace to reign under the heart of El. That is the way that all will be free."

"I don't understand. Why does that mean he has t'die?"

"Like I said before, the meaning of the prophecy is unclear. But the *Brendel* is a man of war. For humanity to be free, for all races to be free, we will need a man of peace."

"He can't be both?"

The old man hesitated, closing his eyes. "It is difficult for man to change once he begins on a path."

"But not impossible."

"With El's help, nothing is impossible, but … very difficult. It would be like a death to change that path."

Aden rose onto his elbow. "Maybe that's what the prophecy means," he said. "Maybe Caleb dies as the man of war and can then become the man of peace. Maybe he can change."

"Maybe." Reyan didn't sound very convinced, however. The old man turned over again, away from Aden, who barely heard the next words. "That would be his greatest victory."

The town was empty.

It was a much larger town than the last few, but it was empty of humans.

Thoros stood in the middle of the widest street in the town, and he could feel the confusion of the demics in the area. Where were the humans? They found several herds of sheep, cattle, pigs, even some horses, enough to feed them for a day or two … but no humans.

Thoros knew now that someone had escaped and warned this place, and they had fled. It didn't matter. They would run to somewhere, and if they ran north, he would catch up to them. The Key was all that mattered, anyway. The Key and the blood of a *Sohan-el*. It was close, a pulse in his mind, drawing him stronger than ever. The Demilord gripped the unforged sword in his claw, baring his teeth and ready to destroy all that the living had built with the very weapon the Creator gave to protect it.

He would give the demics time here to feed. Then they would move on. Soon.

———

Eshlyn dreamed again that night.

Part of the nightmare was the same: Kenric trapped within a deep cavern, in pain, crying out to her behind a black prison. He reached out from the cell to hold a sword, his face a sneer, focused. The evil figure held him there, torturing him somehow. But beyond Kenric, she could sense other voices, other people, also ensnared by the darkness. They cried out to her, as well. It was dark, and she couldn't see their faces but thought she knew them, too. Ken's face was washed pale by the light of the sword he held. Was it the same sword? He still bared his teeth, but his eyes glanced at her, pleading with her, then back at the sword.

"I don't understand," she said to him.

I'm fighting, Esh, she heard him say, although his lips didn't move. He was in so much pain. *I'm fighting him as much as I know how. But he's on his way. He's coming.*

She stretched out her hand to the people in the dark. She saw another person in the prison, a shadow, move next to Kenric. The shadow looked like a man, burning and suffering, too. He reached through the bars and grasped the sword, helping Kenric keep his grip.

We're fighting, Kenric said. *We'll do all we can.*

The evil figure appeared before her, and her vision was filled with black eyes.

She awoke saying Kenric's name.

Chapter 23

Biram

"We gonna get shoggin' drunk in Biram?" Joob asked as they passed a small farm on their left.

The road to Biram led straight east for half a day along the River Rumer before winding southeast to hug a great lake. They had camped a hundred mitres from the road, south, last night, and Xander couldn't say how much sleep he had acquired. He kept seeing things in the trees around him, hearing noises. They decided against a fire, which meant he also chilled a bit as the three moons hovered above. Xander camped before, had been camping for days leading up to Ketan, so he lectured himself about the silliness of his nerves. It didn't help. Something changed when they camped under the ominous walls of Ketan; his heart had sobered in a way it never had before, so his mind raced through the night, and he slipped in and out of slumber. Esh and Macarus' talk of bandits on the road didn't improve his mood, either.

Joob had snored from bedding down 'til an hour after dawn, when he jumped up awake and refreshed.

Xander was proud of his sister, and he loved her. She was smart and beautiful and good.

She had also been a tough shadow to dodge. Xander could never compete with her greatness and character. Even as much as people talked behind her back and thought her condescending, they respected her, regarded her highly. So Xander had always been the fun one, the mischievous little brother that made the adults in town roll their eyes with a knowing smirk. And he watched his sister shine.

He bore no resentment toward her, wished her the greatest happiness, but he knew his father missed her input in the business when she moved south to live with Kenric. Xander could do the computations and run the store, but he would never be the negotiator she had been. But that would have been his life, a good and comfortable life worthy of contentment but lacking adventure.

Until now. Eshlyn had her part to play in all of this, and he didn't begrudge her that. But he had to find his own, as well, not just for adventure but a way to show he wasn't the silly boy with a good heart that everyone believed him to be. Here in the midst of this crisis, he knew he would have his time to shine, as well.

The midmorning sun was hot, and Xander's tunic was soaked through with sweat in several places. Joob perspired even more than

Xander did but didn't seem near as uncomfortable. The air was humid coming off of the lake to their left, but the breeze blew cool.

"I don't know if we'll have time for that when we get there," Xander answered. "We'll have to get up early and get on the road again, try to make Taggart fast."

"Ah," Joob groaned. "We didn't bring any ale with us, so I'll need a mug or two once we get to Biram. Sure to be a tavern or two in that crit-hole."

When Joob said "a mug or two," he meant fifteen or twenty, or until he could hardly stand, or until a woman stopped rejecting his crude advances. Xander had stopped trying to keep up with his friend in their teens. Joob could have a night like that and wake up ready to take on Eres. Xander's head would feel like it was up a cow's arse for at least half the next day. Xander frowned at his friend, but he knew that Joob would find a place to have his ale ... and be ready to wrestle a crizzard the next day.

Joob eyed Xander sideways and frowned back at him. "What wrong with you?" he asked.

Xander scoffed. "Not sure," he said. "I just know this is important, and I need to know you understand that."

"You think I'm some grut-monkey?" Joob said. "Like I don't know what it means to go to the elven army and try to get them to help?" Joob snorted. "You always be the smart one, we know that. You read books and crit like that. But break it all, Xan, I'm no fool." He shrugged. "I know I act it sometimes, but I never really hurt no one, did I?"

Xander smiled at his friend. "I'm sorry," he said. "You're right. I'm just ... thinking about Kenric and Eshlyn and everyone else. For the first time, Joob, I'm ... worried. I don't know, but I had to do something."

"Why the shog you think I'm here?" Joob said. "I couldn't take sitting on my arse one more moment, either." Joob grunted as he shifted in his saddle. "You don't have to worry, Xan. We've been through crit together. Nothing as big as this, I knowin', but we'll get through this, too."

Xander laughed at his friend. "I'm glad you're here," he said. "And you're right. We'll be okay." Then he scowled at Joob, pointing over at him. "But remember, when we get to Taggart, I do all the talking."

Joob laughed. Xander didn't.

Aden peered out over the large body of water on his right as they rode towards Biram, a large town between two lakes, one to the east and the other to the west.

After the tragic destruction at Acar, Biram had grown as the major town before the great city of Ketan. Farms stretched to the south, and fishing came from the river and the lakes to the north. A road south also began in Biram, a road that stretched through the plains of Manahem and wove around the outskirts of the forest of Saten to lead into the lands of Lior and Veradis. Few took that crossroad anymore past the farms on the plains.

Soon Aden could see the buildings of the town rise in the distance. The whole group noticed, as well, and while they remained silent, everyone sat a little straighter in the saddle. They would find friends in Biram and sleep under a roof for the first time since Anneton. That name brought with it unpleasant memories, but the evening of sleep on a real mattress haunted his thoughts in a different way.

Thinking of Anneton was appropriate, since the town of Biram laid along the road much the same. Although it extended farther to the south along the crossroad, the road west through Biram led through a large central field that was used for gatherings, celebrations, markets, and the executions, which Reyan said were quite rare in the western areas of Manahem. An inn and the administration buildings surrounded the central field. They rode through the center of town, however, and continued through the main road to take a side street to their right that led to a smaller inn on the bank of the River Rumer. The sign above the door of the inn said, *The Crying Eagle*, and they arrived there just before dinner that evening.

A young tall man with pocked face came around the side of the inn as he heard travelers arrive, but his eyes bulged when he saw the old man climbing down from Ingrid's saddle.

"Master Reyan!" the man said, freezing at the sight, then took them all in with a quick stare. "Sir! Let me help you!" He rushed to Reyan's side to take the saddlebags and other things from the back of the horse.

"Thank you, Seckon," Reyan said as the rest of the group dismounted and gathered their things.

Aden watched as Reyan made introductions, the young man bowing and shaking everyone's hand.

Seckon bowed again to all of them. "Let me take the horses now. You go in and see Master Re'Syz. He'll be all the pleased to see you."

Reyan smiled at Seckon. "Thank you," he said. "Join us for dinner, if you would."

Seckon smiled as he walked back around the inn to the stables with the horses. "Oh, I will, I will," Seckon said.

Aden carried Reyan's things along with his own, and Reyan led them through the door into *The Crying Eagle*.

The common room was spacious enough with several tables and chairs, although the room was empty now but for a short, thin woman behind the counter against the far wall. The aroma of mutton and baked bread filled the room from the kitchens. Aden's mouth watered at the thought of a hot meal around a table.

"Oh, good and mighty El!" the young woman exclaimed from behind the counter, raising her arms above her head, one of them holding a white towel. "Reyan!" She hurried around the counter and embraced the old man.

Reyan grimaced at the embrace. "Hello, Myrla," he said. "Good to see you."

Myrla stepped back and hollered over her shoulder. "Da! Come out here!"

A short, wiry older man with a pug nose came from the kitchens, wearing an apron and wiping his hands with a towel. His eyes also widened. "Well, I'll be a son of a grider," he said. "Long time, my friend." The man came around the counter, as well, and shook Reyan's hand.

"Good to see you, old friend," Reyan said to Drew. Reyan turned and extended his hand to the rest of the group that had entered the inn. "Drew, do you remember Caleb and Carys?"

"Caleb?" Drew said. "We thought you were dead."

"No," Caleb said. "Not yet."

Aden smiled as Reyan pointed at him. "And this is a good friend and companion, Aden."

"Ah, well met," Drew said to Aden.

Aden took Drew's hand and shook it. Reyan had told them on the road earlier today that *The Crying Eagle* was one of his regular stops as he traveled the lands of men. Drew and his daughter Myrla were kind people, running a fine little inn, but they also believed in El and always gave Reyan and any companions with him a place to stay and a nice meal, or whatever else was needed. Drew and Myrla met with a handful of other believers, in secret, here at the inn when they could. Seckon, who worked at the inn, also believed in El and hoped in the redemption of men.

"What brings you to Biram?" Myrla asked.

"Oh, don't bother him with that now," Drew chided. "They've just arrived."

"It is all right," Reyan said. He turned to the young woman. "We are here in Biram for many reasons, which we will tell you at length after we go to our rooms for a moment. Then we can all sit together and have a fine dinner. I smell your father's mutton and bread, and it makes me hungry."

She smiled back at him. "You are welcome to it. It is always a blessing to have the Prophet at *The Crying Eagle*."

———

Caleb put his things away upstairs and then returned to sat with Drew, talking, while the others came down to the common room for dinner later that evening. A few tables were pushed together, and Myrla and Seckon set out plates of food and mugs of ale. Carys smiled and sat next to Caleb, her hair brushed and hanging loose around her cleaned face.

As the sun set, they ate, and Seckon started a fire in the hearth behind Aden. The conversation turned to what they were doing in Biram and their journey. Caleb showed them his tattoo, told them a shortened version of his quest to the Living Stone.

The room hushed. "So, you're the one, the *Brendel*." Drew said, a mix of awe and sadness in his voice. "The blade of El to drive into the heart of the enemies of truth." Drew took in a long breath, blinking. "We are to see the living hope again."

"We are also here to possibly meet Earon," Caleb said, moving past the comment. Reyan sat, his face without expression. "We will need your help buying another horse, and beg upon your hospitality for a few days to see if Earon will meet us here," Caleb continued. "I have plenty of coin."

Drew frowned at him. "Keep your coin. No good here," he said.

"Please allow us to give you something for your trouble," Caleb said. "The food is excellent. That alone is worth several golden suns!"

"No trouble," Myrla said. "We would be lost and possibly hyped up on Sorcos without the Prophet and his words of encouragement. We owe him so much more than we could pay."

"That is kind," Reyan said, looking down.

"At least money to buy the horse, then," Caleb said. "On that, I insist."

Drew grinned at him. "Very well," he said. "For the horse."

Caleb nodded. "Thank you."

Drew squinted at Caleb. The air was warm from the fire, and between the ale and the full belly, Aden's eyelids were heavy. "So you're going for the unforged sword, to the real," Drew said. "Up mount Elarus." The room grew quiet again except for the crackling of the flames at the hearth.

"Yes," Caleb said, meeting the man's gaze. "A true *Sohan-el* must have one, and the *Brendel* must bring back the *Sohan-el* to the world."

"Of course, I'm sure you're right, but how do you know this supernatural rock is there?" Drew asked. "Much less a supernatural sword? No one has seen an unforged sword in ... centuries. Elves don't go there. They say it is death to do so."

"I am not an elf," Caleb said.

"And for that, I am glad," Drew said. "But how do you know that you will find what you seek?"

"You don't believe it is there?" Aden asked. "Like the Ydu says?"

"I believe the Ydu," Drew said, taking a sip of ale. "But it has been so long since those days. How do we know that it still exists? Or even if it ever did? What did they really mean when they wrote it? Maybe it is symbolic and not meant to be taken so literally."

Caleb leaned back in his chair, the wood creaking at his weight. "I guess I will find out one way or the other," Caleb said.

"You must forgive me," Drew said, leaning forward. "I do not mean to doubt or insult, but if it is time to rally men to the truth, more than the Prophet already has, do you need the unforged sword be a *Sohan-el*? You say you have money. Have a great sword made for yourself and begin to lead. Men would flock to you, I think. It seems a great risk to the future to place your life in the hands of something that might be only a symbol of what used to be. You risk not just yourself, but the future of what could be." He sighed. "It is difficult to follow a dead man."

"My master in Kohinoor believed that the old *Sohan-el* went somewhere to get powerful swords," Caleb said. "Galen remembers King Judai and a few before him."

"But he has never been there," Drew said. "And we are to trust an elf? How do we know he isn't trying to just make a fool of you?"

Myrla laid her hand on his arm. "Da ..."

"I'm sorry," Drew said. "The ale loosens tongues and I have so many questions."

"Galen is an elf," Caleb said, and Aden noticed the dangerous tone in his voice. The man hadn't moved, but he seemed like an animal ready to pounce. Caleb's gray eyes also narrowed. "But I have trusted him with my life. His life is also at stake. He would not knowingly lead me astray or to make look a fool. He is an elf with honor. They do exist." Caleb sat up straight. "You'll just have to trust me."

"And we will all together have to trust El," Reyan said.

"Yes, of course," Myrla said.

"Then that is what we shall do," Drew said. "Together."

Caleb nodded at the man, relaxing. "Yes. Together."

—✦—

The dinner soon ended, and everyone helped to clear the tables and clean the common room and the dinnerware. Seckon and the girls finished up the last bit, and Caleb followed Reyan up the stairs. As Reyan retired to his room, Caleb followed him inside and closed the door behind him.

Reyan sat on his bed and said, "Yes?"

Caleb stared at his boots. "Do you agree with him?"

"With who?"

"With Drew," Caleb said.

"Ah," Reyan said. "What do you think?"

"I know what I think," Caleb growled. Sometimes Reyan could be so infuriating. "That's why I asked you. Do you think I'm being too reckless again? Do you think I shouldn't go get an unforged sword? What if Drew is right? What if there's nothing there?"

"What do you believe is there?" Reyan asked.

Caleb took a deep breath. "I don't know what is there," he said. "But I know I have to go and see. I have to see what is there, if anything."

"Because you believe that the *Ebenelif* is real," Reyan stated.

Caleb nodded. "Yes," he said. "I do."

"Then you must go," Reyan said. "El has his hand in all that you've done, even when you've been reckless. If you hadn't tried to get me from the Pyts, then Aden wouldn't be here among us now. He has a part in this, Caleb. You do see that."

"I know you see that," Caleb said. "Not sure I see it like you do."

"Doesn't matter," Reyan said. "Aden has his own path. But don't let anyone stop you from climbing that mountain and finding the Living Stone. Not anyone. Not Drew. Not me." Reyan held Caleb's eyes. "Not even you."

"You think I will find it?"

Reyan mused for a moment, staring down at the floor. "When Galen offered you the chance to be trained as a Bladeguard, you told me you agreed for revenge. Which is it now? Faith or vengence?"

Leaning against the doorway, Caleb crossed his arms. What was it now? His faith in his father's beloved oracle? Or his anger at the elves that took his parents from him, the opportunity to bring violence against the Kryan Empire?

He sniffed. "Hard to say. Both."

Reyan nodded. "It's alright. To want revenge is natural, but it will destroy you in the end if that remains your motivation. Faith is good. To have faith is to be more than human, however. And we all need to continue working on that, I feel." The Prophet met his eyes. "There is something beyond faith, though."

Caleb's eyes narrowed.

The old man sat up straight. "I believe the *Ebenelif* is there, and I believe that it tests the hearts of all who touch it. What you find there will determine if you are the *Brendel*, and then we'll see if it is the time for men to rise and learn how to be like Yosu again."

Caleb scratched at his beard. "Not easy to know some things, is it?"

Reyan grinned at Caleb. "Some things, no, you have to live before you know." Tears filled the old man's eyes as he looked at Caleb with pride. "Some things we know no matter what happens. Remember that, Caleb."

Caleb frowned, falling silent, his head lowering in thought and doubt.

"Okay," Caleb said. "Good night, Reyan."

"Good night, son," Reyan whispered as Caleb left to go to his own room.

Chapter 24

The Crying Eagle

Xander and Joob rode into the outskirts of Biram late in the afternoon. The town was huge, as large as Roseborough or bigger, big enough for its own Cityguard and Steward.

He led them to a path on their left towards the river just inside of Biram.

"We not going to the big inn in town?" Joob asked.

Xander shook his head. "No," he said. "My Da suggested this inn on the west side. The something 'Eagle,' I think."

Joob frowned at him. "They better have ale," he said. "And food. I need somethin' more than that jerky and dried fruit from the scrip."

"I'm sure it has ale and food," Xander said. "What inn doesn't?"

"I dunno," Joob said as they neared the river.

Xander could see the sign hanging outside the building. *The Crying Eagle*. That's right, Xander thought.

"I never been to Biram before." Joob lifted a leg in his saddle and scratched his groin. "They could only serve tea and prinkets here."

Xander chuckled as he pulled Yaysay to a stop. They both dismounted, hitching their horses to a post just in front of the inn, grabbed their saddlebags, and entered the inn.

The common room was spacious and warm. It felt comfortable to Xander from the start, and he knew he made the right choice coming here. A young woman with curly dark hair approached them from behind the counter. "Welcome," she said.

Xander caught Joob leering at her, and he elbowed his friend.

"Hey ..." Joob said.

"Thank you," Xander said. "How much for a room? And a warm meal if we could?"

"And ale," Joob said. "Don't forget the ale."

"No problem," she said. "But I'm sorry, we have one room available. You'll have to share, if that's okay."

Joob said, "Nope," just as Xander said, "That would be fine." Joob cursed.

The young woman smirked at them. "Ten coppers for the room, and three each for the meals"

Xander sighed. They could afford that. "To the fine," he said.

"Well, good then," she said. A tall young man made it into the common room from the kitchens. "Do you gentlemen have horses?"

"Yes, ma'am," Xander said.

"Seckon, get their horses," she said over her shoulder. The tall man bowed and hurried past them and outside. "My name is Myrla. Welcome to *The Crying Eagle*."

———

Aden read while he waited for Caleb and Reyan to return from their errand to buy another horse, and then he and Caleb went to the small yard between the inn and the stables to continue his lessons with the sword. They were secluded, surrounded by a high fence.

After almost two hours of exhausting work that felt good to Aden's rested muscles, Myrla came out to the yard and informed them that supper was ready. Caleb gave Aden the short wooden weapons from Asya to Aden and picked up the staff resting against the outside wall of the inn as they entered through the back door through the kitchens. Drew stood in the kitchen and told them they couldn't bring the sword into the common room – they had new guests this afternoon – so Aden left the sword just inside the door to the kitchen.

Aden and Caleb sat with Reyan and Carys towards the back corner of the common room where they were served warm sliced pork, more of the bread from last night, and carrots and fresh apples. They had mugs of ale and water.

Two men came downstairs from the rooms above. They were both young, not much older than Aden. One man was tall with dark hair, the other shorter but stouter with a wide brimmed black hat. They sat close to Aden and the others at a separate table, and as they were served their dinner, the stouter gentleman shouted, "Where's the breakin' ale?"

Aden's back was turned to the men, and as he met Reyan's amused stare, he felt it safe to roll his eyes.

———

Xander wanted to get under the table and hide.

The food was amazing, although Xander wasn't sure how much of that had to do with their days on the road and meager, dry provisions; the proprietors were kind. The daughter, Myrla, was pretty enough. Joob had decided that she would be his target for the evening, so as he drank his ale, his overtures to her became louder and more pointed.

The people in the corner close by kept to themselves. Joob made some sort of snide comment about the blond woman in pants that Xander hoped wouldn't begin a fight.

Xander reached over the table and grabbed Joob's arm. "Listen," he said, trying to keep his voice down. "I think we've had enough."

"You mean you think *I've* had enough," Joob's voice boomed in the room.

"Yes, we all think you've had enough," Xander said. "Let's go back to our room and leave these people in peace."

"When did you become such an apron-kisser?" Joob said. "Break it, man, I'm just trying to have a little fun." He leaned in close to Xander as if to tell a secret, but the ale had broken whatever volume control the man did have. His whisper could probably be heard in the stables. "Look, I know we got people counting on us back in Ketan," he said. "And I know this is serious, to the real. But I can have fun tonight, right?" His glassy eyes pleaded with Xander.

Xander shook his head. "Shut up," he said. "Just shut up." He grabbed Joob's wrist tighter.

Joob glowered at Xander as he pulled his arm from his grip. "Look," he said, standing now in the common room and he pointed to Myrla. "We gonna be leavin' tomorrow, right?" Joob's words slurred as he tried in vain again to speak in a hushed tone. The bearded man with gray eyes stood. Slowly. And grabbed the long walking stick near him. "We can tell her that we're goin' for help to Taggart, that towns to the south're dyin' left and right from some crittin' evil monsters and we might need help from Taggart..."

Xander leapt up, knocking over his chair, grabbed Joob by the shoulders and screamed, "Shoggin' shut up!" Joob's eyes widened and his hat fell over his eyes. Joob was drunk, but not drunk enough yet. Xander thought he might have to punch his friend unconscious to get the man to stop.

A voice spoke to Xander's right, the young man who had his back turned to them spun in his chair. He had a beak of a nose and dark bushy hair. "Wait a minute," the young man said. "What did you say?"

Terrified, his heart beating out of his chest, Aden stood to face the two strangers. Carys and Reyan rose to their feet, as well.

"Nothing," the sober man said, his eyes full of fear. "He's drunk. Just rambling like a crit-suckin' maddy." The drunk man pushed his hat back on his head and blushed redder than he already was.

Aden looked over at his friends. They stood ready for some sort of action, but their main concern seemed to be protecting their own secrets and the Re'Syz family from this stupid drunk. Carys had the two wooden weighted poles in her hands as she stood. But that stupid drunk had said something that triggered Aden's brain. Something important was happening.

He turned back to the two strangers. The stout man looked at his friend apologetically as Drew and Myrla came out from the kitchens to see the commotion. The sober stranger turned his friend to start up the stairs with a shove. "I'm sorry," he said, and the drunk one mumbled something Aden couldn't hear.

"No," Aden said. "Wait." He turned to his friends for help, but they all regarded him with confusion. The two strangers continued to walk towards the stairs. Aden darted around them and stood in their way, his hands pressing on the stout man's chest. "No! Wait."

The stout man stopped and swayed, frowning. The sober one looked angry and ready to push past Aden.

Aden looked up into the drunk man's face. "What towns?" he asked. "Where?"

"Huh?" the drunk man said.

"Joob ..." the sober one warned.

Aden looked over the Joob's shoulder and met the sober one's eyes. "It's okay," he said. "We won't get you in trouble. You can trust me." Then he caught the drunk man's face with his stare. Joob tried to avoid it but couldn't. "Please. Tell me. What towns're in trouble? And where?"

Joob turned a greenish color and shook his head. "I sorry," he said. "I –"

"Please," Aden said. "What towns? Where?"

The sober man sighed. He answered for Joob. "It began in Campton," he said. "My sister is from there. Something ... attacked the town. Her husband told her to run to Ketan and get in the safety of the city."

Aden turned to Reyan. "Where's Campton?"

Reyan's eyes tightened. "The town farthest south on the Manahem road," he said. "Just north of the Kaleti Mountains."

Aden faced the strangers again. "What attacked the town?" he asked.

The sober man stood next to his friend. "We don't know. My sister didn't see them. Her husband went to fight them. But she heard ... screams. People dying. Horrible sounds, she said."

Aden lowered his hands from Joob's chest, and the man stumbled. Aden spoke to Reyan. "The mountains of Kaleti."

"So?" Reyan said.

"I read about it today," Aden said. "And you spoke 'bout it in the forest with the Ghosts!" Caleb and Carys viewed him with threats in their gaze.

"What, Aden?" Reyan asked. "What are you talking about?"

"The demics," Aden said. He took a breath. "*Yosu exiled Bana Sahat and his army of demics to languish in the Underland, but he wrote upon the Dark Gate in the mountains a command, that every 527 years, the three moons would align and release the evil of one Demilord and his minions upon the world. The Sohan-el and the world of men hold the duty of protecting the Key to the Underland and destroying that evil."*

"Shog a goat," Caleb muttered. "That's breakin' word for word ..."

"Great and mighty El," Reyan breathed. "You don't really think ..."

"Wait," the sober stranger said. "What are you talking about?"

Aden faced him. "I read about it today. Back when Yosu firs' came to Eres, the demics're a menace upon the world. Bana Sahat created these twisted creatures, and they were destroying th'world, killing men and elves and dwarves'n anything tha' moved. Yosu came and trained the *Sohan-el* to fight th'demics and he imprison them in the Underland."

"And Yosu placed a gate upon the Underland that would open every five hundred and twenty seven years," Reyan said, his eyes distant. "In the Kaleti Mountains. Has it been that long?"

As Aden scanned Caleb and Carys, he saw they began to understand, too.

"You mean you think the demics from the Ydu have been released upon Eres?" Caleb asked.

"What d'you say they wanted, Reyan?" Aden asked. But he knew. He remembered.

"The Key, the Key that would open the gate and set them free from the prison of the Underland," Reyan said.

"Yeah," Aden said. "That's what I read t'day. Do you know where the Key is?"

Reyan shook his head as if in a daze. "No one knows for sure. But the legends say that the Kings of Manahem kept it safe behind the walls that had never been breached. In Ketan."

Carys cursed under her breath and lowered the wooden poles. Caleb sighed. "Myrla," he said. "Get us some tea. Strong tea. Drew, get our weapons." He pointed to the table in front of him, looking at the strangers. "Sit. Please. Tell us everything."

———

Aden listened as Xander took an hour to describe the events over the last two ninedays, from Xander's sister Eshlyn and how they all finally reached Ketan.

Joob entered the discussion towards the end of the hour as the tea helped him become more alert, but then he was a drunk with a great deal of energy. Xander and Joob finished their tale with their mission to go to Taggart with the official letter from the First Captain of Ketan.

"So," Xander asked when they finished. "What do you think?"

"It fits," Reyan said. "And I don't know why I didn't put it together earlier. Aden caught it before I did. Some things that shouldn't be forgotten are forgotten anyway. I think the demics are coming for the Key in Ketan."

"Okay," Caleb said. "Let's say that is true." He didn't seem so sure. "What can we do about it?"

"What d'you mean?" Aden said. "You know who you are."

Caleb glowered at Aden. "But I am still just one man," he said.

"It say that it takes a *Sohan-el* to stop a Demilord," Aden said. "That's what it say."

Xander and Joob both looked at them, lost. "Huh?"

Caleb ignored them and addressed Aden. "That is because a *Sohan-el* has an unforged sword. It takes one of those to defeat a Demilord, at least that's what I remember."

"Yes, that's right," Reyan said.

"I don't have one of those," Caleb said.

"So we leave them to fend for themselves?" Carys asked. "That doesn't seem right."

"They are already going to Taggart to get help from the elves," Caleb said. "They can still do that. An army of elves will be better than just one man."

Carys scoffed. "You're more than just one man, Caleb," she said. "You could help in more ways than you know. They have a critty Steward. They'll need leadership, tactics, all that. You don't need an unforged sword to do that."

"Can I risk exposing myself this soon?" Caleb asked. He shook his head. "I think they should move on to Taggart in the morning and do as they planned."

"That army won't get there in time," Reyan said. "Not if there really is a Demilord and a horde of demics on the way. They may be there already."

Xander grunted.

"But I can't beat a Demilord without an unforged sword," Caleb said.

"Can they beat one without you?" Aden asked.

"El will be good and help you," Reyan said.

Caleb shook his head. "This is too much too fast," he said. "It's all wrong. Don't you feel it?"

Aden cursed in frustration. "Feels right t'me," he muttered.

As Reyan began to answer, the front door of the inn burst open and six Cityguard entered in a disciplined rush and surrounded the humans. As every human in the room—nine of them—stood, three more Cityguard walked in through the kitchens. They wore gray tunics under light silver armor and each had a gladus in their hand.

Aden watched as one more elf walked through the front door, calm and confident in a long white robe cinched at the waist with golden sword belt and a long curved sword in its hilt. He had short-cropped black hair and a thin nose with beady green eyes. Those eyes scanned the room and rested on Caleb.

"Caleb," he said. "So it is you. I track down the Prophet and get a traitor, too."

"Zarek," Caleb said, grabbing his staff.

Aden had heard Caleb and Reyan both say that name before – the Bladeguard that beat Reyan at the Pyts and flogged Caleb at the Citadel.

He turned to see that Carys had her sword in her right hand along with one of the wooden poles in her left. Aden reached back to grab his own sword. Aden handed Xander, who stood next to him, the other wooden weighted pole.

A deadly silence hung in the air.

"It goes deeper than even I realized," Zarek said, and he gestured towards Reyan. "My sources said you're the one that broke him out of prison, and I was somewhat incredulous. I didn't think you had the courage … or the stupidity. And yet I've caught you. I will be quite the hero." Zarek walked forward in front of the Cityguard that surrounded them. "Galen spoke so highly of you, but I always knew you would betray the Empire, one way or another. It is the nature of humanity. And here you are."

Caleb moved forward as well, just in front of Reyan and the others, who arrayed themselves behind him. "I haven't betrayed anyone," Caleb said. "I'm fighting for what is right and true."

Zarek laughed. "Right and true? Aren't you also the one responsible for that scene in Anneton? Killing the Steward and a platoon of Cityguard while interrupting a legal execution? Yes, I believe you are. Treason." Zarek crossed his arms and laid a hand on his chin. "Let's examine your idea of 'right and true.' You've killed several elves on the way here. You broke a legal prisoner out of the Pyts, an enemy of the Empire. All you've done is prove what we already knew: that humanity is violent and corrupt and ungrateful. Full of vengeance and hate towards his betters."

Aden saw Caleb shake his head. "I'm impressed, Zarek," he said. "I thought we were safe here. How did you find us?"

"Oh, yes," Zarek said. "I used the same trick last time I found the Prophet." Zarek turned to the Cityguard closest to the door. "Bring him in." The Cityguard darted out the door into the night and brought in a young man, tall with short dark hair.

Carys gasped. "No," she groaned.

"Earon," Aden heard Reyan say with deep pain. "What have you done …"

Something snapped inside of Caleb when he saw Reyan's son walk through the door. He remembered his message to Earon in Galya, two ninedays ago, and he realized this was his mistake. Earon – a cousin and friend, like a brother – had turned against them.

Other possibilities had run through his mind as Zarek entered the room. Had Freyd betrayed them? Had Zarek gotten to Jyson and Rose? Drew, Myrla, and even Seckon were scrutinized. But none of those were guilty.

Earon had been compromised. He should have seen it from the beginning, but he had been blinded by his own love and trust for the man. Caleb's heart became cold steel within his chest.

As training took over, he observed his surroundings. Three Cityguard were blocking the way out through the kitchens. Six Cityguard stood through the center of the room and barred the front door. A Bladeguard faced him. A traitor mocked him.

Nine humans: Drew, Myrla, and Seckon were to his right, just in front of the three elves blocking the way to the kitchens. The other five humans stood shoulder to shoulder behind him. Carys was well trained. He hadn't seen her in much action yet, except for her archery skills, but she carried herself well, and Athelwulf had her in high regard. She was armed with a gladi. Aden stood next to her with a sword in his hand. He was a talented young man, but talent meant little against training. Aden gave Xander a wooden weapon, but the man was scared out of his mind. Joob was drunk.

Reyan was an old man, injured and unarmed, faced with a son who just betrayed him. He wouldn't fight well; his broken heart condemned him already.

Little more than ninedays ago, Caleb couldn't stand from injuries for more than a few minutes. He was hardly at his best now.

It would be a miracle if any of the humans survived.

Earon stepped forward, just behind Zarek. "I'm sorry, Dad," he said. "Listen, okay? Just surrender and come with us. Zarek promised he wouldn't hurt you."

"Why?" Reyan asked, despondent. "Oh, Earon. Why?"

"You're filling people's heads with lies, Dad," Earon said. "You treat those books, those breakin' books full of myths and bed tales, like they're real. You think you're fulfilling prophecy. That's delusional. The Empire is trying to help. Zarek is trying to help, but you're turning men against them. Come on. Tell everyone to put their weapons down."

Earon wouldn't even look at Caleb.

"He lied to you," Caleb said. "Zarek *lied* to you. They're here to use or kill your father. Zarek will kill every other human here. You believed his lie."

"My lies?" Zarek said. "That is interesting, Caleb. What did you do for fifteen years as you learned all that we taught you? Were you planning to betray us the whole time? After I take care of you here, Galen is next. I guarantee it."

"Oh, Earon," Carys said.

Reyan's son looked from his father to Carys.

Caleb almost pitied him. If he had felt any emotion, he would have.

"You turned him in," Caleb said. "You turned your own father in to the elves and sent him to the Pyts." Speaking to the man forced him to turn to Caleb at last.

"I did," Earon said. "You remember what it was like, all the running, all the death. All of it was for nothing. Then you disappeared. Just gone. And now I learn you've been with the elves the whole time? You have to know we can't win."

"What kind of son betrays his father?" Caleb said. "They threw him in the Pyts, beat him, and they would have killed him."

"No," Earon said, looking over at Zarek with pleading eyes. Zarek stared at Caleb, his face expressionless. They both knew where this was going. "They said they were going to talk to him, try to make him see how wrong he was, keep him from spreading more lies. Zarek said ..."

"They killed your mother!" Caleb bellowed. "They nailed her body to a shoggin' stake and set her ablaze."

"Zarek explained that the Steward went too far," Earon said. "And Zarek was on the way to make sure she wasn't hurt or executed."

"Yes," Zarek said. "How tragic the loss." Zarek's face contained a slight smirk, staring at Caleb. Caleb believed Zarek had been on the way to, but in Zarek's mind, the tragedy was that he hadn't gotten there in time to torture information out of her.

"Did they offer you money?" Caleb muttered, emotionless. "How much money is he giving you, Earon?"

Earon's countenance fell, wounded, and then he sneered at Caleb. "How dare you," he said.

"None of this matters," Zarek said. "Here is what will happen. You will surrender and come with us."

Caleb lowered his head and bared his teeth at Zarek. The elf knew Caleb wouldn't give in. Surrender meant death for them all. "No surrender."

Reyan breathed deeply behind Caleb and pushed forward to stand between Caleb and Zarek. Caleb tried to stop him, but the old man shoved him aside with a strength he didn't think the man possessed.

"Take me," Reyan said. "Only me. I'll surrender now if you let the others go."

As Zarek's eyes looked deep into Caleb's glare, an understanding passed between them. Caleb knew too much about Zarek's methods of deception and manipulation. Zarek might have gotten the Prophet alive, but for Caleb's presence.

But with Caleb here … there would be blood.

"Very well," Zarek said.

Zarek stepped forward in an instant, drew his sword, a long curved blade with an ivory handle, and plunged the weapon into Reyan's chest.

Caleb moved as fast as he could to defend the Prophet, but he couldn't stop it.

—————

Everything happened at once. Zarek produced his sword and buried it into Reyan faster than Aden had ever seen. People were yelling, screaming, crying. Caleb leapt forward, the staff spinning and striking at Zarek and the elves behind the elven Bladeguard. Carys, screaming, rushed forward with the sword and the sharpened wooden pole striking out at two elves to his left.

Aden did the one thing he could think of. He trailed Caleb, the staff causing Zarek to retreat. Within a moment, Caleb had two Cityguard shuffling back and trying to block the staff as well. Aden reacted while the Cityguard to his right had his sword up in defense. Aden stabbed the elf under the arm and up into his lungs. As he pulled the sword from behind the chest armor, blood trailed in the air, and he followed Caleb's staff across to the elf on his left. That elf blocked Caleb low and Aden swiped the sword across the elf's neck, slicing cleanly, and the elf fell back, clutching at the spurting gash across his throat.

Caleb turned around and stalked Zarek. Aden spun to his right and found another Cityguard bearing for him. Caleb was busy with a Bladeguard. Aden would have to take this one alone.

—————

Carys' eyes blurred with tears in rage and sorrow, but she used those emotions to fuel her own training. Caleb was busy with a shoggin' Bladeguard, so she ran forward to fight her way to the front door. They needed an escape, and that front door seemed the best chance, unless another platoon awaited them in the street.

She couldn't worry about that now. Ath had taught her how to use her advantage, her speed, and her athleticism. She moved in between tables, keeping the two elves that were in front of her from coordinating their attack.

Blocking the sword from the Cityguard in front of her with her own blade, she hit him in the neck with the wooden pole at the same time. She heard the impact crush his windpipe, and he fell backwards into his companion. She ducked under a desperate swing from the second elf and stabbed him in his unprotected groin. He fell, beginning to cry out, and she thrust the sword into his open mouth. His cry became a choking gurgle, and he fell, her sword spraying a trail of blood as she pulled it away from his corpse.

Scanning the room, she saw that Caleb was still engaging Zarek, and Aden still had his hands full with a Cityguard. The other three were being overwhelmed. She spied a path to the door, but they wouldn't get there if they were dead. She ran in that direction, keeping her gaze from lingering too long on Reyan, who was lying in a pool of his own blood on the floor.

＋

Drew, his daughter, and Seckon were unarmed and vulnerable as two Cityguard rushed them, their swords stabbing forward. Drew watched Seckon grab Myrla and throw her to the floor behind the table. The young man then yelled and tackled two elves, his long arms reaching to either side of him and grabbing around their necks. He knocked them backwards with his weight.

He ran forward with Seckon, but within two steps, both elves had stabbed Seckon at once, one on his left side, the other into his gut. He cried out but continued to press his body down on them. Drew heard his daughter scream, "No!"

The two elves were stuck under Seckon, who grunted and twitched in pain. Drew picked up a wooden chair with both hands as he reached the pile of elf and human. He raised the chair over his head and brought it down with all his strength upon the head of a Cityguard. Both elves tried to get their arms up, but the chair snapped the arm of the elf on the right, crashing into his forehead with a crunch. He swung the chair down again and again, crushing the skulls of the Cityguard under his dying friend.

＋

Xander tried to block the sword coming at him as he backpedaled, knocking over a table, but the Cityguard's sword cracked the wood. Xander grabbed a table and threw it over at the Cityguard, who tripped over it, grunting, and fell forward. Xander used the cracked pole to bring it down on the elf's unprotected back. The wooden pole splintered as the elf tried to rise awkwardly from atop the skewed table. Desperate, Xander fell on top of the elf and grabbed his sword hand. He was stronger than the elf by a fair margin; so though the elf scrambled to get his sword back, Xander held him in the vise of his grip.

—

Carys saw Joob, drunk as he was, able to grab the sword being thrust at him and twist it away from being plunged into his abdomen, but the sword still swiped across his chest, opening a deep gash there. Carys approached from behind the Cityguard elf and drove her own sword through the back of the elf. He fell a heartbeat after Joob.

She didn't have time to look after Joob, however, since Xander wrestled with another Cityguard on the floor. She ran, jumped, and flipped over a table and sent a knee down into the side of that elf, breaking ribs with an audible crunch. Then she rolled off and spun, stabbing the elf in the same side, silencing his wheezing breath. She twisted the sword before pulling it free.

—

Backing up as the Cityguard kept striking, thrusting, Aden was barely able to defend himself. Within moments, he was at the counter, his back hitting the hard surface and he groaned as he ducked under another swipe. He rolled and twisted on the floor, coming up on his feet and swinging the sword back at the Cityguard, surprising the elf, but he blocked Aden's strike.

From his left side, someone hurled a chair at the elf, and as Aden and the elf both ducked, the chair still bounced off of the Cityguard's back. Aden took advantage of the situation and stabbed the elf in the neck, killing him instantly.

Aden turned, wide-eyed, the blood of elves covering his face and tunic, to see who had thrown the chair. Reyan's son, Earon, stood there, breath coming in heaves, his own face a wide-eyed banner of anguish and terror.

—

Caleb and Zarek faced each other, blade and staff meeting time and again in a barrage of strikes and blocks. They were evenly matched. Caleb thought Zarek might even get the better of him in this fight. Zarek realized the same thing, if his satisfied smirk were any indication.

The Kingstaff turned thrust after thrust, and both elf and human kept their stance and movements fluid, back and forth, forward and back. The tables and chairs of the common room made things interesting, but Zarek's forms flew fast enough to keep Caleb on the defensive and unable to counter with any efficiency.

Caleb rolled over a table as Zarek's sword slashed down, hitting the table instead of Caleb's flesh. He tried a swing at Zarek's head, but the elven Bladeguard ducked it with ease, and Caleb had to use all his speed to bring the staff around for a block, which barely deflected the blade, and it sliced across his ribs.

Cursing, he gritted his teeth and spun, blocking two more short stabs with the staff. Zarek lashed out with his left leg in a kick. Caleb tucked his elbow and absorbed it, leaning into it, and Zarek followed with a slash towards Caleb's neck. He lowered his head and rammed into the elf, his greater size knocking him on his heels. Caleb tried to grab Zarek's robe, but he twisted, escaping and slicing down with his sword. Caleb brought the staff around and deflected the blade, using his momentum to carry him further into a turn and strike with the staff. Zarek stopped the staff with the flat of his blade with minimal effort, then raised the sword overhead for a killing blow.

Duels were like a dance, Galen had told him, and the longer the dance went, the more the expert and the master would be revealed. With two masters, it didn't come down to who was better, but who didn't make a mistake. One hesitation, one slight flaw, and the other master would take advantage and end the fight with extreme prejudice. These dances were often two masters waiting for the other to make such an error.

Zarek brought his sword down upon Caleb's head, forcing Caleb to bring the wooden staff up for a direct block. Zarek didn't know the staff was stronger than steel, and he assumed his elven sword would cut clean through.

He was wrong.

Zarek's blade bounced off the Kingstaff, and Zarek hesitated. Barely noticeable to anyone else, but to another master, the hesitation was all Caleb needed. Zarek was exposed to a forward kick that Caleb delivered with pinpoint accuracy into the elf's stomach. Zarek's eyes widened as he flew backward, the breath leaving his body, and Caleb brought the staff around, spinning, and down upon Zarek's forearms, snapping both limbs.

The Bladeguard dropped the sword, which clattered to the ground, and knelt on the floor gasping for breath, his arms dangling in front of him useless. Zarek choked back a breath, and he looked up, trying to speak. "Well," he coughed. "You seem to have me ..."

He never finished the thought. In an instant, Caleb thought of his parents, Aunt Kendra, executed by the Empire, and Reyan, betrayed by his own son and murdered. He relived losing Danelle, the scars on his back, on his soul. It all converged to create a tempestuous fury within him. Nourished by that rage, he brought the staff around and against the side of Zarek's head, snapping his neck and crushing his skull.

—

As quickly as it had begun, it was over.

Aden left Earon where he was and ran over to Reyan, lying still on the floor facedown. Carys walked to the other side of the Prophet, and they knelt down together and rolled him over. Blood covered the front of him, pouring out of him in spurts. Carys cried out and cradled his head in her chest, pressing her hand against the wound. Aden could see Xander pressing his tunic, ripped off his own body, onto a wound on Joob's chest. Joob lay there, still and pale. Beyond them, Myrla wept and embraced Seckon's dead body. Drew held his daughter's shoulders.

Looking up, Aden saw Caleb kill Zarek the Bladeguard. Caleb's eyes were cold. Then he began to walk towards them, and he noticed Earon, standing in the middle of the room.

Earon was looking at his wounded dying father. "Dad!" he cried out. His fists clenched, and he fell to his knees, bent over with racking sobs.

Caleb walked past Earon, paused in between Earon and Reyan on the floor, and turned to meet Earon's gaze. Earon looked up at him. Aden could not see Caleb's face, but whatever Earon saw there made him fall back, crawling towards the door, a look of terror on his face. And when Earon's eyes found Carys, he uttered a groan and bent over with a cry. After a moment of paralyzed weeping, Earon stood, glancing at Caleb one last time.

He spun on a heel and ran out of the door into the night.

Reyan moaned in immense torment, and that brought Aden's gaze down to the Prophet. Caleb knelt beside him now, and Aden saw in Caleb's face what he already knew. Reyan was dying. No one could survive this.

Reyan's eyes opened, and he looked around himself at the three of them. He reached out with desperate hands, flailing, and Carys grabbed one and pulled it to herself. Aden took her lead and clutched the other. Reyan's eyes were watery and afraid.

The Prophet's grip slackened, and he tried to speak, but couldn't. He couldn't catch his breath, and he groaned and moaned as Carys stroked his face as she wept and said, "No, not now," over and over again.

Reyan found Caleb with his eyes at the end, and Caleb laid a hand on the old man's chest. Reyan seemed to plead with Caleb for something. Some last message? Mercy to end the pain? They would never know.

Reyan spasmed once and then fell back, his eyes empty and looking up. With a final gasp and release of breath, the Prophet left the world of Eres and moved on to the Everworld of El.

Mochus lifted the dark sword he received from the Lord of the Underland, and he faced the Master. "We cannot win," he said to Yosu. "They are too strong!"

Yosu lowered his unforged sword and did not defend himself. "Do what you have come to do."

Mochus drove the dark sword into the heart of his Master.

Yosu gazed at Mochus and said, "This must happen so you may understand that nothing can stop the redemption El has planned for this world." And then Yosu died.

Mochus looked upon his dead Master, and he wept. He fell on the dark sword and killed himself.

The Sohan-el buried the body of Yosu in a tomb they fashioned beneath the Father Tree. They burned the body of Mochus.

The Sohan-el and other men, elves, and dwarves grieved the Master. They lost all hope. In their sorrow, however, they forgot his words. Death has no power over those that are truly free.

But they would soon be reminded.

- From the Ydu, 6th Scroll, translated into common tongue by the Prophet

Chapter 25

Aftermath

Caleb sat there on the floor with the Kingstaff across his lap, looking down at the body of the man he called uncle and Prophet. And most recently, friend. He never thought he could feel close to the man, but in the past ninedays, he had. And now it was gone.

Carys and Aden knelt next to Reyan's body. Caleb heard the weeping, the crying, and it was far away.

Maybe elves were right. Perhaps humanity was incapable of redemption and deserved control and domination to save them from themselves. Maybe man was just violent, too deceptive, and a slave to his own lusts. Perhaps Caleb was on a fool's errand. Did a race that spawned such betrayal, thievery, corruption, greed and even apathy deserve freedom? He had seen all this in the last few ninedays alone. And he lived a lifetime of those around him being sacrificed, one way or another, for a cause that seemed to have no value or hope, no reality.

All he had to do was look at his own actions, to be honest. Zarek was right. Caleb had deceived and lied to everyone for so long, it had become a part of him, something he had to protect, to maintain. How was he any better than the elves? At least they were honest about their racism. He tied up his faults into boxes of causes with neat little bows. That made him worse, hypocritical. And the love and hope he expressed, contacting a man once like a brother to join them in their redemptive agenda, ended in betrayal and the death of a great man.

What a joke. This journey and quest was meant to prove him the *Brendel*, but it had revealed his stupidity and selfishness. At least that did its job. He wouldn't blame El if the Creator just ended his life here and now. But no, it was a greater punishment to let him live knowing both his failure and the consequences. That was just. If El were truly just.

And when he killed Zarek just minutes before, he didn't hesitate, gave no mercy when he could have. Even worse, he had enjoyed it.

It had taken all his willpower not to kill Earon before the man had run from the inn. Even now he wished to strangle the life from him.

Caleb was a weapon, yes. But could he honestly claim it was for El when it was his own hate and bitterness that overpowered him?

Hopelessness threatened to overcome him, but they had to leave. Sooner or later, more elves would come.

Staring at the Prophet's body, he reached out and closed those dead, haunting eyes. Carys sat next to him, continuing to cry as she cradled Reyan's head in her hands. "Not now," she said. "Oh, Earon ..."

She had come with Caleb this far, in part, to see Earon again. Did her love for their cousin include a hope for something more intimate, as Caleb suspected?

He heard noise behind him, movement. He lifted his head and focused.

"Help, please," Xander said to the room. "I – it won't stop bleeding … I can't stop it from bleeding. I think, I think he's dying."

Caleb looked at Carys. She was quiet, her hands stroking Reyan's head, his beard.

"Carys," he said.

She didn't respond.

He reached out and put his hand on her arm. She pulled it away, glaring at him.

"That man needs your help," Caleb said.

Her nostrils flared.

"We need to get going. You know it. More elves will be here any moment. And that man needs your help. We have to get moving."

"I can't," she said.

"Yes you can."

"Leave me alone," she said. "Can't you wait one second? One moment?"

"I can't," he said. "Not right now. That man might be dying. And you're the best medic we have. We need to get moving."

She shook her head, moaning, but then rose to her feet.. She lowered Reyan's head, and Aden took it in his hands. Walking across the room, she knelt and examined Joob. "It's deep," she said. "I need my kit from upstairs."

Xander hopped up. "Where? Can I get it?"

"My backpack, in my room. Third door on the left."

Xander raced upstairs.

Caleb needed to get the rest of them up and moving. No one could stay here. He didn't know what information Zarek had given the officials here in town. He couldn't predict what Earon would do next, what he would say to whom. Perhaps he should have killed him.

He leaned down and kissed Reyan on the forehead. "I'm sorry, old man," he whispered. Then he stood, leaning on the Kingstaff. Aden looked up at him with tears streaming from his eyes.

"We have to move," Caleb addressed the room. "And quick. Drew. Do you have a wagon?"

Drew looked up at him. "I have a short wagon we use sometimes, but it's old."

Caleb nodded. "Good. Come with me. We'll saddle the horses, hitch the wagon. Aden, you grab our things from upstairs and the weapons from down here. Put them in the wagon when you're done. Myrla, you need to get some things together for you and your father, and then get some supplies. We'll need food and water, as much as you can pack fast. Carys, you tend to that man ..."

"Joob," Xander corrected.

Caleb took a breath. "Tend to that man, and then we'll put him in the wagon with the supplies. Then we are leaving."

"Where?" Aden asked.

Caleb shook his head. "I don't know, anywhere but here for now." He gave a quick nod. "Let's go." And he started walking in a straight line to the back door.

Drew stood. "Wait a minute," he said, and Caleb stopped. "What about Seckon and the Prophet?"

Caleb didn't answer right away. He pursed his lips. "What about them."

Myrla sat up. "We can't just leave them here. We need to ... to do something."

"Do what?" Caleb said. "We don't know how much time we have until more Cityguard walk through that door, but we can't waste what we do have."

"What are you?" Myrla said, her breath catching in a sob. "How can you be a man and say that?"

"I am what I need to be," he said. "We will have time to grieve, I promise. But they would want us safe, and that's what I'm doing."

"Look," Drew said, glancing from Caleb to his daughter. "You're right. We need to leave. But we can take time to bury our dead."

Caleb scanned the room. Carys shook her head and wouldn't look at him.

Aden stood with clenched fists. "I'm not going anywhere until we bury him."

Drew took a step nearer to Caleb. "I have shovels in the stables."

Caleb sighed. "Okay. You and I will start digging after we get the wagon ready. The rest of you have your jobs. We need to hurry."

—+—

Plunging the shovel into the earth in the garden behind *The Crying Eagle*, Caleb threw dirt aside to dig a grave for the Prophet, the man who had traveled the land of men, speaking truth, exhorting men to hope.

Now the prophet was dead.

And it was Caleb's fault.

He couldn't escape it. He sent the message to Earon, and Earon betrayed them, led a Bladeguard right to them.

Everything went to crit in a matter of minutes with Earon's betrayal and Reyan's death. He felt lost, blind. Who would teach men the truth of El now? Tragically, the man most capable of taking over that role was Earon. Earon, the traitor.

He took a moment to breathe, to rest on the shovel, and he looked down at the hole in the ground. He winced at the pain from the slice along his ribs. He wanted to quit, just walk away.

Quitting wasn't an option, however. Not yet. He had to get them moving and away from here. But where? Where would they be safe?

Not back the way they came. That would take them closer to Taggart, and if Zarek caught up with them, then more elves were behind him. The safest option was to travel south and back into the forest of Saten. Carys would know how to find Athelwulf or other Ghosts. They could all hide out in the forest, maybe even have a nice life there.

Of all their options, Ketan was the most dangerous. There was an army of demics from the Underworld on its way to find the Key that would unleash the rest of that dark, evil place upon the world, and a Demilord that was invincible unless one possessed an unforged sword. Caleb did not. No one did. The city retained a minimal Cityguard. That place was death.

He closed his eyes. An image emerged in his mind of Reyan on a boat, insisting that he hear the Vow once more, a look of deep satisfaction on his face. I dedicate my soul, my heart, and my life to find the Living Stone. *I will protect the innocent, free the oppressed, and spread light in dark places.* They were just words, he thought, bosaur-crit. But he knew he didn't believe they were worthless. Those words represented something real to him. In any case, what could he do against an army, a Demilord? He didn't have the sword.

He could hear his father's voice reading from the parchment translated by the Prophet. *El will wield him as a sword, a blade to cut out the heart of those who would enslave and oppress.*

Maybe he didn't need the sword. Maybe he was the sword.

If he went to Ketan, however, there would be no more hiding, not for Caleb. The revolution would either begin or man would fail.

He heard Drew speak to him. "Caleb? Did you say something? You all right? You're bleeding."

Caleb straightened, opening his eyes. "No. It's nothing. I'm fine." He began to dig again.

―+―

Aden finished gathering the bags and packs from their rooms, especially careful with the Ydu and the Fyrwrit. Then he and Xander collected the gladi strewn about the common room and piled everything in the wagon as Caleb and Drew finished digging graves in the yard.

Carys had completed her work on Joob and began working on Caleb's side, which was still bleeding. Aden and Xander helped place

Joob, unconscious, in the back of the wagon with the supplies and weapons. It was a short wagon; Joob's feet dangled off the edge.

Taking Drew with him, Caleb picked up Reyan's body gently. They carried it to the yard and placed it in a grave. Aden and Xander did the same with Seckon.

Everyone stood around the graves underneath a cloudless night sky, stars and the three moons shining down upon them. Aden scanned the group of men and women; they were quiet, their heads down.

"Someone should say somethin'," Aden said.

Myrla began to cry again, and her father put his arm around her and pulled her close.

Drew nodded and began to speak. "Seckon was like a son to me," Drew said. "He was a good man. He would have made a good husband and father. The world is a darker place without him." Myrla groaned through her sobs.

Drew's gaze moved to the dead Prophet. "Reyan was known to most as the Prophet, but he was more than that. He was the *Arendel*, the messenger of El, a leader and father to many. He gave his life to teach something good and true." He cleared his throat. "Now it is up to those he taught to carry on. Not to carry on his teachings – those did not come from him – but carry on the fight to spread the truth and message of El to any who will listen, to call on men to something … far greater. The Prophet is at peace. He is in a better place, and our call is now to make this world the better place he believed it could be."

Something swelled within Aden. Pride? It didn't fell arrogant, but resigned and diligent. He couldn't have spoken Drew's words, but it was like they came from his own heart.

"I'm going to Ketan," Caleb said. "If an army of demics really is headed there, then they need all the help they can get. And to help the men of that city, I will have to reveal myself." Caleb's head rose and he looked them all in the eye. "I will be leaving within the next hour."

He stepped forward. "I can't ask anyone to come with me. I won't. You are all free to make your own choice. Xander, it is four or five days to Taggart, if you still want to go. But if they learn you had anything to do with what happened here, your life is forfeit. It is two days to Ketan, and you have friends, family there."

"What about the help from the elves?" Xander asked.

"If this is the will of El," Caleb spat, "then it is time that men learn to fight for themselves. I will not send for an elven army. Men will rise or Eres will die."

Feet shifted in the yard. Caleb turned to Drew. "I am sorry I brought this to your home. I'm sorry you must leave. You can take the road south to the forest of Saten. Carys and Aden can go with you, show you the way to some friends. You'll be safe there."

Carys rounded on him in anger. "Break you, Caleb, I'm going with you."

Aden shook his head. "Me too." To the end, he thought.

"It's going to get worse from here," Caleb said.

"You think you're the only one wants to help?" Aden said, his face growing hot.

"And someone needs to look out for you, Cubby," Carys said, crossing her arms with a frown and glancing at the wound she bound along his side.

Drew took a deep breath and glanced down at his daughter. She closed her eyes and nodded. "The Prophet has good friends in Ketan. We'll go with you."

"Break me," Caleb said. Could he blame them? He was about to ask a whole city to take the same risks. "Very well." Caleb handed picked up the shovel from the ground and handed it to Xander. "Help Drew finish here. Aden, come with me."

Aden followed Caleb into the common room, and they picked up Zarek's body.

"What're we doin'?" Aden asked, grunting and shifting his grip on the Bladeguard's legs.

"We're dumping him in the river," Caleb said, backing his way out the door through the kitchen.

"Why?"

"Cityguard don't just disappear. Bladeguard do. For the guard, dead or missing makes no difference. But a missing Bladeguard will confuse them, unless Earon tells them what happened. Something tells me he's in as much trouble as we are, now, though. He'll run if he's smart."

After dumping the dead Bladeguard in the river, they all left *The Crying Eagle* and were on the road in less than an hour.

———

Macarus made his way into the throne room. He had met with Desiderus many times over the centuries, but this was the first time he had been summoned. Their meetings had always been official business, obligatory reports, or Macarus' own desire to have words with the Steward.

Desiderus sat on the throne, looking as pompous and opulent as always, and Unitian stood beside him. The two guard waited at attention a few steps below the throne. They saluted to their Captain.

Macarus bowed to Desiderus as he made his way up the stairs to stand before the throne. *The position, not the elf*, he had to remind himself. "Steward," he said.

"First Captain," Desiderus said, his chubby cheeks flapping a little as he spoke. "Good of you to take time out of your busy schedule and come."

His sarcasm didn't bode well for their meeting. "Odd to be summoned," he responded. "Is there something you need from me?"

"Yes," Desiderus said, his eyes narrowing. "I hear you've been helping those humans who came from outside the city."

"Only helping them get settled, ensuring their protection, and ensuring they are not a threat," Macarus said. "That is my job."

"Your job," Desiderus said. "Is to serve the Empire, and by extension, me."

"I serve the Empire," Macarus said, his eyes squinting at the Steward. "And have done so my whole life."

Desiderus scoffed at that. "I also hear that you told the guard at the gates to close them if they saw a large force approaching. Care to explain that?"

Macarus' brow furrowed. "Not sure I need to explain anything, Steward. It is standard procedure, and I was reminding the guard of their duty."

"And did you also tell them to report to you if any other humans came seeking refuge?"

"Again, standard procedure."

"I am the Steward!" Desiderus shouted. Unitian blinked, startled. "You will not allow any more humans seeking refuge through the gates."

Macarus hesitated, and one eyebrow rose. "But sir," he began.

"That is an order," Desiderus said, "from your superior. Is that clear, First Captain? No more humans seeking refuge are to be allowed within the walls of this city."

Macarus clenched his teeth. He was being manipulated, he could feel it, but what did the Steward have to gain from keeping the refugees outside the gate? Was he just being cruel?

"Yes, my lord," Macarus said. And since he couldn't bear to look at Desiderus' satisfied smirk any longer, he spun and left without being dismissed.

—◦—

Caleb warned them as they traveled that they might be followed. He was on his guard for any platoons of Cityguard coming up from behind them.

What would the authorities in Biram do? It all depended on what Zarek told them. He was notoriously secretive. He may have told them nothing, merely arrived and demanded a platoon of Cityguard, refusing to reveal why. Zarek was that arrogant. Caleb thought that the likely scenario. It would take longer to find the dead elves hidden in the stables at *The Crying Eagle* in that case, days maybe. And with Zarek's body washed far down the river, the bureaucracy of the Empire would grind in the confusion. No telling what a Bladeguard would do or where he had gone. The disappearance of Drew's family would be connected, but they would have no idea where they had gone or what direction.

If Zarek had told them where he was going and why, however ... Well, he would have to trust El and be on watch. And keep the group moving.

They traveled at a decent pace, eating on the way. Caleb wished they could ride through the night, but they had begun before dawn, and he stopped them a few hours after sunset after riding through the day. The horses needed the rest, and he could tell everyone else was road weary, too.

After everyone camped a few mitres from the road, Xander and Drew watered and fed the horses. They all ate cold rations. Caleb told them to all sleep with swords at their side.

He went up to the road and sat with his back to a tree, facing east, settling in with the Kingstaff lying across his lap. He ran his thumb along the words, To lead with compassion, justice, and strength. He placed it in the grass, away from him but within reach. It made him feel more the failure.

In his hand he held a folded parchment, a document containing the Seal of the Emperor. He was about to play every Tablet in the game, but it was necessary if men were going to learn to fight for themselves.

He heard steps in the grasses behind him, soft and small. He knew it was Carys before she sat next to him.

"What's that?" she asked, pointing to the paper in his hand.

He held it up to her. "This Letter of Regency proves that I am a Bladeguard. With this Seal, I can act in the name of the Emperor."

"Well, crit," she said.

"You need to sleep," he told his sister.

"So do you," she said.

He grunted, but he didn't argue. He just looked back east. Watching. Waiting.

"It's not your fault," he heard her say. "Don't believe that. No one blames you."

He shook his head. Sixteen years apart, and she could still read his mind. "I sent him the message. I should have known."

Carys reached up and turned his face towards her. "Listen to me," Carys said. "I do understand. We all made our choices. Reyan, me, Zarek and Earon. You can't be responsible for all of them."

"How could I have been so wrong?" he asked her. "I was so wrong."

"You were wrong for the right reasons," she said. "We were both wrong for the right reasons. We loved him, so we trusted him and never thought he would betray us. But he betrayed Reyan even before you came back. You can't save everybody, I don't care what you think or what some breakin' prophecy says. You have to let us save ourselves." She sniffed. "Better yet, let El be El. Let him do it."

He peered down again at the letter in his hand.

She searched his eyes, her own filled with tears. "You're a good man, Caleb. And I love you."

Something in him broke then; all the grief and pain he held off all day, and he began to weep. As strong as he tried to be, he couldn't stop it. His sister reached around him, pulled him close, burying her head on his shoulder, her arms around his neck. They cried together.

CHAPTER 26

HEADLESS

Byr had never been to Ketan. He had been to Roseborough once, years ago, with Kyv when they were both still single men, and they attended the festival there. He couldn't see why everyone made such a big deal of it. Besides that one trip, he had never been out of Delaton. He preferred to stay at home, work on his farm. He felt comfortable there. He knew who he was on his farm.

Standing in front of the walls of the city, he wondered who could live in such a place, so large and imposing. But his wife was here – at least that had been the plan. So he had to get inside.

Byr sat in the back of the wagon behind Kyv and Dyra with their boy, Tim, but he and the boy faced forward looking over Kyv's shoulders as the walls of Ketan loomed over them, the eastern sun high in the morning sky. The wagon stopped at the gates, and he felt like hunching over in fear at the impossibly high structures that surrounded him. How could anyone build something that big?

Cocking his eye over at the gate again, he counted the number of guard. Must be fifty, and he swallowed hard. A guard approached them, an elf that appeared to be the one in charge, and he leaned on his long spear when he reached the side of the wagon to speak to the humans.

"Where are you from?" the Cityguard asked.

An odd question to start with; Kyv traded glances with his wife and Byr before answering. "Delaton," he said.

The Cityguard's eyes hardened at that. Why was that the wrong answer? "What is your business in Ketan?" the guard asked.

"Town was attacked a few nights ago," Kyv said. "We running from some monster things comin' this way."

The guard set his green eyes upon the boy in the back and sneered at Byr like he had found a rat in his grain. "You have to move on to Biram," the guard said.

"What your Tablet?" Byr said. "My wife is in there. She from Delaton, too. They in there, right?"

The Cityguard scowled further at him. "I can't tell you that," the elf said.

"Can't tell me where my wife is?" Byr said. He was ready to jump out of the wagon and lay into this elf, Cityguard or no. Then he saw several other guard from the gate walk forward in response to Byr's outburst. He thought better of it. "She my wife, elf," he said. "She in your city, I know it."

"We are under orders," the elf answered. "You can't come in."

Kyv scoffed. "What orders? Why?" he said. "Do you know that if we're outside these walls when those things attack, we are dead? My boy is dead."

The guard tried not to look at young Tim. "I'm sorry," he said. "Orders from the Steward."

"Well, the Steward can go kiss a crizzard's arse," Byr said. "Where are we going to go?"

The Cityguard looked away. "Biram is off to the east," he said. "You could keep running that way. Might be safe."

Kyv shook his head. "These things are right behind us," he said. "We almost killed the horses getting here as fast as we did. We're dead if you leave us out here. You won't help us?"

The guard pressed his lips together before speaking. "I cannot."

"No," Kyv said. "Won't. We'll camp out here tonight, I guess. Or is that against orders?"

The Cityguard shook his head. "No. Not against any orders. You are free to camp outside the city."

Kyv sighed and turned the wagon around without a word, and Byr glowered at the elf and the other Cityguard scowling back at him from the gates.

—┼—

Eshlyn stared at Macarus intently as he stood in front of the building that housed half of Delaton. "What do you mean, he's not letting anyone else in?"

Macarus sighed. He understood her frustration. The late afternoon sun cast shadows on both of them as they stood in the street. "I'm sorry, I am," he said. "I would change it if I could. But he is pushing me, playing a game."

"Why?"

"Not sure I want to know. Perhaps to get me to disobey an official command. But he would only do that if he wanted to get rid of me."

"He can do that?"

"Yes," Macarus said. "If he can prove I went against orders, he can."

"So what happens when Xander and Joob come back?" Eshlyn asked. "That wasn't really following orders. You going to leave them out there?"

"My hope is they will return with five hundred elven militan," he said. "And we'll get them back in."

"But if he comes back alone?"

"We'll deal with that when it happens," Macarus said.

Eshlyn cursed, and he hoped he would have had better news for her. But these humans were safe, for now, and before anything major happened, he would figure out a way to get anyone else inside if there were more refugees.

"How is it here?" he asked Eshlyn. "How is everyone?"

She gave him a sideways look and a half frown. "We are comfortable. Most people are happy to have a roof over their heads. We've developed a routine that works. Mostly. But we'll run out of money for food soon. Some work would be nice so that we can feed our families … if and when it comes to that."

"I'll talk to Chamren about it," Macarus said. "See if he has any ideas."

"Thank you," Eshlyn said.

A young Cityguard came riding up, calling for the First Captain. Macarus led his horse back up the street to intercept the elf.

"Yes?" Macarus said.

Even riding the horse, the guard was out of breath. "Sir," he said. "You have to come see this."

"See what?" Macarus asked. Eshlyn walked up to stand behind him.

"Humans at the gate," he said. "A lot of them."

Eshlyn touched him on the shoulder. "I'm coming with you," she said. She turned and went back to the first floor of the abandoned building, which the Delatonians had turned into a makeshift stable. You could smell the place from outside. She hadn't even waited for an answer.

Macarus smirked. "I guess we'll both be there shortly," he told the elf. Macarus mounted and waited for a minute before Eshlyn came riding out on her horse.

The three of them rode west down the street and through the city. They turned right at the Cityguard barracks and met with the main thoroughfare. When they rode up to the gate, Macarus took in a sharp breath.

A sea of humans, wagons, and horses covered the Manahem road as far back as he could see. The head of the long caravan stopped just mitres before the gate, where several humans were arguing with Lieutenant Ryus. The officer was trying to obey orders, but with all those humans … fifty elves with spears … if there were a riot, that would be a lot of blood.

Macarus rode past the guard and dismounted behind Ryus. The guard held Eshlyn at the gate.

"What is going on?" Macarus asked Ryus.

"First Captain," Ryus sounded both relieved and anxious. "These people are from Roseborough."

Macarus' brows rose. "All of them?"

A fine looking man with nice clothes and short-cropped hair gave Macarus a slight bow. "Yes sir," he said. "My name is Mayor Crystof De'Sy. This is the whole city of Roseborough, and we are officially asking for sanctuary in the city of Ketan."

Macarus' heart sank. "I'm sorry, Mayor, but I cannot allow that today."

The Mayor was shocked. "So I am to believe your Lieutenant here when he says that the Steward has closed the gates to citizens seeking refuge?"

It pained him to do so, looking out over all these people, but he nodded. "I'm sorry to say that is true. How many people do you have here, Mayor?"

The Mayor was still processing the information that his town wasn't allowed in the city, so he took a moment. Macarus waited until the Mayor answered. "We have just over five thousand people in our city."

Five thousand, Macarus thought. Men, women, children, all left outside the walls and kept from safety. He would have to do something.

"Eshlyn!" one of the humans standing behind the Mayor shouted, and Macarus noticed a haggard and dirty fellow jumping and waving at the gate. "Esh! It's me! Byr!"

Macarus turned around to see Eshlyn peering to see who called her name. The First Captain spoke to the guard at the gate. "Let her through," he said. "Come on, let her through!"

Eshlyn dismounted, pushed past the guard, and jogged up to stand beside Macarus. The haggard fellow stood in front of the Mayor, who twisted his nose at the man. "Byr?" Eshlyn said. She looked at him like she knew him, but also with suspicion. Macarus placed his hand on his sword.

"Esh!" Byr said with joy. "So good to see you! First, let me say that we were wrong. We shoulda all listened to you. You were right. Delaton was attacked."

"It was?" Eshlyn said, her voice shaking. She leaned over and scanned the long caravan of people. "You escaped?"

"Yeah, me and Kyv and his family," Byr said.

"Who else?" Eshlyn said, her voice choked..

Byr calmed and his voice softened. "That's it, Esh," he said. "That's all."

Macarus watched as Eshlyn tried to contain her reaction. "Anyone from Pontus? Ca ... Campton?"

Byr didn't answer, but he shook his head.

Eshlyn suddenly bent over in grief. Macarus laid a hand on her to steady her, to keep her standing, and she pushed his arm away. Delaton had been her town, the town she grew up in, and she just learned half of them died. And Campton had been where she and her husband lived, and if no one had come from there, either …

She straightened, holding back sobs, tears running down her face.

"I'm sorry, Esh," Byr said. "I gotta ask about Sirah. Is she with you?"

Eshlyn narrowed her eyes at him. Macarus gripped the hilt of his sword tighter. "Yes," she said. "She's safe now."

Byr smiled and nodded, but his face reddened. "Good, good," Byr said. "Glad to hear it. Will you let her know I love her and that I'm glad to hear she's safe? Will you please, Eshlyn?"

"I'll let her know you're here, to the sure," she said in a firm voice.

"Ah," Byr said. "Thank you."

"I'm sorry to interrupt this reunion," the Mayor said, stepping up beside Byr before Macarus again. "But we have a whole city full of people out here that need food and shelter for the night. They've had a long, hard road, and we need to get inside those walls." The Mayor looked back at the people behind him. "I have five thousand and you have fifty guard. I say we're getting in that city tonight. One way or the other."

Macarus shook his head. "You don't want to do that, Mayor," he said. "I understand your desperation and your desire to protect your people, but five thousand will bottleneck at those gates when confronted with fifty trained elves armed with spears and swords. You might eventually get past us. But you will do so by walking over the dead bodies of your men, women and children. Will you lead the charge?" Macarus stepped closer to the Mayor, lowering his voice. "I require your patience."

The Mayor set his jaw and tightened his eyes. Men like this were more bravado and fear than conviction. Macarus would bet on Eshlyn in a fight over this politician any day.

As if she read his mind, Eshlyn spoke. "What changed your mind, Mr. Mayor?" she asked. "My father and I begged you to come with us days ago, and you dismissed and insulted us. Was it simply Byr's testimony?"

The Mayor turned to her. "You had no evidence, young lady," he said. "I acted as I should. Later I saw some actual evidence."

"Evidence?" Macarus asked. "What evidence?"

"Our evidence," Byr said. He turned and shouted back at the caravan. "Kyv! Bring up the bag."

A man from the front of the caravan jumped down from a wagon and ran up with a canvas back in his hands. He looked almost as ragged as Byr.

"Hey, Esh," Kyv said as he reached the head of the caravan and stood with Byr.

"Hey, Kyv," she said. "Good to see you and your family made it."

"Thanks," he said. "I'm guessin' you wanna see this." He reached into the bag and pulled out the contents.

Everyone took a step back at the sight and the stench. It was a head. A head of some creature Macarus had never seen before. He flinched but stood still. Barely. "Where did you get this?" he asked.

"I had to kill a few of them to get the family out," Kyv said. "Took this one's head with my ax, just to show people. Didn't think anyone would believe me."

Eshlyn's hands covered her mouth. "How many of those things are there?" Macarus asked.

Kyv shrugged. "I dunno," he said. "But it sounded like a big ol' herd of 'em there in town. Lots of screamin'. I could hear it. Lots."

Macarus cursed. "By the nine gods," he said. He faced the Mayor. "Listen to me, Mayor. You stay out here for now, camp as close to the gate as you can. Post a watch through the night. The plains will give you a good line of sight, and you should hear them long before you see them. If they come tonight, you tell the guard at once. At once."

The First Captain turned to Lieutenant Ryus. "Get a lookout on the top of the wall. If you see those things headed this way, you let them in."

CHAPTER 27

DIRECTIVE XVII

Thoros accessed the memories of the other Demilords before him, knowledge of places and landscape, reports of armies and kings and battle after battle.

As the demics huddled in the grasses, Thoros knew what lay before him on the road. A city – a grand city full of humans, a city older than any other in Eres, spread out against a river. Other towns nestled along the river to the east, and a large dam was to the west, a dam almost as old as the city. Beyond the city, to the north, was a wilderness of forest and cold plains before more mountains and tundra.

He didn't know the name of the city, but he could see the walls in his mind. The *Heol-caeg,* the Key, was there. He could point straight to it.

The walls were formidable, but without an army or *Sohan-el,* that wouldn't be an obstacle. Walls could be scaled.

He gripped the unforged sword in his hand, a heavy blade, but he was strong enough to wield it. The weapon transfixed him.

The memory of every Demilord's death ran through his mind, all fourteen of them slain by an unforged sword. Each Demilord was different, and their deaths came after long battles or extended campaigns or within hours of emerging from the Underland. Not one, however, had ever held an unforged sword of his own, the perfect weapon to protect against another warrior of El. He would destroy humanity and get the Key with the very weapon that was meant to protect them. Thoros smiled at the irony.

———

It was late afternoon as Caleb led his group of travelers to the gates of the city of Ketan. That morning, he told them all to wear their swords. Illegal, he knew, and bound to cause conflict of one sort or another, but they had to make a statement right away – shock and awe from the first glance. They had to remember Caleb and the humans with him as outside the norm. Caleb also had them stop and wash and dress in clean clothes, trying to erase the look of travelers under the weight of too many sleepless nights and their own crushing grief.

As they neared the city, the walls and towers visible from far away, Caleb noticed a large group of people just outside the walls. He spurred his horse to a gallop and headed to the gates themselves. Carys, Aden, and

Xander rode behind him. Drew hung back with the slower wagon that carried his daughter and the wounded Joob. People stared at them as they sprinted towards the gate, eyeing the swords. They rode up to the front of the congregation of humans, and one man stood and walked towards them. He was a man of some importance, by the look of his clothes and expensive shoes.

"Who is in charge here?" Caleb asked him.

"I am," the man said, his nose rising a bit.

"That's Mayor De'Sy," Xander said behind Caleb. "Mayor of Roseborough, just south of here."

"You are Eliot Te'Lyan's boy," the Mayor said, his face contorted in confusion. "What—"

"My name is Caleb," Caleb said to him, cutting him off. "Well met, Mayor. Why are all these people outside the walls? Why aren't they inside the city?"

The Mayor stammered for a moment. Few people, few men, ran over him like this, Caleb was sure. "The Steward of the city has ordered us out. The First Captain is trying to help us, but —"

"The Steward has ordered you to stay outside of the walls?" Caleb said. He kept his voice calm with effort. "Did you ask for sanctuary?"

"Did I …?" the Mayor scoffed, flustered. "That was the first thing I did! What kind of –"

"Very well," Caleb said. "Let's go to the gate." This was going to be easier than he thought.

"Xan!" he heard the voice cry and turned to see a very worn and weary man running to meet them. "Xan!"

"Who is that?" Caleb asked Xander.

"That is Byr," Xander said. "From Delaton, my hometown. He didn't come with us when we left. He must have left later."

"Xan," Byr said, catching his breath as he walked up to Xander's horse. His eyes widened as he saw the sword. "Where you been? I thought you were with your sister. She's inside the city …"

"He's been with me," Caleb said. "How long have you been here?" he asked Byr.

"Oh, well," Byr began. "We got here yesterday morning sometime, I say." Another man walked up, holding a canvas bag. Byr turned to the second man with the canvas bag. "Wouldn't you say, Kyv?"

"Huh? Oh, yeah, yesterday sometime," Kyv said, staring openly at the swords at the hips of Aden, Carys, and Xander. "Hey, Xan," he said, more at the sword than at Xander.

"Hey, Kyv," Xander said. "When did you leave town?"

"Your sister was right!" Byr shouted. "They attacked the town and we escaped. Just us, though. Just me and Kyv and his family."

Caleb moved his horse towards Kyv. "Who attacked?"

"Those monster men," Kyv said. His eyes brightened. "You wanna see one?"

Caleb's eyebrows rose.

Lifting a hand to his forehead, the Mayor backed away.

"Yes," Caleb said.

Kyv reached into the bag and brought out a hideous head. It was the head of a demic.

"Great and mighty El," Carys said.

Aden cursed next to him. "It's real," Aden said. "Crit on a frog, we were right."

"Right about what?" Byr asked.

"That," Caleb pointed to the head. "is a demic from the Underland."

The Mayor's eyes bulged and his jaw dropped. "You know what that is?"

"Yes, and that is why we are here," Caleb said. He looked at Kyv. "Put that back in the bag and give it to me."

Kyv hesitated, caught an encouraging cock of the head from Byr, and then complied.

Caleb placed the canvas bag in his lap and turned to his companions. "Come, let's go to the gate." Caleb again rode off at a gallop, and they were at the gate in seconds. The Cityguard had fifty armed elves there at the gates. Observing the humans with swords, the guard pointed their spears at him. One Cityguard walked up to them.

Xander spoke under his breath, telling Caleb the name of the officer.

Caleb nodded, speaking to the officer. "Lieutenant Ryus?"

The officer's face was blank, but he recognized Xander. "Yes."

"You must let these people in the gate," Caleb said.

"I can't," the elf said, his voice weary. "Under orders from ..."

"Yes, the Steward, I heard," Caleb said. "I need to speak with the First Captain. Now."

"I don't know where he is right now, but I'm sure ..." Ryus began.

"Then I suggest you find him," Caleb said and rolled up the white sleeve of his cotton shirt, showing Ryus the Bladeguard tattoo. The elf stumbled backwards. Caleb pulled the staff forward into a spin on either side of the horse and leveled it at the Lieutenant. At that signal, Carys, Aden and Xander drew their swords. "I will give you fifteen minutes before we fight our way into the city. There will be blood, I can assure you, and I'd rather not have to do that."

Ryus froze, staring at the tattoo.

"Lieutenant," Caleb said, gazing up at the setting sun. "You have just over fourteen minutes."

Caleb met the angry and fearful gapes of the Cityguard at the gate with his own confident and calm glare. For about ten minutes.

The First Captain raced up to the gate with the Lieutenant and three other humans. Two of them were related to Xander, so Caleb identified the sister and the father; the other human he couldn't place, but he was no warrior.

Dismounting, the First Captian walked up to Caleb, looking at the tattoo. Caleb made sure he saw it. "Ashinar breakit," he said.

"Xander!" the sister, Eshlyn, called from the gate, but the guard held her back. Xander stoically nodded back, acknowledging his sister without a word. Good man. Just as instructed.

"First Captain," Caleb said. "You will allow these humans full access to the city."

But the First Captain was still recovering from the sight of the tattoo. "It can't be," he said.

"I assure you it is," Caleb said. "Now let these people in the city."

"I – I can't," the First Captain said. "The Steward …"

"Yes, I keep hearing about this Steward," Caleb said. "I'll deal with him next. For now, you will let these people in."

A human giving commands to an elf was near impossible, even here in Manahem. It was unthinkable for a man to reverse the direct orders of a Steward.

It was time. He reached into his belt and pulled out a piece of parchment. "Read this."

Galen had procured a document, signed and sealed by Tanicus himself, which would prove Caleb's position as a Bladeguard. The Master had given it to Caleb the day he left from Kaltiel. Because of the nature of their work, all Bladeguard possessed one. How Galen got the Emperor to sign and seal it, he wouldn't say, but Caleb learned over the years to trust him.

The First Captain stepped forward, reached up and took the parchment, a subtle shake to his hand, almost hid well enough. He unfolded it and brought it close to his face. He read the document.. "Chamren!" he called. "Come here."

The other man got down from his saddle, and the guard parted to let him through. The First Captain gaped at Caleb while he handed Chamren the paper.

The man squeaked a curse when he read it.

"Chamren," the First Captain said. "Is that what I think it is?"

"A Letter of Regency," Chamren spoke fast. "And it names the bearer as a *human*."

"And is that the Seal of the Emperor?" the First Captain asked.

"I … uh, um, well, I believe it is, sir," Chamren said. He held the paper as if it might bite him.

The First Captain breathed deeply. "Is it…" it took some effort to finish the query, "is it authentic?"

"Yes, sir," Chamren said. "It most certainly is."

Caleb's companions did as he told them. No reaction. Nothing surprises you, he said. You expected it all to happen just as it did. Be ready for anything.

He looked to the First Captain. "Let these people into the city and take me to the Steward. And I'll take that parchment back, as well."

Chamren shuffled up to Caleb and handed him the parchment. Caleb placed it back in his belt.

It took almost a full minute for the First Captain to process it all. Caleb allowed him the time. The elven Captain turned to his Lieutenant, still at the gate with Eshlyn and her father. "Let them in," he said. "Let them all in."

The Lieutenant hesitated, but he gave a bow and obeyed.

The Mayor performed a little hop like a child before he ran back to tell people to get ready to move into the city. Enough people had heard, though, and word spread faster than he could run. The town of Roseborough bustled with noise. Some cheered.

The First Lieutenant mounted his horse. "I've been trying to see the Steward all day," he said to Caleb. "He's been … otherwise engaged."

"One way or another," Caleb said. "He'll see me. Who is that man? Chamren?"

"He is the Second Assistant to the Steward," the First Captain said.

"He comes with us," Caleb said. "As does Eshlyn and these with me." Caleb pointed to his companions. "Lead us to the Steward. What is your name, First Captain?"

"Macarus," he said.

"Lead on, Macarus," Caleb said.

Chamren shuffled back to his horse and mounted clumsily. As they neared the gate, the Cityguard parted, their spears pointed Caleb's direction. Caleb spoke to Eshlyn's father. "You are Xander's father?" he asked.

"Um, yes," the man said.

"Your name?" Caleb asked.

"Eliot, sir," he said.

"Eliot, may I trust you to take these people from Roseborough to where your people are currently staying?"

Eliot nodded. "Not sure there is enough room, but I can show them."

"Just for the night," Caleb said. "We will find better lodgings in the morning. That I promise you." Caleb turned to where the Mayor was leading the first group of people toward the gate on his horse. "Mayor," Caleb called to him above the din. The man looked his way. "I have placed Eliot in charge. You will do as he instructs or you will answer to me."

Caleb didn't wait for a response. He spoke now to Macarus. "Let's go."

Macarus acknowledged by wheeling his horse around and moving up the main street of the city of Ketan at a trot. Caleb and the others followed.

"What is the name of the Steward?" Caleb asked.

Macarus didn't look back as he answered. "Desiderus." Macarus was the single elf among seven humans. He didn't seem nervous enough, but Xander had spoken well of him. Caleb watched the elf and noticed he wore a master's blade.

Within minutes they were at the palace, and they all dismounted. Caleb took his staff and the others wore their swords scabbarded.

Macarus stopped just before the stairs up to the main doors to the palace, and he shook his head at the swords. "Those are not allowed on humans," he said. "I don't care who you are, and not in the palace with the Steward."

"Things are changing today, Macarus," Caleb said. "They are with me. Lead on, First Captain."

Xander and Eshlyn embraced behind him.

Macarus grew pensive for a moment. "Come, then," he said.

They entered the palace while the nearby Cityguard stood by in shock. Macarus motioned them to stay still.

"Have two of them come with us," Caleb told him. "Elves that you trust." Macarus did as instructed and chose two guard to follow them.

A stately elf rounded a corner, and as he beheld the group in the hallway, he dropped the papers in his hand and yelped. "Macarus. What is this?!"

"Unitian," Macarus said. "We have come to see the Steward. Please have him come to the throne room."

Unitian looked at Macarus as if he had just been informed that pigs flew on the ramparts of Ketan. "What?" Unitian said. "I've told you several times that he is not available today … *those humans have swords!*" He jumped back.

"Take us to the Steward's apartments, then," Caleb said. "I assume he is there."

"You can't go to the …" he started and shrieked. "He has a Bladeguard tattoo?" Caleb thought the elf was going to faint.

Caleb turned to Unitian, hefting the staff. "Yes," he said. "I do."

"Macarus!" the elf said. "Do something! This human …"

Caleb struck the First Assistant in the forehead with the Kingstaff. The elf fell to the floor, unconscious.

Caleb turned to Macarus. The guard had their swords out behind him. Chamren wrung his hands and hopped from foot to foot in fear. "Let's go," he said.

"You just attacked the First Assistant," Macarus said. "You cannot do that!"

"I told you," Caleb said. "Many things are changing today. Shall I find the Steward's apartments myself?"

Macarus scowled at him. He walked farther down the corridor and took a winding stairwell up. The humans and four guard followed the First Captain. The stairs were made of stone with intricately designed iron bannisters, and they wound up several floors in shadow. The lamps had not been lit yet.

The First Captain took them down another corridor with tapestries on either side, one of an overweight elf lounging on a golden couch. He stopped at a tall golden door. Macarus turned to Caleb, speaking low. "Listen," he said. "This is the Steward of Ketan, and you will respect him."

Caleb cocked his head at the First Captain and raised an eyebrow. "Do you respect him?"

Macarus did not answer.

"Now you listen," Caleb said, his voice even lower, leaning close to the elf. "I will do what I feel is necessary to save and protect this city, human and elf alike. Will I have your cooperation?"

"Just be careful," Macarus pleaded, glancing back at the guard behind him. "The way you're acting … you could start a riot. A war."

Maybe more than that, Caleb thought. "Did you not see the head of the demic?" Caleb asked, raising the canvas bag at the elf, who flinched and grimaced. He had. "We are already at war, my friend. That is why I am here. Do I have your cooperation? I would very much like it, but I do not require it."

Macarus frowned, shaking his head. "Yes," he said. "You have my cooperation. For now."

"Good," Caleb said. He opened the door to the Steward's apartments.

He distinguished the scent of incense and ale and fried pork. They walked through a receiving room, and Macarus led them to a hallway. He pointed down the corridor, lowering his eyes. A bedroom. Caleb walked into the hallway and down to the bedroom. He heard giggling and low voices from beyond the door. He opened the carved wooden door and stepped inside.

The Steward, an overweight elf similar to the one in the tapestry outside, lay on a bed with two young women and a little human boy. All of them were naked. The Steward started in surprise. Pitchers of ale and half eaten plates of food littered the room, and three large candles burned and filled the room with a strong aroma.

"Steward of Ketan," Caleb said. "My name is Caleb De'Ador." He showed the Steward his tattoo. "I am a Bladeguard of the Kryan Empire. I will wait in your receiving room for you to get dressed. We will have a discussion." Caleb eyed the humans in the room. "Get dressed and leave."

The women and the little boy scurried as the Steward remained frozen. Caleb turned and left the room, closing the door behind him and returned to receiving room with the others.

Within seconds, a half dressed boy ran past them, away from the apartments. The two women followed close behind.

Desiderus emerged from his back bedroom, dressed in a long white silk robe. His fingers were covered in jewelry. The Steward took in the humans and elves in the room, and he sneered at them all, baring his teeth. "Macarus! What is the meaning of this? Who is this –"

"Steward Desiderus," Caleb said, standing straight. "Is it true that you ordered the Cityguard to keep humans from entering the city during a time of crisis, citizens of a colony of the Empire?"

Desiderus scanned the room again, his eyes resting on Eshlyn for a moment. He turned to Macarus. "First Captain …"

Chamren leaned over and whispered into Macarus' ear. Macarus nodded that he understood. "Answer the question, Steward Desiderus." The two elven guard looked around, agitated, their swords still in their hands. Caleb's companions stood calm and still, their hands clasped in front of them, confident.

Desiderus regarded Caleb with disdain. "I don't believe you are a Bladeguard, no matter what tattoo you have," he said. "The Emperor would never …"

"Show him the letter," Chamren said.

Caleb pulled the parchment from his belt and handed it to Desiderus. The elven Steward read it and gasped. "No," he said. "It can't be."

"The Seal of the Emperor is legitimate," Macarus said.

Caleb stepped closer to the Steward. "Did you refuse sanctuary to citizens of the Empire under protection of the Emperor Tanicus?"

Desiderus crumpled the parchment in his hand and regarded Caleb with a sneer. "No one informed me of any crisis."

"That is a lie," Eshlyn said. "I was in the throne room not four days ago."

"Is this true?" Caleb said. "Did a citizen of this colony inform you of a crisis? And be careful with that parchment. Destruction of Imperial property is a crime. Here, let me take that from you." Caleb reached out and grabbed the paper.

"She came to me with some bed tale about her little town in the south," Desiderus said. "She had no evidence that there was any real threat …"

"But she did inform you," Caleb said. "And your response was to keep humans out on the fields of Manahem instead of safely in the city?"

"She had no evidence!" Desiderus said. "And I am Steward. I have the authority to do as I wish."

Caleb pulled the demic head out of the canvas bag and showed it to Desiderus, who recoiled from the sight. The two elves in the room, having not yet seen the demic head, also shrank back, covering their noses with their forearms. "Holy Ashinar!" Desiderus exclaimed. "What is that?" The elf turned green.

Ignoring the question but still extending the demic head towards Desiderus, Caleb said, "By the power vested in me by the High Evilord Tanicus, Emperor of Kryus and ruler supreme over these colonies, I hereby invoke Directive XVII. I remove you from your position as Steward over the city of Ketan." Caleb lowered the demic cranium. "In the presence of the First Captain of the Cityguard of Ketan, the Second Assistant to the Steward, and two witnesses of the Cityguard, I hereby take full authority over all the Empire's resources during this time of crisis. First Captain, do you concur?"

"Wait," the Steward said, raising the palm of his hand. "You must be Sorced. You cannot invoke Directive XVII. It does not apply."

"But it does," Chamren said. "As a Bladeguard, proven by the Letter of Regency and Seal of the Emperor, he has the right to take authority during a crisis – war, natural disaster – if it can be proven that the elf in power is not acting in the best interest of the citizens of the Empire."

The Steward glared at Chamren. "Yes, but ..."

Caleb pointed to Eshlyn. "We have just established that you were told of such a threat. You not only ignored that threat, but you ordered your First Captain to keep human refugees from entering the city."

"We have established nothing," Desiderus said. "I demand a hearing! This cannot ..."

"All I need at this point," Caleb continued, "is the witness of another major Kryan official. I believe the First Captain is such a person. First Captain, do you concur?"

"I concur," Macarus said after a pause.

"Just to be fair to you, my Lord Steward, we have two officials. Second Assistant Chamren, do you concur?" Caleb asked.

"I concur," Chamren said without hesitation.

"Then Directive XVII has been ratified. Gentlelves," Caleb addressed the guard, deep in shock, their eyes saucers and jaws slack. "Place the former Steward under arrest and place him in a cell in the prison. A cell by himself, if you please." The guard looked at each other and then appealed with their eyes to Macarus. He nodded an affirmation at them.

"No," Desiderus said. "You ... you cannot do this!"

"It is done," Caleb said.

Desiderus' face turned to a mixture of horror and anger as the two Cityguard, just minutes previously responsible for his protection and under his authority, took Desiderus' chubby arms and dragged him from the room. "No!" Desiderus said. "You can't do this!" He still yelled his protests from the hallway.

Macarus turned to face him, his lips pressed together. He had known Caleb would invoke the Directive. Caleb could see it on his face. "Desiderus has … friends down at the prison," Macarus said.

"Then replace them," Caleb said. "And place his friends in a cell next to the Steward if they give you trouble."

Macarus performed a curt bow. "Yes, sir. Is there anything else?"

"Yes," Caleb said. "How many Cityguard do you have in the city?"

"Right at five hundred," Macarus said.

Caleb grunted. The other major cities in the Kryan colonies billeted whole legions. Asya had two. More opportunity for the men of Ketan, Caleb thought. "I want half of them on that wall, watching the fields overnight. Have the rest dressed and ready for action, even when asleep. And close and bar those gates after the humans from Roseborough are through."

"Yes sir," Macarus said.

"What military resources do we have to defend the city against a siege?"

"Besides the Cityguard and their weapons? None. The city was stripped of those things after the surrender – no siegeworks or anything of that nature. We only have the Cityguard, and they are a minimal peacekeeping force. The Empire never believed such a remote location would ever need to endure a siege or fight a battle without encountering Taggart first."

"Well, then, we will see what we can do about that tomorrow."

"Yes, sir."

"And I will need a place to stay," Caleb said. "Not here. In the military barracks, perhaps? Are there extra rooms?"

"We can make them for you," Macarus said.

"Excellent," Caleb said. "I'll need an office to plan and work from, to meet with you and other city leaders through this crisis."

"You may have my office," Macarus said. "It is designed to be a war room."

"We'll share it. Will the Cityguard take orders from me?"

"That … may be difficult," Macarus said. "But I will speak with them."

"Will you have trouble taking orders from me?" Caleb asked.

Macarus hesitated, pursing his lips. "No sir," he said. "Not for now."

"You let me know when it becomes a problem," Caleb said. "And I will have you give the orders to the Cityguard, if you are amenable to that."

"I am," Macarus said.

"I want you to know, First Captain, that I was trained to do this. I studied for years and read more books than you can imagine to earn this tattoo and that Letter of Regency. We will get through this if you trust me. Do you understand?"

"Yes," Macarus said.

"Good," Caleb said. "Then please, show us where we are staying tonight."

Chapter 28

The Rise of Men

Dawn broke over the walls of the city as Eshlyn was escorted to the office where the man, Caleb, now ran the city. It had all happened so fast. She still couldn't believe it. Within an hour, everything had changed.

She walked through the door of the office within the military complex that consisted of a few large buildings for barracks, a training yard, an armory, and administrative buildings. Caleb's office, or the office he shared with Macarus, was long and rectangular, but sparse and bare but for a large desk and several chairs around the desk and about the room. Maps hung on the wall, large maps of the world of Eres, of Kryus, of Manahem and the city of Ketan. A window let in light from the ceiling, but since dawn still peeked in, a lamp burned low on the desk. She wondered if Caleb had slept. Blankets sat in the corner. She thought he had.

Macarus stood with Caleb at the desk, leaning over a map of the city and another map of Manahem, smaller cartograms than the ones on the wall. Caleb and Macarus both looked up at her as she entered. "Come in," Caleb said as he stood upright. He turned to Macarus. "Can you give us some time?"

Macarus straightened as well. "Of course," he said.

"Meet me back here in a couple hours, please," Caleb told the elf as he walked away. "We have a lot of work to do today."

"Yes sir," Macarus said, gave Eshlyn a thin smile, and walked out of the room, closing the door behind him.

Eshlyn stood over the maps, looking at them intently. The city map was a maze of detail, streets and buildings and names and places. The map of Manahem showed the cities of Biram and Ketan and also marked the towns to the south along the Manahem road. She touched the dot that marked Campton.

Caleb pointed to the mountains below Campton. "The Ydu says the Dark Gate was here in the mountains," he said. "It opens every five hundred and twenty seven years when the three moons of Eres lined up over the gate."

"The Dark Gate?" Eshlyn asked, not taking her eyes off the map.

"Yes. A gate to the Underland. It opens and lets out a Demilord and a few legions of demics, those creatures that attacked your town, out into the world."

"What do they want?" she asked.

"10,000 years ago, the demics lived in the world. They were nocturnal beings, constantly at war with humans, elves, and dwarves. They eat the flesh of the living."

She grimaced.

"After a long and costly war, the demics were finally exiled by mankind, led by a man named Yosu and his warriors. The demics were imprisoned within the Underland. What do they want? They want back in the world again, to have their rightful place. The ancient testimony mentions a Key that opens the Gate and allows the whole of the Underland upon Eres."

"There were storms, earthquakes a few nights before Campton was attacked. You think that was the moons?"

"Sounds right," Caleb said. "Eres goes through that kind of natural turmoil every time the moons line up." He pointed to the towns. "So then they moved north from Campton to Pontus ... and on and on."

"Why north? Why not south to Lior?" She pointed down to the southern colony.

"Well, we think because the Key I told you about is here somewhere. But we aren't sure. That is more a legend, I think. Not in the Ydu."

"Kenric mentioned they were after a Key," Eshlyn said, the night in Campton filling her memories. "Could we find it?" Eshlyn asked. "If we knew where it was, we could take it from here, and take these demics away with it."

Caleb shrugged. "It would be like finding a pebble in a cornfield," Caleb said. "We don't even know where to look. It is a big city. A good idea, I agree, but how do they know it's here? Do they know from legend or something else? I would like to know where it is, though just in case, but I wouldn't even know where to start."

She frowned at him. "What is this Ydu you talk about?" she asked.

"The testimony of the creation and history of Eres. It is about El. Do you know of El?"

"Only one god, right?" she asked.

He nodded at her.

"I hear but don't pay much attention to gods."

"That's okay," he said.

"But it sounds interesting. You're saying the Underland is real? Not just hearth stories?"

"If the demics are real," he began, "then they came from somewhere. Stands to reason the Underland is real, too. Seems the testimony is telling us the truth."

Eshlyn peered down at the map again and drew her fingers north along the Manahem road. "Campton, Pontus, Delaton ... I knew these places. I knew people that were there."

"I know," Caleb said. "And you traveled north with just your son to warn people?"

"Kenric told me to," she said. "I'm not as brave as you might think. I just left him there and ran like he said. I told people, but few listened."

"I think you're braver than you give yourself credit for," Caleb said. "Your brother, Xander, seems to think so."

"My brother is best friends with a fool and just six months ago tried getting a pig drunk," she said. "I wouldn't put too much stock in what he says."

"Your brother is a good man," Caleb said. "There's a lot of worth there, I think. It runs in your family, it seems. And that fool friend ... well, he almost gave his life for your brother."

"True," she said. "I never would have thought that about him, growing up."

"How is Joob, by the way?" Caleb asked.

"He is improving," Eshlyn answered. "Thank you for the doctor you sent. Joob is annoying me already."

His face turned dark and pensive. "A lot happened in Biram."

"I heard," Eshlyn said. "Xander told me."

The grin was gone, and he seemed years older in an instant. Was he even thirty? Unexplained grief aged him in a moment. "These are dark times, times that test you. Show what makes you. Exposes what is deep within. Most of the time we are surprised at what is laid bare."

Eshlyn looked up at the man, his gray eyes like steel in his soul. "Have you been so tested?" she asked.

"Yes ... but even after all this time, I think I've a long way to go," Caleb said.

"Maybe we all do," Eshlyn said.

"Maybe we do," Caleb said. "Please. Sit."

They sat across from each other at the corner of the large desk. "Why did you ask me here?" Eshlyn said.

"Two reasons," Caleb said. "First, I hear you're the leader of the people from Delaton."

"My father is an elder of that town," she said. "I wouldn't say ..."

"I would," Caleb interrupted. "And eventually, I think you'll have a similar position among the residents of Roseborough."

Eshlyn scoffed. "They have a Mayor."

"They have a politician," Caleb corrected. "What they need is a leader. You will be that leader, believe me."

Eshlyn shook her head at him. "Second reason?"

"Tell me about your journey, what happened in your town and what led you here," Caleb said. "Xander relayed much of it, but I wanted to hear it from you, to see if I could pick something up that might be important."

"It is a simple story, to the real," Eshlyn said. "Xander couldn't have breaked it up."

"Oh, he probably didn't," Caleb admitted. "Just humor me. Please. Tell me everything."

She took a deep breath. And she told him. But not everything. She didn't tell him about the dreams, or that Kenric claimed to be from a line of kings.

—

Returning right before his allotted hour, Macarus waited outside. The door opened and Eshlyn exited the office, her eyes red from crying. "Are you okay?" Macarus asked.

She smiled at him, such a beautiful smile made even more so by the sadness within it. "I'm fine," she said. "He's ready for you now." Eshlyn walked away.

Macarus entered the office. If this man had hurt her in any way, Macarus might get to test his mettle against a Bladeguard after all.

Bladeguard. "Where is your sword?" he asked the man.

"Excuse me?" Caleb said.

"You are a Bladeguard, and they are notorious for their fine swords." Macarus patted his sword as he walked towards Caleb. "I have a fine sword. And you do not. Where is it?"

Caleb waved a dismissal. "The staff is my weapon now. I'll get my sword soon enough. Now are you ready to get to work today? We have to get ready for a siege."

"Fine," Macarus said. "Since you've taken authority, are you going to send pigeons for help now?"

Caleb regarded him without expression. "No."

"What? We have five hundred Cityguard and a wall to protect. We need legions from Taggart!"

"And how long will that take, First Captain?" Caleb asked. "It took us seven days to travel from there to here, and we were a small group; and once we heard of the possible attack, we pushed ourselves and the horses to travel."

They had a wounded man with them when they arrived, with what appeared to be a gladus wound. Macarus still wanted to ask him about that.

"By the time the elves in Taggart get the message, decide to respond, and get here with troops, it could be two ninedays. The battle will be over by then, I think, one way or another," Caleb said.

"Fine," Macarus said. "Then send a boat. One of the fishermen can spare his craft, or you could requisition it as Regent, and sail down the river to the lake and then Biram. A small group could make Taggart from there."

"Same problem," Caleb said. "The boat would get to Biram faster, but then that person, or small group, whomever we sent, would have to ride or walk to Taggart, slower than the original pigeon." Caleb cleared his throat and rubbed his beard. "We have to mobilize this city, elf and human, here and now, to fight whatever force of demics shows up at the gates."

It took a moment for the implication to set in. "You're going to arm humans?" Macarus asked, his tone high.

Caleb looked down to the tattoo on his arm, and said, "Does that surprise you?"

Macarus sighed. With all that happened in the last twenty four hours, no, it did not.

"We have the wall of Ketan," the man said. "Dynitian said …"

"That a good city wall is worth legions of militan," Macarus interrupted. "But he also said that you need capable defenders to man that wall."

"We were not given enough Cityguard for the whole wall. We'll need more bodies up there. And defenders are one part of what we need to organize. The city must prepare for a siege, to support those defenders – food, healthcare, and the like."

Macarus nodded. The man was right. "What are we going to do first?"

"We're going to the prison," Caleb said.

"To see Desiderus?" Macarus asked.

"Oh, we might check up on him," Caleb said. "But that is not why we are going."

"Then why are we going?" Macarus said.

Caleb didn't answer. He just grinned and gestured that Macarus should lead the way. Macarus found himself anxious.

They exited the office, mounted their waiting horses, and rode northward to the west of the palace complex to the prison. Macarus had a skeleton crew there to make sure he had as many elves as he could at the wall through the night, which had thankfully passed without incident. Caleb and Macarus entered the prison, a long, rectangular building with four floors of cells. It was half full.

"Take me to the prison yard," Caleb said. "And have all the human prisoners gathered there."

"We have twenty-five guard here total. They could overpower us."

Caleb shifted his staff in his hand. "I can take care of myself," he said. "Just do it."

Macarus shook his head and gave the instructions to the guards, who looked at him as if he were insane. He shrugged and instructed them again. They gaped as they obeyed. Macarus then led Caleb out to the prison yard. Soon four hundred and sixty-two prisoners in chains were marched out into the yard by elven guard carrying clubs and gladi.

Standing close to Macarus, Caleb spoke under his breath. "Four hundred and sixty-two?" he muttered. "In a city of this size? Macarus, I'm impressed."

Caleb stepped forward and addressed the prisoners. "Good day, gentlemen," he said. "My name is Caleb, and I am now the authority in Ketan." That produced a few nervous chuckles from the prisoners. "I would like to make a proposal to you. This city is about to find itself in a battle. And we will need men on the walls of this city. You've all heard of the unbreachable walls of Ketan. Well, those walls are only strong if there are soldiers on that wall, men and elves to repel those enemies."

Macarus walked forward. "No, Caleb," he said. "I cannot allow ..."

"It is not for you to allow," Caleb said, putting a hand out to halt Macarus. Macarus stopped but glared at the man. His gray eyes communicated confidence and calm. Macarus scanned the prisoners. He had placed a few of these men in chains himself.

Caleb turned to the prisoners again, the convicts far more attentive now that the First Captain had backed down at Caleb's order. Macarus' heart beat fast. "My proposition is this," Caleb said. "If you agree to fight with us on that wall, with the elves that put you in prison, yes, but also with me, then you will win your freedom. Do any of you know how to fight?"

A few exchanged glances with one another. Macarus could point out several that could handle themselves well, but he wasn't about to help Caleb in this fool endeavor. Several men stepped forward, however. Caleb walked forward to intercept them. "Good," he said. He walked past the small group to a large man behind them.

Oh, no, Macarus thought. *Not him*.

"You look familiar," Caleb said. "Like I've seen you in some picture drawing or something. What is your name?"

"Zalman," the large man said. He was over two mitres tall, towering over even taller men, with bulging muscles and a dark brown complexion, Veraden skin.. He had smallish nose and ears, thin lips, and light blue eyes. His head was shaved.

"From where do I know you?" Caleb said.

Zalman didn't answer. He just glared at Caleb.

Macarus answered for him. "Qadi-bol," Macarus said. "He was a star for Asya for years until he ran off."

"Yes!" Caleb said. "That's it! You ran away from big money and fame." He squinted at the large man, unafraid. Didn't he know Zalman could crush him with one blow? "Why?"

"I wanted to be free," Zalman said. "I had money and fame, but I was a slave."

Caleb glanced down at the man's hands in heavy iron chains. "I can get those chains off you. Are you willing to fight with me?"

Zalman looked away. "How much money you got?"

"How much do you want?" Caleb said.

"Not much," Zalman said. "Just a little."

He liked the crinklehouses, Macarus knew. That was how they had caught him. Women were his weakness.

But with Directive XVII, Caleb now had access to all the coin in the Bank of Kryus. Again, Macarus wasn't about to offer that information.

"I'll tell you what," Caleb said. "You fight like you played Qadi-bol, and I'll see you get some money. A little, at least. Enough."

Zalman looked down at Caleb. "Okay," he said. "Deal."

"Good," Caleb said. He backed away. "Now ... anyone want to learn how to fight?"

Macarus shook his head. This was a mistake. He considered himself an enlightened elf, but teaching humans to fight? Human criminals? Insanity.

Every criminal stepped forward. All four hundred and sixty-two.

"Well," Caleb said to Macarus. "Looks like your prison will be almost empty after today. Get these men out of their chains and into some clean clothes." He addressed the prisoners. "Meet me in the central market this afternoon, second hour after noon. We'll have weapons for you."

Caleb and Macarus walked out together. Macarus spoke passionately but in a low whisper. "What are you doing? You know the Empire's policy on humans and weapons. Tanicus cannot be okay with this."

"I'm building an army to protect the citizens of Manahem," Caleb responded. "I told you that I'm trained for this."

"But those are prisoners. Convicts. Some of these are very violent men," Macarus said.

"I hope so," Caleb said. "I'm counting on it."

"I put some of those men in chains myself, and you want to place weapons in their hands and place them next to elves? That's insane."

"Macarus," Caleb said. "I have a feeling that when the demics attack, and they will any moment now, elf and human won't matter on that wall. It will be about survival. Come. We have more to do..."

Macarus shook his head and rubbed his jaw.

Caleb mounted his stallion and grinned at Macarus. "You're an elf of honor and principle. You will do what is right when the time comes. You are rare in Kryus, but I believe we work towards the same goal, even if you don't understand it yet."

Macarus glowered at Caleb with suspicion and mounted his own stallion.

"Get Chamren and meet me back at the office in an hour," Caleb said.

"Why?" Macarus asked.

"We have soldiers for our army," Caleb said. "Now we need weapons."

Caleb rode off. Macarus realized he was in way over his head.

———

Aden sat on his horse outside the office as Caleb rode up to meet him. Caleb wore his leather trousers and boots and a sleeveless white cotton shirt. The sleeveless shirt allowed him to expose the tattoo on the inside of his forearm, Aden knew.

"You wanted me?" Aden asked.

"Yes," Caleb said, pulling his horse to a stop. "How did it go with Eshlyn and Carys?"

Caleb had sent Aden and Carys to go with Eshlyn to recruit fighters among the people of Delaton and Roseborough.

"Carys is with about two hundred and fifty men, and a couple women, in the central market square now, training them," Aden said. "Although they don't have any weapons yet. They're training with sticks and chair legs, that sort of thing."

"Good, but we're going to need a lot more from the city itself," Caleb said, then looked over to his left. "Ah, here we are."

Macarus and Chamren rode up on their horses. Aden noted Macarus' angry visage and Chamren's nervous eyes as the red mustache on his face twittered when he sniffed. Caleb greeted the newcomers, and the elf didn't respond while Chamren bowed and called Caleb "sir" three times in two seconds.

"How goes the recruiting in the city?" Caleb said.

Chamren shrugged. "A thousand, perhaps twelve hundred so far. They are meeting in the central market with Carys, as well."

Caleb frowned. Aden knew Caleb wanted more than those numbers, in a city of well over fifty thousand. They didn't know how many demics were coming, but they needed well over the five hundred Cityguard to man that massive wall.

"Are the doctors set and ready?" Caleb asked.

"They are not, um, very pleased that you closed down the infanti," Chamren said. "But yes, they are ready."

"Things change," Caleb said. "Tell them to get used to it."

"Where to now?" Macarus asked with accusation and impatience. The tension between he and Caleb made Aden almost as nervous as Chamren.

Caleb ignored Macarus' tone and faced Chamren. "We are going to the forge," he said.

Chamren became still in an instant, and even his horse seemed to catch the mood and froze. "What forge?" he asked, his voice thin.

Caleb leaned forward in his saddle. "My master, Galen, told me of an ancient forge here in the city, a place where Blademasters come to buy the best swords in the Empire. Once, the Bladeguard would travel to the nearby Mountains of Gatehm to the Living Stone. But instead, the elves now come here, to Ketan, in secret, to a hidden forge. Besides the Steward, I suspect that the two of you are the most likely to know where it is."

Macarus shook his head. "A secret forge? That is ridiculous."

Aden stared at Chamren, who stayed silent with his eyes wide open at Caleb. "Chamren?" Caleb asked. "Do you know of the forge?"

"I've been here for more than three centuries," Macarus said. "No offense to the Second Assistant, but he's only been alive for forty five years. If I don't know, then he can't know." But Chamren looked down, pursing his lips, and doubt crept into Macarus' face. "Chamren? You don't know what this madman is talking about, do you?"

"Well, um," Chamren began.

"Spit it out," Caleb commanded.

"Uh, you see, I, uh, have noticed elves traveling to the city," Chamren said. "Strange and suspicious elves that have met with the First Assistant or the Steward." His eyes darted from Caleb to Macarus and back again. "They were shown right in, where you, the First Captain, are put off for days or ninedays at times. They never speak to me, and they try to hide it from me, but ... "

"I get the feeling people don't hide things from you for long," Caleb said. "Not in this city."

Macarus gawked at Chamren as the Second Assistant blushed. "Um, well, uh, I checked out where these elves were being sent."

"And?" Caleb encouraged.

"And it is under the second building in the palace complex, the administration building just inside the arch." Chamren paused, then spoke in a torrent of nervous words. "I don't know what's there, mind you. I just know that's where they went. If there's a place that fits what you're saying, that is the place." Chamren's eyes lowered and he muttered, "But the elves do come away with new swords ... "

"Please," Caleb said to Chamren. "Lead the way."

Chamren looked at Macarus for some sort of affirmation, but the First Captain continued to gape with his jaw hanging askew. Chamren hesitated a moment and heeled his horse back out of the military complex and into the main thoroughfare of the city north to the palace. Aden followed behind Macarus and Caleb.

As they passed through the arch and the inner walls, Chamren took them to the left of the grassy field surrounded by tall trees, and towards the administration building. Aden wasn't sure why they needed a whole separate building since most of the offices were bare. A few had writing on the doors for the various ministries of the city: education, health, and sanitation. But the building seemed half empty to Aden.

Chamren led them through the main hallway. They took a right at a crossway that led them past empty offices. This area of the building was dusty and dark, unused. An unmarked doorway, as nondescript as the others in that hallway, was Chamren's destination, and he paused there, pulling a long golden key out of his pocket.

He smiled and said, "Master key," as he held the object up.

Slipping the key in the lock, he opened it to a dark hallway of black stone, different from the white and gray stone of the administration building. Chamren led them down that black hallway to a wide stairway that led down, turning at a wide landing three times before coming to a wide iron door.

"This is as far as I've come," Chamren said in a whisper. A low rumbling and humming came from beyond the iron door. "I believe it bolts from the other side."

"Well," Caleb said in a normal voice, stepping past Chamren. "Let's knock." Caleb pounded his fist on the door three times. Aden heard muffled voices, and after a moment, Caleb pounded again.

Bolts clanged from within, and the door opened to reveal a short, stout man waiting for them inside. He was shirtless but wore linen trousers and had on a leather apron. His arms were muscular and thick. He had wide shoulders and straight red hair that was pulled back from his face. His bushy red beard contorted as he frowned at them with suspicious dark brown eyes. "Who are you?" he asked Caleb.

Caleb pushed his way past, and Aden and the rest followed him.

The forge extended for twenty mitres past the iron door, the walls black stone, and the ceiling ten mitres tall with vents for the smoke that came from several vats of molten metal over flaming coals. Aden counted six of those vats, three on either side, with a walkway down the middle.

Along the walls, however, weapons of every kind were displayed, the finest weapons Aden could imagine, even though his experience was limited. Most of them were swords, hundreds of them, but some were spears and axes. Aden even saw a few sets of armor. Caleb breathed, "Great and mighty El."

"Who is that at the door disturbin' my work!" came a shout from the far end of the forge, a woman's voice … or sounded like. Aden peered through the dark forge, glowing red and yellow by torches and molten metal, and he saw a small figure bounce down from a stool over an anvil near the furthest vat on the left and strut over to them.

She was a dwarf. Aden had seen a dwarf or two in his time. Hairy and stout, dwarves were another head shorter than elves. They came every now and then to Asya, but not often. And they were always male dwarves, usually with some sort of theatre or circus. He had never seen a female dwarf before. She possessed fine, long, curly red hair, and her wide face could be considered pretty with bright blue eyes over her short frame. She wasn't as stocky or hairy as the male dwarves Aden had seen. She wore a sleeveless leather dress, and her arms were thick with muscle.

She was also angry. "Who might you be?" she stood a few paces down the center aisle with her hands on her hips. "Always an elf here or elf there comin' down here to get them a sword, always a sword. Never had no humans down here except Hunter." She pointed towards the man that had opened the door. He appeared amused.

Caleb made the introductions. The dwarf didn't seem to care. "I be knowin' the First Captain," she said. "Seen him time enough with his pretty eyes and fine body riding through the city, and I heared of Chamren, but you two I don't know. Tell me what you're doing here 'fore I bounce you outta here on your arse."

He stepped closer to her and showed her his tattoo. "You've seen these before, haven't you," he said.

She looked from the tattoo to his face three times. "Maybe," she said.

"I am a Bladeguard, and the city is in danger," he said.

"A human Bladeguard?" the dwarf said. "Ha! Now I've seen it all."

"What is your name?" Macarus said behind Aden. "How long have you been down here?"

The dwarf frowned at the First Captain. "They call me Bweth Ironhorn," she said. "I'm a swordsmith from one o' the lesser dwarven mines 'cross the pond. I been here for almost two hundred years. This be my assistant, Hunter."

"But he's a human," Macarus said. "He hasn't been your assistant all this time."

"No," Bweth said. "Don't be a maddy brain. I pick my assistant three hundred years ago, and his sons have been my 'prentices every generation."

"And I've never known about this place," Macarus said as he looked around.

"Quite the family secret," Hunter said, smirking with his arms crossed.

"Why isn't the swordsmith here an elf?" Macarus asked, his face still confused.

"T'was," Bweth said. "At first. When the elves took over. But that elf did not like to be so far into the colonies, so he asked for a replacement. No elf came to replace him, so he … find me and train me so he could go. I been here ever since."

"Amazing," Caleb said. "And you've made all these weapons?"

"These and more that elves take when they come," she said. "Me and Hunter's family."

"How quickly can you make more?" Caleb asked.

"I dunno," Bweth said. "What you thinkin'?"

"Swords, in the main," Caleb said. "But spears will be nice. And bows. And arrows."

Bweth nodded at Macarus. "He gots an armory," she said.

"It is there to stock for five hundred elves," Caleb said. "There's extra, but not enough for what I need." Caleb pointed at the weapons along the wall. "I'm going to arm the humans, Master Ironhorn. These will help, but we need more."

"You be armin' humans?" She gave her head a sharp shake. "I take it back. Now I seen it all." She snorted and spat on the ground, eyeing Caleb. "You can use these you see here, and we can make more, whatever you like," Bweth said. She glanced at Hunter. He shrugged back at her. She faced Caleb again. "Arrows ain't nothin'. Anyone can learn how quick. Get me enough wood and enough people and you'll have arrows comin' out yer ears. The rest, we can make quick, not fine as all these, but quick enough for war in a day or two."

Caleb turned to Chamren. "Get the woodcarvers and smiths of the city involved. We'll need to teach them, mobilize them."

Chamren nodded. "Yes, sir."

Macarus stared blankly at him.

Caleb's eyes glistened as he smiled. "Aden," he said. "Pick out a sword."

—+—

Carys had over a thousand people to train, all by herself.

Caleb was out gallivanting around the city, talking to people, even visiting the breakin' coliseum – something about lights - and he left her here to babysit a bunch of farmers, ranchers, fishermen, and half-Sorced city dwellers. And all without any weapons. Sticks and table legs swung awkwardly all around her. They found her a large platform, used for small theatres, so that the people could see her go through some basic forms and show them how to keep their balance. She didn't think that the demics would be master swordsmen, so she hoped the basic stance and forms would do. They would have to. Slash and stab. Killing points.

As she watched some men join the group, about three hundred of them, many of them rubbing raw wrists. Prisoners? What was Caleb thinking?

Then she thought she recognized one of them.

She called out to the hundreds in the crowd. "Keep practicing that form! Keep low and balanced! Don't stop until I tell you!" Then she leapt down to the brick covered ground and walked over to the man with almost black skin. Liorian skin.

"Esai?" she said. Then as she got closer, she knew it was him. "Esai."

He was a hand taller than she was, and almost as thin. His wide smile appeared as he recognized her. Esai was thirty-two years old with strong wiry limbs and a head of kinky black hair that had grown longer since she last saw him. His head was a little too large for his body, and he had a wide nose, large dark eyes, a wide mouth and a high forehead. He had been one of the Ghosts of Saten.

"Carys," he said as she neared him.

She grabbed his arm and pulled him away from the crowd. "Where have you been? We looked all over for you."

Esai's head lowered. "I was scouting with Oldre and we came upon a platoon of militan near Taggart," he said. "They surprised us. It was my fault. I was point man. Oldre died and they injured me. They had spears and shields. There were too many of them."

"I'm so sorry," Carys said. She had known Oldre, too. Sometimes platoons of militan would raid the northern edges of the forest. They knew men lived and hunted there without permission, and they considered any humans found fair game. "How did you get here?"

"I would not talk, so they did not know what to do with me," Esai said. "They held me in Taggart for some time, first to heal and then to beat me. The First Assistant here, Unitian, came to the prison in Taggart and bought me as a slave. I wouldn't work for him, either, so he placed me in the prison."

"How long ago?" she asked.

"Three ninedays ago," he said.

Carys smiled at him. "I'm sorry about what happened," she said. "But I'm so glad you are here. We need some good fighters. Do you know what's going on?"

"A man came to the prison and told us if we fought to defend the city, we would be free," Esai said. "Someone is attacking?"

"Not yet," Carys said. "But they will. That man who came to the prison, he's my brother."

"Your brother?" Esai said. "He had a Bladeguard tattoo ..."

"Yeah, I know," she said. "It's a long story, but you can trust him." She looked over at the crowd of people practicing a slash and thrust, and she plead with Esai. "Will you help me? Please?"

Esai nodded. "I will help you," he said. "But are we to fight with sticks? Where are the weapons?"

A wagon pulled into the central square, driven by Caleb with Aden at his side. Caleb drove the wagon up to the platform Carys had been teaching on. He stood. "Everyone!" The crowd stopped. "Come and choose a weapon."

The crowd hesitated, unsure. Then they moved forward to the wagon.

———

Zalman stood still as the crowd moved to the wagon of weapons. He had just arrived, and there had been some little girl trying to teach men how to fight. This looked like a plan destined to fail. He clenched his fists. He thought about going back to the prison. He would probably die fighting alongside these people. He had played the highest level of Qadi-bol, and in that sport, your team mattered. The best player in Eres on a team of worthless men would lose the game. Badly. But if the players were good enough and learned how to work together, they could beat any team any day. To be honest, this looked like a bad team in the making.

Caleb, the man who had been at the prison a few hours ago, climbed down from the wagon with a small young man. The small young man carried two weapons in the hook of his elbows and had a fine sword at his hip. They both walked towards Zalman.

As they reached him, Caleb said, "Zalman, this is Aden. Aden, this is Zalman." The young man's eyes bulged.

"*The* Zalman Be'Frial?" Aden said. "It's really you! I saw you play in Asya five years ago! You were th'best!"

Zalman didn't answer.

"Give him the weapons, Aden," Caleb said.

Aden extended his arms, and Zalman looked down to see two large-bladed battleaxes. He grabbed the handles and lifted one in each hand. The weight was perfect, almost like the paddles in Qadi-bol. The handles felt made for his large hands.

"I thought those might work for you," Caleb said. "And you probably don't need a lot of training to use them. I'll see you on that wall tonight. I'll be standing next to you."

Zalman met Caleb's eyes, gray eyes of cold confidence. Maybe it wouldn't be such a bad team after all.

CHAPTER 29

DEMICS AT THE GATES

It was late, the red moon of Vysti bright and high in the western sky, and Eshlyn was talking with Caleb outside his office near the training yard in the military complex when Macarus and his horse galloped up to them, his eyes wide and his face pale white.

Macarus wore a full set of armor, silver and shining, but not new. That was not Cityguard armor. That was the armor of an officer in the Kryan legion, light but strong sections that moved with a Blademaster, fashioned for his body. Macarus' fine sword hung at his side.

"They're here," he said, and his meaning was clear: the demics.

Eshlyn didn't think she hesitated, but Caleb was on top of his horse by the time she thought to do the same. She mounted Blackie and rode behind Caleb towards the gates.

"You should stay behind," Caleb shouted back at her.

"I have to see this," she answered.

He did not press the issue, and they stopped before the gate at the base of the battle tower to the east of the gate. Caleb followed Macarus up the circular stair of the tower. A thick iron door opened to let them out on top of the wall.

The top of the wall of Ketan was wide, six mitres from front to back with thick stone parapets on either side. An arrow loop cut into the parapet every three paces looking out from the city. Several Cityguard and men already stood atop the wall with spears, swords, and shields. Macarus took them to a stand over the city gate, and they looked out together into the large field outside the gates. The wind blew strong at this height.

Eshlyn gasped.

It was dark, the world in shadow, but even in the moonlight, she could see the field covered with teeming dark shapes, a blanket of gray flesh roiling and moving. She could hear distant sounds that brought back that first night in Campton to her mind. Tears began to stream down her face, and she touched the golden bracelet on her wrist. For the first time, she was sure that her husband had died that night. No one could survive that. No one.

"Bring up the lights," Caleb said. Macarus repeated the order.

Every major city in the Empire had a coliseum with lights made by the alchemists, bright burning torches that burned even through rain, burning in front of large round mirrors to spread the light over the playing field for the major sport of Qadi-bol. Earlier that day, Caleb had men bring those lights up to the top of the wall to shine out from the city to expose the demics in the field if they had to fight at night.

A Cityguard each stood at the eight large mirrors and lit the torch, sending light out into the field beyond the city. The demics shied away from the light; it seemed to make them angry. They bared their teeth at the light and pressed forward toward the wall.

Eshlyn groaned in fright. There were thousands of them. Farther than she could see even with the coliseum lights. She looked around and saw perhaps two hundred Cityguard with five hundred humans interspersed among them.

Caleb moved to the parapet and leaned over with a peerglass in his hand. He looked over the demic horde.

"How many?" Macarus said.

"Hard to tell," Caleb said. "Five thousand? Ten? Could be more. They are small and all bunched up like that. No organization."

Aden walked up from her right and stood next to them, his boots scraping against the stone. She heard him swallow. "It's happening," he said. She couldn't tell if he was frightened or relieved.

Eshlyn noticed a figure towards the back of the horde, a man-like figure towering over the demics around it. It lifted something that reflected the lights brightly.

"Hand me the peerglass," Eshlyn said and held out her hand. Caleb looked at her curiously but complied.

Quickly putting the peerglass up to her right eye, Eshlyn took a moment to adjust it. She saw nothing but chaos until she looked to the shining light from that tall figure and followed it to its source. He had red skin, tall and muscular with black tattooed writing all over his upper body and had long black horns on his forehead, but as gruesome and horrible as he appeared, the intelligence in his eyes chilled her.

She knew that creature. It was him. It was the evil figure from her dreams. And in his hands was a sword.

"Oh, no," she said.

"What?" Caleb asked, concerned.

She lowered the peerglass. "He has Kenric's sword," she said. "My – my husband's sword."

Caleb took the peerglass from her and looked at the figure, as well. "That's the Demilord, I assume," he said. "And I see a sword in his hand. It shouldn't be reflecting the light that much … no sword does that. No sword …" He stood straight, brought the peerglass down, and gaped at Eshlyn. "That is an unforged sword," he said. He turned and suddenly had a hold of her shoulders. He shook her. "Where did your husband get an unforged sword? What didn't you tell me?"

Eshlyn stammered, scared and confused. She heard Aden call Caleb's name with a warning, and Macarus do the same with greater urgency.

Caleb held her still, his eyes bright and intent. "Eshlyn," he said. "Tell me. What did you leave out of your story?"

"Kenric said …" she began, but she didn't know how to say it. It was so maddy. She hadn't told anyone, not Xander, not her parents. It wasn't important.

"Tell me." Caleb's hands and arms were like iron.

"That night in Campton, Kenric told me that he descended from a line of kings," she said as she held back a sob. "He told me that our son, Javyn, was to be protected and brought here to be safe. Kenric's father must have passed the sword down to him. Kenric said that Javyn was the ancestor of King Judai."

And he called me a queen, she wanted to say. But didn't.

Caleb's eyes were huge with horror. "The last *Sohan-el*," he said. He released her and pulled away, his right hand covering his forehead.

"Caleb," Aden said. "Are you alright?" Aden placed a cautious hand on Caleb's shoulder.

Caleb looked down at Aden. "That Demilord has an unforged sword," he said.

"I know, I heard," Aden said.

"And I don't!" Caleb said.

Aden's face fell.

"First Captain!" came a cry from the left. "Look!" A Cityguard pointed down at the base of the wall.

Eshlyn, Caleb, Aden and Macarus all leaned over the parapet and stared straight down.

The demics were clinging to the smooth stone, piercing it with their sharp, black claws. They climbed the wall.

—✦—

Caleb turned to Eshlyn. "Get down and back with your family," he said.

She looked at him, hurt and confused. He pushed her back towards the tower and the stairs down to the city. "Go!" She cried out, but she ran.

Turning to Macarus, he said, "Get everyone on this wall. And your best archers should be in those towers."

"The archers are in position," Macarus said and turned to a nearby Cityguard, ordering him to gather the rest of the guard.

Caleb looked down the wall-walk. Aden stood next to him, a new sword in his hand. Zalman spun the battleaxes in his hands ten mitres to the west. Carys' friend Esai, the Liorian, was to the east of Caleb, two short swords in his hands in a pose that said he was more than capable.

Carys was up in the battletowers with the archers to Caleb's left in the east tower. He faced that direction and could see her blond hair through an arrow loop. He had put her in charge there. One of Macarus' sergeants was in charge of the other tower.

"Wait for my signal," Caleb said to Macarus, and the elf nodded. Caleb leaned over the parapet again and watched as the demics crept up the wall. They moved deliberately, snarling, anxious to get up the wall. One demic tried to hurry and couldn't catch hold and fell, knocking three more off the wall as he did. None of the others tried to hurry after that.

Caleb waited until the demics had climbed three fourths of the way up the wall. Macarus held his tongue. Caleb turned and whispered to Macarus. "Now."

Macarus stood and gave the signal to both towers: *Archers, fire at will.*

—

Carys saw the signal from Macarus and screamed, "Fire!" She let loose her arrow with the first volley from her tower. Fifty archers stood in her tower and fifty in the opposite one. They aimed at the demics on the wall. Several fell in their first volley, and the arrows from the other tower did as much damage.

"Some of you elves missed!" she yelled. "Better aim! We don't have all the arrows in Eres." Her own arrow had passed through the cranium of a demic.

Fifty or more demics had fallen in the first volley, but the walls were still covered with them. The archers loosed arrows again and again. The demics were afraid, looking back and forth, caught as targets, but they kept coming like something drove them. Something that caused them more fear than arrows raining down upon them.

"Keep shooting," she said. "Take them all down!"

The Cityguard elves didn't need her encouragement. She could almost smell their fear – or was it her own? – amidst the press of battle and the vision of little monstrous vermin scaling the city walls. They shot over and over at the demics, and hundreds fell. But hundreds more came behind them.

After twenty minutes of constant firing, Carys realized they would run out of arrows before the horde ran out of demics. They would reach the top of the wall within the hour, and they would reach her brother.

She screamed at the elves, cursed at the demics, but none of her frustrated words kept her from getting to that moment where she reached down into her quiver and found it empty.

Carys dropped her bow, picked up her gladus – she had been offered new weapons from the forge, but why try to learn something new now? – and she yelled once more at the elves around her as they also came up empty. "Come on. To the wall!"

⊢

Caleb saw the last of the arrows fly from the tower to his right. No more came. A few seconds later, the last of the arrows flew from the tower to his left. He looked down at the wall. The demics climbed over their dead brothers at the base and leapt up to clasp onto the wall with their claws and kept coming.

They would end up fighting hand to hand.

Caleb turned to the men and elves around him. The elves had their spears and swords and shields. Most of them had never seen any real action, no real battle. Macarus had, that was clear, even though Caleb didn't know when or where. A person with battle experience was easy for him to spot. The calm, the stillness, the anticipation in them that accepted the fear and chaos as a part of life. Not welcome or wanted, but accepted.

He had been in three major battles before, as an observer, but never as a participant. The Empire would never have allowed it, but Galen made sure that along with Caleb's studies of military tactics, ancient and modern, Caleb had the opportunity to learn the leadership of armies within the chaos, the adjustments that took place as plans went awry. He was never allowed to lead, so while he had fought hand to hand and taken life – elf, human, and dwarf – all on chaperoned missions for Kryus— being responsible for the defense of the city was a first—and perhaps the last.

Master Ironhorn had offered him one of the fine sets of armor down in the forge, or to make him one, but he had refused. The Cityguard armor had been made for elves, too small for most humans, and the vast majority of the men on the wall would have to fight without any such protection. So neither would he.

"They will reach the top of the wall," Caleb said, stepping closer to Macarus. "We must hold."

Macarus raised a brow at him. "We will see how your criminals and farmers react. I've seen trained militan run at the first sight of conflict."

Caleb looked down the wall, to his right and left. The humans understood what was about to happen, their eyes wide in terror, mouths agape. A few began to take steps back from the parapet. He looked behind, turning to stare over the darkness of the city, rare lights glowing dim from this distance, lamps in windows, torches or fires at a street corner.

"They know what they're fighting for," he said. "They will stand. Did you always know what you were fighting for?"

Macarus sniffed, moving his eyes back at the field before the city. "Doesn't matter. Battles are chaos, luck, full of random moments you cannot predict."

"El will help us," Caleb said.

The First Captain chuckled. "A battle is no place for faith of any kind. The only thing a battle proves is that life is cruel and violent; that there is no reason or logic to life. Yor, the God of death, reigns here."

Frowning, Caleb stepped back from Macarus and leapt upon the front parapet, raising the Kingstaff over his head and facing the men and elves on the wall-walk. "Men and elves!" he shouted. "Listen to me." He pointed with the staff back to the city behind them, dark and quiet. The only sounds were their own breathing and the distant snarls and hungry growls from the demics below. "The demics are going to reach the top of the wall. If they get beyond us, the city is doomed. We will not fail and we will not run. Not here. Not tonight. Fight for the city. Fight for one another. Elf and human, we make our stand here!"

He could see a few faces shift away from fear and become tight with resolve while others dropped their shoulders but nodded their heads with resignation. They would all see violence this night, fighting for the lives of their families and the people within the city. Caleb prayed that they would stand.

Glancing down, Caleb could see Aden's visage, hard and determined, his nostrils flared and open. He was a good young man and had survived bloodwolves, Cityguard, and a Bladeguard. Caleb hoped he would survive tonight. He hoped they all would. But he knew many would fall. Whether they stood or ran or survived or fell, Caleb knew the men of Manahem would be forever changed.

It took another ten minutes for the demics to reach the top of the wall. The elves and humans waited for them, leaning over the parapets and stabbing and striking down, trying to keep them from reaching the top. Carys appeared next to him now, sneering and grunting as she killed demics and knocked them from the wall. He wanted to tell her to go, run and find a safe place, but he kept himself from expressing that selfish thought. She deserved to be here as much as he. He also noticed that several men and elves regarded her courage, and they fought with more vigor.

Demics began to reach the top, however. There were not enough people to cover every pace of the wall, and the elves and humans were soon fighting for their own lives along the wall-walk. For the demics, their weapons were their numbers and claws and teeth and horns, but a few had clubs made of some smooth black rock.

Caleb continued to spin the Kingstaff, crushing skulls and knocking demics over the parapet to their deaths below. The demics seemed to have no battle plan other than desperate feral attack with whatever they could use to cut or bleed or hit an elf or human. Sometimes they attacked in groups or pairs, but perhaps that gave them too much credit.

A man ten mitres to his left panicked and tried to run in fear, but two demics overtook him and brought him down, ripping at him with their claws and teeth. He screamed, but one of the demics pulled back the man's head with one claw and sliced open his neck with the other, silencing him.

"Don't run!" Caleb yelled, his voice booming and echoing in the night. "Your only hope is to stand and fight!"

Caleb's training and instinct overtook him, and he made sure to keep moving, keep up the brutal strikes at the little imps. He became the weapon he was trained to be. He struck one across the face, the monster's jaw ripping right off from the force of the staff, black blood spraying in a wide arc. Turning and spinning, he brought the staff around and against the torso of another, folding the creature in half, sounds of bones crunching filling his ears. As that one flew back over the parapet, Caleb didn't stop moving, crushing the skull of the next one, the staff sinking down between the demic's black eyes, eyes that popped from its head as it crumpled and died.

He killed without thought or conscience, his clothes covered in stinking, black demic blood. A lull in the fighting gave him a moment to catch a breath, and in that moment, he grinned. He was enjoying this.

But he was one man. He couldn't kill them all. He couldn't stop them all.

Zalman fought in the corner of his vision, a beast of a fighter. The skill of his hands with those battleaxes was flawless. After a few minutes of violence and carnage, the demics tried to avoid him. He began to wander and hunt them down, chopping the imps in half or decapitating them. He covered a large enough area of the wall for ten men.

Esai also sliced through the demics as if he had been born to do it, his quickness and skill like a continual dance as he cut down one after the other, carving through the throng.

Caleb heard screams and cries from beings other than demics along the wall. Elves and humans were dying around him.

It was chaos. Aden had been taught forms and balance and the art of swordsmanship. This was a brawl, a frantic fight for survival where only the brutal and the merciless would make it out alive. And perhaps not even then.

Aden realized thirty seconds into the battle on the top of the wall that choosing a new sword was a mistake. He hadn't trained or fought with it at all. His brief experience had been with a shorter sword like the

Cityguard around him used. *I should have stayed with that.* Somehow he remained alive.

He swung the longer sword more like a club, hacking and cleaving the demics around him in pieces, heads and limbs flying amid the screams. They came at him from everywhere. One or two of the demics had clubs, swinging at him, others with their claws or biting with their tusks. Everything happened too fast, even faster than the other night in Biram. That had been a dream next to this nightmare. His arms were numb from the fighting. How long had it been? He kept fighting, though he didn't know how long he could last.

A Cityguard fell to four or five demics at Aden's right, screaming as claws and teeth tore into his flesh and feasted upon him. Carys appeared suddenly and struck at the demics and killed them all, trying to save the elf, but he lay dead in a pool of his own blood despite her efforts. Aden saw all this in his peripheral vision. There was no time to grieve or react to these horrors, just fight. The noise of the screeching demics and the shouting and crying of others rang in his ears.

Aden's arms begged to hang at his side. He forced them to move, but his strikes came slower and slower, more and more clumsy and awkward. Caleb saved his life more than once, the long staff snapping against a demic that got too close or came too fast.

He was up against the parapet that backed to the city. Demics surrounded him. Aden noticed that a gray light had begun in the east, but he didn't register its meaning. He fought off one, then two of the demics that surrounded him. Another he cut in half, the legs still wiggling as it died. But more came. His eyes were heavy. A demic drew close, claws out and striking towards his face. He didn't know if his sword would come around in time.

Then the sun broke over the eastern horizon, and the first sunlight hit the demics.

The demic that bore down on him screamed and covered his eyes with his arms, shrinking from the light. Aden found some hidden reserve of energy and slew several demics that cowered before the sun. As they all fell to human and elven blades around him, Aden went to the wall and looked down. The demics howled and covered their eyes with their arms as they climbed the wall, and a few hundred fell to their death.

Caleb stood next to him, soaked with sweat and splattered in blood. The man spread his feet and looked out from the city as if he could fight for hours more.

On the field in front of the gate, those thousands of demics still alive wanted to curl up and hide in the grasses, but they dragged themselves further out from the wall before doing so. The tall figure of the Demilord stood as they passed him and retreated for the day. Aden didn't know, but he thought the Demilord smiled.

Aden collapsed into a sitting position and leaned against the parapet. His sword was stuck within his grasp; he couldn't get his fingers to open. Blood and gore covered him. He didn't care. He closed his eyes, thinking he might fall asleep right there.

——————

Exhausted and distraught, Caleb looked out over the field in the morning light. The Demilord had smiled because he knew what Caleb understood. If not for the sunlight that blinded the demics there at the end, the city of Ketan would have been overrun. The Demilord would have overcome these unbreachable walls, protected for over twelve millennia by men and *Sohan-el*. The sunlight had saved them. Thousands more of those little monsters waited to climb the walls even though the humans and elves had slaughtered, what, a thousand? Maybe two or three thousand of the things between the arrows and the butchering on the top of the wall. But several elves and humans had died; many Cityguard lay torn, crying and bleeding … or dead.

If the demics attacked at sunset tomorrow night … with the numbers they had left … the city would not survive the next night.

But they had survived this night. More men and women were being trained and would stand the wall with them tomorrow night. The city bought one more day of life with death.

Zalman strode over and stopped, hovering over Caleb. Caleb's eyes rotated to look up at him. "You owe me coin," Zalman said.

Caleb lifted an eyebrow at the mercenary gruts on the man. Here, amongst all this death. And the man asked for money?

Placing a bloody hand into the front pocket of his leather trousers, Caleb handed Zalman a silver moon.

Zalman took it from Caleb's hand, both of their hands black with demic blood, and he lifted it to Caleb in salute. Caleb did not say a word as Zalman walked past him and left the wall of Ketan.

CHAPTER 30

THE BATTLE FOR KETAN

An informal council gathered, leaders of the city and those Caleb trusted. He called them to Macarus' office. Macarus, Chamren, Eshlyn, Aden and Carys all sat around a large desk, and a map of Ketan covered the desk along with other papers, reports and numbers from Chamren.

The morning light bent through the glass window. Any other day, it would have been a hopeful sight, but not today. The sun was a reminder that another night was unavoidable. Their safety had a limit. Caleb sat at the far end of the desk. They were all fatigued and somber. Eshlyn kept her distance, but as long as she did her part, he didn't care.

"We need more arrows," Carys said, breaking through the silence. "And more archers. Several died last night as we ran down to the wall. We could keep them from the top with more arrows and archers."

"How many arrows did the woodcutters make yesterday?" Caleb asked Chamren.

Chamren fumbled a piece of parchment with hastily written numbers on it. "Almost three thousand," he said.

Carys shook her head. "Not enough," she said. "We need ten thousand, twenty thousand. It is a long shot at small targets. Those things are a crinkle to hit. We need hundreds of archers each in those towers, at least, and thousands of arrows. That would keep them off the wall."

"We don't have hundreds of archers," Caleb said to Carys. "Unless you're willing to teach them."

Carys rolled her eyes at him. "With untrained archers? We'd need thirty thousand arrows, a hundred thousand. It would be luck, blind shots. The strategy would have to be pure volume."

"I agree," Caleb said. "Macarus, how many bows do you have, in the armory and from the forge?"

"A few from the forge," Macarus said. "And 250 from the armory."

"Chamren," Caleb said. "How many people are making arrows?"

Chamren looked down at his parchment. "Ah, that would be 65," he said.

"65?" Caleb said. "Are the carpenters and smiths helping?"

"All," he said.

"We need more. This is a town of thousands. We need more help. Chamren, I want hundreds making arrows. They can be taught quickly, and we'll need them. Find as many as you can and divide them up between the carpenters, and have them work together."

"Yes sir," he said.

"Macarus," Caleb said. "How goes the Cityguard?"

"My elves are broken," he said. "We lost a hundred of the Cityguard last night, to injury or death."

Caleb's jaw tightened at that. One fifth of the trained fighters they had. Lost in one night.

"We need anyone who can hold a weapon up on that wall," he said. "Anyone."

"Untrained?" Carys said. "They won't last five minutes."

"Well, then we'll have to train them," Caleb said. "And fast. They're stronger than you think."

"But you've got me training more archers," she said. "I can't train fighters for the top of the wall at the same time."

"Your friend, Esai, and I will do that," Caleb said. "And maybe Zalman. We can find some axes. You take some of the volunteers and teach them the bow. I'll take the rest and teach them a couple spear and sword techniques. We'll take the shields from the fallen Cityguard and give the rest from the armory out. Space them out along the wall. That should help."

Caleb turned to Chamren and Macarus. "We need something to pour down that wall; oil or something to make it slick, more difficult for the demics to climb. Chamren?"

"I'll have some people collect some lamp oil, research what we might have in storage, but that is a lot of wall."

"Pitch and tar will need to be heated first, but they will stick to that if we can make it work. Anything slippery will do. Animal fat, oils, even sewage. We need to slow them down, keep them from the wall as much as possible."

Chamren grunted. "I will do what I can."

They all looked despondent. Beaten. They had lasted the night, but they knew it was a fluke.

"We weren't prepared last night," Caleb said. "Not really. And that is my fault. I didn't suspect they would be able to climb the walls so easily."

Macarus shook his head. "We wouldn't have been prepared at all if not for you," he admitted.

"Doesn't matter," Caleb said. "The survival of this city matters. We'll be better prepared tonight. I promise." He turned to Chamren. "I want you to have the people of this city clean off the wall of the dead. We'll need room to maneuver up there."

Chamren paled. "Uh, yes, um, sir."

"Have them carry stones and rocks, any stones and rocks you can find in the city, or bricks or chairs or any heavy debris – have them carry it to the wall and place them in piles every two mitres," Caleb said. "Then they can help they carry off the dead. That should take most of the morning. Between the arrows, archers, oil, and debris we can throw down from the top of the wall, we can hold out longer than last night. For as long as we can. Macarus," he turned to the elf. "Your elves fought bravely last night. Make sure they rest and eat. The way those demics reacted at sunset we won't need to be ready until late afternoon. We have all day. Aden, Macarus, you both sleep. You need it."

"I'll help you train the volunteers," Macarus said.

"And you need to sleep sometime, too," Eshlyn said. "You'll be no good without."

"Okay, then, we'll all rest until noon," Caleb said. "Then we train volunteers and archers for tonight."

Carys shook her head in disbelief.

"It will be enough. You'll see. We can hold out."

They all nodded an affirmation. Chamren and Eshlyn rose to leave, the man with a bow and Eshlyn without a word or look. Caleb spoke to her as she left. "I need to speak with you later, Eshlyn," Caleb called after her.

Macarus lingered. He looked at Caleb. "The Nican would like to talk to you."

"The priests?"

"Yes," Macarus said. "They are an important symbol for the elves in the city, and you've ignored them."

"I've had better things to do," Caleb said.

"With all due respect," Macarus said. "You should go talk to them, seek their input."

"I have no desire to hear their input," Caleb said. "But if they feel they need to talk to me, have them meet me outside of the coliseum this afternoon."

"But you've turned that into the infirmary, they will not like ..."

"I don't care what they like. Tell them that's the best I can do."

Macarus sat back, frowning. "I've been in battles before," he said. "Many. And fought under great First Generals and even Tanicus himself. We got lucky last night, and you know it. You think we can last a whole night with those things?"

"I don't believe in luck," Caleb said. "I believe in El. And I believe that with El, we can do the impossible."

Macarus groaned. "Stupid," he said. "But what can we do? Your plan is as good as any." He stood up. "I have to go see to my elves and relay your message to the Nican." He walked out, leaving Caleb alone with Aden and Carys.

Caleb looked at his sister. She sat there, brooding. "Talk to me, Car."

"These are people who've never held a weapon in their life," she said. "And you're gonna train them and tell them to stand on a wall and kill?"

"Yes. We will do what must be done."

"You know it won't work."

"I don't? What you said on the road the other night got me thinking. You said, *let us save ourselves, let El be El.* We should have died the other night at the inn. A room full of untrained humans stood off against a platoon of Cityguard and a Bladeguard. A couple of us knew how to fight. I had taught Aden here to barely hold a sword."

Aden scowled with a huff.

"And people died, I know. People we loved. But think about it. We should all be dead, but we fought." Caleb frowned. "I know more people will die. This is a battle. It's not pretty. But these are men. They are farmers and ranchers. They've never held a weapon, but they've used a hoe in a field, or an ax on a tree, or a dozen other things we can use to teach them how to fight. And I will. I will teach them all I can so they can save themselves. El will have to do the rest."

She crossed her arms. "Using my own breakin' words against me. That's just mean."

"Sorry. As an older brother I'm out of practice."

She took a deep breath, stood, and kissed him on the forehead. "I've got some farmers to teach how to shoot and not kill themselves or each other while they do it." She walked out, leaving him alone with Aden.

Caleb turned to Aden.

"Are you all right?" he asked.

Aden looked over at Caleb. "Why'm I here?"

"What?"

"I know why everyone else's here," Aden said. "Macarus, First Captain. Chamren, administrator. Carys, your sister and one o' Ghosts of Saten. Even Eshlyn, a fine woman and leader o' people from down south o' here. But me? I dunno …"

Caleb leaned back in his chair. "He gave you his books," he said.

Aden set his jaw and stared at Caleb.

"Before he …" Caleb cleared his throat. "He gave you the books. Put them into your hands. I don't know why yet, but it means something to me. Means a great deal to me. And he thought you were important, a part of all this. So you're here. If you want to be."

"Wanna be?" Aden asked. "I don't want. But I feel I have to." Aden looked away and down, his eyes embarrassed and sad. "I dunno if I can go back out there, though," he said.

"I understand," Caleb said. "You can help with the wounded or something else. Other things need to be done."

"But you just said that we need more people on th'wall."

Caleb sighed. "And we do. But a man who will freeze of fright up there… battles do things to people and it's better for everyone if you don't go back out there."

"I won't freeze," Aden said. "Are you kiddin' me? Did I freeze with the bloodwolves? Did I freeze in Biram? I'm not worried about freezin' up there."

"Then what?" Caleb said.

"I … I didn't like who I had t'be up there," he said. "No mercy, no emotion, just … killing. How can you stand it?"

Caleb's brow furrowed. Stand it? He didn't want to tell the young man he had enjoyed it. "You get used to it. It happens all at once, and the training takes over. You get used to it."

"Maybe that's it," Aden said. "I don't wanna get used to it."

———

The first night the elves had let them into the city, Byr had sought out his wife, Sirah, until he found her. She stood there with her parents, watching the thousands of people from the south come by the building they inhabited and pass them to camp out next door. When she saw him her eyes tightened, and she hid behind her parents, refusing to talk to him. He tried to call out to her. He pleaded for her forgiveness. Sirah's father, Brend, kept intercepting him. Finally, Brend said, "Come on, Byr, just leave her alone. She doesn't want to talk to you right now. Give her some time."

So he had left her alone. But he couldn't anymore. He needed to talk to her.

She was in her room in that building, a candle burning low as the sun fell behind the walls of the city, casting a shadow on Ketan. He walked in through the open door, and she turned away.

Byr stopped halfway into the room. He lowered his head. "Look," he said. "I just wanted to say I'm sorry. I just want you to forgive me." He took a deep breath. "I'm going out on that wall tonight. I did the training this afternoon. They even give me a sword. Kyv and I will be up there together." She didn't respond, her face to the wall. He looked at his wife's back. "Anyway. They say it might be bad. For the real. So I wanted to see you one last time. Tell you I love you and that I hope you can forgive me. I was wrong. We should have come here together. And I shouldn't have …" He cleared his throat. "And I shouldn't have hurt you. I'm sorry."

Byr clucked his tongue in frustration, turned and left.

———

"I can't believe you're arguing about this," Eshlyn said to the two elderly men in front of her.

She had been walking to the Ketan Square from the tenement now filled with people from Delaton and Roseborough, and these two gentlemen intercepted her on the way. They began the morning working at the infirmary, the makeshift one set up in the coliseum, but now they were asking for a different duty.

"I don't care how difficult it is," she said to them, keeping her voice stern. "Everyone has a hard job. Perhaps you'd like to clean the dead from the wall tomorrow and clean the blood and crit from the wall."

The men exchanged a glance, men she shouldn't have to coddle. "No, Miss Eshlyn," the one on the right said. His name was Pylar. The other, Manach, lowered his eyes and shook his head.

"You have dealt with sickness and blood and flesh on your farms, right?"

"Yes ma'am," Pylar said. "But not of humans, to the sure."

"And our friends," Manach muttered. "They our friends dyin' in there. We dealt with sickness, accidents, the like. That more than we ever seen done to a man." His eyes never lifted.

She took a deep breath to gather herself. "We've all dealt with death and blood recently," she said. She thought of Kenric, and Pylar winced, probably remembering her dead husband, as well. "And I daresay we'll deal with more. You're grown men of the Manahem plains. You work hard and take care of your own, do you not?"

"Yes, ma'am," they said together with quiet voices.

"Then you follow the doctor's orders, save who you can and hold the hands of those who die. Or I will have Chamren or Caleb assign you to clean off the wall, do you understand?"

"Yes, ma'am," the two men said again and walked away.

Eshlyn shook her head and continued to the square.

Upon arriving, she saw hundreds of people, maybe more than a thousand. They were in three different groups, although all in neat lines. The far group had spears, and Esai was teaching them how to fight, wide circular swings back and forth with the long blades cutting through the air. A big man, shirtless and bald, taught a second group, lifting their swords or axes over their heads and bringing the weapons down in a violent motion.

The third and closest group had spears and swords, and Caleb stood before them, stepping into a thrust and retreating with a block. Caleb held that staff of his. Xander was in Caleb's group, a long sword in his hand.

Eshlyn stopped a few paces behind Caleb. Some of the men in his group looked her way, and Caleb paused to look over his shoulder. Facing the group again, he paused and nodded to Xander. "Keep them practicing," he said. Xander stepped forward and took over. It surprised Eshlyn how confident Xander appeared – and how good he was.

Caleb joined Eshlyn, wiping his brow with the back of his shirtsleeve. His hair was tied back with a leather cord. He greeted her.

She gestured towards the people in the square. "How are they doing?"

Caleb shrugged, peering out at them. "They are fishermen, farmers, and ranchers, but they are strong. My father was a farmer, and he was one of the strongest men I've ever known."

"A farmer?" she asked. "Where?"

"Out east in Erelon, a tenant farm south of Anneton. He worked it for a local elven landowner." His gray eyes met hers. "These men are used to hard days of labor, and their bodies are rugged and tough. Now they have to trade those tools for weapons and learn to be warriors. Some will take to it and others will shrink. You never know until the battle. But they know what they're fighting for."

She nodded, her stare on Xander. "You said you needed to speak with me."

He leaned on the staff. "Yes. I wanted to see if there was anything else about Kenric you remembered that might help us, give us a clue to finding the Key."

She cleared her throat. "I don't know 'bout the Key," she said. She bit her lip. "But there is one other thing. I think it is important. But it will sound maddy."

"Maddy?" He chuckled. "There is an army from the Underland waiting outside those gates. We are putting weapons in the hands of men and women and teaching them how to fight. I just took over an elven city. Legends are coming to life before our eyes. How maddy can we get?"

She met his eyes. "I've seen him before."

His brow furrowed. "Who?"

"That creature that leads the demics. The Demilord. I've seen him before."

"I thought you said you didn't see anything that night in Campton."

"Not there," she said. "I've seen him in my dreams."

Now his eyebrows rose. "Keep talking."

"I've been having these dreams, dreams about Kenric mostly. Nightmares where Kenric is being held by a dark figure, imprisoned somehow. I think ... I think that dark figure is the Demilord, and Kenric is trying to tell me something."

Caleb rubbed his beard. "What do you think he's trying to tell you?"

She took a deep breath. "There's a sense of urgency, for me to get to Ketan. But now that we're here," she shrugged, "it's like he is fighting the Demilord somehow. But I don't know how, if he's dead. But in the dream, Kenric is holding onto that sword. And another man is helping him. You said you needed one of those swords to beat the monster."

"Yeah," he said.

She bit her lip and searched his face. "Maybe Kenric is bringing you the sword somehow." She shook her head and looked away. "I don't know. I thought I should tell you, but maybe I'm just grieving."

Caleb grunted. "It's possible," he said. "But the Demilord is carrying that unforged sword. They are supernatural weapons, and it's been centuries since someone has known how to use one or what they can do. Maybe Kenric is still connected to the Demilord through the sword, his soul somehow. And if so, then the sword could let him communicate with you."

"In the dream he's in so much pain," she said.

"The blood of kings," he muttered. Reaching out, he touched her arm. "It was right to tell me. Thank you," he said. "I believe you, and it feels important. I wish there were…" But he faltered and fell silent.

Eshlyn cocked her head at him. "Wished what?"

His eyes glistened, and he forced a grin. "I'll ask Drew and see if he can find something in the Fyrwrit or Ydu about this. But I have a feeling this is something new. We'll have to trust while we keep fighting."

———

His body more exhausted from the fighting last night and the training this morning, Caleb knew he needed rest, at least an hour or two of sleep, but there was one thing he needed to do first.

Looking up, he marked the sun as two hours past noon, and he made his way through the streets of Ketan to the coliseum. Hovering at the wide arch at the entrance, two robed figures stood. The Nican. He rolled his shoulders and gripped the Kingstaff in his right hand as he neared them. They noticed him, standing straight and tall, as tall as an elf could, which was to his shoulder. Stopping close to them, he towered over them, but they had learned to intimidate with more than their stature, their stares looking deep within him with condescension and annoyance.

Even from just outside the coliseum, though, he could smell death.

The elf on his right had short white hair, the one sign of age for the elder elves, and he wore a black robe, a priest of Motali, one of the three moons. The elf inclined his head in greeting. "I am Blinus," he said. "We are here to represent the Nican of this city."

Caleb's response was to turn to the elf just before him. He was younger with short blond hair and the red robe of Yor, the god of death. "Patris," he said, attempting to stretch himself to more than his full height.

"Well met, gentlelves," Caleb said. "I am Caleb De'Ador, Bladeguard of Kryus and Regent of Ketan during this crisis."

"Could we see your Letter of Regency?" Blinus said. "You must admit a human Bladeguard is quite odd. It would set our hearts at ease to see it for ourselves."

"No," Caleb said. "I do not have it with me. It was good enough for the First Captain, as I'm sure he explained to you. You can take it on his authority, surely. That will have to give your hearts peace enough for now."

"Yes, well," Blinus said, catching annoyed looks from the other priest. "Nevertheless, we must speak with you ..."

"Fine," Caleb said, and he began to walk, pushing his way through them. The two elves grunted as he passed. He stopped to speak over his shoulder. "I am visiting the city infirmary now. You'll have to speak with me while I talk with the injured."

"We would prefer to speak with you back at the Temple," Patris said.

"We are under siege, gentlelves," Caleb said. "It is not a time to worry about what we prefer." And he turned and strode forward, entering through the wide arch, past the open gate into the tunnel that led to the field. He heard movement behind him, the whispering of cloth, and he glanced for a split second to see Blinus following him, Patris at his heels.

The grass of the coliseum was covered with cots and beds. Along one end, a handful of larger tents had been erected. At the other end of the field, dead bodies lay wrapped in tan canvas, stains of black blood seeping through the wrappings. Straight ahead of him, Caleb could see through the cots of injured, a pile of severed limbs festering in the heat of the day.

The First Physician of the Ketan, an elf, glided to intercept them. He was bald with a hooked nose and large pointed ears. He was one of five elven physicians in the city clinic, which Caleb had closed down and moved here for more space. The clinics employed twenty-three physician's assistants, humans trained in surgery and basic healing arts. The First Physician appeared as exhausted as Caleb felt.

"Good afternoon," he said.

"Hello, Doctor," Caleb said. The elf glanced past him to see the robed elves halting behind him. "I'm sure you know the Nican."

"Yes, of course. I do," the Doctor said, wringing his hands. His white robe was covered in blood, red and black, and he wiped his hands on a worn rag that didn't seem to help much. "Good afternoon to you, as well."

"How is it here?" Caleb asked.

"We are doing what we can," the First Physician said. "But the wounds are so ... extensive, that most are losing limbs, the ones that survive. Others we can make comfortable until they pass."

Caleb frowned, clenching his jaw. "I understand. I'm sure you are doing your best. What do you need?"

"Not much," the Doctor said. "Chamren and that new woman ..."

"Eshlyn."

"Yes, Miss Eshlyn they call her. They both are quick to provide any that we request." The Doctor sighed. "We've learned to just amputate as soon as possible, and clean out the wounds quickly so infection doesn't set in."

"Don't let me keep you," Caleb said.

"Thank you," the Doctor said. "Actually, there is a man who has asked for you several times. Since you're here …"

"We'll join you," Caleb said.

"We'd rather not," Patris said.

Caleb raised an eyebrow at them and spat at their feet. "I'm going to visit the wounded, men and elves that have sacrificed to defend your lives. Go back and hide in the darkness of your temple if you wish. Pray all you like there. But if you wish to speak to me, here is where I will be."

Patris filled his chest with air, but Blinus laid a hand upon his shoulder. "We will come with you."

Caleb turned and followed the First Physician, weaving through cots of people moaning and groaning, crying out as they passed. The Doctor reassured them that someone would help them soon. They were mostly men, but Caleb noticed an elf missing an arm and a leg, black veins reaching out across his white skin. Caleb tried to look each of them in the eye and greet them as they walked. The Nican ignored the wounded.

"How many wounded still survive?" Caleb asked.

"Forty-nine," the Doctor answered. "But many are in critical condition."

They passed a young man, not much older than Aden, both legs gone, gripping the sides of the cot, whispering as he stared to the empty sky. "Kept coming … just kept coming …"

Caleb cleared his throat. "How many dead?"

The Doctor turned towards a canvas tent and paused. "Three hundred sixty one. So far." Then he continued to the tent, pushing open the flap and ducking inside. Caleb followed.

The tent was dark inside, lit with a single lamp, a middle-aged man with long, thinning dark hair. He had pock marks all over his face, his eyes closed. His arm ended at the wrist, wrapped in bloody bandages, and his left leg ended at the knee. The ground was covered in blood.

The Doctor touched the man on the neck, the skin pasty and pale. "Still has a fever. Weak heartbeat."

Caleb walked around and stood at the other side of the cot. "What is his name?"

The Doctor shrugged as if it didn't matter.

The injured man's eyes fluttered open, and he grunted in pain.

"There, now," the Doctor said. "Can you hear me?"

"I … I … yes," the man said.

"You've asked for the Imperial Regent, the human Bladeguard," the Doctor said, his eyes darting to Caleb and back down. "He is here."

The man cried out, whether in pain or relief, Caleb couldn't say. "Here?"

"I'm here," Caleb said.

The man took ragged breaths, his eyes glassy, open and searching. Caleb leaned over. The man's eyes narrowed at him. "Is it you? Are you the one?"

Caleb stood straight, catching the gaze of the Doctor and the two Nican on him. He nodded to the tent flap. "Wait for me outside. All of you."

The Nican didn't need any more instruction, hustling out the door. The Doctor cocked his head at him, glancing down at the man, hesitating, but he also left.

"Are you?" the man asked again.

Caleb leaned over him once more, close enough to smell the infection and his rancid breath, see the black lines along the man's face here in the dim light. "Who?"

The man swallowed hard, wincing, his mouth hanging open. "I heard a man, years ago. Came to Ketan. Here. They called him the Prophet..."

"Yes?"

"He spoke ... spoke of a man who would come and lead us, teach us how to fight, how to ... be free."

Caleb blinked.

"You came, and I heard you were a human Bladeguard, but so many humans are just elves in human skin, think and act the same. Odd but thought you probably like them." The man's eyes cleared all of a sudden, and he stared into Caleb's face. "But you're not like them, are you."

Caleb shook his head.

"Didn't think so. You gave us ... swords, spears, taught us how to fight. No elf ever do that. Ever. And I saw you fight. Like death itself came to those monsters." The man grimaced, spasming in pain. Caleb rested the Kingstaff against the cot, reached down and grabbed the man's shoulders, to comfort him, to hold him down and keep him on the cot. The man settled, stretched his remaining hand across his body and grasped Caleb's. "I'm dying. I know it. I can feel it. But I want to know. Are you him? Are you the man the Prophet talked about?"

How could he answer? He didn't know for sure, not yet, not until he reached the Living Stone, if he lasted that long anyway, with an army of demics and a Demilord with an unforged sword outside the gates. And even if he did know, how could you say a thing about yourself?

"Please," the man said. "I'm dying."

He thought about the Vow he took, about his dedication, his willingness to sacrifice his life, all that he had been through. If not him, then who? Was it arrogance to speak what was true?

"What is your name?" Caleb asked him.

"My name is Kormac," the man said. "Kormac Te'Kafar."

"Well met, Kormac. My name is Caleb De'Ador." He leaned even closer, his mouth centimitres from the man's ear, and he whispered, "The Prophet you speak of was my uncle. The man he told you about is called the *Brendel*, the Sword of El. And yes, I am he."

The man smiled. "Thank you," he said. "I knew it. When I saw you fight and stand on that wall last night, I knew."

The man cried out, his stare going blank, uttering sounds of pain and desperation. Caleb stayed with him, clutching the man's hand, calling the man's name as he died. It took ten minutes for the man to lay still, the tent filled with an overpowering stench of crit and piff and sickness. Caleb released the man's hand and closed his eyes.

Three-hundred sixty-two.

Sniffing, Caleb gathered himself, picked up the staff, and exited the tent, the sun bright on his face, and he squinted. The Doctor had gone, and the two Nican stood outside. Patris grimaced at him in disgust, and Blinus stared with a blank look.

Placing the staff in the crook of his right arm, he sneered at the Nican. "What did you want to speak to me about?"

Patris stepped forward. "We are the spiritual guides of this city, with the authority of the High Nican of Ashinar in Kryus. We speak for the gods and to the gods for the city here. You need our blessing, for the lives of the people in the city."

Caleb did not move or respond.

"You have leaders making decisions for this city, humans." Patris scoffed. "Even a human female from some village without a Steward or Temple to Ashinar and his host. We must be given leadership during this siege, control of the city."

"If you've been trained at the Citadel," Blinus said, standing next to his fellow priest. "Then surely you understand that we have the authority that both elves and humans will recognize. Chamren is a fine administrator, but these people need a leader. Your action with the Steward was regrettable but understandable. You and the First Captain are busy with the defense of the city. It is logical that we be given control of the city. At the very least, we should be included in your little leadership council."

Caleb looked from one Nican to the other for a long moment. "No," he said. "As you just heard the Doctor, Chamren and Eshlyn are doing fine. Thanks. But I will tell you what you can do, if you'd like to help."

Blinus lowered his head. Patris curled a lip in anger, his breath coming short.

"You can stand on the wall, pick up a sword or spear and fight. Some of the dead and injured here are elves. I'm sure we could find some armor that will fit you."

Patris paled.

"If that doesn't seem a good fit for you, then you can help clean the dead off the wall in the morning. You can head up that detail. Be good for the Nican of the god of death, I think. Or stay here and learn how to heal or comfort the men and elves that are dying around you. There are dozens of things I need. Find a place to do something and serve. Or don't. But you will not be given control of the city. Is there anything else?"

Patris gritted his teeth and clenched his fists. Blinus gave a short bow. "No. You have made yourself clear."

"Good. Now if you'll excuse me. I have forty-eight other injured men and elves to see before I fight on the wall again tonight."

He turned his back on the Nican and walked to the nearest cot, an older man with balding white hair gazing up at him with tears in his eyes. He had heard Caleb's conversation with the Nican.

"What is your name?" Caleb asked the man.

"Rab, sir."

"Well met, Rab. Well met. I am Caleb. How are you?"

He might not be getting much sleep after all.

—

"Ketan was once the greatest city in all of Eres," Caleb said, leaning against the parapet of the wall, just over the gate, watching the sunset. Aden frowned and looked at him.

Caleb crossed the wall walk and peered out over the city. Aden joined him.

"When Ketan was built, the elves were nomads, hunting and gathering, and the dwarves were cave-dwelling scavengers. The first city became the greatest city. Men, elves, and dwarves made pilgrimages to the First Temple to El near the palace." He pointed to the northeast. "Ketan was known for more than her great wall. She also boasted the first and greatest university in the entire world. Any and all could come and learn about any subject. Masters of all disciplines gathered here. Only the best could teach at the Ketan University. Theology, law, medicine, philosophy. And it was all free. Strenuous, the education required the greatest of discipline and sacrifice, but it was free."

Aden was silent for a moment before speaking. "What happened to the school?"

"Over time, men weren't willing to make the sacrifice, to endure the discipline. Many felt that it was unfair to have such high expectations of those who studied, and so Ketan University lost its prestige. The elves took what we taught and started their own schools, but none ever compared with what Ketan had once been." Caleb watched as dark fell. "Upon King Judai's surrender, Tanicus razed the First Temple and the University to the ground, placing a temple to Ashinar in place of the former. A coliseum stands where the University once dominated the landscape."

Macarus lowered his head behind them.

Caleb leaned closer to Aden and spoke low. "It makes sense that El would begin the revolution here, the first city of the First Men, the home of the first *Sohan-el*, where so much of it began the first time."

Aden grunted. "Reyan would have liked to see this."

Chuckling, Caleb felt his eyes mist. "Yes. Yes, he would have loved to be here. But he sees it. Perhaps better than we do, now."

"I miss 'im. Is that strange?"

"No, not strange," Caleb said. "Not strange at all."

Within moments after dark fell across the field, they could see the shapes begin to crawl forward, impish bodies making their way to the base of the wall. They began to grab the bodies of their brothers and pull them away from the wall.

Macarus looked at Caleb. "Are they burying them?"

"No," Aden said from Caleb's other side. "Look. They're eating them."

As Caleb looked closer, he pursed his lips in disgust. Aden was telling the truth. He turned to Aden. "So you decided to join us tonight," Caleb stated.

Aden didn't respond. He gazed off after the demics as they dragged the bodies of their own into the grasses to feast upon them. Caleb knew the young man wouldn't freeze. He would fight as well as any man or woman. But the young man had been through so much, seen so much in a short amount of time. He would have to survive this night, too.

3500 men, and a few women, had appeared that afternoon for training with weapons, a mixture of humans from Ketan, Roseborough and Delaton. Even a few of the elves in the city decided to do their part and train to stand on the wall. Teams of people made arrows throughout the day. They had a few thousand tonight, and along with the piles of debris along the top of the wall, he thought they should be able to keep the demics at bay for quite some time. And with the extra people, they could better man the wall.

But Caleb knew that it would come to hand to hand fighting. The demics would reach the top of the wall again, and people would die. He scanned to his right and left, and he saw Xander down to his right standing by his father, Eliot. Eliot held a spear awkwardly, and Xander held his long sword. That young man might become a fine swordsman one day. He had the potential. If he lasted the night.

Macarus grunted. "Maybe this will buy us some time," he said. "If they are so hungry they eat their own; maybe they will be weak from hunger."

"Or more desperate," Caleb muttered, and Macarus frowned.

Aden shook his head.

Macarus was right, however; it did buy them some time.

Two hours after sunset, the demics came charging back at the wall at full speed.

"Lights," Caleb murmured just loud enough for Macarus to hear.

"Lights!" Macarus called. And the lights from the coliseum shone bright over the field. The demics hesitated for a brief second, but they reached the wall at a sprint. The demics leapt at the wall, clung to the stone with their claws, and scrambled up the wall, even faster than the night before.

"So much for the hunger making them weak," Caleb said under his breath, then louder, "give them the crit."

Macarus lifted his sword and waved it, shouting down the line to dump the oils and other substances down the wall. Men and elves took buckets and small barrels of oil, lard, fat, and sewage and poured it down the wall. Caleb even saw a few people emptying heated pitch and tar over the parapet. Within minutes, the walls were covered with crude substances, either slippery or sticky.

Caleb watched as the demics tried to find purchase on the wall again, but it was difficult. Many fell from the wet and slick surface. After ten minutes of attempts and failures, the demics began to take their time, latching on with more care and deliberation. A few were also caught and stuck in the tar.

"It smells like crit and piff up here, but it's slowing them down," Caleb said.

Macarus didn't reply, but the elf captain looked out over the field of demics. "Did we even make a dent last night?" he asked. "By the nine gods, I still can't see the end of them."

"We'll find the end of them," Caleb said. "One by one." The demics were almost halfway up the wall.

"They're more spread out along the wall tonight," Macarus said, scanning east and west. "Not just bunched up here. They are adapting."

"The Demilord is adapting, I think," Caleb said. "But we will adapt, too."

"I said I'd see it to the end," Aden said.

Caleb faced the young man with a questioning look.

Aden slowly turned to him. "I promised myself that I would see it to the end, no matter where it took me," Aden said. "It was one of the few things Jo said to me, the man who took care of me on the streets, one of the few things he said that I remembered." Aden looked back over the parapet to the field of small, red creatures ready to eat their flesh and willing to eat their own. "That's why I'm here. I'm not quitting. I will see it to the end. No matter what."

Caleb nodded.

After an hour, Macarus said his name, and Caleb turned to see the demics had reached three fourths of the way up the wall. "Yes, First Captain," Caleb said. "Now."

The First Captain lifted his arm and signaled the battle towers.

And the arrows flew.

—

Carys had 126 people in her battletower, many of them untrained humans, and they were split facing both east and west along the wall. The other battletower had 133 people, also untrained humans. The elves from the Cityguard were still among them.

The bows were fine, and well strung, but the quality of the arrows left much to be desired. Carys wondered if they would even reach the wall, much less kill those demics. Taking advantage of her brother being in charge, Carys had gathered the straightest arrows for herself. Besides the elves, she would be the most likely to actually hit something. She hoped the rest of the humans shot well enough to hit a demic once out of five or ten.

Carys watched the demics climb the wall. Again. The creatures were crawling slowly up the wall, and that made them easier targets. There seemed like more of them tonight, but she didn't know how that could be. A trick of the eyes or her own fear. Either way, she nocked an arrow and waited for the signal from Macarus.

She took even breaths, calling out to the people around her and behind her with encouragement and instructions. "Wait for the signal. Wait for me to tell you to fire. Remember to keep your arm straight and aim with your eye." And your heart, she thought to herself. But they weren't good enough for that yet. She thought if she lived through this, she might make the joke that some people "couldn't hit the broadside of the wall of Ketan." But it wasn't funny tonight. She hoped to El they could.

And when the First Captain waved his arm, Carys cried out from her gut, and the humans let loose their first volley. Surprised, Carys watched the arrows fly and hit several demics, and if the arrow didn't kill them, at least the little crits were knocked from the wall to plummet to their deaths.

Carys told them to fire at will, and ultimately, her predictions held true. They hit one out of five at best. But they kept the demics from the top of the wall for an hour, maybe two.

Out of the corner of her eye, Carys noticed a tall figure walking farther forward than he had last night: the Demilord. She turned toward him and fixed him with her eye. Even at this distance, Carys could see the Demilord focused on the gates with intense concentration. He was an ugly figure, but bigger than the little demics. She wondered ...

She had two arrows left, so she nocked the straightest one. This would be a difficult shot. She held her breath and waited until she measured, anticipated, aimed with her heart, and then she let the arrow fly.

It felt like a good shot when it left her hand, and she watched it arch over the lit field and come down at an angle at the Demilord. The arrow raced towards the chest, the left front breast of the creature. And it hit.

And bounced off to the ground beside him. The Demilord looked down at his chest, then the ground, then back up at her. He grinned.

"Shog a bosaur's momma," she said.

—✝—

The last of the arrows flew, and Aden waited until Caleb gave the order, through Macarus, to begin to throw the debris. Caleb leaned over the parapet and peered down at the monsters coming towards them. He glanced at Macarus with a nod, and Macarus gave the order. "Now!" he said. "Now! Throw it down!"

This took little skill but proved to be effective. Aden picked up a stone, hefted it, and dropped it over the side of the wall. He watched as it took out two – no, three – demics as it bounced along the wall. Aden kept lifting stones, rocks, and old wood from trashed furniture or unsafe buildings and throwing them over. At first, his body was glad to be doing something, but he began to tire. And it became an act of will to keep it up. And they weren't even fighting hand to hand yet.

Time stretched, and an hour or so passed until the debris at his feet was gone. Others had paced themselves well, as Aden had tried to do, and kept up the deliberate defense by throwing rocks. Others, in their desperation and fear, moved through their piles of debris too fast, but that was understandable – more than 2000 of these people had never been in a battle before, or held a weapon, or had to look in the face of actual creatures from the Underland. The result, however, meant that the demics could race up in certain areas without obstacle sooner than others.

Demics began to reach the top of the wall, even while some still had stones to throw down, but those men had to pick up their weapons and fend off teeth, claw, horn, and tusk from tearing into their skin.

Aden picked up his sword, a gladus tonight, and began to fight for his life and the survival of the city behind him.

—+—

Taking the stairs two at a time, Carys bounded down from the battletower to the wall-walk in a matter of seconds. She held no weapons in her hands; she left the bow and empty quiver above, and she gave her gladus to one of the men on the wall who didn't have one. So she would have to find something on the wall-walk or fight with her bare fists.

The demics were close to the top of the wall by the time she arrived, even with the debris being hurled down at them, and she helped two men for ten or fifteen minutes before the humans had to switch to weapons to knock them from the parapet. Without a weapon, she kept tossing what little debris was left at the demics as they crossed over to engage the humans face to face. She hung back, crouching low in a defensive stance, wondering why she didn't at least bring a club or something, but it was too late to worry about that lack of preparation now. One demic got past a human with a spear, and Carys was able to catch the creature mid-air, turn on her heel, and throw the demic from the wall to his death. It squealed.

For the first time in her life, Carys fought something smaller than herself. She usually had to use quickness and skill to beat an opponent, but here she could use brute force against the demics. It was awkward for her to adjust, since part of her strategy had to be keeping away from those black claws and teeth, but overall she enjoyed the feeling of strength.

The human with the spear went down with a scream, and as he died, she pulled the spear from his grip, broke it in half over her knee, and attacked the demics around her with the blade of the spear in one hand as a sword and the butt of the spear in the other as a club. She cut half through the neck of one demic with the spear, smacking another in the face with the butt of the spear, following the strike with a kick, moving forward.

She began to fight her way to her brother.

—+—

Nafys had a sword in one hand and a club in the other, swinging away at the imps at the top of the wall. The club was his from Roseborough. The sword belonged to a dead elf from the night before, and it felt small in his large hand. But it cut through demics sure enough, and the club helped him fend off the things until he could stab them or slice a piece off of them.

He was covered in sweat and blood within the hour, and his muscles and bones began to ache with the effort and the strain. He did not slow, however, and he did not relent. Nafys bared his teeth at these creatures and crushed them again and again.

But they kept coming. Nafys had to fight both the beasts from the Underland and his own hopelessness at the same time. Would there ever be an end to them? He won that battle, though, filling his thoughts with his love for his wife as the demics surrounded him, of protecting her now and getting back to her later.

Somehow he stumbled after two hours of fighting and blood and killing, and that one human mistake cost him. His club didn't have time to fend off a demic from latching onto his left leg, the tusks ripping through the muscle in his calf. He screamed in pain and went down to one knee as he frantically clubbed the demic latched onto him, the thing coming off with half his calf in its teeth.

Crying out, he was distracted by his injury, and within moments, another demic had hold of his right arm, the one holding the sword. Another jumped past the one on his arm to sink teeth into his neck and claw at his face, ripping at his eyes and the flesh from his cheek.

Nafys died screaming and thinking of his wife.

—+—

Shirtless, Zalman wore long leather breeches and black leather boots. The night air felt good against his skin, the wind high above the city whistling past him. The battleaxes again gave him the sense that he had been born for this battle, for this moment, and with both hands he swatted and squashed and sliced through the mass of creatures around him. Zalman even began to use his feet and knees to kick and knock the demics from his presence.

Last night, they had begun to avoid him. Tonight, they took a different tactic. They crowded him, hoping to overwhelm him. While last night they ran from the threat, tonight they ran to him. He welcomed it.

Six demics launched themselves at him at once, two from behind and four from the front. Zalman reacted with a spin of his body on his left foot, kicking out with his right and swiping with the battleaxes. With the battleax in his right hand, he clove one demic in two through the torso and the ax sunk deep into the cranium of another. He swung with the broad bladed weapon in his left, beheading one and taking the legs from the second. He kicked out with his left foot, watching a demic fly back over the wall to the ground below, but one got through from the rear and slashed at

Zalman's right shoulder with his claws, scoring a deep cut and drawing red blood from the large man.

Zalman backhanded the demic, breaking bones in the thing's face, and barely registered the pain. He was in a brawl. He had been born fighting, and he would die fighting. Although he had never been in a full battle before, constant conflict had been the character of his whole life. These demics would regret changing their tactics tonight.

Still bleeding from the shoulder, Zalman threw himself into the gathering of demics before him, startling them and scattering them as he bashed and chopped them to blackened, bloody pieces with the battleaxes.

———

Macarus was a master swordsman. He felt wasted in a battle such as this.

His training did help him, however. The need for constant motion, to be unpredictable in his movements, on the offensive and defensive all at once, it helped him in this turmoil. But the demics were a storm around him, and he was the eye within it. Macarus fought and struggled to be that eye.

Hours passed. He saw elves fall. Humans fall. Their blood mixed on the top of the wall with the black blood of the demics. A few of the humans panicked and went down under the ferocious demics in moments, but most of the humans fought with bravery and heart. Macarus remembered the battle for the defense of this city hundreds of years ago. Brave men and elves had died then, too, fighting one another in a brutal and cruel conflict. At least this battle was to save the innocent, to save lives.

That did not feel wasted. This battle was unique to the First Captain. He had fought for his country, to conquer, for the pride of an Emperor. Now they fought for survival, against real evil. Macarus was in a battle that felt good and pure. And a human was leading them.

Caleb fought to his left, and even though the man didn't have a sword and wouldn't wear armor, Macarus believed that the man was a Bladeguard. While the tattoo and the seal on the parchment checked out, Macarus had still had his doubts. But watching the man fight and move— no one could do that without the right training. And while Macarus had fought more battles than Caleb – the last campaign of the War of Liberation had been extensive and grueling – Macarus didn't want to test his mettle against this Bladeguard. Not unless he had to. He wasn't sure of the outcome.

Macarus heard a cry from his right, and on the edge of his vision, he saw Ryus collapse under a fierce attack from several demics. Ryus was a fine swordsman in his own right, but in a battle like this, anyone could fall.

Yor, the god of death, didn't skip an elf because he was a fine swordsman. He took whom he would.

Trying to get over to help his lieutenant, Macarus spun and swung wildly with his sword, cutting through the shoulder of one demic and removing the heads of two more, getting to Ryus in three steps. But he wasn't in time. Ryus was dying when Macarus arrived, and while Macarus was able to keep the demics away from Ryus, he couldn't keep his lieutenant from bleeding to death at his feet.

But by the nine gods, those things wouldn't eat him.

———

After what seemed like days or a ninedays, the sun rose, peeking above the eastern horizon. Caleb's eyes had been drawn to the east for some time now, even unwittingly glancing in that direction as if he could will the sun to rise and end this dance of death. While more people on the wall had allowed them to prolong the battle and keep the demics from breaching the walls, it had also increased the chaos and noise. And casualties.

The demics screeched and fell back from the sunlight. The humans and elves that remained on the wall cleared the top of the wall with final desperate bursts of energy. Within seconds, what had been a cacophony of sound dropped to a quiet interrupted by the distant cries of the demics as they retreated for the day and those men or elves still within the throes of injury or death.

The Demilord stood tall and strong upon the field before the gates of the city for a time, gazing at Caleb as if he somehow knew. Perhaps he did. Who knew what beings from the Underland knew or understood. After another few moments, the Demilord performed a flourish with the unforged sword in his clawed hand and backed away, turning after a few paces to join his demics.

Aden, Carys, and Macarus stood nearby Caleb. "What a shogger," Carys said. Where had Carys gotten that broken spear?

He wondered if Eshlyn was correct. Was her husband somehow still connected to the sword and the Demilord? Was he trying to get the sword to someone so they could kill the beast with it? He shook his head. Even that were true, none of them could fight through the legion of demics and then take it from him. The demic strategy was to wear them down, and it was working. Could he draw the beast out somehow?

Caleb thought of the Vow. He had promised not to touch a sword until receiving one of his own, but the pledge also called him to fight for the oppressed and the innocent. If faced with the choice, he would break the Vow either way. He would do what he could to save the city.

Looking around, Caleb noticed far more demics dead than elves or human, but he saw the humans and elves more clearly than the monsters.

They had made it another night. But at a great cost.
    Perhaps too great.

Chapter 31

At the Feet of Dragons

Watching the demic retreat, Zalman breathed a heaving sigh and wiped his face with the back of his hand, still holding the battleaxes.

As he walked back to the door to the battletower and the stairs that led back down to the inside of the city, he stumbled, tired and light headed.

A small blond woman wearing brown pants and a green tunic walked up to him and placed a hand on his chest. "Hey," she said. "Sit down. You're wounded."

Zalman shook his head. "Others wounded worse. Get them to doctor first."

"Oh, I'm not taking you to the doctor," she said as she pushed him down. Even as his head swam, she didn't have the strength to make him do anything, but he allowed himself to be guided to his haunches and leaned against the back parapet of the wall-walk. "I'm taking care of you right here. You're bleeding a lot."

Zalman twisted his head on his neck to glance at his shoulder. His whole right side was covered in blood. "Ah," he said. "Just a scratch."

The girl rolled her eyes at him with a frown as she pulled a needle and thread out of her belt pouch. She looked around herself, tore a clean sleeve off of a dead elf nearby, and wiped down his side and shoulder, also using the remaining water from a bucket a few paces away. Zalman sat still and quiet as she sewed the gash closed. He winced once, but she was fast and good with the stitching. Zalman watched her green eyes as they narrowed intently at her work.

"What is your name?" he asked.

"Carys," she said.

He gave her his most mischievous smirk and leaned his head back against the stone parapet. "Well, Carys," he intoned. "Once we finish here, maybe you'd like to come with me somewhere nice and quiet ... and private."

Her jaw set, she took a final moment to finish the stitching of his wound. Carys balled up her fist and struck him just below the ribs. Hard. His breath left him in a rush and his eyes bulged.

"You're done," she said, standing and placing the needle and the rest of the thread back in her belt pouch. "I'd suggest some rest." She walked away, calling over her shoulder. "And put on a breakin' shirt!"

Zalman grinned, once he caught his breath.

＋

Xander and Eliot, exhausted, walked in the morning shadows with Caleb to the office he shared with Macarus, where they would debrief again from the fighting that had recently ended.

"I am sorry you lost your friends," Caleb said. "They fought well."

"And they were good men. Good friends." Eliot's eyes were empty and distant. "I have to go talk to their wives now. I have to tell them."

"We'll tell them, Da," Xander said.

"Be sure to get some sleep and rest while you can," Caleb said. "And food. How is the food? Is there enough?"

Eliot nodded. "Chamren is doing a fine job with rations," he said. "And he's been kind to include us."

"Good," Caleb said as they reached the door to the office. "Go back and get some sleep."

"Will there be training again today?" Xander said.

"If so, maybe a short session," Caleb said. "Surviving last night was training enough. Rest will do you better than training for another night." Caleb said his goodbyes with his hand on the door and watched the two men trudge away.

Entering the office, everyone was present, waiting on him and sitting around the large desk. Aden, Carys, Macarus, Chamren, and Eshlyn sat there with vacant, fatigued stares. Eshlyn had brought her son, Javyn, to the meeting.

Eshlyn noticed his eyes on the baby, and she said, "He was having a bad night," she said. "He cried a lot last night. I thought he might be missing me, so I brought him."

"It's fine," Caleb said. "I'd rather have you here."

She smiled at that.

Not for the first time, Caleb noticed her beauty. He had heard of her courage and intelligence days before meeting her, and Xander had mentioned her loveliness, but it was natural for a brother to think his sister a beautiful woman, just as Caleb thought so about Carys. But even upon first meeting her, she astounded and disarmed with how fair she was. Xander hadn't exaggerated; he had undersold her. Even as she sat with disheveled hair and a dirt smudged yellow cotton dress, Caleb's eyes were drawn to her unwittingly, as they had been to the east for the sun just an hour ago, although for different reasons.

But she was a woman grieving a dead husband, and Caleb didn't have time for such things anyway.

Shaking his head free of those inane thoughts, he sat between Eshlyn and Carys and leaned back in his chair, wearier than he had ever been before.

"Let's get it out of the way," Caleb said. "Losses."

"I lost 53 elves last night," Macarus said. "A few injured survived."

"We lost four hundred humans, give or take," Caleb said. "Although several are wounded. Another hundred, maybe. I'll have to check at the infirmary later."

Carys raised her eyebrows. "That's a lot of people," she said.

"But better percentages than the night before," Caleb said. "The extra numbers are helping."

"But they will be wounded or tired tonight," Macarus said. "The line will be thinner around the wall."

"We'll have to adjust," Caleb said. "Suggestions?"

"I'll say it again – more arrows," Carys said. "We could keep them off the wall longer with more arrows. The new archers got better as they went last night, but it is still a game of volume. But the oil and other crit down the wall slowed them down, made for easier targets."

"Some of that will have dried out or hardened in the sun by tonight," Caleb said. "Chamren, do we have more of that?"

"We used much of it last night, but not all. I'll find what extra I can," Chamren answered.

"And more debris," Aden said. "And we need to tell people to pace themselves. Some threw everything down all at once."

"Good point," Caleb said. "It was uneven last night." He turned to Chamren again. "How are the stores for food?"

"We are fine for now," Chamren said. "The people are used to a certain amount of … control. But we didn't really prepare food for the siege. It won't last long. A couple ninedays. After that, we'll be relying only on the fish from the river."

"It may not matter," Macarus said. "We'll be spread thin and even more tired tonight."

"Then we do what we can and rest," Caleb said. "And pray. Despair and doubt will kill us faster than those demics. We are the ones the people in this city look to. We must give them hope. We lasted another night. We'll do what we have to. Are those elves working on catapults?"

"Um, well, you see, uh, okay," Chamren began. "They built one yesterday, but when they fired it … well, one elf now has a broken arm and another was thrown five mitres." He lowered his voice. "They're both in the infirmary with the wounded."

Caleb sighed. Throwing stones large enough to cause damage with hurried trebuchets was a long shot anyway, especially over those enormous walls. Caleb instructed Chamren again to have people clean the walls of the dead and bring up more debris.

Javyn began to fuss, a little cry and moans at first, but then he began to wail. Eshlyn rose and took the boy to the far corner at the other end of the office while they continued talking and making plans for the day.

Caleb heard Eshlyn begin to sing to her son in a whisper. Javyn settled, groaning.

Caleb stared at Eshlyn and Javyn in the corner. Eshlyn rocked the baby and continued to sing.

"Caleb?" he heard Carys say. "Are you listening?"

Caleb stood. "Yes," he said. "But not to you. What are you singing?"

Eshlyn turned and looked at them apologetically upon noticing Caleb's gaze on her again. "I'm sorry," she said. "I'll take him outside."

Caleb walked towards her. "No, don't. That's not what I meant," he said. "What are you singing to him?"

"Just a lullaby that Kenric used to sing to him," Eshlyn said.

Good and mighty El, Caleb thought, and he stood still three paces away from her. *Could it be that simple?* "Kenric used to sing it to him?" he said under his breath.

"Yes," she said. "Why?"

And he remembered her story, the first time she told it to him here in this office. He thought nothing of it at the time, but hadn't there been … He closed his eyes. "You mean the lullaby he told you to sing to the boy the night he died?" he asked.

"Yes," she said, dragging out the word.

It was beginning to make sense. "And let me guess," Caleb said. "Kenric learned that lullaby from his father, and his father before him."

"Well, yeah," she said, and her face went blank. Her eyes widened.

"Tell me the words," he said.

———

In another age, the children lead
The sons are kings, and daughters queens
The crowns will bow at dragon's feet
And thrones will fall to find the Key

The words rang in his mind as the group of them entered the throne room, an immense and bare room that accentuated the throne up on the dais. Caleb stopped inside the double doors and the others filed in behind him. "What are we doing here?" Aden asked.

Chamren's eyes flew around the room. Macarus was also agitated, but he held it well beneath his soldier's calm. Eshlyn still held her son in a sling at her breast, her face full of fear. "You think it's here," she said to Caleb.

"What is here?" Carys asked. "I don't get it, Caleb. Are you all right? Maybe you need to rest …"

Caleb hushed her. "Quiet," he said. "Do you hear that?"

"Hear what?" Aden said.

"Chamren," Caleb said. "Has anyone else been in the throne room since Desiderus was arrested?"

Chamren shook his head and shuffled his feet. "No sir. Not even a few days before then."

There was a pulse, a faint pounding.

"I do hear something," Eshlyn said. "Or feel it." She stood still and closed her eyes. She opened them again and pointed to the dais, to the throne. "There. I think it's coming from there."

The group was quiet, and Caleb saw they all heard and felt it now. He looked up at the throne, at the dragons that formed the armrests. Those golden dragons wound around the iron seat of the throne, and their golden feet became the feet and legs of the king's chair.

"Yes," Caleb said. "The throne." He began to walk towards it. "Come on, everybody. I'll need your help."

They followed him cautiously, and he didn't wait for them. He made his way up the stairs to the platform at the top. He paused as he stood next to the throne; the high back in the form of a lush tree felt smooth under his fingers. He gripped the right side of the throne. And pushed.

Chamren gasped, and Macarus said, "Wait!"

But Caleb didn't wait. He kept pushing. Soon Eshlyn was next to him, Javyn hugging close in the cotton sling at her breast, and she pushed as well. It budged beneath their weight. Carys and Aden followed, pushing against the side of the throne. Chamren danced from foot to foot for a moment before joining them. He was a large man on his own, and the whole throne tipped a few centimitres.

"Come on, Macarus!" Caleb said through a grunt and gritted teeth. "Help us!"

Macarus shook his head, confused. "What are you doing?"

"It's here," Eshlyn said. "Help us, please."

Macarus moved at her words, and soon he had his hands on the head of a golden dragon and heaved with all his might. The throne began to tip even further, accompanied by a scraping sound against the marble of the dais. Caleb shouted, and Carys and Aden and Eshlyn joined his guttural cry. The weight of the top of the throne was now enough to help them topple the substantial base, and the whole throne fell over on its side with a crash that echoed through the enormous room.

Everyone else stepped back, breathing heavily, but Caleb squatted down and looked at the floor exposed beneath the throne.

"Breakit," he said.

He saw a steel circular panel set into the marble, about a half mitre in diameter. Along the edge of the panel were the ancient runes that belonged to the initial writing system of the First Tongue. Painted on the marble just outside the panel was a red arrow.

"What is it?" he heard Eshlyn ask.

"It is a lock," Caleb said, and the rest of the group knelt or sat around the steel panel. "Those runes are the first writing system of Eres. And to open this panel, we must have the combination, lining up the runes in a particular order to open it."

"What kinda combination?" Aden asked.

"Usually a phrase or word," Caleb answered.

"King Judai placed this here," Macarus said. "Try his name."

"I'll try. But that seems too easy," Caleb said. It took him a moment to remember the meaning of the runes, translating back twice from common to the First Tongue then to the runes. The first phrase didn't work.

The group suggested other words like Manahem or Ketan, but nothing worked.

"The lullaby," Eshlyn said. "If he went to the trouble to pass on the sword and the lullaby, then the combination would be there, too, right?"

Caleb grinned. "Yes. But which part."

Aden sniffed and spoke with confidence. "*Dragon feet*," he said.

Glancing at him, Caleb's eyebrow rose.

"Just try it," Aden said.

Caleb turned the panel to line up the runes that spelled "dragon feet." He heard a series of clicks, and he withdrew his hand and leaned back as the panel split into four pieces and sunk into the marble, exposing a compartment underneath. Within the rectangular compartment, something lay wrapped in white linen cloth.

Caleb reached in and grabbed it out of the rectangular space. It was very heavy, but he could lift it with one hand. He unwrapped the object. A black object was housed within the white linen. It was a rounded shaft, a handle that ended in a flat circle. The whole thing was made of some black stone, like onyx but much heavier.

He turned the object over and peered at the circular end. Runes had been etched into the stone.

"Is that writing?" Aden asked, kneeling down next to him.

Caleb nodded. "In the First Tongue," he said. "An old rune version of the First Tongue. I can barely read it."

They waited while he tried to decipher the meaning. "I can read something about blood," he said. "And I think this word is the word for *Sohan-el*, but it is hard to make out. I think … I think it means the life or soul of a *Sohan-el*."

"The Key," Aden said. "This is it, right? The Key to the Underland?"

"The *Heol-caeg*," Caleb said. "Yes."

"So what is it about the blood of a *Sohan-el*?" Eshlyn asked.

Caleb didn't take his eyes off of the Key. "I think it means that in order to use this Key, you need the soul of a *Sohan-el*," he said.

"Who needs the soul?" Eshlyn asked.

"The Demilord," Caleb said. He looked up at Eshlyn. "Demics eat flesh, but Demilords eat souls."

She gasped. "Kenric," she whispered.

"If I'm reading this right, a Demilord must have the soul of a *Sohan-el* to use the Key," he said.

"What is a *Sohan-el*?" Chamren asked.

Aden pointed his finger at Caleb. "He is."

"A warrior-leader of El," Caleb spoke, but his mind was elsewhere.

Macarus' face turned dark and dangerous.

"I'm curious," Caleb said. "Did Tanicus look for this? We know Judai surrendered, but in the end, if Tanicus had known it was here, he would have done everything to get his hands on it." Caleb turned to Macarus' scowl. "Do you agree?"

Macarus collected himself, drew in a deep breath, and blinked. "Tanicus would have taken this for himself, yes, if he had known of its existence."

"So we can assume that Tanicus didn't know about it, or couldn't find it," Caleb said. "After the siege of Ketan."

"But why did King Judai leave it here?" Aden asked. "Why not give it to the elves to protect once he surrendered? He just hid it here for anyone to find."

"No," Caleb said. "Not just anyone." He peered at Eshlyn. "He gave one of his descendants his unforged sword and a lullaby to lead them here. He didn't give it to the elves because it wasn't theirs to protect. It belonged to humans, to men to protect it. So he had faith and hope."

"In a lullaby," Macarus muttered bitterly.

"No," Caleb said. "Not in a lullaby. In El. In his design for humanity to rise again. In the midst of the greatest defeat, a defeat that seemed final, he had faith." Macarus groaned at him. "And amazingly enough t worked."

"But the question is," Aden said. "What we do with it now?"

———

Eshlyn clutched her son close to her as they all sat speechless for a long stretch of time around on the floor of the throne room. In their midst lay the *Heol-caeg*, pulsing from within the black stone, the Key that opened the Dark Gate to the Underland. She laid her hands upon it once, a cold slippery surface that shook and throbbed. It made her nauseous.

She spoke first. "We have to get rid of it," she said. "Can we get someone on a boat and send it into the river? Or one of the lakes?"

"I think that pulse is what calls to them," Aden said. "They'll find it anywhere we send it."

"And anyone we send with it will be exposed against all of them," Caleb said.

"But can we keep it here?" Eshlyn asked. "This is what they're after. If we get rid of it, we can be safe."

"That's true," Caleb said. "There's too much we don't know, though. If we send it into the river, will they still get it? If we run with it, how far can they follow?" Caleb sighed. "But I do know this. The Key was put into the hands of men to keep safe, to protect. It was put into the hands of the very men whose soul it needs to work. I don't intend to give up that responsibility. I don't intend to run with it or throw it away."

"But the men of today, if they ever were like you say, they are different now," Macarus said. "This place is different. We don't have the resources, the training in the city to deal with this. They could breach those walls tonight. Even if we fight better than we have been, they might make it past the walls into the city. And then they will get this Key." Macarus sighed. "Send a pigeon. Send a boat. Send for help. Please."

Caleb shook his head. "I'm sorry, Macarus. I can't. First of all, you just admitted we might not last the night. We need to finish this sooner than later. But more important, Yosu and El placed this Key into the hands of men, into the hands of *Sohan-el* to protect. Judai did what he could to put it in the hands of men again. And here it is. I have to believe El will help us. We have to have faith. We can be those people again."

Macarus shook his head in disbelief, and Eshlyn lowered her eyes. "Faith in what?" Eshlyn asked.

"Faith that if we fight, El will help us," Caleb said. "Faith that this hasn't all been an accident of fate. Faith that we are here for a reason, that situations and events haven't been coincidence or chance. That I am here for a reason. And I think this is it."

"So, help me understand," Eshlyn said. "Your faith in this god of yours tells you to put all of our lives at risk, to put my son's life at risk, all to prove a point?"

"Think about it," Caleb said. "Please. You survived, Eshlyn! Out of all the people in Campton, you survived with your son and a lullaby that led us straight to the Key. Not anyone else. You." He turned to Carys. "And I found you again, after all that time apart; we're here again, together." Eshlyn watched Aden's eyes glisten as Caleb turned to him. "And I found you, just when I needed you, and we were able to help ... an old friend. I was simply going to the mountains to get an unforged sword, to complete my journey to become a *Sohan-el*, and yet I'm here, after meeting Xander and Joob in an inn on the outskirts of Biram."

He looked each of them in the eye. "King Judai taught his son, or grandson, or somebody a lullaby and gave them an unforged sword and here we are in the first city in the world, once the greatest city in Eres, with the Key among us, with humans and elves standing on a wall together."

Caleb shook his head. "No," he said, staring at the Key in front of him. "I'm not sending a boat or a pigeon for help. Not now. El has been a part of this whole journey, and I must believe he will help us here and now. This has all been by design. We are here for this time and purpose. It is up to us. But I can't make any of you stand with me. You're free to stay or go."

"That's bullcrit," Macarus said. "You're making this decision for all of us and you know it. If we divide our resources and leadership now, we are definitely done. I guarantee it."

Aden looked from Macarus to Caleb, a tear in his eye. "I'm with you, Caleb," he said. "I believe. I do. I say we stay and protect the Key together, as men were meant to."

Carys regarded Aden for a moment, a look of respect passing over her face at the young man, then she turned to Caleb. "You know I'm with you, Cubby," she said. "It's like we're in an ancient story where everything happens for a reason. For the first time, it all makes sense to me. I wish ..." Eshlyn watched the young woman struggle with her emotions for a moment, then recover. "I wish our ... old friend were here with us now. I'm with you wherever you need me to be."

Caleb grinned at his little sister, and Eshlyn thought about her brother. "People were slaughtered in those ancient stories, too," Eshlyn said. "And good men died last night. Men I knew, grew up with. Is that part of this amazing story? Is that the will of this god you believe in?" Eshlyn's heart fell with the very despair Caleb had warned against. "How can you know this decision is right? " she asked Caleb pointedly. "For sure? Help me understand."

"There's no guarantee," Caleb said. "But I will trust that El has a will and a plan and the rise of men again here and now is part of that plan. I believe he wants us to be men again even more than I do. And so I believe he will help us." Caleb caught her gaze, and Eshlyn could see deeper into the man than ever before. "And we all might die. Even if I save the city, I might die doing it. But I'm willing to die for that, to give my life for that." Caleb lowered his eyes and breathed heavily, wearily. "I have for a long time, now."

Eshlyn shook her head. Men. Caleb's resolve reminded her of Kenric in that moment, his resolve to go and fight those monsters instead of run with her, but Kenric had been right that night, just as Caleb was correct now. Why had she been the only one to survive? The wife and son of the man who might know that there was real danger? She didn't know the answer, but she did see the iron and stone in Caleb's gaze. She didn't know why, but as crazy as he sounded, she had never seen a man lead like this man, fight like this man, and live like this man with people around him that carried swords and imprisoned elven Stewards.

She ran to Ketan based on Kenric's wishes, even though a part of her wished she had stayed to fight with him. There was a time to run and a time to stand and fight. She felt the truth of Caleb's words. She wouldn't run.

"I want to see my son live to grow up and grow old, maybe fall in love and have children of his own." She found herself crying. "But what do I know of guarantees? Our lives are so fragile anyway ..." She faced Caleb again, her vision blurry, but her stare was hard and determined. "We stay and fight ... and protect this cursed thing."

Caleb turned to Chamren, the only one who hadn't spoken. His nervousness gone, he bowed his head and spoke, his voice soft, "I don't know what to believe, but I've seen something in you, Caleb, sir, that I have longed for my whole life," Chamren said. "Whatever happens, I'm yours."

Turning to Macarus, Caleb said, "First Captain, I believe you are an honorable elf and a friend to the humans here in Ketan. If you wish to take a boat with the rest of the Cityguard, or anyone else that wants to go, and sail to Biram or walk to Taggart, you have my leave. You have acted honorably, and I will not keep you here against your convictions or your will." Caleb grinned. "But you are also a fierce warrior, an amazing leader, and someone I'd like to keep at my side, if you'll stay. I leave the choice to you."

Macarus looked at Eshlyn, and she reached out and laid her hand upon his. "Stay, Macarus," she said. "Please."

He shook his head at her and then at Caleb. "Faith has always produced zealots and fools," he said. "And I believe you are both. But I will do as you ask, on one condition."

"Name it," Caleb said.

"If we live and survive this," Macarus said. "You tell me everything. you tell me how you came to be a Bladeguard and what you are really doing, what your real agenda is. There are things you haven't explained to me and kept from me. If I stay, you tell me everything."

Caleb nodded. "That's a deal. You deserve that much and more."

Macarus and Caleb stared into each other's eyes for a long moment, two warriors measuring each other, and Eshlyn was glad to see Macarus nod back. "Very well," he said. "I shall stay."

"Good," Caleb said. "Now, who's gonna help me put the throne back?"

———

Night fell with the setting sun, a beautiful red and orange display across the western horizon that would have inspired any artist. But the men, women, and elves on the top of the wall that night watched it with dread.

Like the night before, the demics came and dragged their brothers out from the base of the wall and into the tall grasses to feed upon them. The protectors on the wall waited patiently over the next four hours, even longer than the night before. For most of them, the anxiousness was gone. Exhaustion put a damper on their worry and concern.

That was until something long and dark moved through the grasses of the field before the gates.

"Lights," Caleb said. He knew it had taken too long. What were they up to?

Macarus relayed the order, and the field below was flooded with light.

The demics had somehow cut down a tall tree and carried it on their backs towards the wide Manahem road that led straight to the gate. They turned at the road - there must have been hundreds of them carrying the log that measured at least thirty-five mitres long and two mitres in diameter - and marched the fallen tree as a battering ram against the gates. The demics carried the tree with the branches that still stuck out from the tree. They hadn't trimmed it.

Caleb heard the impact more than felt it. The gates should hold. They should. But how had they managed to get a battering ram? Then Caleb saw the Demilord in the back of the horde, gesturing his smaller cohorts forward, waving the blazing unforged sword. It was said the unforged sword could cut through anything. Had he felled a tree with it?

No—two trees—since Caleb could see another battering ram coming from the shadows and into the lit field.

He gave the order to pour the oil, fat, crit and piff down the walls, praying the city would survive the night.

—†—

Bweth Ironhorn stood on the top of the wall with a spiked mace in her right hand and a shield in her left. Her apprentice, Hunter, wore a fine breastplate he had made yesterday. He hefted a sword with a wide blade and a shield of his own.

That human Bladeguard tried to talk them out of fighting on the wall tonight: their skills were too important to the battle to be lost. But he argued to no avail. Once Bweth got an idea in her head, she had to see it through, which was why there were so many weapons down in the forge. She would see a sword or ax or spear in her mind and she had to create it.

A part of her felt that being here, here on the top of the wall to defend the city with her own life, was important. Some whispered that as bad as the battles had been the last two nights, tonight would be the worst. That made Bweth more determined to join them.

Bweth glanced over at Hunter, and he grinned back at her with a knowing look. The man always seemed to be able to read her mind. It unnerved her, when it didn't comfort her. A man male shouldn't know you that well, especially a human. Well, break it all, he did.

And he knew her secrets, things that shamed her. But none of it seemed to bother him, especially the fact she was half-elf, a mutt of a person rejected and ostracized by all three races. But he had never rejected her or treated her with disdain once he discovered the truth. None of his ancestors had known. She thought she hid it well, but Hunter possessed an ability to perceive things she wanted to keep concealed. Like her thoughts.

With another glance, the fool man chuckled at her, as if he discerned what was in her head. She glared at him, and he grinned.

Focusing her mind on the battle at hand, Bweth stepped forward to the edge of the wall, looking down at the monsters gathered there. She had been in battles before, long ago. Fortunately, as they made weapons, she and Hunter had also been able to practice with those weapons. More secrets.

She didn't have to look to her right to see Hunter stand next to her; she felt his presence hovering over her. She would do what she could to keep him alive.

—┼—

Caleb and Macarus stared out over the field of demics. "There are less of them tonight," Caleb said. "Do you see it now?"

Macarus nodded. "There are still thousands," he said. "But yes, we have made a dent, to the sure. But will it be enough?"

"We'll see," Caleb said. "The battering rams were bad strategy. They had us near overrun for two nights and now they've wasted hours getting those trees into the field. The Demilord had to wait for evening to fall. The night is half over already."

Caleb saw Macarus grab the hilt of his sword, still sheathed. "But we still may be spread too thin," Macarus said. "We cannot win battles on miracles."

"This time we will," he said.

Soon the demics began to climb the walls as others rammed the trees into the portcullis of the gates. Besides the battering rams, the night went much as it had the night before. After Macarus gave the signal, volleys of arrows flew from the battletowers. They would wait to throw debris until the arrows ran out.

—•—

Davyn had been born in Roseborough. He was twenty-five years old. He had no wife or children. He was young, and the opportunity for adventure overwhelmed the fear of these beasts from the Underland attacking the city. He had volunteered to learn the bow with that pretty girl, Carys.

As he saw the demics bring up those trees to ram into the gates, an idea formed in his head. Even before they began to fire away at the demics on the wall, the idea grew and became a complete plan. After a few minutes of killing demics on the wall, he put his plan into action. He thought Carys would love the plan. But he didn't check to make sure, he just assumed that he knew what the woman would say. He presumed the fire would weaken the battering rams and kill those demics.

Taking his flint and stone out of his pocket, he tore the sleeve of his tunic off and then into strips. He wrapped one of the strips around the end of an arrow and lit it with the flint and stone. It caught fire on the third strike. He nocked the arrow and aimed for the branches, still full of leaves, on the battering rams at the gates. He let the arrow fly.

The burning arrow didn't hit as square on the tree as he would have liked, but it did get caught in the branches and smoldered in them.

"Hey!" the man next to him said. Mathe hadn't grown up here in the city, but he and Davyn became fast friends over the last couple days. He was from one of those towns to the south. "Lemme see that flint and stone," Mathe said.

"Wait a minute," Davyn said, and he wrapped another strip around his arrow while Mathe imitated him by tearing off both his own sleeves and into strips. Once Davyn lit his arrow, he gave the flint and stone to Mathe, who in turn made his own flaming arrow.

Davyn got three shots off and Mathe two, and both trees were in flames, when Carys ran up to them and screamed at them. "What are you doing? Don't worry about those gates! They've withstood far worse than this, I'm sure. Keep them off the top of the wall!"

He was so surprised, he froze and stammered as the young woman glowered up at him waiting for an answer, and he didn't see what Carys began to see out of the corner of her eye. The glower vanished, and she turned slowly with widening eyes and a slack jaw to view the field below.

"Good El in Everworld," she breathed.

And when Davyn felt brave enough to look, following her eyes, he gulped and cursed aloud in a high-pitched voice, like a squeak. The flames engulfed the trees, and the demics had dropped them in the fields, but the fire didn't burn or kill the demics. They bathed in it with joy, like it fed them. It gave them bursts of energy, and once they had enjoyed themselves within the flames long enough, they began to leap ten or more mitres over the field and up to the wall, the demics leapt higher and moved faster up the wall.

———

The battle was once again plunged into chaos, worse than ever before.

Aden watched the flaming arrows fly towards the battering rams, and Caleb yelled out towards the battletower, his hands upon the rampart. "No! The walls! The walls!"

Noting the effect the flames had upon the demics, Aden uttered a prayer at the same time as Caleb. "El, save us," they both said, glancing at one another briefly before peering again down the side of the wall. The demics scaled the wall faster than ever. The arrows wouldn't hold them at that speed. The archers would have a more difficult time hitting them.

Then the flames from the tree against the gate hit the oil on the wall, and parts of the wall began to catch fire. Over time, other sections began to smoke. The arrows continued to fly, but a few burning demics reached the top of the wall, bounding over the battlements.

Chaos erupted all along the wall. Men shouted and began to panic as more demics launched themselves at the defenders.

Aden gripped his gladus. This was going to be bad.

He steeled himself against the creatures as they were emboldened and strengthened by the flames.

Wait, he thought. *Strengthened by the flames …*

He turned and sprinted to the bucket of water at the back side of the wall-walk. Picking it up, he spun and raced back to the front of the wall. Without looking, he dumped the bucket of water straight down. He heard the screams of demics before he saw the results, and when he peered down, the demics seemed to react to water the same as sunlight. They made horrendous, pained noises and shrank back, releasing the wall and falling down to the field below.

"Caleb!" Aden said. "Water!"

Caleb turned with a confused look to Aden, and then when he saw the bucket in Aden's hand, his eyes widened. "Macarus!" Caleb said to the elf as the First Captain was preparing himself and his men to engage the demics. The First Captain turned to Caleb. "Send some of your men down to the city and organize a way to get water up here to the wall! We need buckets!"

Aden raced back to another bucket of water behind Macarus as Caleb gave instructions, and he dumped that bucket down as well. Macarus heard the wails of the demics and cast his eyes down.

"Water hurts them," Aden said.

Macarus didn't hesitate. He moved to two nearby elves, one of them Second Captain Aetos, and gave his orders.

Eshlyn stood in the street near the front gate, coordinating efforts to gather the wounded from the wall. She heard screams from above, and looked up to see a cloud of smoke surround the city. Something was on fire.

Shouts came down to her from overhead. She made out the calls for water, and just as she turned to give orders, burning bodies began to fall from the wall. She moved aside to dodge a small figure, a demic, splattering to its death at her feet. The stench and sight caused her to retch. Another body hit the ground a mitre on her other side – man still holding his sword, smoke rising from the singed form.

She looked up again. Bodies fell along the wall, mostly demics. But some of the creatures were crawling back down the wall and into the city.

Eshlyn froze in fear for an instant, but then she forced herself to move, grabbing the gladi from the dead man nearby, prying his charred fingers free. The demics were halfway down the wall, covered in flames.

She turned to the people next to her, many of them also transfixed by the horror crawling in their direction.

"Sirah!" she cried out, and her friend turned her way. "They need water up on that wall. Start organizing some of these people to get it up there, anyway you can!" Sirah grabbed several individuals and led them to the wells in different parts of the city.

"The rest of you," Eshlyn said. They looked at her with blank stares. She raised the short sword in her hand. "Grab spears and swords from the wounded and the dead. Or find something you can use as a weapon, a club, anything. They are breaching the walls, and we need to fight for the city. We hold them here."

She wheeled around to face the wall again as the humans scattered. Hoping they returned to fight, she thought of Kenric and his last moments, and Javyn in an abandoned tenement not far away with her mother. *I will not run this time*, she thought. *I will fight.*

A demic flew at her from the wall, and she advanced with a scream, holding the sword behind her with two hands. She brought it around in a wide strike that clove the demic in two.

The demics reached the wall, and Hunter De'Vyn threw himself into battle to protect his home and his city.

He struck at the little monsters with the heavy, wide blade in his hand. It was a fine sword, weighted well, and he cut through a fierce demic with one swipe. The shield protected him from another that came from his right. He spun around, hitting the next creature with the sword, taking its head clean off.

While he knew Bweth had fought in battles a few centuries before, he did not expect her to be so good. The spiked mace in her hand decimated demic after demic, their bodies or heads unrecognizable as such after a bash from the weapon, explosions of black blood and red skin accompanying each blow. Her shield always seemed perfectly placed, even when a little monster tried to jump her from behind.

The battle raged, and Hunter soon faced a herd of demics all at once. He swung his sword and shield in desperation, but one got through his defense and swung a claw at his face. Hunter flung his head back to dodge, but it wasn't enough. A claw ripped through his left eye, taking the eye and half his sight with it. His skin stung from the flame.

In the moment, he ignored the wound and struck and fought the rest with a sense of urgency, feeling a cut along his left thigh as he heard Bweth cry out, "Hunter!" And in a moment, her mace and shield destroyed the remnants of the herd of demics that surrounded him.

"Hunter!" she said, looking at him with dismay. "Great gods, get to the infirmary."

He could feel the blood down the side of his face. The pain threatened to cripple him. Instead, he tore the sleeves off his tunic and ripped them into strips of linen cloth. One he folded to cover the wound, the other he wrapped around his head to hold it in place.

The half-dwarf turned to slay three more demics that came after them while he tended himself.

"I'll be to the fine," he said, twirling the sword in his hand. "But perhaps you should stand to my left."

—

Xander fought beside his father as the demics reached the top of the wall. They were near the eastern battletower, and they hacked and stabbed at the creatures once the fighting began, Xander with his gladus and Eliot with is spear. After a half hour of fighting, turning, twisting, constant motion and violence, Xander saw Carys pass them in a sprint with a gladus in each hand towards the center of the wall.

Eliot made simple and efficient moves with the spear, and Xander was impressed with his father's newfound skill. Xander slew demic after demic, and another hour or so passed in a blur. Men and women began to make their way up to the wall with buckets of water that were poured out at the demics.

Xander heard his father yell in pain, and as Xander turned, he saw a flaming demic with his tusks and claws clamped onto Eliot's left leg. Eliot was in pain and tried to get the demic off of his leg with the spear, but at an awkward angle, the demic now stabbing at the calf with its claws, singing the leg of his trousers. Xander leapt to his father and killed the demic, but as he extended his arm for the stab, another demic jumped from the side and bit into his right forearm and clawed at him all at once, flesh and muscle ripped away.

He heard his father call his name, clubbing at the demic on his son's arm with the spear still in his hand. He heard a wailing scream, and Xander realized it was his own voice as his arm was mangled by the demic. Eliot managed to stab the butt of the spear into the open mouth of the demic on Xander's limb, choking and killing it.

More demics neared them, and Xander tried to grab the sword with his left hand; but he almost passed out bending down.

A figure emerged on the wall next to them and threw a bucket of water and the approaching demics. "Xander!" the man said.

Joob had a sword in his hand from somewhere, and after throwing the empty bucket at a little monster, he began his own hacking at screaming and pained demics. Other demics were drawn to the blood and noise, however, and Joob found himself surrounded.

Xander tried to get his father on his feet. Both of them cried out in anguish, and Xander stumbled. Joob shouted some spontaneous war cry as he fought off the growing number of demics around him in desperation. Xander could barely stand and didn't have time or energy to ask his friend where he had come from or why he was here on the wall after being sustaining a serious injury days ago. Xander took off his father's leather belt and wrapped it around Eliot's upper leg. Eliot had to help since Xander had one working arm. Eliot tugged at Xander's belt and they did the same with his own on the wounded arm. Xander heard his friend cry out, not in anger or frustration, but severe pain. Even in Biram, Xander hadn't heard Joob make that noise.

In helpless horror, Xander turned watched his oldest, dearest friend succumb to the demics around him. One by one, demics found their way onto his flesh, tearing chunks of skin and muscle and cloth. First his back, then an upper arm, then his knee, and Joob dropped the sword and fell to the vicious demics.

Xander had his father up and hopping now, his own head clearing enough to let Eliot lean against him. Xander dragged his father towards the door back down to the city. But he stole a glance behind him and saw demics rushing them. Joob had bought him time, but it wouldn't be enough. He kept dragging his father, both of them losing blood fast despite the belts cinched on their wounds.

From behind them, they heard another man yell his name. "Xander!" the man said, and as Xander stole another glance, he saw the man that now engaged the demics that pursued them.

Byr had a gladus in one hand and a spear in the other. He swung the spear wildly, taking out three demics at once. He followed the swing with a stab of the gladus, slaying another. "Run!" Byr said. "Go, Xander, go!" Xander thought he imagined it at first, but Byr's barking command broke him from the spell and he dragged his father to the door and down the stairs back into the city of Ketan.

—┼—

The Demilord managed another new strategy besides the battering rams. As the demics reached the wall, they not only attacked the humans and elves but the lights as well. The demics surrounded the lights and pushed them over the wall into the field before the gates below. The mirrors shattered, and the torches exploded against the debris and crit and oil at the bottom of the wall. The chemicals within the torches burned hot enough to set large sections of wall and ground aflame.

Caleb watched Carys and Aden fight at his side. Even as the battle fell apart and the tide turned against them, he couldn't help but be proud of both his sister and Aden. Carys fought with such abandon and skill, even Galen would have been impressed.

As he finished the thought, Carys was engaged with two other demics while a third leapt from the top of the parapet to stick its claws into her lower abdomen. She gurgled and fell on her back.

Caleb yelled, "Macarus!" and was standing over his sister in a second, batting away the demic at her stomach with one end of his staff, snapping both of its arms, and sweeping the other two away with a return swing, bones crushing and creatures squealing. Macarus was near him now, as was Aden, both of them fighting off demics as Caleb bent to pick up his sister with one arm, the staff spinning in his right hand. Carys had the presence of mind to hang on to his neck.

"Macarus!" Caleb said. "You have the wall!"

And he proceeded to fight his way across the wall, carrying his wounded little sister to safety.

—┼—

Bweth saw the first rays of light beam across the top of the wall, and her breath caught in her throat for an instant.

They had survived after all.

Bweth hadn't believed they would; not after Hunter's injury, not after seeing so many dead.

Once the last of the demics had been killed or thrown from the wall, Hunter collapsed to a sitting position at the front of the parapet, his head hanging down in weariness and pain. He was covered with blood;

his own and the black blood of the demics. But he had fought like a great warrior, not simply with skill, but heart and will.

She knelt beside him, and he looked up at her. Hunter grinned.

And Bweth kissed him full on the mouth.

———

Macarus thanked all of the nine gods and – break it – even threw in a grateful prayer to Caleb's god once the sun peeked over the eastern sky. They made it another night, but as he looked around himself, he knew by the bodies piled up around him that the losses were great.

It took another hour to knock all the demics from the top of the wall, despite the fact that they huddled against the sunlight. There were just too few men and elves, too few left. Macarus heard cries down below, inside the city, and he looked over the side. Some demics had crawled back down the wall to the streets, lurking in the shadows. He saw Eshlyn dispatch an imp as it tried to hide from the sunlight.

The rest of the morning was spent extinguishing the flames along the wall.

Chapter 32

The Kulbrim

Watching his sister laying sown and bandaged on a canvas cot in a private tent in the midst of the makeshift infirmary that was once a coliseum, Caleb sat on a low wooden chair that creaked underneath his weight.

Were his bold words of faith yesterday mere bluster? Everything had fallen apart last night. Many had been wounded and killed, too many for them to successfully mount another defense. Caleb had seen Xander and Eliot last night as the First Physician tended to Carys; Eliot's leg ended in a stump, as did Xander's right arm. He guessed Xander wouldn't have much of a future as a swordsman now.

And what of all his talk of sacrifice and faith? In a single moment, as he helplessly watched his sister fall, his one thought was for her safety. What of his leadership? The greater cause? The safety of the city? All forgotten the moment that demic tore into her body.

Perhaps Macarus, the ultimate pragmatist, had been right. Faith produced zealots and fools, and he was both. Hundreds of men, women, and elves had died because he believed something. It almost cost him his sister, and he wasn't sure he could survive losing her.

"Hey," he heard a hoarse voice from the cot next to him. He looked at her. So pale. She had lost so much blood, but the First Physician said she was strong and should make a full recovery.

Caleb leaned forward and touched her arm. "Hey," he answered. "How you feeling?"

Carys blinked, her eyes fluttering at him. "Like I've been stabbed in the belly," she said, licking her lips. "Thirsty."

Grabbing the canteen from the ground next to the chair, he gave her a sip of water. She spit up the half she didn't drink.

Carys opened her eyes, squinting and breathing at the pain. "How bad was it last night?"

"The worst so far," he said. "We lost a lot of people."

Carys reached out her hand. Caleb took it in his own.

"Do you believe?" she asked him.

"What do you mean?"

"I never asked you, you know. Ma and Da believed, Reyan and Kendra believed; we were born to believe, almost. But sometimes I'm not so sure. Do you believe it all? In El, in Yosu, in the testimony and the scriptures, the prophecies? All of it?"

Caleb rubbed his beard with his hand, blinking. "More now than ever. I've seen an unforged sword. Those nightmares from the Underland are outside these walls, trying to get at that Key. They're not just words in a book anymore. It is real." He stretched his arm; the cut across his ribs from Zarek was sore. "I don't know if we'll survive another night, but yes, I believe it all."

Carys nodded. "You remind me of him," she said.

He didn't need to ask whom.

"And I mean that in a good way. You just keep going," Carys said. "You were like that as a kid, too." She tried to move but winced in pain. "Annoying as crit sometimes, but you were always moving, always pushing for something. If you're the *Brendel*, El picked the right guy. You'll die before you give up." Carys sniffed. "Uncle Reyan was the same. He wasn't perfect; he just never gave up."

⊢—

It was midmorning by the time the remaining leadership got together at the office in the military complex. Eshlyn had to be pried away from her brother and father, as well. The usual members sat around the large desk, none able to look another in the eye. The absence of Carys nagged at Caleb.

Exhausted, he rubbed his beard and sat up in his chair.

"We probably won't have the numbers to hold the wall tonight," he said. "We survived another night, but at great cost. They destroyed the lights. However, they'll be coming at us at nightfall again in a few hours, and we need to figure how to stand and survive."

"Water worked well," Aden said. "We could hold them off longer if we had enough water."

Eshlyn sat straight. "If we take the day to prepare, we could have lines of water supply across the city and to the walls. We did well last night, but it could be better organized."

"Can you work on that today?" Caleb asked.

"Yes," she said.

"Good," Caleb said. "Between the water, the archers, and even a minimal presence along the wall, we should be able to keep them back."

"We're just delaying the inevitable," Macarus said, scowling. "And you know it."

Caleb paused before addressing the elf. "What do you mean?"

"One more night? Maybe?" Macarus said. "They have numbers and we could be doing this for weeks. Look how they've worn us down after three nights. We're exhausted and talking about throwing breakin' buckets of water down at them."

"What do you suggest?" Caleb asked.

"We could evacuate the city."

Caleb shook his head. "We've had this discussion. We are not running."

"No, Macarus," Eshlyn said. "We stay and fight."

Macarus took a deep breath. "We have boats along the river, for fishing, some cargo. Put as many as we can in the boats and get them downriver to Biram. Get help from the elves there while we hold out here."

Caleb frowned back at Macarus. "I'm not running to the elves."

"Do we even have enough boats for everyone?" Eshlyn asked.

"Between fishing boats and other merchant ships, no," Macarus said. "Maybe half. But they would be safe from the demics on the water, right?"

"I'm not going to evacuate only half the city," Caleb said. "How would we choose who leaves?"

"They could choose," Macarus said. "Since you like giving men the choice. It might give some a chance, right, Chamren?"

Chamren's mind, however, was in another place. "Water," Chamren said. "Oh, my, water."

Caleb turned to Chamren, his face confused. "What?"

Chamren woke from his thoughts and scanned the room. "I, uh, may have another option," he said.

Caleb leaned forward. "I'm listening." The whole room's attention was on Chamren, which made him nervous, wringing his hands in his lap.

Chamren looked at Macarus. "The Kulbrim," he said.

"The Kulbrim?" Macarus asked. "The dam? What?" Then Macarus' eyes narrowed. "The Kulbrim ..."

"Wait," Aden said. "What's the Kulbrim?"

"The Kulbrim is the dam farther up the Rumer River," Macarus explained. "It was built a couple centuries after Ketan by the people you call the First Men. They built it because the river would flood once or twice a season and destroy crops. The Kulbrim keeps the river flowing at a steady rate they could control."

"But it has valves, floodgates that control the water from the northern lakes," Chamren said. "If we could ... open those floodgates at the dam, the river would flood the whole valley surrounding the city."

"How much water we talking about?" Caleb asked.

Chamren shrugged. "It's never been done that I know of," he said. "But beyond the dam is a lake. I would say an enormous amount."

Macarus also lifted his shoulders. "It's been years, a century perhaps, since anyone from the city has even traveled up there. It's worked well as long as I've been here."

"The city, I believe, would be insulated from the flood behind the walls," Chamren said. "It was built to withstand flooding before the dam was built. We could tell everyone to congregate on higher places or on top of the higher buildings, just to be safe."

"Are we actually thinking about doing this?" Macarus asked. "Chamren, this is part brilliant and part maddy."

"Will it kill the demics?" Eshlyn asked.

"If they afraid of it like the sun," Aden said. "Makes them weak and hurts them, don't matter. Surround the city with water and we won't have t'fight them. Not at full strength, and not all at once." Aden faced Caleb. "Although we not know what th'Demilord will do."

"I'll deal with him, when it is time," Caleb said without hesitation. "How far is it? How long would it take us to get there?"

"It is less than a day's walk," Chamren said. "A few kilomitres."

"Be more specific," Caleb pressed. "How far."

"Eight kilomitres," Chamren said with confidence.

Caleb could run that in a few hours. "And can we get across the river?" Caleb asked.

"You could get to the docks and get a boat across the river," Macarus said. "It might expose you to the open for a few minutes, but the docks are well protected. I don't see the demics getting to you easily or quickly."

"Do you know how to open those floodgates?" Caleb asked.

Chamren was nervous again. "Th – there might be a schematic in my office," he said. "It will be simple but physically difficult. You will need someone strong."

"Then we'll take someone strong," Caleb said. "How many crops will we kill? Harvest hasn't happened yet. If we survive, this city will need food for the winter."

Chamren's face went blank. "I don't know," he said. "I agree, it's a risk."

"I'll take it," Caleb said. "I'll lead a small force across the river in an hour, and we will run the eight kilomitres up the river to the dam where we will open the valves and flood the valley here."

"The fate of the world hangs on this decision," Macarus said. "The Key – and your soul, you say – has the potential to unleash something that threatens elf, human, even dwarves."

"I can't decide the fate of the world," Caleb said. "None of us can. That is El's decision to make. But what I can decide is what kind of person I choose to be. I cannot guarantee the results of my decisions. I leave them in the hands of El. But will I be the man who fights to save us all or some?" Caleb's teeth clenched. "I choose to fight to save us all. That is who I choose to be."

"The dam will work," Eshlyn said.

"Let's open those floodgates," Aden said. "I'm with you."

Chamren's brow furrowed. "I would also choose the Kulbrim," he said.

Macarus gazed long at Eshlyn. "It is insane," he said. "But how is that different from everything else we've done? If it works, we can hold out for much longer. I'm with you."

Eshlyn nodded. "We will get the city ready to defend the wall tonight," she said. "with barrels of water and a system to resupply. We will get others on the roofs for when it floods." She stared deep into Caleb, searching something deep within him. He didn't know what she found, if anything.

"Let's hope you get your miracle from your god today, Caleb," Macarus said.

———

Ba and Qo huddled against the back wall of the city in the shadows at the base. They did not want to be awake in the light of day; the sun hurt them in ways they did not understand. It would not kill them, the Demilord assured them, but their minds only understood pain or fear ... or hunger. And they were hungry. But the Demilord had sent them forward as scouts to look over the river, and demics knew they would suffer great pain if they disobeyed. So they suffered less pain to avoid more.

They looked over the river, as was their mission, and the sun began to grow high overhead. They hated this part, shaking in fear, pressing frantically against the warming stone of the wall. They also stayed as far away as they could from the river, a raging and roaring threat of a substance that also froze them to their core and sapped them of their strength.

Movement along the river. The two demics could see humans in a boat, rowing along the river, fighting the current. They couldn't count or interpret what they saw, but they didn't have to. Bo and Qo established the telepathic link with the Demilord. As he could send them images and impressions through the link at will, they could send him images and their own fears and feelings, as basic as they were. They sent him the images of what they saw.

———

Thoros received the images, surprised by the telepathic interruption to his thoughts.

He had lost several thousand demics in the recent attacks, but thousands more still populated his army. The humans were broken, and the city was almost his last night – and the Key! He could taste it! If he had been given a few more hours last night, a thousand demics would have caused violence all over that city. He would lose all of his demics to get a hold of the *Heol-caeg*. That was the purpose for their existence, that and to wreak havoc and destruction upon the world of the living races.

The images came to his mind, humans on the water, on the river, landing a small boat on the other side of the river. They were all armed. He could count five of them. They turned northwest and began to run along the bank of the river.

One man, a strong and athletic man, wore a leather vest on his torso, so Thoros got a good look at the inside of his right forearm and the tattoo set into his skin.

Thoros roared, anger and hate and joy all balled into one expressive cry. The demics asleep in the grass screeched and cowered, their eyes covered.

A *Sohan-el*.

He split off a group of 200 demics from the remnants of his force, rousing them with the appropriate threats and fear. They kept their eyes closed, and he had to guide them with his thoughts, which divided his own attention. But he was going after that man, that warrior of El. He drove the 200 demics, as hungry and tired as they were, northwest along the other bank of the river. He held the unforged sword in his hand.

A *Sohan-el*.

But if he were a *Sohan-el*, where was *his* sword?

—

Caleb ran through the grasses, brush, and trees along the bank of the Rumer River, the Kingstaff in his hand. He had to pace himself, though. Not everyone in the small team he put together for this mission could keep up, and the bulk of the trip was slightly uphill.

Each man had been handpicked by Caleb. Macarus had wanted to come along, as well, and Caleb could have used the master swordsman if they encountered any trouble. Caleb had seen the elf in action and would never want to face the First Captain and expose the better between them. But Macarus and Chamren worked so well together, Caleb wanted to leave a capable leadership in the city along with Eshlyn in case he died or failed at the Kulbrim. El could still deliver them somehow, and Caleb wanted to give them all the chances he could.

He chose Esai because the man fought for three nights like an artist, didn't have a scratch, and Carys trusted him implicitly. Zalman battled like a beast and was stronger than three men, even with that wound on his shoulder. Byr had proven himself another good man in a fight, although his training was minimal, and he was a stout, strong man they could use for the levers at the Kulbrim.

Aden hadn't been chosen. He was always going to come along. Caleb didn't know if he could get rid of Aden now if he tried. Live or die, their destinies were intertwined.

He had said his goodbyes to the people in the city, but mostly Carys. She had improved through the morning and was sitting up by noon. He kissed her on the forehead as he left her in quiet tears. Too many serious goodbyes between them.

His training allowed him to recognize the deep fatigue that racked his body. He could push himself for days, but his reactions would slow and his mind would falter. He might hesitate, which was death when faced with a real opponent. He would will himself to do whatever he needed for the mission. But he wondered, in the back of his mind, how the others would fare. They had to be as spent as he was, if not more.

The kilomitres passed, and he could see, far in the distance, a large, smooth, curved construction of stone and iron that held back a lake. The dam was set against a high cliff of rock and trees hanging down to the area below.

The Kulbrim.

As they got closer, Caleb saw the dark stone of the dam and an iron bridge across the top, steep iron stairs leading to the bridge from the ground below. The large iron levers were visible from even this distance at the top and accessible from the iron bridge.

Within a few hundred mitres now, Caleb perceived figures upon the bridge. Small, red spastic shapes. Demics. And behind them, climbing the tall iron stairs from the other side of the river, was the Demilord.

Caleb heard Aden's voice from behind him, cursing. Now fifty mitres away, Caleb slowed and stood, breathing heavily; the rest of the group also stopped, Byr and Aden leaning over with their hands on their knees, sucking air into their lungs. Caleb watched the Demilord walk across the iron bridge at the top of the Kulbrim, the unforged sword in his hand.

For the first time, Caleb could see the tattoos across the bare torso of the Demilord written in a language not common or dwarven or the First Tongue. Was it a different language of the Underland or an even older language? Caleb didn't know, but the Demilord displayed them with pride. Two hundred demics crept along that walkway, as well, leaping down the stairs and headed toward him.

"The Demilord is mine," Caleb said, placing the Kingstaff across his shoulders. "The rest of you fight through the demics if you can and get to those levers."

Zalman took deep breaths, moved next to Caleb, peered up at the Demilord and said, "You wanna trade?"

Caleb looked up at the large man with two battleaxes in his hands. Zalman was serious. "You're good," Caleb said. "But not that good."

"And you are?" Zalman said with a smirk.

The demics raced towards them, screeching and keeping their heads down to duck the sun as much as they could, and the Demilord made his way down to the ground on their side of the Rumer.

"Not sure," Caleb said, spinning the staff from his shoulders to heft it in front of him in a low guard. "'Bout to find out."

"Gotta play the game," Zalman grunted, pulled another big sigh, and bolted off towards the demics that galloped towards them. Esai, with two gladi in his hands, and Byr, carrying a spear in his left hand and a gladus in his right, followed Zalman. Aden stood where he was.

"What are you doing?" Caleb asked.

"You think you gettin' rid of me that easy?" Aden frowned and shook his head as if Caleb should know better, twirling his gladus in his hand.

Stubborn young man, Caleb thought as he ran towards the Demilord, several demics in the way.

A large, flat clearing marked the bank of this side of the river, descending to the wide, still water that collected at the base of the dam like a large pool. The demics and humans met in the middle of that field, and Caleb saw Zalman slay ten demics within a matter of five seconds. Byr met the creatures with a similar ferocity, his tactic of sweeping with the spear, keeping the demics from any concerted group attack, and then stabbing behind the spear with the gladus, was immensely effective. Esai did not take out as many at once, but his quick and fluid form was too fast for the demics, and his strikes too perfect.

The Demilord said one word, a roaring echo across the cliff behind him. "*Sohan-el!*" The Demilord's voice was deep, blasting through the air and vibrating into Caleb's chest.

Caleb and Aden also had to join the fray, but Caleb kept the Demilord within his field of vision. For his part, the Demilord moved straight to Caleb, the unforged sword hanging at his side.

In the midst of the fighting, Byr launched himself at a group of demics close to the Demilord. Caleb cried out a warning, but it was too late. The Demilord diverted his attention for a moment, lifting the unforged sword at Byr and swinging awkwardly. A grimace filled the Demilord's face, and the muscles of his right arm bulged with effort. Byr noticed the strike coming his way and lifted the spear at his left side to block the sword. The unforged sword sliced through the spear and the middle of the man, cutting him clean in half.

"No!" Caleb shouted and launched himself at the Demilord, the staff striking.

The Demilord's eyes widened in surprise at the sudden attack, and as he tried to block the staff, several times the staff struck home, including a mean blow to the side of the face of the Demilord, which knocked him back a step. He looked up at Caleb, smirking, but then he frowned as he regarded the sword in his hand, as if he were frustrated with the weapon.

Aden got past a couple demics on his side and stabbed the Demilord in the back, but the gladus simply slid off the Demilord's skin. The Demilord roared, and as Aden paused in horror at the lack of effect, the Demilord used his left arm to backhand the young man, who flew ten mitres into the shallow water of the river near the bank with a splash.

Caleb tried to overwhelm the Demilord with as many blows as he could manage, and Caleb could manage quite a few. But besides driving the Demilord back a few steps, the large creature still recovered and dragged the sword around in a desperate swipe that Caleb ducked.

Being the veteran of several battles and duels, Caleb could see the Demilord fight against the sword for some reason, force it with brute strength to move against Caleb. The sword was fighting against him. The sword held the Demilord back.

Emboldened, as he ducked the wild swing, Caleb struck at the Demilord's knees and torso and groin within two seconds, each of them debilitating blows for any creature or man, but they had no effect on this one. Cursing, Caleb kept moving, taking a quick moment to notice that the demics left him and the Demilord alone to clash.

The Demilord stood two heads, almost a full mitre, taller than Caleb and outweighed him by half again. He was powerful, so Caleb tried to use quickness and surgical strikes. But it was like hitting a rock. Although they annoyed and gave the Demilord some pain, they just bounced right off.

Another wild swing, this time faster and stronger, and Caleb couldn't duck and had to block with the staff, bringing the middle of the staff in and up to block the sword as it came around. The staff splintered and broke in two as the sword connected, and Caleb fell back to his knees to dodge the follow through, the Demilord still fighting with the blade. Caleb scrambled to his feet again with a half of the Kingstaff in each hand.

He turned and attacked, beating against any surface he could find with the two halves of the staff. The Demilord tried to shrug most of them off, but a few to the head caused him to stumble, and another slash from the sword was slow and wide. Caleb stepped back and brought both halves of the staff down upon the right wrist of the Demilord. Caleb struck with full force. He heard a slight crack, and the Demilord roared.

And dropped the unforged sword.

Caleb didn't hesitate, energized by his success of getting the unforged sword out of the Demilord's hand. He spun and struck, even jumped and kicked the Demilord hard across the jaw. Again, like kicking a rock. But now that the Demilord didn't have the unforged sword to fight against, he was free to move his own hands and black claws.

And he was fast.

On the defensive now, Caleb blocked and weaved and dodged, no longer able to counter. The Demilord's strength, speed, thick skin, larger size, and deadly claws bore down on him. The Demilord scraped a claw across Caleb's upper left arm. He ducked and rolled to recover, coming up on the right side of the Demilord in a crouch and striking as he could, his left arm screaming in pain.

His eyes flashed to the unforged sword on the ground, mocking him. He growled, thinking of the Vow he would break either way, but he couldn't get to the sword. The Demilord was quick and moved to keep him from the weapon. Surely El would help him. Somehow.

———

Zalman batted two demics away from him with one swing. On the edge of his vision, he could see Esai dispatch two nearby. The creatures were slow and blind in the sunlight, and Esai fought them with ease.

Esai turned to him. "I've got this. Go and open the floodgates."

Cutting his way through three more, Zalman nodded and grunted. This was why Caleb had recruited him. Zalman didn't even ask for money this time.

He sprinted to the iron stairs and took them two at a time. He glanced back, and ten demics hastened after him, their black eyes closed, feeling along the railing. He reached three flat iron levers along the walkway. He stopped and spun at the demics behind him. Within moments, he had killed them all.

Zalman placed his shoulder underneath the first lever, and he pushed upward with all his might. It caught at first, and he yelled, straining, while he pressed again.

It began to move.

———

Wet. Muffled noise. Aden came to consciousness, random sensations punctuating his recovery. The side of his face hurt. Badly. He touched it and winced, and his hand came away wet with blood. His own.

He shook his head and sat up from being on his back in the shallow water. Noise of battle, all too familiar to him now, the grunting of effort, the screaming of demics.

The dam.

As he sat up, he still held his sword. He scanned as well as he could. Esai was holding his own. Where was Zalman?

Aden's eyes fell on Caleb engaging the Demilord. Caleb blocked three successive strikes with the broken pieces of the staff, and as the Demilord turned, Caleb took the opening and stabbed forward with both wooden pieces. The splintered wood pierced the skin in the middle of the

Demilord's chest. Howling, the large creature kicked Caleb in the midsection. The man flew back five mitres, his arms flailing, the pieces of the Kingstaff falling with him. Caleb landed on his spine, and his head bounced off the ground. He lay still.

Aden raised his sword and ran to help his friend.

———

Thoros smiled as the *Sohan-el* tumbled to a stop and did not respond. He advanced to finish the man with the tattoo and eat his soul. From the side, a young man raised a sword and rushed him, yelling out something Thoros could not understand.

He did not strike the young man this time. He caught him by the neck and lifted him, light and easy. The young man struggled and slashed against him with a sword, but his red skin deflected the blade each time. Thoros squeezed the neck of the boy, grinning as he thought to crush him to death.

But as his talons broke the soft flesh of the boy, Thoros could taste his soul. So pure. He was purer than any of the others, more than he could have ever imagined. Thoros glanced over at the *Sohan-el*, who was still motionless. He gave his full attention then to the boy struggling in his grip. He had to devour this life. He brought forth his other claw and pressed it to the boy's chest, the talons digging into the skin.

Thoros began to eat the young man's soul. The taste was overwhelming; it transfixed him and he lost all sense of time as the sweet pleasure overpowered him. His head leaned back.

———

Caleb opened his eyes with a start. He rolled to his knees, coughing and staggering to confront the Demilord, whom he knew would be attacking. He had lost consciousness for a moment – how long? Caleb cried out in pain as he tried to breathe with several broken ribs. He held one end of the Kingstaff. The other lay in the grass of the riverbank. The unforged sword lay just beyond.

Just beyond the unforged sword, the Demilord held Aden in the air with one claw, the other pressed against his chest. Aden's eyes rolled up in his head, and his mouth open, his body shuddering. The Demilord's head leaned back, his eyes fading from black to white. The Demilord was going to consume Aden's soul.

A broad column of water began to pour from the dam into the river.

Still a little dazed, he shook his head and crawled as fast as he could on his hands and feet, clenching his abdomen against the pain, dropping the end of the Kingstaff that was still in his hand. He passed by the other end lying in the grass. He reached out and clasped the hilt of the unforged sword.

With the unforged sword in his right hand, he forced himself to his feet, holding his breath. The Demilord didn't avert his focus; he appeared engrossed with Aden. A mist began to form over the young man's skin.

Caleb hefted the blade and shuffled into a clean strike, swinging up and carving through both wrists. The Demilord shrieked, staggering backwards, his eyes changing to black once again. Aden's body collapsed to the ground, the claws falling off of him.

The unforged sword hummed in his hand, and Caleb pivoted on his heel, a sudden strength building within him. The pain left him for that moment, and he swung the sword around and against the Demilord's neck. The unforged sword severed the head from the body, and the Demilord fell dead to the ground.

He heard voices in his head; there were no words, but they communicated gratitude. From the neck stump of the Demilord, a thick white mist poured along with black blood. The mist dissipated. Caleb did not hear the voices anymore.

He stood for a heartbeat, then crumpled to his knees. It hurt to breathe again, and he was able to see Aden two paces away, unconscious.

The level of the river was rising. He could feel water pooling around him.

He heard a voice near him, sensed hands under his arms. "Get up," Esai said. "Come on."

Caleb allowed Esai to help him to his feet. "Get the staff," he said. Esai bent down and collected both ends of the staff, reaching to help Caleb again. The river water was rising. "No," he said. "Get Aden."

The river was up to their calves as Esai gathered Aden in his arms and out of the water. Caleb trudged onward to the stairway, urging Esai ahead of him. The man arrived at the stairs and transported Aden up, carrying him on his shoulders.

A second column of water joined the first, and the flood intensified. He had to get up those stairs.

The water rose to Caleb's waist as he gained the bottom of the iron railing. He pulled himself to the top with one hand, the other still holding onto the unforged sword. As he climbed, he screamed in pain. Once reaching the walkway, he groaned and sat down with his back against the dam. Esai lowered Aden gently, then he sprung to help Zalman open the third gate.

A third column of water flooded the river. The deluge demolished trees, ripping them up by the roots, and the countryside became a muddy ruin as the lake emptied into the land below.

Caleb closed his eyes.

CHAPTER 33

AFTER THE FLOOD

Eshlyn stood on the top of the wall, her son wrapped in cloths and clinging to her in the sling against her breast. Others stood around her: Macarus, Chamren, Kyv, Sirah, Xander pale with his bandaged stump of an arm, Second Captain Aetos, and people from Delaton and Roseborough. Humans and elves stood by barrels of water and buckets all down the wall-walk, weapons nearby. Carys sat next to her in a wooden chair that allowed her to lie back. The stubborn woman insisted on coming up here when she heard people talking about a group standing on the wall to watch the field and wait for the flood. If it came at all. Or wait for the sunset and the demics if it didn't.

The wind blew swift and strong, whipping her hair in locks that snapped against her cheek, stinging. The breeze brought a scent of death and smoke and crit from the field below.

No one spoke for hours. She stood on the wall, her thoughts drawing downward into her grief and helplessness. Grief for her husband and the numerous people that had died over the last few ninedays, towns that had been destroyed, men that had died upon this bloodstained wall, her father and brother's injury. And after all that, Caleb left her here, helpless and waiting for whatever result of his insane mission up to a dam near an unnamed lake.

She, Chamren, and Macarus had spent the afternoon organizing and preparing the city to transport buckets of water through the city to the wall in case they needed to try to hold off the army from the Underland tonight.

The sounds of demics in the distance came across the plains, remote screams and screeches as if they were in terrible pain, tormented by something they couldn't see. Everyone on the wall shifted their weight or cleared their throat as they strained their sight to look over the field. But nothing happened. Nothing came.

Carys looked up at her, pale and weak. She smiled. Eshlyn forced a smile in return and reached down. Carys grabbed her hand.

She stood like that for a long time, staring back again out at the field before the gates of the city of Ketan.

The sound preceded anything else, barely distinguishable at first with the ripping wind around them in the late afternoon sky, a rumbling sound that accompanied a tremor beneath them, reverberating through the stone and iron of the walls.

"Get me up!" Carys said from below.

Eshlyn reached down and put her hands beneath Carys' armpits. Macarus moved to help her. "Should you be moving ..." Eshlyn began.

"I wanna see!" Carys said, and Macarus and Eshlyn propped her up against the parapet. Everyone on the wall now leaned forward and looked east.

They saw trees falling, the tops of them disappearing in a wave along the river in the distance. Then Eshlyn could see it, and her heart beat within her ears. Water. Muddy rushing water destroyed everything in its path for hundreds of mitres on either side of the river Rumer. She gasped. Carys grabbed her hand on the parapet again. Tears rose in Eshlyn's eyes, and she touched the golden marriage bracelet on her wrist. The muddy water, now filled with logs, fallen trees, and other forms of detritus, crashed with a loud noise against the walls of Ketan, water spraying upwards for mitres upon mitres. The valley filled with the muddy water over the next few minutes, swirling and breaking in every direction. The brown water and debris were ugly, but in that moment, it was the most beautiful thing Eshlyn had ever seen.

Sirah stood to Eshlyn's left. "Oh, Byr," she whispered. "You did it."

Caleb's god did produce his miracle after all.

—+—

Caleb winced as Esai's hands examined his ribs, the water roaring into the river below them. "Three cracked, one broken," Esai said above the din. "I've bound the arm, but those ribs just need some rest."

"What about Aden?" Caleb asked.

Esai glanced over at the young man. "He's breathing fine, but still unconscious. I don't know what that thing did to him."

Caleb did, but he lacked the knowledge to help. Did that knowledge exist?

A memory came to him, a time not long ago when he was wounded after battling Cityguard and a grider. He remembered Reyan's hands upon his shoulder, the Prophet's words full of compassion and faith. Leaning over Aden, Caleb placed his hand on Aden's forehead and spoke quiet words, asking El to help the young man. Esai nodded and rested his own hand upon Aden's shoulder, joining him in the prayer.

Three hours after opening the floodgates, Caleb rose to his feet and helped Esai and Zalman reverse the levers. Zalman did most of the work, but Caleb used his weight with his good arm to provide some assistance. By the time they were done, dusk had fallen, and the land below them was covered in water. Caleb decided to take Esai's advice: he rested.

The next morning, Caleb heard Aden begin to groan. Aden lay on his side, and Caleb sat near him, rolling him to his back. Aden squinted at the sun as his eyes opened.

"Whu – what happened?" Aden asked, throwing an arm over his face.

"The Demilord caught you and started chanting," Caleb said. "He was feeding on you."

"Well, shog me," Aden said. "Everythin' went black. And I felt … stretched. Like my whole body bein' pulled apart." He coughed. "And I heard voices. Not you, but in my head."

Caleb nodded. Had they heard the same voices?

"Did you kill him?" Aden asked, moving his arm to look up at Caleb. "Did you open the dam?"

Caleb put a hand on the young man's chest. He noticed he held the unforged sword with the other. He had broken his Vow, but that was inevitable, he realized now. He had saved the boy without thinking, and he could not regret that choice. The two pieces of the Kingstaff lay nearby, rent between the words *To lead with compassion* and *justice and strength*.

He smiled down at Aden. "Yeah, I killed him. And look," Caleb cocked his head toward the body of water below them.

Aden grunted and rose on an elbow, leaning over to see. "So we won," he said.

"We won," Caleb said.

The water receded through that day, but it wasn't until the next morning that it was close to normal. The countryside was flat with destruction, razed by the flood. The men ate some jerky from Esai's pack that he shared with the rest, and they drank from the two canteens that had survived, but they didn't try to trek back until the middle of the morning of the third day when it appeared dry enough to pass. Another night of sleep felt good, even there on the iron grating.

Caleb wondered how it was at the city of Ketan as they trudged through sludge on the way back. They traveled on the opposite side of the river than the one they took to get to the Kulbrim. They couldn't find the road but kept within sight of the river, muddy and dangerous. Because of the landscape, it took them the rest of the day to make the trip. They arrived at the field before Ketan and the gates by the evening, shin deep in muck and water.

Hearing a cry from the top of the wall, Caleb looked up but couldn't see who yelled, nor could he tell what they said. But as they neared the dark arch of the opening gate, a group of people ran out to meet them. Macarus, Eshlyn, and Chamren led the march of horses from within the city. Caleb saw Carys on a horse to the rear, riding slow and cautious, her face beaming like the others.

A crowd surrounded them within the next few minutes, embracing them, but Caleb waited for his sister. She made it to him, and he helped her dismount straight into his arms. She cried, and he held her, whispering into her ear.

Caleb pulled away from Carys as Eshlyn neared them.

Eshlyn shook her head at him with a grin. "So maybe miracles do happen," she said. Then the grin melted from her face as Caleb handed her the unforged sword.

"I believe this belongs to you," he said. "And your son."

She took it with care, both hands on the hilt, staring at the blade with tears in her eyes. "But ..." She raised her gaze to him.

He gave her a short bow. "You have the heart of a warrior," he said. "It is yours by right."

Eshlyn clutched the sword to her chest. "Thank you."

"No," Caleb said. "Thank you. And thank Kenric if you dream of him again."

Her brows furrowed, and she leaned over, nodding.

He heard a voice in the crowd. "Where's Byr?" the woman's voice called. He found her. He forgot the woman's name, but she was Eshlyn's friend.

Eshlyn's eyes turned to him, questioning. All he could do was shake his head. Her face, radiant and smiling a moment ago, fell to grief for her friend as she walked to the woman and communicated the same message with her own shake of the head. Byr's wife collapsed into Eshlyn, and they wept together.

—+—

Five of them met the next morning in the same office around the same large desk. Clean and rested, Caleb scanned the faces. Eshlyn, Aden, Carys, and Chamren all sat there refreshed as well, better rested and calmer than ever.

He realized this was the revolution: the people in this room and those in the city that rose up and learned to fight. But it was only the beginning.

"Why isn't Macarus here?" Eshlyn asked.

"He won't be a part of this discussion," Caleb said. "I owe him an explanation, and I will give it, but I wanted to speak with the four of you first. As the city moves forward, they will need your leadership more than ever, especially Chamren and Eshlyn. Human leadership."

That sank in for a moment. Chamren narrowed his eyes at Caleb. "Are you not releasing Desiderus, reinstating him?"

"No," Caleb said. "I'm releasing him, but I'm sending him back to Kaltiel, to give Tanicus a message."

Eshlyn's eyes bulged. "What message?"

"That men are free again," Caleb said, and he pointed down at the desk in front of him. "Right here in Ketan. They fought for their own survival and the survival of this city. We put weapons in their hands and taught them how to use them. They have seen men and women lead them instead of elves. We have awoken the souls of men, and we cannot return them to slumber. This is now a city of men, completely free from the Empire, and the freedom will spread from Ketan."

Chamren gulped and Eshlyn grunted as she almost fell from her chair. Carys and Aden didn't move, their faces blank, and Eshlyn looked over at their calm face. "You knew already," she said. She turned to Caleb. "Was this your plan all along?"

"This has been decades in the making," Caleb said. "But I can't say this was my plan. I planned to travel west to find the Living Stone. All this, the demics, the Demilord, saving the city, it was all part of El's plan. I can't take credit for that. It's happened far faster than I thought it could. But here is where we are. And I need to know if you're with me, if you are committed to making this city a free city of men again. It won't work if you say no."

"You keep asking impossible things of me, Caleb," Eshlyn said.

"That's because I believe you're capable of what you feel is impossible," Caleb responded.

The room grew quiet and pensive, the calm replaced by anxiety again, but a different type of anxiety. A hopeful one.

"I'll stay here with you," Eshlyn said. "So much has been destroyed. It is time to rebuild."

Chamren appeared as if a crizzard were on the other side of the desk about to attack him and eat him alive. "Like I said before," he began with a cleared throat and several seconds of stammering. "I am ready to see what you see in us. And I believe we've caught a glimpse of it already."

"And you owe us an explanation, too," Eshlyn said. "If Macarus gets one."

"Of course," Caleb said. "I'd rather do it all at once, though. Let's get down to business first. We need to organize a few things."

Over the next hour, they discussed getting crews together to go down to the farms around Campton, Pontus, Delaton, and Roseborough to harvest what crops they could and bring the food back to the city before the crops spoiled. The demics didn't seem to eat anything but meat and flesh, so Caleb thought those crops would still be there. They also needed to organize a watch in case the elves did come with some sort of force. Caleb didn't think Kryus would be able to react and mount any sort of real response in months, so they had time to prepare. They discussed leadership, and Eshlyn mentioned how the Mayor of Roseborough was already lobbying for his own power again now that the battle had died down. Politicians. Caleb brainstormed with Chamren for a way to officially declare Eshlyn Caleb's choice for the head eldership of the city. Other elders would be chosen by some sort of election.

Caleb also told them they needed to choose men – and women, Carys noted – from the city that had fought in the battle, people that they trusted that could keep peace as needed or protect the gates if the elves reacted quicker than Caleb predicted. Carys and Esai would take care of organizing that force, and other names to help with leadership and organization began to crop up. Caleb suggested someone, possibly Esai, travel back to the forest of Saten and ask for volunteers from among the men and women of the Ghosts, which took some preliminary explaining. Caleb wanted to request Athelwulf's help.

"Overall, we must empower the people of the city to take care of one another, give them ownership in the city in various ways as the authority of the elves vanishes. It will be up to them to change. They must learn what their individual responsibilities within that freedom will entail," Caleb said. "They must be shown and taught, not forced. It will not work any other way."

Then he turned to Chamren. "Last thing. Get all the Sorcos of the city and put it in the market square," Caleb told him.

"Why?" Chamren asked, his eyes continual saucers.

"Something I have to do," Caleb said. "And I'm the only one who can do it."

"But you're leaving," Carys said, sorrow tinting her voice. "Right?"

Broken Vow or not, he knew his journey demanded he find the Stone. It called to him, or was that his imagination? *The sword that gives him life will take his life.* Or was it *the sword that takes his life will give him life*? He would find out.

"I'm leaving in a few days, before autumn can sets in," Caleb said. "I'm headed west to the mountains of Gatehm to find the Living Stone."

Aden frowned and lowered his eyes.

"And you're going to leave us here to do all this?" Eshlyn exclaimed. "Without you?"

"El willing, I'll be back," Caleb said. "You are more than capable of leading and organizing while I'm gone." Caleb sighed. "Don't get me wrong, though. This will be difficult. You'll need to pray. A lot. And if you don't know how, learn. We'll all need to learn. It will take another miracle the likes of which Eres has never seen. People don't willingly give up their security and safety for true freedom again. But El can help us. And that is the only way they can be free."

Caleb nodded to Chamren. "Now go get Macarus," Caleb said. "I've got some explaining to do."

—+—

It took three hours, far past lunch, and help from Aden and Carys to explain to Macarus, Eshlyn, and Chamren the last twenty years leading up to the events of Caleb becoming a Bladeguard and returning to Ereland to call humanity to rise again and be who they were created to be. There were several tangents to the conversation, and much confusion that needed to be cleared, but Macarus sat there with a blank look on his face, his legs crossed, his left arm around his belly and his right hand stroking his chin.

"An intriguing story," Macarus said as Caleb finished. "Gives me much to think on."

"We need to decide how to move forward with the elves in the city," Caleb said. "If you have any ideas ..."

Esai burst into the room, interrupting. "Caleb," he said. "You have to come."

Caleb trusted the man and reacted, grabbing the two halves of the broken staff on his way out, still good weapons ... if one was not combating a Demilord.

Esai took him out to the horses, and all five of the humans and Macarus mounted their horses and followed Esai through the city west to the market square. Carys even demanded to go along, even though the ride was hurting her. Could stubborn run in a family?

As they came into the market square, it was full of men, women and children, and the crowd stood in silence and looked towards the large platform that Carys had used to train the defenders of Ketan. On that platform, two humans stood around a gathering of five elves, Desiderus and Unitian in the midst of them, chained and beaten, bruised and bleeding. He assumed the others were heads of ministries in the city. A small congregation of humans before the large platform clamored and cheered a man in a wide hat.

A bonfire raged behind them.

Caleb thought he recognized the man with a wide brimmed hat. Had he fought on the wall a few nights ago? He had fought well, but now he led some sort of public execution with two short swords in his hands.

The stallion under Caleb responded well to his forceful maneuvering through the crowd. A few people were knocked aside, but no one was injured. Caleb slowed the horse as he neared the platform, dismounting on the run, landing and leaping in one move upon the platform next to the man in the broad hat, the two halves of the broken staff in his hands.

The man in the wide brimmed hat faced off against him, but fear filled his eyes. Caleb must have developed a reputation. "What are you doing?" Caleb asked the man through clenched teeth.

"Finishing what you started," the man said, and Caleb winced as if he'd been struck.

Macarus sat on his horse, ready to leap from his saddle, his face calm but his eyes murder, his hand gripping the hilt of his sheathed sword.

"No," Caleb said. "You're not."

"You placed these elves in prison, our oppressors," the man said, his voice rising so it could be heard above the noise. "These elves that took our freedom and abused the power given to them. Shouldn't they pay with their lives?"

"That is not for you to decide," Caleb said.

"Is it for you to decide then?" the man said.

"Tell him, Shan!" one of the men below shouted with a raised fist. Three or four others joined him.

"No, it is not," Caleb said. "Not alone, and not like this. But it is for me to stop you, if I so choose." Caleb's eyes tightened and his face hardened at this man, Shan.

Shan suppressed an urge to step back in fear and instead blinked. But he continued to speak, his voice above the crowd, more silent now. They knew Caleb, too. "Don't you know what these elves have done? Especially Desiderus. How many have disappeared from the city after being used for his pleasure? You would try to protect these evil elves from justice?" Shan said.

"This is not justice," Caleb said, his own voice rising, but his eyes never released Shan's. "This is mob rule. And all this will do is prove that what the elves believe about us is true, and that we deserve the very oppressions they seek to bring upon us. This is not how you begin a real revolution or express your freedom."

He turned to the crowd now, all of them silent, even the men in front of him still and pensive. "You want to be free? I shouldn't have to stand here and fight this man to stop him." He pointed the half of the staff in his right hand over the crowd. "You should all be standing in his way instead of gawking at him and doing nothing." He spat the words. "Either that or come and slit his throat yourselves, if you think that's what it means to be men!"

Caleb turned back to Shan. "Justice is standing against those that would use their freedom for revenge or personal vendettas. So I will stand, and any are welcome to stand with me. Believe me, one way or another, Desiderus and the Kryan Empire will pay for their sins against the innocent. But we will not seek revenge and act like them."

Shan stared into Caleb's eyes for a long minute. Caleb did not move. A bead of sweat dropped from the brow of Shan's hat, the hot afternoon sun beating down upon both of them. Shan heaved a sigh of frustration and turned, dropping from the platform to the bricks below, and walked off.

The crowd dispersed, one by one. After ten minutes, Caleb turned to Esai, who had ridden up close while the crowd scattered. "Take these men back to the prison," he told the Liorian. "Please. And release their chains and tend to their wounds."

"Gladly," Esai said and began to comply.

Caleb also jumped down from the platform, mounting his horse, placing the halves of the Kingstaff into his belt.

Macarus moved next to him. "That was the Rat," he said, frowning. "I've been trying to capture him for years. That is what you've set free."

Caleb nodded and their eyes met. "We will deal with the rats. The light exposes them, too."

The First Captain scoffed at him.

Caleb rode to face Eshlyn and Chamren. "You have to teach the city, show them," he said. "Leadership is not control and power. Show them the difference."

—✦—

Chamren had the stockpile of Sorcos within the city heaped in the square as Caleb had requested. It took the rest of the day, and now Caleb walked towards it. The three moons of Eres were bright in the sky, one of them full. Eshlyn, Chamren, Carys, and Aden stood behind him. Caleb carried a torch.

People were scattered around the square, keeping their distance but eyeing the stack of Sorcos with suspicion and worry.

Caleb lit the mountain of Sorcos in the middle of the city square and watched it burn. He noticed tears in Aden's eyes.

Turning to the crowd, Caleb projected his voice, and it carried across the square with an echo. "Ketan survives. We have won. We fought evil from the depths of the Underland itself and won. Thousands of men and women rose up and fought to save their families, their friends, this city. The First Men built this city, and men have defended it.

"Man has known oppression for too long," he continued. "It is time for humanity to throw off the shackles of the Empire and rule himself. Tomorrow, the elves will leave. But for us to be free, we must not partake of poison. It is only another type of bondage." He pointed back to the growing flame. "Let this be a symbol, and a sign. Ketan is free again. We will be free."

As the blaze behind him reached high in the air, Caleb produced the Letter of Regency from his belt. He lowered the torch and set it aflame. The Letter burned in his hand for a moment, and he dropped it to the cobblestone, watching it turn to ash.

Zalman and Esai separated from the crowd and joined Caleb. Zalman shook his head. "You may have just killed some people in the city, burning that Sorcos," Zalman said, his voice low. "Or started a riot."

"Perhaps," Caleb said. "But no more crutches."

"You going to keep them all from ever doing wrong?" Zalman asked, gazing around the square at the other humans, people who sat and observed the drug go up in smoke.

"No," Caleb said. "Just making a statement. There are other places they can go if they feel they need Sorcos. We will not keep them here."

Zalman scoffed. "That crit is death in a bottle. You get no argument from me 'bout that. Not as many addicts here as other places, but enough that many could leave."

Esai spoke up then, watching the drug burn. "We'll set up tombs here," he said. "This is good thing. For those to understand what it means to stay."

Zalman didn't seem so sure. "How many you expect to stay?"

"Only those that want to be free," Caleb said.

—+—

That night, Eshlyn slept in a large, comfortable bed. She had been offered a room in the palace, but she declined. She wanted to be with her family and friends, those that were left. So they moved the bed from the palace to the tenement for her. She held her son with one arm. The other hand held Kenric's unforged sword.

She dreamed. In the dream was a bright light, like the sun but more radiant, white and clean. A figure stepped before the light, and she was filled with a great warmth. Kenric. She reached out to him, but he shook his head. She understood. He had to go.

"I love you," she said to him, those words she had failed to say a month ago. She said it over and over, desperate for him to know. She wanted to hold him, feel him close. He smiled as if he knew it all, and a warmth filled her.

I love you, she heard his voice for the last time. He spread his arms and was consumed by the sun.

—+—

The next morning, Caleb stood outside the gates of the city in the mud, not near as deep now, and faced Macarus and almost a hundred elves behind the First Captain. Every elf had a large backpack full of supplies – dried fruit and jerky, blankets – and a canteen of water. Fifty-two Cityguard, out of the original four hundred, had survived. Desiderus, Unitian, and forty other elves – administrators and ministers, physicians and Nican of the city – all stood among them, too. Most of them glared at Caleb.

Eshlyn, Carys, Chamren, and Aden stood behind Caleb.

"I wish it didn't have to be this way," Caleb said.

"I understand," Macarus said. "You feel the humans need to do this alone. It is honorable, as foolish as it may be."

Caleb leaned into the First Captain. "You're the one I wish could stay," he said. And he meant it. Macarus' knowledge of the Kryan military and experience in the Legions would be invaluable.

"I wouldn't even if I could," Macarus said. "Kryus is my home, even though I am a stranger to it; the elves are my people. I will go back and talk with them about what I've seen here."

Caleb pointed south along what remained of the Manahem road after the flood. "You know the directions?" he asked.

"I have the map," Macarus said. "And you've been more than kind with supplies and our weapons."

"They are yours, and you may need them for protection," Caleb said. "And the bows will be good for hunting."

Macarus nodded and stepped past Caleb to shake Chamren's hand. "Goodbye, my friend. You will do well here," Macarus said. Chamren's eyes were moist. Macarus shook hands with Aden. He went to shake Eshlyn's hand, but she embraced him, as did Carys, all saying their goodbyes. Macarus moved closer to Caleb; he extended his hand and Caleb shook it.

"Tell Tanicus, when you see him," Caleb said. "That humanity has risen again. That we are free here in Ketan, in the oldest and first city of the first men. Tell him that elves were friends and allies in Eres, long ago. I wish to be friends again. I do not wish to fight or go to war for freedom we should already enjoy. Tell him to allow us our freedom by right, and we can sit down again as brothers, as we were meant to be."

Caleb's voice became low and firm, his eyes fierce. "But also tell him that if he comes to stop us with his legions, he and those with him will pay for the blood of the believers and innocent that he has shed. Ask him to repent and accept freedom or face the wrath of El."

"I will tell him," the First Captain said, and his smile contained a hint of sadness. "I count you all as friends," he said, then to Caleb. "And I knew King Judai. He was an amazing man, a phenomenal warrior, and a great king. If Erelon had accepted his help against Tanicus, men in the north would still be free of the Kryan Empire. He did the right thing to surrender and negotiate the safety and some measure of freedom for his people. He was wise."

Macarus sighed. "I also watched as Tanicus did unspeakable things to his family and murdered them while Judai watched. Then Tanicus had the king's eyes gouged from his head so those atrocities would be the last thing he would ever see. I saw the man scream in agony few will ever understand. I saw him rot of starvation and abuse in the prison for two years until he died. I almost had pity on him a few times and ended his life myself with this sword." He patted his sword at his hip.

"You are a man like him," Macarus said. "I have seen you do things here that I never thought I would see. I have seen miracles happen, Caleb, and I thank you for that. I have much to think on because of it. If anyone can lead and teach men to be free again, it is you."

Macarus peered at Caleb and the rest of the humans behind him. "And so I must also tell you that you will fail. You do not know what you face. I will buy you what time I can, I swear it, and you will never face me in battle – that I also swear. But I beg you, when Tanicus responds, and he will respond with a force like you've never seen or could imagine, surrender to him as soon as you can. Do not fight him. You will lose."

"You forget, Macarus," Caleb said, soft and calm. "I lived amongst the elves for sixteen years. I was trained among the best of them. I've even beaten the best of them. I know what I'm up against."

Macarus shook his head. "You know what they showed you," he said. "There is much you do not know, nor have you seen. Do not test this, my friend. I beg you. I do not wish you to end as King Judai did, as much as that might already happen, even for what you've done to get here. You think you've started a revolution, but all you've done is awaken the wrath of a god."

"The Tablet has been played," Caleb said. "We shall pray to El. He will deliver us."

Macarus grinned. "His deliverance looks a lot like your action," he said.

"For us to live different than we lived before, to change our actions, that is his deliverance," Caleb said. "Tell the Emperor what I said."

"I will," the First Captain said.

"I gave Desiderus a letter for Tanicus, as well," Caleb said. "See that the Emperor gets it, will you?"

"You have my word," Macarus said.

The First Captain of Ketan waved and led the elves on the long walk south.

CHAPTER 34

The Sohan-el

Caleb stood outside the gates to begin the final leg of his journey to the Living Stone. It was a ninedays since Macarus and the elves left. Ketan had grieved and buried its dead, and everyone stayed to help rebuild the city, at least for now.

The sun peeked over the eastern horizon a few minutes ago, and the wind was cooler. Autumn had come.

Caleb wore his usual leather pants, but the rest of his garb was special for this journey. His boots had been made for climbing, and his tunic was part of a plan for added layers as the elevation increased. The backpack tied securely upon him carried various supplies, added clothes with fur linings, basic tools he might need on the climb, and a tent. Two halves of a staff were strapped to the pack as well. Although his ribs were sore, his injuries were healed enough to travel.

A group of people gathered there to see him off. Eliot rested on crutches with his wife, Morgan next to him. Xander seemed healthy and strong again, as if indeed making a good recovery. Caleb would never be able to see either one of those men without feeling like a failure, valid or not. Drew and Myrla smiled with an odd mixture of sadness, pride, and hope. Chamren was there, calmer than usual, but twitching, Esai serene at his side. Eshlyn stood with her family, her son in that sling again. She wore her husband's unforged sword in a scabbard Bweth had fashioned for her. Caleb thought he might have to teach her how to use it, if he returned. He heard of how she roused the citizens in the city the last night of the battle to fight the demics coming over the wall.

He turned to see Carys watching him.

It had all happened too fast. Galen trained him extensively on how to use Reyan's contacts to garner more support, train an army, use people he trusted like Carys and Earon to spread the ideas that fostered freedom: a revolution. That would have taken years. But El had his own plan, and El knew more than what little Caleb's training could give him.

Looking here now at the humans arrayed before him, men and women of strong character, his heart found hope.

Through the small crowd, Aden pushed his way to stand before Caleb, outfitted and supplied like him. Aden wouldn't meet his eyes.

Caleb wanted to tell the young man that he wasn't ready, he hadn't gone through the teaching, hadn't committed himself to the Vow. But could Caleb really say that? He had broken the same Vow to save the boy's life, and he did not regret it. Maybe all the traditions were changing; maybe they were never necessary. He wondered what would happen to the young man when they reached the Living Stone. Break it, he wondered what would happen to them both.

Aden scowled up at him, as if he knew what Caleb was thinking. "All the way to the end," Aden said as if that explained everything, adjusting the straps of his backpack on his shoulders. How long would the young man say that?

Caleb and Aden found their way into goodbyes. Drew laid his hands on Caleb and prayed for him before embracing him. Caleb thanked the man. He moved on to give some final encouragements to Esai and Chamren. He charged Esai with taking care of his sister. Carys' pout deepened.

Eshlyn shook Caleb's hand. Their eyes met, and an understanding passed between them. "I want to say be safe," Eshlyn said, chuckling. "But I don't know if that is the right thing to say."

Caleb returned the smile. "It is a kind thing to say, and kindness is good enough," he said. "Just bless our journey and have hope."

"Then I do bless it and hope that you return with … whatever you need," she said. "And remember the people of the city here need you and love you."

"Need me? They need something far greater than I can give. And love me?" He stood close to her, lowering his voice. "These people will hate me before it is over, Eshlyn. I will ask of them things they do not want to give, and I have made them a target of the most powerful Empire in Eres.

"But it was never about their love or need for me. And it never will be." He grinned at her again, gripping her hand.

He turned to Carys now, and he wanted to laugh at her petulant look. But he was wise enough to resist it.

"You're leaving me," she said. "Again."

"Have faith. Were the demics legend and myth? Was the *Heolcaeg*?" He shook his head. "The Demilord had an unforged sword, and now Eshlyn carries it. It is real. I'm surer than ever that the Living Stone waits. It will give an unforged sword again."

"And you're letting him go with you?" she asked, glancing at Aden. "I want to go."

"You're still too injured, and I need to do this before the snows," Caleb said. "And it is his choice, ultimately. It has to be. You know this. Why are you breaking my gruts?"

"Because I love you and want you to stay," she said. "But I know it is something you have to do." She sighed. "And that maybe he has to be there with you. I don't know. I know it is right. But it still piffs me off."

He embraced her, and she uncrossed her arms to throw them around his neck, grasping him with a desperate strength. He loved the feel of her face buried there. "If all goes well, I'll be back in a ninedays," he said into her ear.

She scoffed at him. "You know how your plans have gone recently," she mocked. "I'll see you when you get back. However long that needs to be."

He pulled away from her. "Thank you," he said. "I love you."

"And I love you, Cubby," she said.

He rolled his eyes with a smirk, and as Caleb and Aden began to walk over the soaked ground due west towards the mountains of Gatehm, where the road was washed away.

He heard Eshlyn's voice behind him. "Cubby?"

<hr/>

Carys had her arms crossed again, and as the rest of the group filed away, she turned to Eshlyn. "Wait a minute," she said.

Eshlyn's brow furrowed, but she lingered. Carys held her words until everyone else was out of earshot, even Caleb and Aden, slogging through the wet, muddy ground.

"He needs you, you know," she said to Eshlyn, low so no one else could hear. "He's going to need you."

"What?" Eshlyn said, blushing. "I'm ... a recent widow ... I ..."

"Oh, that's not what I meant," Carys said in an annoyed huff. "What I meant was ... that man can fight a war and beat the Sahat himself when it came down to it, I think." Carys shook his head. "But he needs others around him to help him, to keep him honest, to help him see what he can't see sometimes, to help him be ... human."

"He has you," Eshlyn said.

Carys laughed. "I'm his sister," she said. "He loves me. He needs you."

"He needs you, too," Eshlyn said. "Don't forget it."

"Maybe," Carys said.

After a moment of silence between them, Eshlyn said, "And he isn't human now?"

"Not like you think," Carys said. "Not like you might think."

<hr/>

It took them two days of walking to reach the foothills of the mountains of Gatehm. Caleb led the way, and after trudging for hours in mud and puddles, the ground began to rise and dry. They crested hills and saw trees again, trees with leaves starting to turn. The travelers continued straight west. On the morning of the second day, it rained, a heavy downpour that soaked them through.

"We could have used this a ninedays ago," Caleb muttered.

Both men were quiet and subdued, their minds processing and decompressing from the events of the past few ninedays. Caleb thought of Reyan often, thankful for time with him, and guilty for leading the betrayer right to him, guilty for his death. He could still remember countless things Reyan had said to him as a boy, and much of their travels in the last month were fresh, perfect in his memory.

Caleb also meditated on Earon. He had been so sure that Earon would be an integral part of this, with his love of the Ydu and the Fyrwrit, with his intellectual acumen, with his knowledge of the importance of the cause. Who better to travel and teach and inspire with Reyan, or even take his place, than the son who had intimate access and experience with those teachings? He had been so sure that Earon and Carys would be together and be the man and woman of prophecy. It all made perfect sense. Frustrated, his heart broke as he thought of Earon's betrayal.

As Caleb walked in the rain, his thoughts also turned to the city, how to defend it again if needed, against a real army. What would they need? How would they prepare? His brain was awash with images and details and resources and plans. After hours of this, he chuckled bitterly when he thought of his sister's words. His plans hadn't panned out very well so far. What made him think he could prepare well enough for the next step on this journey? He would still try, though.

The rain stopped just as they reached the foothills on the afternoon of the second day, and Caleb turned north, remembering the ancient directions in his head. By evening, he found the Stake Stone, which was a tall narrow brown rock that looked like a giant finger pointing to the skies. At the Stake Stone, a path turned to the left, to the west, and up into the mountains. That was the path to Elarus, the mountain of the Living Stone. They camped that night at the Stake Stone.

The sun broke through the clouds, and as they bedded down for the night, Caleb perceived a rustling in the bush to his right, about three mitres. He caught Aden's eye, placed a finger to his lips, and he picked up a small flat rock. Aden froze, calm, and Caleb waited to find the glimpse he needed of his prey. A low branch of the bush shook, and Caleb reacted, throwing the rock sidearm and hearing the accompanying thud with a direct hit.

Caleb walked over to the bush, reached his hand down and pulled out a rabbit, still twitching from the blow. He wrung its neck. Dinner.

——

Unfortunately, the rain had also made the surrounding vegetation too wet to make a fire, so they ate the rabbit raw. It was still warm enough to lay out their clothes while they slept in dry blankets, and they traveled with damp attire for the first part of the morning. Caleb explained to Aden the dangers of the cold they would soon experience as the elevation increased. The sun baked them through the afternoon as they took the path from the Stake Stone into the Gatehm Mountains, and Aden was grateful. While the terrain became rockier, there were still trees and brush around them as they hiked up a steep path. They were both wearing their gloves and another layer of clothing by the evening, and Aden was able to make a fire that night out of wood not doused by the rain the day before. He stalked and killed two snakes that evening before sunset, and they had roasted snake for dinner.

While the path did not steepen the next day, the trees and bushes were sparse. Caleb informed Aden they now climbed the Mountain of Elarus. It was more difficult to breathe on the second day's journey from the Stake Stone, and several times Aden heaved and coughed enough air from his lungs that Caleb noticed and made them stop, much to Aden's shame. Caleb tried not to act annoyed or frustrated, but Aden knew the man too well by now. Caleb's gray eyes betrayed his anxiety at getting to their destination.

The two men barely talked even as they hiked up Elarus. Caleb didn't offer much information – he probably didn't have much of it to submit – and Aden didn't feel the need to ask any questions. Aden brooded alone with his own thoughts. He thought of Jo, the man who cared for him on the streets of Asya. Aden pondered his own improbable escape from the Pyts, his short but influential time with Reyan, and Reyan's tragic death. He wondered how he could feel such grief over a man he had known for less than a month. Did he grieve the man? Or did he grieve the promise of a life of learning from him, of questions he could ask that no one else could answer? He concluded it was both, which compounded his grief.

He had read more of the Ydu over the last few days before leaving for the Living Stone. The information and answers he sought only led to more questions. If he understood it at all, this was bigger than just the freedom of men. El desired the freedom and faith of all, men and elves and dwarves together again as one. But how could that be? How would a sword help against kings, armies, and empires? Against the ugliness of man itself? His believing seemed to lead him to more truths he found even harder to believe.

Aden also thought of the battle of Ketan, the blood and violence on the walls. He had asked to learn the sword without any real knowledge of what it meant to wield one. Caleb was a weapon. He had been trained like a weapon, moved like one, and thought like one. Aden didn't know if he wanted to live that life. It seemed lonely. And ironically, here he was on a trek to get a sword.

But would he get one? It was quite an assumption on Aden's part for several reasons. It wasn't about the sword, though. Not really. It was about seeing where this path took him, with Caleb. He had a feeling it wouldn't be about a sword. But he felt he must keep moving forward. He knew his own path would be clear to him soon.

That afternoon, Aden looked up and saw a tower rising among the cliffs of the mountain. Aden stopped and pointed at the steeple. "What is that?" he asked.

Caleb shook his head. "I don't know," he said.

They reached the tower by the evening. It was a ruin of stone, two hundred mitres high, with several sections missing. Wood had long rotted away. It did not look safe.

"Seems like a good place to camp," Caleb said, and they entered the bottom level, a round room made of cold stone. Aden had difficulty finding enough wood for an effective fire. The pitiful flame tempted with minimal heat. At least they had shelter for the night.

Eating through a third of their provisions, they left the ancient ruins and made their way up the path, much steeper now, even having to use hands and knees to traverse a particularly steep part of the way. Aden could see no vegetation, and their canteens became low throughout the day, which was dangerous. All that surrounded them was frigid gray rock, sharp and dangerous even on the path. The cold seemed to reach into Aden's very bones, and he found himself nauseous by noon. Threatening to make him go back, Caleb made him eat. Aden forced down some dry jerky and a hard, small biscuit before Caleb would allow him to continue. Caleb had to give Aden a few sips from his own canteen.

Aden saw steep cliffs far ahead and a narrow pass between them. He could not see what existed on the other side, and he didn't know if it was the darkness beyond or his own light-headedness. His vision narrowed once, and he almost stumbled. But he didn't cry out or tell Caleb.

Caleb reached the narrow pass first, and he walked through with shoulders straight. Did he know something he wasn't saying? Aden was trying to stay on his feet at this point, and he hoped he could make it to the evening so he could rest, which should be an hour away or less.

Following Caleb through the pass, Aden came through and stood motionless at the sight before him.

CHAPTER 35

THROUGH THE DARK

The dry rock spread out before Caleb into an open area after he strode through the pass. Bones of men and elves scattered throughout the place, lying in awkward positions as if they had been tossed there, broken and dead before decomposing. It smelled of death, even though the bones were dry and clean, hundreds of years clean if the legends were to be believed. As ominous as those carcasses were, the sight beyond chilled what was left of the warmth in Caleb's heart.

A roiling, tempestuous black cloud extended before them, thick with soot and smoke, and ascended hundreds of mitres into the air. The sky above it was clear ebony and starless, as if day had become night in a moment. The dark cloud moved continuously, billows fighting and colliding and overwhelming each other. A growling thunder, low and rumbling, sounded from within it, hungry and threatening. Rock rose high on either side, and the only way forward was through the maelstrom.

He looked behind him to see Aden backed against the flat rock to the right, his eyes wide and glistening with tears. The young man's movements had been slow and weak all day, and now he was faced with this. And Caleb understood. He looked up at the dark cloud, sure it would kill him.

He was angry, frustration rising in him as he squatted in fatigue. He had come so far. For this? He yelled a curse. He faced the cloud of death before him. He felt himself being drawn, not to the black cloud, but beyond it.

The Vow, however broken, still guided him. … *dedicate my soul, my heart, and my life to find the Living Stone.*

Live or die, forward was his one option. Doubts tried to creep into his mind, but he denied them like he had denied the demics on that wall, one by one, beating them back.

He dropped his backpack to the ground near Aden. It was so cold here, far colder than the other side of the pass, unnaturally cold. Caleb still had almost half a canteen of water and laid it nearby. Pulling the two halves of the Kingstaff of El off his pack, he stuck them in his belt.

Caleb moved between Aden and the dark cloud, intercepting his gaze. "I'm going through that," he said. "Now, listen to me." Caleb had to put his gloved hand on Aden's jaw to force him to pay attention. "Listen! This is not a place you can stay. You must go forward or back. It is too cold. Do you understand? If you stay here you will die."

Aden's eyes focused on Caleb, not so distant and empty now, and the young man nodded.

"Good," Caleb said. And he turned to the dark cloud and walked until it engulfed him.

———

Silence. Darkness. Stillness. Caleb had no perception other than his own existence. Did he walk? Did he stand? Was he even alive? There was no evidence from his natural senses. He possessed no abilities or power. But he knew that he was.

Do you love me?

It wasn't an audible voice, more like an impression in his mind, a communication within, but not from him. The message came from another source, soft in tone but firm in intent. Although he had no evidence other than an ancient instinct and other moments when he felt the Creator communicated with him in times of prayer, he knew it was El.

Do you love me?

He visualized his life, choosing at a young age to give his life for the cause of freedom. The faith of his parents and Reyan, the sacrifice of those he loved, it all fueled his dedication. He could see his father sitting with the prophecy in his lap, his eyes closed, speaking the prophecy like a prayer with a longing Caleb could not understand but was desperate to fulfill. His return will be a sign that man will rise and claim their freedom from the chains of others and the bondage they place upon themselves, and that his father and mother and Reyan would not have died in vain ... He gave his life, willingly, for that oracle.

I am the source of that prophecy. Do you love me?

Caleb recalled the words he had spoken to Aden not long ago, how the revolution would ask men to do the impossible, to trade the slavery they knew for freedom. It would require a great cost.

Loving me is the only way to live the impossible. That is my freedom. There is none greater.

He thought it must have been faith or hope that motivated the Prophet. The man believed, and he suffered so much, even to death. He hoped in things that most counted insane. But was that all? The night before he died, at the inn in Biram, Reyan had mentioned that there existed something even greater than faith. He realized now that Reyan's fight wasn't based on faith or hope. He was willing to fight, suffer, and even die not for a cause but because he loved El. He loved El more than anything else. And El was the root of that cause.

What if there were no cause, no revolution, no memory of his parents or aunt and uncle?

Freedom is not the ability to live or die for men or a cause. You must love me enough to live and die for me alone. Love reaches beyond death. That is the revolution. All transformation is born from there.

He searched his being; he knew he had faith and hope. After all he had seen, how could he deny it?

But did he have love? Did he love El?

As he continued to explore his own heart, he realized he did.

I do, he said. I do love you.

Am I enough? Right here and now in this moment, if you never took another step forward, am I enough?

In the stillness and quiet, a great shaking rose within him, an anguished cry that made no sound, a release of years of burden and weight. He had carried that weight with faith and hope, and that had sustained him. But the burden evaporated as he embraced the love. He would suffer anything to feel this forever.

Yes, he said. I love you. This is enough.

Then rest here with me. You have nowhere else to go.

And for the first time in over twenty years, Caleb rested. He didn't feel like he had anywhere to run to or from, didn't have to hide; he didn't need to fight or argue or stay strong. He could rest and be at peace.

And so he was free.

—

Aden watched the dark cloud stretch forth from its center and swallow Caleb whole.

He thought about taking his things and heading back down the mountain. He had the supplies to make it, although water might be a problem, but there had been a little stream a day and a half ago where they found good, clean water. He might be able to make it there and rest for a while before making it back down the mountain and back to Ketan.

As frightening as the cloud before him was, he felt a call to move beyond it. He was drawn forward against his fear.

He forced his feet to take a step and take off his own pack and lay it next to Caleb's. His own canteen still slung over his shoulder and lay against his hip. He willed himself to breathe, closing his slack jaw, and he walked forward. Aden passed the bodies of elves, well trained and brave elves, he was sure, as he pressed toward the dark cloud.

The dark cloud waited for him. How could a cloud seem both hungry and calm? Step by laborious step he entered the cloud as it reached out and pulled him in.

The voice surprised him, and he imagined someone close and intimate, but someone immeasurably strong. Maybe strength itself.

I love you.

Who was that? He couldn't hear it with his natural ears. None of his senses seemed to be working in his place, an unnerving silence and darkness, but also peaceful in a way he could not understand.

I don't understand, he said.

I love you.

In an instant, he knew this was El. He had heard or felt something similar that night in the forest of Saten when Reyan spoke, a soft voice that was not a voice, an impression that was pure and real and frightening all at once.

You love me? Aden said. I don't know what love means. No one has ever loved me, not that I knew.

How? What does that mean?

I will tell you things you do not know.

Still lost in confusion, Aden saw a picture of a man running with a baby son in his arms from a mother that was about to give him to the infanti to be slaughtered. The man had begged with the woman to let the baby live, that he would work extra, whatever he could find, but she called him names: worthless, lazy, homeless, street trash. But the man had heard another man, an older man—the Prophet they called him—and he knew that he had to save the baby's life. So he stole it and ran. He ran and began to raise it on his own, on the streets of Asya. The woman would later die alone, overdosed on Sorcos.

Then he saw Freyd, the man that had given him work, illegal and dangerous work; but then Aden saw the compassion Freyd had shown him after his escape from the Pyts. Almost a father's heart. Almost.

I've never known a father's love, Aden said. A mother's love.

You have my love.

I've always been alone!

I have always been with you.

I don't even know my real name!

I do.

Aden envisioned meeting Caleb, the words that Jo had told him reverberating within his mind as he knew he must go with Reyan, a man he had seen years before in a shady back room. Aden beheld his training by Caleb, his questioning of Reyan, the long and dangerous path of the last month from Asya.

It was all to get you here.

Why me?

I have chosen you for great and mighty things.

But I am only an orphan from the streets of Asya! I am nothing!

You are not nothing. You are not an orphan. You have the Creator now as Father.

He screamed in whatever way he was communicating – Why me?!

I choose the small to be great. I make wonders out of nothing.

But I can barely read. I barely have any training! I don't know anything!

True strength is not your ability but your humility. My strength is enough.

Aden's heart broke. An orphan boy without a name felt loved by the very Creator of all things, and he knew he would never be the same.

I will always be with you. Remember this moment in dark times. Now go. There is much to do.

That voice was meant to be obeyed.

So Aden moved himself to pass beyond with a strength not his own.

———

Aden emerged into a narrow grassy clearing that led to another pass through large white stone. It was warm here. Aden could breathe again with ease. He looked behind him and the dark cloud was now a white misty fog.

Caleb was nowhere to be seen.

Chapter 36

The Living Stone

Had Caleb gone on without him? Just as Aden felt as if he should linger for a moment, Caleb emerged from the white mist.

Caleb said nothing, but Aden saw something he hadn't seen before within those deep eyes of steel.

Peace. He saw peace.

Caleb raised his eyebrows at Aden, surprised to see him there, but the peace in his eyes never wavered.

"Come then," Caleb said. "We're almost done."

Caleb walked through the narrow pass between the white stones. Aden followed.

———

The narrow pass lasted three steps, and upon coming through, Caleb emerged into a large area full of rolling hills, grasses, trees and brush. Above him, he could see warm, bright sky. This was the summit of Elarus. The summit spread out in a round shape, about a hundred mitres in diameter. The wind blew soft and warm. Caleb was comfortable and at perfect peace.

Straight ahead of him, at a dozen paces, he could see it. The *Ebenelif*, the Living Stone. He was here.

The Stone itself surfaced from the ground about chest high, the rest of the massive round gray stone buried deep in the earth. A third of it could be seen above turf, jagged edges and small craters suggested danger within the beauty of the Stone. Before the Stone was a clear pool of water set into the earth, a still and crystal body of water five and a half mitres wide.

Out of the Stone grew a tree, the gnarled roots digging deep into the stone itself. The *Aeselif* rose high into the air, larger than any tree at the summit, giving pleasant shade and swaying in the soft breeze, the rustling of the wind through the leaves like a long forgotten song. The trunk was dark brown underneath the shadows of the luscious and full leaves that were shades of forest green. The leaves themselves seemed to promise hope and life.

Within the gray jagged Stone, veins of a silvery metal intermingled with the roots of the Living Tree, a pure and bright metal that reflected the light at the summit, distinct from the dark gray of the Stone.

Caleb did not look behind him as he walked with a satisfied grin upon his face. He waded into the pool, dipped his cupped hands into the water, and drank. He was instantly refreshed, filled. Caleb reached up to a low hanging branch of the Living Tree and grabbed a handful of leaves. He placed them into his mouth, chewed them, eating the sweet tasting fronds.

He did not thirst. He did not hunger. He was not tired in the least.

Caleb pulled the two halves of the Kingstaff of El from his belt and placed them within the water of the pool. Aden stepped forward, and they both watched as the staff reformed, the splintered ends moving towards each other, fitting as one. Caleb laughed and drew the Kingstaff of El from the water, healed and whole again.

He looked back now at Aden, the young man's eyes as wide as his heart. They smiled at each other with childlike joy. Caleb tossed the staff over to the side of the pool into the grass.

Another step brought Caleb within arm's reach of the Stone.

Lay your hands upon the Living Stone, the old verses said, *and you will receive the unforged sword if found worthy.*

So Caleb removed his gloves, threw them off to the edge of the pool, reached out and laid his bare hands upon the Living Stone.

A silvery double-edged blade shot out from the Stone and stabbed Caleb straight through the heart.

—┼—

"Caleb!" Aden cried out without thinking, breaking the idyllic silence of the summit of Elarus, and he ran forward. The blade that extended from the Living Stone passed all the way through Caleb's body. Caleb jerked with a gasp, his hands laying hold of the blade, and it came away with him as Caleb fell back and into the pool with a splash.

Aden reached Caleb as the water covered his closing eyes. He bent to grab Caleb's shoulders to haul him out of the water, but the lower branches of the Living Tree grew and stretched downward toward Caleb, cradling the man, lifting him out of the pool, and placing him on the thick grass nearby next to the Kingstaff. Other branches pulled the blade from his chest and laid it across the front of the man. It was a sword, hilt and all, the blade smooth and flawless, gleaming in the overhead white light.

An unforged sword.

Aden stumbled backwards, crying out in astonishment. Where had that come from? Hilt and all? Aden fell to his knees next to Caleb; the man did not breathe, completely still. But Aden could not see any blood in the wound, despite the hole sliced through Caleb's clothes.

The words came to his mind. The blade that gives him life will take his life. Or was it: The blade that takes his life will give him life? Reyan said it could be translated both ways.

Caleb spasmed and sucked air into his lungs and moaned on the ground, his clear gray eyes popping open. Alive.

Aden looked over at the Living Stone.

He rose to his feet, breathing heavily out of fear and excitement, not effort or exhaustion. He took off his gloves and let them fall to the ground. Aden strode forward into the pool and drank, just as Caleb had done. He ate the leaves of the tree. He felt the complete satisfaction within his very being that accompanied the mystical substances. As if at a great distance, he thought he heard Caleb speak his name behind him, but he ignored it.

Aden put his bare hands upon the Living Stone.

—

Caleb sat cross-legged at the edge of the pool, an unforged sword, perfectly suited to his hands and body, lying across his lap. The Kingstaff of El rested just beside him in the soft grass, whole again. He waited for Aden to open his eyes, the young man groaning as he woke. Aden roused from his slumbering death, and he sat up, his own unforged sword in his hand.

He took the hilt of the *Anfyrbrend* in his right hand, and the blade seemed to ache and hunger for blood; the blood of those that opposed the truth and oppressed the innocent. He heard a voice in his mind as he watched the light shining and beaming from the supernatural steel.

He is not a man, but a sword, and El will wield him as a sword …

  The Brendel.

The Blade of God.

Epilogue

The Journey Back to Kryus

It had been two and a half ninedays since Macarus and the elves had left the city of Ketan when they entered the town of Campton.

Macarus led them down the Manahem road through the towns to the south, or what remained of them. Most of the buildings still stood, although windows and doors were torn through. Grisly remains littered the towns, most of them recognizable as human. The demics had feasted at these places. Beginning at Delaton, Macarus forced the elves to dig a mass grave and fill it with the human remains they could find. Desiderus and Unitian complained and protested more than anyone, but one stern look from Macarus, as he fingered his sword hilt, and they would do what he told them to do.

He couldn't completely shut the old Steward up, however. The Evilord would search the towns for a horse, an ox, begging to find anything he could use to ride and spare his poor feet. Desiderus stumbled along and cried out every five minutes as if the long kilomitres of traveling by foot were torture. Macarus supposed that for Desiderus, it was. But they had supplies enough, and water in wells in each of the towns to refill canteens and water bags. Desiderus lost weight, though, and the Steward glowered at the First Captain when he pointed it out. But they were all thinning a little. They had to have care for the provisions.

Thankfully, Macarus and the rest of the Cityguard from Ketan had killed several rabbits and groundhogs, even a snake or two. They ate well enough.

Every few days, teams of men and women on wagons passed them on their way to harvest the crops of one town or another. These teams would sometimes pass again on their way back to Ketan. The men were friendly enough and would give the elves some turnips or potatoes if asked. Desiderus saved his most gregarious begging for these times, offering jewels and the riches of Kryus to any who gave him a horse, better yet a wagon. But either Caleb told the humans to ignore the Steward, or they did it out of their own character. Macarus would chuckle when the humans left and Desiderus would be despondent about his ongoing miserable fate.

The air had cooled over the last ninedays, and Macarus enjoyed the brisk coming of autumn. He walked to the southern end of town where the large warning horn still sat on its stone tower. He sighed, gazing further south to the distant mountains of Kaleti. *Perhaps another four or five days away.* They would have to be sure they had enough provisions and hope for good hunting as they made the foothills of those mountains. For they would follow them all the way to the coast.

He would buy Caleb as much time as he could, but Macarus knew that the revolution was futile. It would be another month before they reached a major Kryan settlement that was able to send messages, even if those messages could be believed by anyone with any real authority to do anything about it. Macarus and the other elves would be called to Kaltiel to give a report to Tanicus himself, Macarus was sure. He wondered if the High Evilord would even remember the First Captain he had once hailed as such a hero. Regardless, by the time they reached Kaltiel and gave a full report – the Empire always required full reports before any decisions were made – it would be the middle of winter, if not late winter. And Tanicus knew as well as Macarus the misery of launching a campaign in Manahem in the middle of winter. The Emperor would wait until the fall before his bureaucracy would act, sending the Imperial legions forward from Taggart or Asya or both. Tanicus would act with swift and overwhelming force. That would be the only way to keep the peace in the colonies, in his mind.

There would be rumors before then. Men and elves in Manahem, Biram and maybe Taggart, would know that something had changed. But Kryan legions did not move without orders from on high. First Generals that made independent decisions, and failed, faced punishments whispered about in back corners of taverns.

So Caleb would have until the spring to build an army, entrench himself in the city with walls that had never been breached save for a stray demic or two.

It would all be for naught, Macarus knew.

Tanicus held secrets that the common man or elf would never know. When he finally brought his full power to bear upon Caleb, the man would need more than mere miracles from his god to defeat the High Evilord of Kryus.

Caleb would need to be a god himself.

Acknowledgements: .

The Living Stone began as a simple idea, but an epic story emerged from that idea as I took four years to build the world of Eres. What you have read is the culmination of years of work and research before I even began to type out the story on my computer. And this is the first chapter of several to come as I explore the redemptive history of the world of Eres.

A book like this cannot happen without help, and if you enjoyed it at all, then you also have these people to thank.

My first Beta readers, Matt and Gina. Both intelligent and well read, they gave the first feedback. They were an invaluable part of the process.

My editor, Chris White. Worth every penny, he was honest and brutal at times, but in the end, he helped me make this the book I wanted it to be, both darker and more redemptive.

The graphic artist, Paul Gary. The first to begin playing with the visuals for the book, he has been a friend, a fan, and an absolute pro.

Jeremiah Briggs, who put paint to canvas and worked with a demanding author to come up with a mind-blowing painting for the cover.

To the friends and family who continue to encourage this crazy dreamer, thank you. Especially to those that gave to the Indiegogo fundraiser – Alex, Stephen, Stacy Walker, Ben and Gina, Shawn, Matt, Jodey, Stacey Roberts, Francine, and Jesse.

My wife, Rebecca. When we got married, she promised to always be my biggest fan, and she has NEVER disappointed. There are many amazing women in the world, but she excels them all. Her sacrifice and continued encouragement is in every page of this novel.

And last but not least, Jesus, my Yosu, my El. Yes, he is more than enough. Always.

About the author:

M.B. Mooney has traveled extensively and writes novels, short stories, and songs. He lives in Lawrenceville, GA, with his wife, Rebecca, and three children: Micah, Elisha, and Hosanna.

If you would like to see more of his work, check out his website at www.mbmooney.com.

Also like him on Facebook: MB Mooney.